HOPE ON THE PLAINS

HOPE ON THE PLAINS

The Dakota Series • Book 2

Linda Byler

New York, New York

HOPE ON THE PLAINS

Good Books books may be purchased in bulk at special discounts for sales promotion, corporate gifts, fund-raising, or educational purposes. Special editions can also be created to specifications. For details, contact the Special Sales Department, Good Books, 307 West 36th Street, 11th Floor, New York, NY 10018 or info@skyhorsepublishing.com.

Good Books is an imprint of Skyhorse Publishing, Inc.®, a Delaware corporation.

Visit our website at www.goodbooks.com.

10 9 8 7 6 5 4 3 2

Library of Congress Cataloging-in-Publication Data is available on file.

ISBN: 978-1-68099-311-0
eBook ISBN: 978-1-68099-313-4

Cover design by Koechel Peterson & Associates, Inc., Minneapolis, Minnesota

Printed in the United States of America

TABLE OF CONTENTS

CHAPTER 1

THE BRISK WINDS OF AUTUMN FADED, LEAVING THE NORTH DAKOTA
plains silent, dry, and dusty, the grasses that never ceased their
brittle rustling hanging limp and brown. The sky took on a yellowish gray color, hanging above the Detweiler homestead as
if it might crack and fall. The air crackled the atmosphere still
and ominous.

Sarah shivered, rubbed her arms as she crossed them tightly
to her waist, standing on the edge of the porch that looked
across the level land to the barn, gray, weathered, its roof cap-
ping the logs with rusted tin, the fence around it brown and
splintered. Every morning on that porch, the widow repeated
her early morning ritual of gazing between the second and third
posts of the barnyard fence, where her husband, Mose, had met
his early death, gored by a displaced and angry cow with horns
like sabers.

And she spoke to him. To his memory. She told him she loved
him still, that today was another new day without him, but she
was all right. She had the children. Hannah, strong, indepen-
dent, a mind of her own; Manny, growing into another version
of his devout father, conscientious, obedient; Eli and Mary, still
so innocent, playing and playing on the endless prairie; Abby,

the baby, growing, crawling, her little body a comfort to her mother when she held the child in her aching arms.

She turned, her eyes misty, her dark hair parted in the middle, the white head covering set on her sleekly combed tresses pulled into a bun on the back of her head. Still slim, her worn, faded dress a soft blue, a black apron tied at her waist, her feet encased in black stockings and sturdy leather shoes.

She stepped off the porch, her eyes drifting to their beacon of hope, the windmill, its rotating blades pumping the water necessary for a fledgling herd of thirteen cows and one magnificent bull. But the blades were still now, and the up and down movement of the pump silent.

There was no wind.

Sarah prayed, asking God to bless them with the wind. She never imagined praying for wind; in times past, its endless blowing could test the limits of her sanity.

She felt her daughter's presence before seeing her. Tall, disheveled hair as dark as midnight, her dress hanging loosely, surrounding her thin frame in ragged patches, worn thin beneath her arms and along the sides of her chest. And no apron—again.

Sarah didn't understand her daughter's aversion to the required black apron. It was part of the *Ordnung*, which was highly regarded in her own mind, the lack of it meant being partly undressed. No head covering this morning.

"No wind?" Hannah asked, her large dark eyes black with anxiety. Sarah shook her head, shivering.

"Well, we're going to have to go to town for gasoline. The tank was half empty last night. We have to get that engine started."

Sarah stifled a whimper. The engine terrified her. To think of pouring gasoline into a tank, the dreadful machine churning away out there surrounded by unpredictable cows and grass dry as bone, filled her with dread. But she hid this away, for Hannah's sake.

They ate their breakfast of fried eggs and homemade yeast bread, bowls of oatmeal spooned up and appreciated.

There was a time when breakfast consisted of barely enough watered-down cornmeal porridge to stave off the lurking hunger that made their stomachs, cramped and empty, growl with voices that drew down their courage and hope, leaving them to endure their days in wide-eyed incomprehension of what to do next. Until Hannah rode to town and worked for Harry and Doris Rocher, who paid her in enough flour and cornmeal to keep their stomachs filled and their courage up.

The 1930s were lean, the Great Depression causing hardship even in prospering areas of the United States. On the Dakota plains, stark reality was crying children, hurting with hunger and dark-brown questioning eyes asking silently for what no one could provide.

Sarah spread the fragrant butter on toasted bread, thanking God with every bite, her mind reaching out to her Heavenly Father as her spirit sang its praises.

"Hannah, when you go to town, will you wear an apron and your white head covering, please?"

Hannah's dark eyes met her mother's anxious ones, a quick rebellion thrusting its way between them, filtering out the love and obedience. "Why? There's no other Amish for miles, hundreds of miles. Who cares what I wear?"

"God sees. He cares. You are an Amish person, subject to an *Ordnung*. Hannah, your father's words should mean more to you than they do. You cannot still them by your disobedience."

"I am not Amish unless I choose to be, Mam." This with a proud toss of her head and a shrug of her wide, capable shoulders.

Fear clenched Sarah's stomach, a cold lump lodged in her chest as her oatmeal turned into a gray, inedible mass of anxiety. She longed for Mose's calming presence, his gently spoken words as wise as those of the biblical Solomon.

Nothing more was said, the dread in Sarah's mind obliterating further conversation.

Hannah rode off with Manny on the spring wagon, the triangle of a blue men's handkerchief fluttering from her head, and no apron in sight. Shameful, that patched dress worn thin.

Sarah knew that any further words of discipline would only fuel the fire of rebellion, so she let it go, turning to the dishes and her day's work, the crushing weight of her daughter's disobedience taking away the joy of the washing and ironing.

The mismatched team, one steady, thick muscled and plodding horse from Lancaster County named Pete, was hitched with a lean and rangy brown mustang, a gift from their neighbor, Hod Jenkins. He never acquired a decent name after Hannah said he looked like a goat. So Goat he was. Goat and Pete, a pathetic pairing, driven by a girl dressed in little better than rags, that ridiculous kerchief tied on to the back of her head, her shoulders wide and proud, her goal keeping her head high, her eyes alive and questioning.

She was a homesteader, the owner of the Bar S. A cattle owner. No one would have a finer herd. No one could get better prices at market time. They were well on their way, with the generous loan from her grandfather, the ten first-year heifers dropping calves next year.

They had a bank account, a checkbook, and cash in her pocket to buy gasoline. They needed coffee and baking powder and chicken feed. Laying mash for the flock of precious chickens was an unimagined luxury after the generous lending from their grandfather.

She drove the mismatched pair as if they were fine thoroughbreds, and the patched, jingling wagon with the loose wheel spokes a grand carriage, the picture in her head differing greatly from the actual lowly form of transportation, the endless gray dust that squelched out from the steel rims of the wheels launching into the still air before powdering the papery grass.

Hannah shivered in spite of herself. Her coat was too thin, too patched and worn.

On either side of the grass-lined dirt road, the prairie fell away, level, unmoving, and endless. As far as the eye could see, after the clump of cottonwoods and jack pines in the hollow where the winding creek was deepest and widest in normal weather, there was nothing but grass and sky.

The next road right led to the Klasserman ranch, a neat assembly of low buildings surrounded by heavy black Angus cattle, run by Owen and his wife Sylvia, a couple of German descent, hardworking, hard-eating and larger in size than most other folks who ran cattle and lived spare, lean lives that wore them down like polished wood, and creased and fissured their leathery faces. Not the Klassermans. They remained florid pink, smooth-faced and portly, their clothes pressed to perfection, washed until the whites shone blue.

After that road, a few miles farther, was the road that led to Hod Jenkins's spread. He had resorted to some barbed wire, the corner post leaning haphazardly, the wires rusted and sagging, like everything else around their place.

The sight of the corner post took away Hannah's proud thoughts and replaced them with a sort of humbling.

More of a put-down, she thought grimly, thinking of Hod's oldest son, Clay. Blonde and handsome, desperately in love with her, he was as bothersome as a determined green-headed horsefly. But he made her feel wanted and beautiful, everything she had planned to resist.

Would resist. For one thing, he was a person raised according to worldly standards. A non-Amish. An English. A chasm stood between them, a divide that Clay simply did not understand or try to. His comprehension of all things spiritual was distorted by his infrequent church attendance, Hannah thought. He claimed he went with his parents, Hod and Abby, but knowing them, they went on an irregular basis themselves.

Well, the neighbors' church-going particulars were none of her affair, so she wasn't going to ruin her morning thinking about Clay. If she was inclined to marry, which she was not, he wouldn't be included in the list of possible suitors. She'd have to travel back home to Lancaster County, join the Amish church, then take up the serious vows of church membership, which meant giving her life to God, accepting Jesus Christ as her master and the author of her faith, a prospect that seemed a bit daunting.

The Detweiler homestead was situated on 640 acres smack in the middle of nowhere, with not one other Amish family living closer than hundreds of miles, giving Hannah reason to question her future as far as staying Amish.

She put all of this out of her mind as they approached the dusty little town of Pine, situated among clumps of half-dead trees and rusted out cars, broken-down farming equipment, and peeling signs.

There was a livery stable, Rocher's Hardware, the feed store, two cafes, and a few bars, places of evil that Mose had warned his children were the devil's watering holes and to stay away from them.

There was a gas station on the edge of town by the railroad tracks where the redroot and tumbleweed sprawled among each other, both sifting dust and dirt and whatever blew past. Hannah stopped the team, gave the reins to Manny and pushed open the heavy door covered with cracked white paint, fly speckled, the long window splotched with grease and fingerprints. The loud bell that jangled above her head made her jumpy.

She didn't smile at the young man behind the counter, just looked him square in the eye and said she needed five gallons of gasoline and a can to put it in.

He looked back at her, then leaned on the counter, his elbows propping up his long bony shoulders, without smiling.

"You that Detweiler girl?"

"Yes."

"Hmm."

"I need the gas. Cows out of water."

"Oh, you got the engine, do ya?"

Hannah nodded, irritated, watching his slow movements, getting the metal gas can, dusting it off by blowing on it, wiping the top of the can with a greasy rag, then methodically thumping the numbers on the buttons of the high-backed cash register.

"That'll be two bucks and fifty-four cents."

Hannah counted out the money, ten quarters and four pennies, placing them on the counter before turning to pick up the empty gas can. She walked to the pump, waited and waited, then went to find the youth, who was bent over a red metal tub, his pant legs hitched above his ankles, fishing around in the cold water for a bottle of root beer.

"I need my gas can filled," Hannah said loudly. He came up with his drink, turned, adjusted his pants and said, "Git it yerself."

Ashamed to tell him she didn't know how, she stalked off, figured she could learn, unhooked the nozzle, and pressed a button.

Nothing happened. Red-faced, she tried again. Still nothing.

"Manny, get down offa there and help me with this thing," she shouted, holding the pump nozzle in one hand and the gas cap in the other.

Obediently he leaped off, hung the reins across the splintered dashboard, walked over, pressed not one lever, but two, and an aromatic stream of clear gasoline shot into the can. At the proper moment, Manny stopped the flow, capped the gasoline can, and hoisted it onto the back of the spring wagon.

At the hardware, they made their purchases, promised Harry she'd be back the following week, said hello to the wan Doris, who clasped her hand in both of hers and begged her to return.

The hardware store was more of a general store, stocking all kinds of groceries and housewares, fabrics, boots, and shoes.

The place had returned to its usual disregard for order of any kind, but Hannah knew there would only be time for an occasional day's work done there. The ranch required most of her time.

The ride home was even colder, the dry air slicing through their thin outerwear, cold and cruel. Manny said they could have brought a horse blanket. Hannah shook her head, chapped hands to warm them, and drew back a nose-full of mucus, her teeth chattering.

"This weather is odd," Manny remarked.

"Nothing's odd out here. If you expect the worst, it's normal. Terrible cold, high winds, drought, heat that scorches the grass, hailstorms—that's all normal. So why would we worry about a still day?"

Manny nodded, his eyes lifted to the yellow light that came from gray clouds, the air so cold and still. He didn't like it. The hairs on his forearms prickled with electricity.

The engine chugged away, propelling the pump into the well. Water gushed from the cast-iron hydrant, filling the galvanized tank to one half, three fourths, then to overflowing.

The cows smelled the fresh water, came from every direction, hopping, trotting and bobbing through the trampled brown grass. The sound of the engine stopped them in their tracks. Heads lowered, they stood grouped together, sniffing the air, ears forward like black flaps, their fear of the engine overpowering their thirst. The large cow, the one who had turned on their father, shook her head and pawed the ground, her breath whistling through distended nostrils.

"Watch her, Hannah," Manny said, tense and alert. Hannah nodded, shutting off the engine.

Snorting, blowing, the cows surged forward, dipped their noses and dry tongues into the tank brimming with cold water. Hannah stood watching the milling cattle jockeying for position, butting heads, tossing a smaller heifer like a half-empty sack of feed.

They started the engine again, leaning, yanking on the starter rope until it popped, backfired, sparks flying. The cows took off, panicked, bawling short, sharp sounds of craziness, their tails held aloft like baseball bats.

"Hey! Watch those sparks!" Manny yelled above the roar of the clattering engine.

"It'll be all right," Hannah yelled back.

When the tank was full, they shut off the rattling contraption, glad to regain the sense of solitude and sweet lonesomeness that clumped together out in this boundless land without end, bringing substance to an unstable world. It was always like that. A town, a loud engine, company coming, letters from Lancaster—everything was a tangle of noise and uncertainty. Alone on the prairie, everything came together and made sense. The sky, the earth, the cattle, hopes and dreams. Thoughts became reality, and reality became thoughts. A oneness with the land materialized over time, a fine, sweet message that flowed back and forth without effort. To feel the level dirt beneath her feet, knowing it held an uncountable amount of roots that would push new growth to meet the undying sunlight every spring without fail, was a promise of the future, a substance she could feel in her spirit.

If she listened to the neighboring ranchers, their past, their predictions of the future, she lost sight of this reassurance with the land. Folks just talked too much. They made her so tense and irritated. Take that Hod Jenkins and his boys. They'd as soon make fun of any new idea as try it out, stuck on that ranch that didn't know the meaning of the word maintenance. If a hinge on a door broke, they merely lifted the door to swing it open or shut on one hinge. Every empty tin can was plastered with buck shot, left to rust in the grass for someone to cut themselves on. Their herd of cattle was slatted with protruding ribs, pot-bellied, scrawny-necked and ugly, coarse hair hanging off them like dead grass. That didn't keep them from telling Hannah her fancy cows wouldn't winter over good and would need help birthing calves.

But she knew that without the Jenkinses, they would not have survived that first year. Generous and plain good-hearted, they took the Detweilers under their wings like a mother hen. Everything they had given, everything they had done, had been with the Detweilers' best interest in mind. Even as they begged them to return to Lancaster County because they weren't cut out to be homesteaders, the Jenkinses eyes were liquid with sympathy.

The cows watered sufficiently, they walked back together, the stillness of their companionship the only thing necessary.

They came up on the squat, brown and weathered house, the dark smoke curling toward the ominous sky. Without speaking, their pace increased, anticipating the warmth of the cookstove, secure from the cold. They clattered up on the porch and yanked the door open to the smell of simmering chicken potpie, the children's chatter like birdsong, and the sound of Sarah's low singing at the table, where she sat darning a pair of stockings.

Sarah served them the chicken potpie in deep bowls of stone ware, and sides of applesauce and spicy red beets. She frowned when Hannah lifted her spoon and began to eat without the usual bowing of her head, eyes closed in silent prayer. Manny sat waiting.

Sarah reminded Hannah to pray before eating. After a whoosh of impatience and a shrug of her shoulder, she folded her hands and dipped her head, Manny following suit. They ate quickly, shoveling the hot food into their mouths, shaking their heads to cool their tongues when too much heat produced quick tears.

Hunger, or the sating of it, was not a matter taken lightly. "Why'd you kill a chicken?" Hannah asked after she wiped her bowl with a bread crust and jammed the whole piece into her mouth.

"I didn't. It's canned chicken from Doddy Stoltzfus's cellar."

Hannah raised her eyebrows and kept her comment to herself. Sarah lifted the cover on the cookstove, added two sticks of wood, and squinted at the billowing smoke before replacing the lid.

Eli played with blocks of wood and tiny bundles of grass tied with string, building a barnyard and feeding imaginary cattle. Mary pushed the wooden wagon, loaded the bundles of grass and took them across the floor, making galloping noises as she imagined a team of horses.

"Winter's coming," Eli piped up. "Better get more hay, Mary."

Abby crawled fast, wrecked the barn, and scattered the hay with baby squeals. Eli jumped to his feet, his hands grasping her soft, plump waist as he pulled and dragged her back from the cattle ranch. Abby set up howls of protest as she wriggled against the restraint. Hannah slid off her chair, bent to pick her up and held her on her lap, cooing and stroking her back.

"They should let you play. Mary, why can't she play with some of your blocks?"

"We need them."

"Our barn needs to be closed in," Eli chimed in.

Manny got down on the floor and helped them build a better barn, with blocks left over for a barnyard. He promised to build some cattle for them from blocks of wood with nails for legs.

"Grass for a tail! Grass for a tail!" Eli shouted, until Sarah held a finger to her lips, shushing him.

Night fell, darkening the windows with a smear of black. There were no stars, no wind, only the breathless silence. Inside, it was warm, their stomachs were full. Contentment lay in the folds of the white curtains, the simmering of the hot water on the back of the stove, in Sarah's drooping eyelids as she set cups of sugared tea in front of them. Night was closing in and she was ready to rest, weary with the work of the day.

Hannah said the engine worked well and the cattle had their fill of water. Now they would not need to worry about calm weather.

Sarah smiled sleepily, her mind only absorbing a portion of what Hannah was saying. She was thinking of long winter evenings with Mose, the times of happiness in Lancaster County when she was a new bride living in the small rental house at Uncle Levi's, her husband dark and handsome, their love so perfect and unspoiled, like a delicate rose. His kindness, his loving devotion, everything a man should be. She was blessed beyond measure in those days.

It was only her absolute devotion to the Bible and the art of submission that had taken her through the dark times that followed. She had not been blind to her husband's poor management of the family farm, but she felt it was not in her rightful place to assert herself.

Cows milked late, milk production dropped, and checks in the mail dwindled, leaving unpaid feed bills, horses dying of colic, mold in the grain, and wet alfalfa they should not have been fed. Sarah milked the cows until her arms were numb, her fingers stiff like newly stuffed sausages. And still she milked, trying to ward off the lurking mastitis, the dreaded clumping of the milk, and the blood mixed with the yellowish lumps as it came painfully through the teats.

When the Great Depression hit, the cows were sold to pay the feed bill. When the price of a good milk cow barely reached one hundred dollars and corn wasn't worth anything with no livestock to eat it, the slide into losing the farm became inevitable.

Yet he dreamed and refused to face reality, a cloud of goodwill and a rosy future would appear just around the next bend. They still had five good milk cows, a much smaller feed bill, plenty of hay, and corn to husk.

The bishop sent the deacon to talk to Mose about unpaid bills and the offer of allowing men into their house to "Go over the books," in his words. In his courteous manner he spoke of this being a help to Mose to relieve him of the burden of not being able to meet the monthly payments that were past due. Mose bowed his head, acknowledged that he needed help, and then went out and made his own arrangements. He set up the illegal whiskey still and turned all his grain into the *verboten* alcoholic beverage.

He felt despised, stomped on, hunted, and shamed. Excommunicated for this gross *ivva drettung*, the overstepping of set boundaries, he experienced public shaming to the fullest, his soft heart and easy-going manner wrecked, twisted, and wrung out to a fine pulp.

Still Sarah remained loyal and supportive. When the men went through their accounts, there was no alternative. The farm had to be sold for much less than it was worth. Mose made *frieda*, was taken back as a member of the church, his sins forgiven. Then, already, the decline of his good sense had begun.

Sarah sat, the darning needles clicking, her face serene in the glow of the kerosene lamp. But the dark circles that saddened her eyes into a shade of gray betrayed the pain of remembering, so intense at times that she felt as if she could not bear up beneath it.

Had she done wrong by being passive? How much could she have prevented?

Manny looked up from his building of a better farm, his eyes resting on his mother's, the sadness a common knowledge between them. Manny's was caused by his *zeit-lang*, and Sarah's by the pain of wishing that things had been different.

Still, she had carried his love and preserved it valiantly, in spite of his shortcomings, and for this, she felt rewarded and redeemed.

Sighing, she put away the darning needles, folded up the half-finished socks, and set the basket on the side cupboard. Her eyes felt heavy with sleep as she bent and lifted up Abby to wash her face and hands. Confused, she noticed an odd pink glow in her bedroom window. Was there a storm approaching so late in the evening?

CHAPTER 2

Sarah's shaking hands parted the curtains. She strained to see. Her mouth opened, but no sound came from it. . Then she called loudly, "Hannah! Manny!"

The pink glow turned into an orange line, low and wide, in the direction of the windmill.

The sound of their mother's voice froze both of them. They knew instantly there was something serious. They fell over each other, rushing to the bedroom. Both of them let out a hoarse, primal scream. Sarah directed as they moved swiftly through the house.

"Feed sacks. The sacks!" Hannah shouted. Manny burst through the front door, flung himself off the porch, and disappeared into the night, leaving Sarah and Hannah to run toward the dry burning grass surrounding the windmill.

Eli and Mary held Abby, their eyes large and frightened, Abby reaching toward the front door, wailing and crying for her mother.

They realized the situation was dire. The line of fire increased too fast to stop. Somehow, they had to reach the tank and immerse the sacks. They had to try.

Hannah stood at the edge of the fire, the heat sending a hard stab of fear through her sturdy leather shoes and into her stomach, feeding their desperation to stop the fire. The homestead was all they had.

"The tank. We'll flog a path through," Sarah shouted.

"There's no wind," Manny yelled.

"We can do this," Hannah ground out between clenched teeth.

The heat seared the soles of her feet as she dashed through the scattered flames. She saw the breaks in the line of fire, where the cattle hooves had trampled the grass.

Was there hope?

She threw the sacks into the tank, prodded them down as the greedy flames licked at the dry grass around them. As Hannah gripped a feed sack with clenched fingers, sucking air through clenched teeth, her nails bent backward, creating a searing pain. She brought it down on the low, crackling flames with a hard whoosh, the flames dying and leaving a black, charred area, stinking smoke and ashes showering them. One area blackened, and the flames leaped out of control in another.

Clearly, they had created a path to the water tank now. The dash to wet the sacks was possible without wading through a line of fire. The flames died down, only to leap up, hissing, brilliant. The sight of the fire devouring the dry grass banished any hope.

The night was still, the only sounds the crackling of the burning grass and the wet burlap sacks flogging the orange flames in bursts of smoke and ash. There were no stars or moon, only the canopy of black night sky and the eerie orange glow of the flames.

How long did they keep throwing those wet sacks around? Hannah didn't know, couldn't speculate, her world suddenly turned into a searing nightmare of heat, flame, and the stench of smoke and black ashes.

She noticed that the burnt grasses turned into bits of white, like tiny worms that appeared for only a second then disappeared. For a fleeting moment, she saw the homestead, its puny buildings tinder dry, gone up in smoke like a blade of grass.

They became hopeless when the surrounding line of flames grew in spite of the blackened path, the avenue of charred grass mixed with hot dust and dirt.

Hannah flogged on, beating the earth until her face burnt, her shoulders and arms numb with fatigue. The ever widening area of burned grass was only an unstable victory. She sensed the dancing, licking greediness of the blaze devouring dry grasses so easily, increasing the red and orange flames.Manny's face was as black as the night sky, with white lines zigzagging along his cheeks where the tears of desperation had fallen. He was like someone gone made, running and flogging with a maniacal speed of despair, a pace he could not hope to keep up.

Sarah worked grimly, a determination born of panic driving her on. They had to save the buildings. There was hope, in spite of the futility of these wet sacks beating on the flames. She cried out as she saw a new line of fire breaking out toward the direction of the house.

Dear God, is this your will? Are we simply not meant to be homesteaders? Are we meant to reside among others like us, secure together in body as well as spirit?

She knew the situation was dire long before Hannah and Manny did. But she figured that, as long as God gave her strength, she would fight on. The path to the tank grew longer and longer, the blaze spreading wider. How long until Hannah saw this?

She watched her daughter beating and beating, stomping on flames, her skirt charred and blackened, her face a caricature of herself, her hair, coming loose as the pins fell out, surrounding her face in tendrils, like a wild woman. Her eyes were swelling from the heat and smoke.

Sarah stood still, making raspy sounds as she breathed in and out, her chest heaving, her throat feeling charred and burnt.

Taking stock of the situation, the panic rose in her chest, filling her senses. They need to flee, to get away now. She calmed herself, not wanting the children to see absolute abandonment in her need for a headlong dash away from this heat and uncontrollable dry grass. She needed to think and speak rationally.

"Hannah!" she called loudly, her voice carrying above the sound of the crackling prairie fire.

Hannah was deaf to her mother's voice, lost in a world of agony and defiance, her determined nature now leading her to the brink of foolishness.

Sarah screamed in a high and desperate voice. "Hannah!"

Manny stopped beating the flames and ran over to his mother, his eyes dark with rings of white in the eerie glow.

"It's no use. We can't do it," Sarah choked.

Manny nodded, ran over to Hannah, and yelled in her ear. She elbowed him away and kept up her demented flogging and beating with s gunny sack half eaten away by the flames. She stomped and danced, her head down, her arms outstretched as if the power of her own determination would yet deliver them from this horrible evil.

Manny grabbed her arm, yelled and pulled her away. She fought him off, the gunny sack flung in his face. She beat his shoulders with her fist, kicked his shins, his legs and feet, screaming hysterically.

"No! No! Come on, Manny! No! No!"

Sarah ran and grabbed Hannah by the waist, pulling her away with supernatural strength. Hannah twisted and yelled, shrieking threats and beating the air with her fists. Manny grabbed her kicking feet and held on.

Without speaking, they gave up the fight. They had all they could do to get Hannah away from the flames. Sarah could not think of what this would do to her daughter, knowing what can happen to a person so unusually determined to be pushed over the brink.

The thought of her Aunt Suvilla sent shudders of fear through her. They hadn't known what was wrong. No one did. Put away, they called it. Put away in an insane asylum. Please, please, please. Her pleading came with her gasping breath as she begged for deliverance from so harsh a punishment.

In the end, their strength gave out. They had to rest. Crying and screaming, Hannah tore out of their grip and took off into the night and the disastrous orange flames. There was nothing they could do but lay spent and gasping, their muscles burning with fatigue. It was only the thought of the terrified children and the need to get away, that roused Sarah and set her on the path of action.

"Manny!" she panted. "Get the horses hitched. Take the lantern. Bundle the children into their coats. Go. We have to get away."

"Will it take everything?" Manny gasped.

She could not soften the blow. "Yes! Go!"

She thanked God for Manny's obedience and began walking in the direction of the fire. "Preserve Hannah's mind, Lord. Preserve her spirit," she prayed. Soon enough she saw her, stomping on the flames, as useless as she had ever seen anything. The windmill behind her, the arc of blackened earth, the ever-widening wreath of burning grass and white smoke against the cold, black sky—the hellish scene etched in her mind forever.

"Hannah!" she screamed. "Hannah!" Sarah went to her, wincing at the heat coming through her skirts and on the soles of her shoes, the fire's searing brilliance ever powerful, ever increasing. Sarah drew on Hannah's sleeve, tugged at her skirt, begging, crying, her breath coming in painful puffs of air. "Hannah!"

The sound of panic in her mother's voice broke through Hannah's maudlin stomping. She stood stock still, her dark eyes staring without seeing. Dear God, have I lost my eldest daughter? Suddenly a fierce and undeniable hatred of Mose's ill-timed journey to North Dakota speared its way into Sarah's mind.

She had submitted, had obeyed the whole way, the whole senseless, ridiculous way. She cried and screamed, lifted her face to the dark sky and allowed herself the luxury of regret and remorse. The power to save her daughter from this awful fate fueled the confrontation of who she was.

To this end, then, she had blindly obeyed. Her screaming broke through Hannah's sense of shock. With a broken cry, she threw herself down, groveling and clutching Sarah's blackened skirts, whimpering, a lost sound devoid of courage.

Sarah bent down and lifted her up. Supporting her with an arm around her waist, she drew her away. Pliant now, her head fallen forward, Sarah guided Hannah with an arm about her shoulders and then around her waist.

Murmuring half-prayers and half-endearments incoherently, Sarah stopped and turned to kiss Hannah's cheek. She tasted soot and ashes, and the salt of Hannah's tears. Broken, they stood together weeping hoarse sobs of pain and defeat, acceptance and helplessness.

"Come, Hannah," Sarah murmured gently. Hannah nodded. And then, in a gesture Sarah would never forget, laid her head lightly on her mother's shoulder. Dry, hacking sobs and coughs tore from her raw throat.

"It'll take the buildings," she croaked.

"Yes."

Mother and daughter, united now, turned back toward the house, tears mingling with ashes from their a baptism of fire, introducing the uncharted territory of homesteading in the West. So far, determination and the help of family and neighbors had kept them afloat. But from here on, on this terrible night, there was no direction.

They looked back and saw the ever-widening circle of flames. Spurred on by fear, they ran to the house, stumbling painfully on leather soles half burned away. Up on the porch, they grabbed the little ones, hushing, cajoling.

What to take? What to leave? No matter. The windows reflected the orange glow. Hurry. Oh, hurry. Will the horses outrun it?

A high yell from Manny in the direction of the barn. The wind. The wind was getting up. Sarah snatched quilts, blankets, towels, the checkbook, the coins in the crock.

For what? For what? Blindly they ran out into the night. She felt the wind. Plainly, she heard the distant crackling, the yellowish glow lighting the dark.

"The chickens! The cow!" Hannah shouted.

"I let them loose! Manny shouted back, hanging onto Pete's bridle. Goat snorted, his hooves digging into the earth. Fire terrified horses.

They threw themselves into the wagon, stuffing quilts under the seats. As Manny let loose, the horses reared and leaped, knocking him onto the seat. He grabbed the reins. The wild dash into the night began.

Hannah looked back at a wall of crackling orange. The buildings etched in black harbored their belongings—the cookstove, the plank table made by Mose's own hands, the beds and the washtubs, the dishes and pans. All of it would be devoured by one spark from the new gasoline engine.

She turned away, the picture of all her hopes and dreams an unbearable vision. She clung to the seat and hung on to Eli, wide-eyed and crying.

"You have to slow them down, Manny," Sarah called hoarsely.

He nodded. "Klassermans?" he croaked.

"They're closest."

Owen and Sylvia were deep in their first slumber of the night when Owen dreamed there was a woodpecker talking to him, his mouth in a smile, telling Owen he'd better check the front door soon. He woke with an unnamed dread and a cold chill, aware of his wife's soft hand shoving at his shoulder and saying, "Owen. Owen. Owen."

He swung his legs down from the high bedstead, his feet scrabbling for the stool he used to get in and out of bed. He missed it and fell hard on his hands and knees, a whoosh of air and a grunt pushing from his mouth.

"Ach, Owen. Get up." Sylvia, talking to him from the folds of warm blankets. Fumbling for his trousers, he placed one pink foot into an opening and jammed his toes into a pocket before untangling himself and trying again. The knocking was louder and faster now.

Muttering, he let himself out the bedroom door, wondering if he should grab the rifle or what. Such a pounding on his front door!

His eyes stretched enormously to see the blackened huddle in front of him. The story came tumbling out in swift sentences, sending Owen to the telephone to call the fire department and all the surrounding neighbors. He held the mouthpiece and yelled into it, the dim electric bulb from the ceiling making the desperate group appear more burned and terrified.

Sylvia appeared in her fluffy pink housecoat, her eyes popping then streaming with tears of pity. She couldn't help but think of the time spent on her hands and knees wiping the linoleum on the floor, and now here it was, covered with black soot. They smelled terrible, just terrible. But *ach*.

The wind confused them after days of silence. It moaned and sighed in the cold night and tore at the corner of the roof where the downspout wasn't fastened properly. It whistled around the corner of the porch, lifted the door mat and folded it in half, sent a half-dozen barn cats scurrying for cover.

Back at the homestead, it whipped the burning grass into a fury of heat and light. The flames danced across the plains, eating away at the dry, unpainted logs of the buildings. It licked greedily now, gulping wood and mortar, growing hotter and hotter as the wind rose in strength, riding before the storm that had been lurking in the gray bank of clouds for days, waiting to unleash its pent-up power.

The work of Mose Detweiler's hands was ravaged, gobbled up in less than an hour by the raging inferno, whipped by the oncoming storm. There was no one to observe, no one to record the actual time.

The fire engines arrived clanging, but by now the fire had spread wider and was completely out of control. Telephone wires crackled with the news until the poles went down, annihilated along with everything else in the fire's path.

The laying hens cackled and squawked as they ran before the wall of fire with the gophers and rabbits and prairie hens. The milk cow ran clumsily, her poor udder swinging and her eyes wide with terror until she succumbed to the power of the smoke and heat, like every other living thing in its wake.

When the ice and freezing rain started, appearing as wet splotches the size of dimes, driven sideways and slanting against the night sky, pelting the house's sturdy German siding, they all thought it was only the wind increasing. But soon they realized what the sound against the glass window panes was.

Manny's face lit up, the hope burning in eyes so like his father's, believing, with faith like a rock, that his prayers were answered. The homestead would be saved, there was no doubt.

Sarah turned her head and saw the ice and cold rain sluicing down the window panes. She silently calculated the distance between the windmill and the buildings and was afraid to hope.

Hannah stood still and listened. Bitter. Too late, likely. So much for God helping you out. And yet, for a fleeting instant, she hoped.

The freezing rain and the wind turned into a maelstrom of sight and sound, pounding against the north side of the house, then the south. The wind shrieked and roared. The cold deluge clattered against the windows, flung on the house as if giant arms were throwing it.

Eli held both hands to his ears, palms sweaty with panic and little boy agitation. "Mam, Mam," he whimpered, his black eyes like wet coals.

Mary went to him and held him in her thin arms. She stroked his shoulder and said, "It's only rain, Eli. And wind. *Yusht da vint.*"

Owen sat at the kitchen table, his round face sober, his eyes glinting in the electric light. Sylvia was in the closet, rummaging for clothes for Sarah and the two oldest children. They smelled bad. She could hardly breathe.

She filled the claw-foot tub with hot water from the spigot, the stopper to the drain attached with a small chain. She gathered clean towels, a bar of soap, washcloths, and two flannel nightgowns she had outgrown. Holding one up to her shoulders, she shook her head in disbelief. Had she really been that small once?

Back at the homestead, the wind whipped the fire into a hellish frenzy, its power growing until it could gobble up anything in its path. The greedy blaze devoured acres of dry grass, reducing it to flat, black ash that left little puffs of gray smoke and white dust whirling away into the night.

When the thunderous black clouds finally unleashed their pent-up rain and hailstones, the sky poured unlike anything the huddled ranchers had ever seen, and they thought they'd seen everything.

In only a few hours, the out-of-control burning turned the land into a black, stinking, mushy slime dented with ice pockets, hailstones sizzling and steaming in seconds. The clattering ice and rain made hissing and spitting sounds as it fell on the raging flames, firing shoots of white steam toward the roiling black sky.

Ranchers and firefighters stood by their various forms of transportation until the power of the deluge sent them inside.

Hail bounced off metal rooftops and windowpanes, and the torrents of icy rain made driving impossible.

The flattened brown grass bent to the onslaught. The cracked earth took on piles of ice and water sluiced into the broken, parched soil. The rain was too late for the crops, but it restored the water table beneath the grass.

Years later, the ranchers would speak of the fire, the sizzling and steaming clouds of it that people spotted as far away as Pine. The storm had saved them all. Hard telling where the fire would have stopped had the rain not come. They would have needed to dig trenches to save ranch buildings. Stretched to the limit by the local gossip, the night of the storm was told and retold, around dinner tables, in church yards, and in cafés and bars. Hashed and rehashed, until it was chewed to a pulp.

At the Klassermans, Sarah lay in the clean guest bed that Sylvia had made, little Abby held snugly in her arms. She was exhausted. Weary beyond anything she had ever experienced. The muscles in her arms burned with the extended force and movement of the wet feed sacks that had pushed her to her limits and beyond. Her legs ached and felt like stumps. Her lips were numb, scorched by the heat and smoke. Her face was chapped and dry. She reached up to feel the lashes on her eyes and eyebrows and was met with smooth, hairless skin.

She cried, then, hot scalding tears of hopeless despair, the loss of her eyebrows the final shove that sent her headlong into a chasm of anguish. She drew up her knees as she whimpered and sobbed, stuffing a fist against her mouth to keep from waking Abby.

The rod of God's chastening had fallen hard, more than she could bear. What had she done to deserve this? Must one person reap what another had sowed? When she became Mose's wife, they had become one. Was punishment meted out bit by bit to her as an accomplice in Mose's follies?

She squeezed her eyes together, moaning softly with the pain
and humiliation. She had followed him, this wild land an anchor
for his dreaming. Footloose, unstable he was. Oh, he was.

The future loomed, a bitter cup. Sarah's family could not
be expected to come forward yet again. All Sarah and the children had were two worn out horses, a rusted wagon that jig-
gled, clothes that reeked of fire and smoke, a few quilts, and she
hoped, a handful of bewildered cattle that had been bought with
her father's money. She prayed to keep from blaming Mose. She
prayed that God would purge her heart and show her the known
and unknown sins she coveted. *Vissa adda unvissa.* To be beaten
back time after time, surely God was showing her something
about her life—a wrong, a sin, a rebellion.

In the adjacent guest room, Hannah lay with Mary and Eli
beside her on smooth and spotless sheets smelling of lavender
and mothballs. The quilts pressed her ravaged body into the
mattress.

She was bone tired. She could be dead the way her body felt,
but she guessed that as long as her heart was beating and her
lungs were breathing, she was still alive, so that was something.

Stupid old gas engine. That Ben Miller didn't install it right.
Probably Ike Lapp did it. One spark, two or three, whatever.
If the storm had arrived even a few hours earlier, the buildings
would have been saved. She railed against God about how the
Higher Power handled what she couldn't control. But her sensi-
tivity to sin and wrongdoing steered her away from blaming the
family's misfortune on God.

Well, all right then; here is what it was. The homestead was
a soupy black mess that smelled worse than Sodom and Gomor-
rah. One windmill. Some frightened cattle. Two horses and a
wagon. Everyone safe. They'd need to make a phone call to Lancaster. Her grandfather's neighbor could find him and bring him
to the house.

News would spread. The biggest hurdle, as Hannah saw it, was going to be her own mother's need to return to the safety of Lancaster County. To persuade her to start over was the closest thing to an impossibility Hannah had ever encountered. Who could do it?

An iron fist closed around Hannah, the will to stay and start over flowing in her veins, revitalizing her fatigue. She envisioned a new house, long and low, a real ranch house, a barn, the grass lush and green and waving; the cattle fat and black, multiplying like rabbits, being driven to Dorchester where the auctioneer's gavel crashed down on the highest prices.

Everyone would know the superiority of the Bar S brand. Somehow, she needed to procure another loan. First thing in the morning she'd make that telephone call without Sarah knowing about it.

CHAPTER 3

THE COLD CAME WITH DETERMINATION, RIDING IN ON THE WAKE OF the storm a month earlier than usual. It came at night, freezing a lid of ice on the cow's water tank and coating the crumbling dry grass with hoarfrost resembling sugar crystals. The dry creek beds welled with turgid brown water that seeped into the cracked, parched earth and left slabs of thin brown ice along its banks that looked like torn slabs of moldy bread.

The cows grew winter coats and stood hunched against the cold, their eyes slashes in their faces, warding off the frost. Acres and acres of burnt prairie grass froze to a blackened permafrost, a sort of nighttime Arctic, someone's overwrought imagination come to life.

Owen and Sylvia kept them all safely tucked in the warm ranch house, the fire burning and crackling cheerily in the two wood stoves. As news of the fire spread, farmers and townspeople bearing bags of clothes and boxes of pans and plates, glasses, knives and forks, blankets and towels stopped at the Klassermans in their chugging cars and trucks.

Hannah made the phone call home, relating the events, her voice strong and without emotion. The word spread quickly, ears bent toward the shocking news. That poor Sarah. They shook their heads, clucked their tongues. Hadn't the poor woman had enough?

Ei-ya-yi. And they stepped forth. They couldn't blame hard times. In the time of tragedy, you gave freely, never questioning. Give and it shall be given unto you, packed down and flowing over.

And they did. The relatives gathered clothing and furniture. Some gave money. Samuel Stoltzfus, Sarah's father, sat at his kitchen table with tears flowing silently down his face, glistening in his white beard, the humble gratitude overflowing.

Jeremiah Riehl was shoeing a horse for a customer, Henry Esh, the horse leaning all his weight on the hoof tucked between his knees. Henry kept up an endless volley of local news peppered with gossip. Jerry's shoulders burned with the strength needed to keep the hoof intact. He was tired of listening to Henry's blather, and this horse was about the most contrary creature he'd shod all week.

He heard North Dakota. Immediately, he let go of the hoof, straightened his back and stared at Henry, his dark eyes intense.

"Yeah, burned up. They say there's nothing left. Burned up the house and barn. They say it wasn't much to begin with. That Mose Detweiler was an *aylend*. They say his wife will come back now, but the oldest daughter won't. Ray Miller said the only reason they're out there is because of her. She's something else. Must be like her old man. You know they say it rained so hard the fire was out in five minutes. Five minutes! I guess the way it sounds the weather out there is hardly to be trusted.

"So I don't know what's gonna happen. Old Samuel Stoltzfus is getting ready to go out again. Folks are giving things and he'll probably end up with a railroad car load of stuff."

He stopped and went over to the open barn door to send a stream of tobacco juice into the crisp November air.

"Weddings going full sing, right now. Don't you think you better start courting someone? You're not getting any younger."

Jerry didn't hear that part of Henry's string of words. He was still thinking about North Dakota. About Hannah. "So how'd this fire start?" he asked.

Henry roared and slapped his knee. "Boy, you're a slick one! Avoid talking about what I just said."

Henry took his leave, driving the newly shod horse and leaving Jerry in a fuzzy state, his mind hundreds of miles away, out on the plains of North Dakota. He didn't understand his need to go and see for himself what had actually occurred, to see for himself what they had come through. Mostly, though, he wanted to see Hannah.

Was she suffering? Broken down? Where was the family staying? How could he go without raising suspicion?

When he heard of a group of men and boys going to help rebuild, he put his name in. He met the raised eyebrows of his sister and her husband with a bland questioning look, one of innocence, so that she told her husband perhaps there was nothing to her wondering if Jerry had been attracted to Hannah that day she had been caught in the rain. After all, it wasn't unusual for a young man to get the fever to go West. Not unusual at all.

Emma wanted to go. She felt she could persuade her sister to come back and live a decent life among God-fearing Amish instead of yoking herself to the world. Those western heathen were no good for the family, especially that Hannah.

Samuel said point blank there was no work for the women until the house was up. Emma blew up, enraged at her father for even thinking of helping them rebuild. What in the world was wrong with him? If Sarah planned on staying out there for Hannah's sake well, then, she was going to wash her hands of the whole affair, and she certainly hoped he wasn't too generous in his giving.

Samuel told his daughter in a patient, even tone that no, he wasn't too generous; other folks had given so much that he believed he'd need most of one railroad car to take it all.

Sylvia Klasserman had a minor breakdown that resulted in the neighbors erecting a sort of shack to house the family while they worked on rebuilding.

Sylvia was from an old aristocratic German family and was given
to extreme cleanliness, a way of life that decreed that certain jobs
be done on certain days. Washing on Monday, ironing on Tuesday,
and so forth. Her washing was done in her Maytag wringer washer,
rinsed twice, once in vinegar water and once in water containing
blueing, her whites so white they shone blue. She ironed everything,
even her bed sheets and Owen's underwear. Every six weeks she took
down her white curtains and washed them, rinsed them in blueing,
and ironed them. She washed walls and floors and furniture. She
scoured the claw foot bathtub and the small sink beside it.

Her bread baking was done on Wednesday, her pie baking on
Thursday. All her belongings had a place and were always in it
or on it. Cast iron frying pans were hung by size, her turners and
spatulas in certain compartments in certain drawers. When the
tin of lard was brought out of the pantry, it was never returned
before a good washing with soapy water.

When her immaculate house received two children and a
baby, it scrambled all her ingrained priorities. The laundry was
washed haphazardly, the ironing not even close to her specifications, not to mention the cleaning and dish washing.

And oh, that baby!

Sylvia didn't want to be this way. She wanted to relax and
give over for the dear homeless family. But in the end, she just
couldn't do it.

Abby Jenkins snorted and shook her head. She invited the
family to stay at the Jenkins ranch. But Sarah declined; it would
not be proper with Hannah's attraction to Clay.

When Owen and Hod got a group of locals to help construct
a temporary dwelling where the family could live there while the
building was going on, Sylvia did her best to hide her pent-up frustration until the glad day when they all moved out of her house.

The temporary dwelling was a shack, nothing more. Sarah
shook her head at the irony of it. Here she was, back to where

they began and probably with even less. All around them lay the blackened land. A dark desolation, the stark windmill creaking and spinning endlessly, the gray sky above it like pewter.

They had a good cookstove, and for this she was grateful. They made their beds on the floor each evening, but she was thankful for the heavy blankets and quilts. They made due with a rickety old table and chairs and clothes packed in cardboard boxes.

They carried their water from the tank, heated it in the agate canner, and used it to wash dishes and clothes. The rough planks that served as flooring were soon covered with black ashes and soot. It was everywhere. There was no way to avoid it. The land surrounding the dwelling was scorched and blackened, the gray skies and the cold prohibiting any new growth.

The cattle stayed on the prairie where the fire had been stopped by the storm. They found sustenance in the dry brown grass and for water made their way to the tank, where Hannah or Manny faithfully broke away the rim of ice.

The cattle had all survived, easily able to fend for themselves, standing far away from the fire on that awful night. Resilient, bred to fend for themselves, they went about the business of eating grass as if nothing had happened.

The locals had given without restraint. The family had no other clothes, so they wore whatever had been given.

Sarah looked funny in a too-short red shirtwaist dress with a collar. Even if she buttoned it all the way up, it still seemed as if her neck was exposed. She wore her covering and always pinned up her hair, laughing with Hannah about her ridiculous get-up. But she was clothed, and for that she was grateful.

Hannah reveled in the newfound luxury of rooting through boxes and choosing her own clothes. She tried on blouses and skirts, shoes and thin stockings. Sarah frowned as Hannah tried rearranging her hair and told her to stop it. That was enough of that.

Manny wore denim jeans. There were no buttons to attach suspenders, so he went without them, finding a leather belt and wearing it. He looked apologetic and knew he was not obeying the *Ordnung*.

One day, a black dot appeared on the horizon. It turned out to be a rattling truck, then another, and another. A freight train carload of material, a miracle in real life, had recently arrived from Lancaster.

Sarah stood in the doorway of the shack and listened to the chugging of the engines. As she watched them approach, she wept.

Across the edge, where the blackened earth lay frozen and dormant, the windmill rose cold and harsh, the paddles whispering of the desolation and loss, the gears creaking, the foundation charred and blackened.

There was her father, Samuel Stoltzfus. With him were Ben Miller, who had installed the windmill, Elam Stoltzfus, and a few men she did not recognize. Single men, without beards, none of whom she knew.

She grasped her father's hand, bit her lips to keep from crying, and blinked back the tears that threatened her composure. She had to remain strong in the face of these men. It was bad enough they were here to see the loneliness and devastation.

Sarah squared her shoulders, her mouth trembling, giving away the agony of what she'd been through, the vulnerability and weakness in the face of what God had wrought. Not a few of the men marveled at this woman who had an ability to carry on. For the life of them, they couldn't see it.

They heard hoof beats. Hannah and Manny, riding in, the cold air flushing their faces, their horses sweating, lathered where the saddles rubbed against them, threw themselves off, the blackened earth puffing up like smoke. Hannah wore jeans, a short dress over them—Sarah made her do it—and a heavy denim coat.

Her blackened face was edged in soot, her eyes dark in her flushed and exhilarated face. Manny smiled, his teeth white in his dark face.

Hannah watched the group of men warily, without smiling. She took in the three trucks, the impatient drivers hanging out of the windows saying, "Let's go. Let's go. We don't have all day!" She saw her grandfather and recognized Ben Miller. She dropped the reins of her horse and strode over to greet them with long strides, tall shoulders flung back, a tower of pride and strength. Her eyes mirrored the black devastation around her, shrouded well, or so she thought, by the pretense of her self-confident swagger.

She greeted only her grandfather and nodded curtly to the rest. She recognized Jerry Riehl. What was he doing here?

A blast of irritation shot through her. He had no right to come out here and see this burnt land and a pile of twisted metal, the hellish scene of failure and disappointment. She wished she could reach out and erase that day when she told him her foolish hopes and dreams.

She would not meet his eyes.

The men spoke with Sarah. Where would the house be built? Hannah stepped forward and began to speak, overriding her mother's voice. She had planned the house. She went through the door of the shack and came back with a folded white paper and gave it to her grandfather.

The men turned and began to unload, heeding the drivers' impatient shouts. Unload close to the charred metal, Hannah said. Under a cold, gray sky bloated with snow, the men worked feverishly, knowing that when the snow began to pummel the charred earth, their job would become twice as hard.

Samuel Stoltzfus wished they could dig a cellar. What was a good sturdy house without a cellar, especially on a level land prone to storms of every description? Ben Miller eyed the clouds and said they had best get on with it.

They erected a lean-to of sorts for the men's quarters. Sarah cooked soups and stews from morning to night. She baked bread, fed the group of men from the donated store of food, the men consuming vast quantities at each meal.

The house was framed before the snow began. Fine pellets of snow blew through the air, pinging against the lumber and their bare hands and faces.

Hannah looked up; her eyes watched the lowering clouds and the resulting bits of snow and ice. If this turned into a full blown blizzard, they'd all be packed into that shack like a bunch of rats. Well, she wasn't going to be stuck in that tar-paper shanty with those men, that was for sure. She'd ride over to the Jenkins.

That Sylvia Klasserman was crazy as a bat. She'd never step foot in that house, ever again. You didn't have to go through life eating off your floors and sanitizing everything you wore. Them and the Jenkins were exactly the opposite.

With all of Hannah's forthright thoughts swirling around in her head, the wind picked up, scouring the prairie. She knew within an hour that she would not be riding to the Jenkins. The snow intensified and fell like white curtains across the burnt earth.

Ben Miller and his crew worked on. Samuel Stoltzfus lifted his face to the sky, his white beard separating in the wind, the black felt brim of his hat flapping. He said they'd best make sure there was firewood, the way Sarah described these storms.

With the power of the driving snow, they abandoned the work. The only safe haven was the tar-paper shanty, a small drafty hovel much too small to house the nine men plus Sarah and the children.

Hannah sat in her allotted space beside the cookstove. She glowered at everyone and kept quiet, not listening to the men's ceaseless talk. Worse than women at a quilting, they talked constantly, no doubt thinking this was all a grand adventure that they could go home and joke about for the rest of their lives.

Sarah moved between the stove and the table, cooking beef stew and chili, cornbread, and fried potatoes. She was glad for the men and the endearing company of her father. Let Hannah smolder in her corner. Let her pout and hiss like a bad-mannered cat. She would happily feed these men for the gratitude and the aura of protection they afforded her.

Manny was a part of these men. He sat with them, listened to their talk, the way they expressed themselves, soaked up the latest news on politics. The times in which they lived were a clear sign of God's displeasure, taking away their money and chastening them with unsavory, undisciplined leaders in Washington, D.C.

In spite of herself, Hannah found herself listening. When the subject turned to cows, the way everyone in these parts made a living, Elam expressed his incredulity by saying he couldn't see how, if this storm was an example, these cows survived the winter.

"Yeah, and it's only November," Ben Miller chimed in.

"They won't make it. There's no way," another concurred.

That was too much for Hannah, harboring all that uncomfortable ruined pride and resentment, stuck in this disgusting little shack with these odorous, unwashed men who flashed yellow teeth like slabs of cheese every time they laughed, which was much too often.

"They will too!" she burst out.

All eyes turned to the prickly daughter, beautiful but covered in quills like a porcupine. They'd soon learned to stay away. Her grandfather smiled his slow smile. He knew her well. "How do they do it?"

"It's bred into them. They're tough, same as the people here. In a storm like this they hunker together facing away from the wind and wait to eat until it passes. They paw the snow and eat what's underneath if they have to. Ranchers have hay and some of them have shelters. Our hay's all gone, though, so we'll have to keep any eye on them."

"What happens when the storms become too frequent and the snow too deep?"

Hannah shrugged her shoulders. In the lamplight, from his corner, Jerry watched her eyes lose their flash of enthusiasm, becoming dark and brooding. He could feel her covered-up vulnerability, her fear of the coming winter.

He wondered how they would survive, much less prosper, in a land where even the elements seemed to crouch on the horizon, waiting to wipe out even the most resilient.

"Well," Elam said finally. "One way or another, we're going to give it a go; huh, Hannah?"

Her lightning smile and grateful eyes vanished, replaced by condescension and the cold, lofty lift of her chin. "Yeah." Her voice was low, a certainty laced with doubt.

The storm blew itself out during the night. Everyone was roused by the quiet, the stillness that pervaded their thin walls, the sound of the wind and scouring snow gone.

Sarah dished up bowls of oatmeal, slabs of fried bread, blackberry jam, and honey. The men pulled on rubber boots, brown work gloves, shoveled snow, and continued building the house.

The locals rode over on horseback. Abby Jenkins dismounted stiffly, the mule she had ridden tired out from his trek through the drifting snow. She brought a cardboard box of cookies, bread, and broken pies that she had lashed to her saddle.

She was yelling about the indecency of staying in this little outhouse, as she put it, wanting to know whose hare-brained idea this was? She thumped the baked items on the makeshift table, pulled up a chair to the cookstove, and held out her hands to its heat.

"Almost froze," she said, searching Sarah's face for signs of suffering. She gathered Abby into her lap and wrapped another blanket around her, rocking her gently with her thin arms. "Poor baby. Poor, poor baby," she crooned.

"So you found out about Sylvia, did you? She's crazy. She ain't right in the head. Sumpin's wrong if'n a woman irons her husband's underwear and rinses her washing twicet. Ain't never heard the likes. Ya shoulda come on over, stayed with me. I'da took keer of all of ye. Don't know why ya didn't. This shack ain't fit to live in. Reckon them men can't all fit inside, fer sure not to sleep. It ain't right. You leave these men to theirselves an' you an' the children come on over an' stay with me."

Hannah shook her head. Sarah told Abby it was a generous offer, but, no, the house would soon be finished. It was better this way. The men needed warm food.

Abby sighed. "Wal, I'll tell ya one thing. If'n this was my men, the house wouldn't be finished any time soon. Come spring, it still wouldn't be. You know Hod an' the boys." She took off layers of clothing, rolled up her sleeves, helped Sarah dice carrots and potatoes, and told her what the locals were saying regarding the fire. She chuckled.

"I thought I should tell you this, Sarah. That town in the Bible that burned so bad, the lady looked back and was turned into salt? That coulda been you, you know."

Sarah laughed, the sound genuine, always to glad to be in Abby's company. "Well, Abby, hopefully God wasn't punishing us for the sins of that town. My goodness!"

Abby laughed her own happy cackle. "No, yer a good woman, Sarah. Yer too good fer the rest of us. Yer like a angel come to live among ordinary folks."

Sarah blushed and shook her head vigorously. Hannah put clean plates on a stack as she watched her mother and Abby and felt the easy flow of their talk, the binding of their love. She was sure her mother would take offense if she dared mention that they were more like sisters than her blood relatives, so she said nothing.

"Now, yer daughter here. She's pretty normal. Full of spit and vinegar, ain't cha?" She jostled Hannah's shoulder companionably.

Hannah grinned. She thought Abby would make an admirable mother-in-law. She hated being in close proximity to Jerry Riehl. If she could wipe away every sensation of that thing he had called a goodbye kiss, she'd be fine. She couldn't look at him without thinking of it, which, truth be told, threw her into an inward struggle she couldn't stand, feeling as if she was out to sea, or something like that.

So she didn't look at him. In fact, she avoided him as if he had some disease he could easily transmit. She planned on showing him somehow that Clay was the one, not that she ever planned on getting married, but it would certainly throw him off. If he came out here thinking of any romantic involvement—well, it was just too bad. It wasn't going to happen.

The men came to eat dinner and could barely all fit. Hannah stepped back to allow Elam Stoltzfus to pass, stumbled backward, and fell into Jerry's lap. His hands went out instinctively to keep her from falling, catching her slim waist as soft as a dove's back. He laughed, enjoying her discomfiture, his hands falling to his sides as she shot up, outraged, crossing her arms tightly about her waist, then going to stand behind the cookstove, her face flaming.

Clay saw the disturbance. His eyes narrowed, drawing his mouth into a straight line of disapproval. That Jerry was far too good-looking. Brash, handsome, a threat—and Clay didn't like it. He still fully intended on claiming Hannah someday. He was willing to wait for the duration. Yes, he was. He could never forget about her. She inhabited his thoughts constantly. And here she was, dressed in English clothes, although her mother made her wear that ridiculous kerchief on the back of her head.

Sarah watched the incident with a mother's intuition. Jerry was far too handsome, far too suave for any normal girl to resist.

She knew that, like Clay, he was used to plenty of girls trying to get his attention.

Well, all too soon, Mr. Riehl would need to know that Hannah was different. She was not like other girls. She had her mind made up. Was this God's answer for Hannah's life? Because here was another roadblock, like Clay not being Amish: Jeremiah Riehl would never leave the prosperity of Lancaster County to come out here to these lonesome, unsettled plains, with their unpredictable elements and disasters, which, bit by bit, ate away at the pioneer spirit.

CHAPTER 4

The sun shone as soft and warm as a fine spring morning, melting the snow and ice and creating a gray, blackened slush-like tundra. Another load of people arrived from Lancaster County, gawkers, curious onlookers who came simply to satisfy their nosiness, their snooping, their wanting to find out for themselves how dire these leftover Mose Detweiler folks actually were.

Sarah's sisters were among them. Emma and Lydia. Sarah pushed back the irritation, projected the sisterly bond, shook hands, and smiled saying, "So good to see you." But inside, she felt much differently.

"We have lodging in Pine. We're not staying overnight," Emma informed her. They wrinkled their noses, drew sharp breaths, asked how she could live like this. It was disgusting.

Sarah felt her courage rise up within. She drew herself up to her full height, which was taller than Emma, looked her full in the eyes, without a trace of her usual bowing, and told her she was doing what had to be done under the circumstances, and if she couldn't accept it, well then, she'd have to go back to her lodging in Pine.

A volley of accusation followed, raining down on Sarah like bilious hail. She was only doing this for Hannah, and where would it get her? they wanted to know. And if she thought her father was going to give her one penny to rebuild, she was badly mistaken.

Sarah did not give out any information, nor did she give them the pleasure of her usual apology. It was, quite simply, none of their business where the funds came from, or why she chose to live in North Dakota, or what she was planning for the future.

Her father had given her the funds from Lancaster County, his soft, dark eyes welling with tears. She would not need a loan for the house or the barn. There was more than enough right here.

Sarah had been seated, but now she rose in agitation, wringing her hands, shaking her head and saying, "No, no. I can't take this. How can *Herrn saya* be received if there is always charity? We are always taking, taking, taking, Dat!" Her voice rose on an edge of hysteria, saying it wasn't right, yet again, to be recipients of other people's money.

Her father spoke quietly, calmed her by saying that God's blessing lay before her in the form of this money. All she needed to do was reach out and take it, thanking God with a pure heart.

And she had, until now. She was shaken by the deep dislike of her sisters, condemned by it, yet rose above it, receiving the courage she found deep within herself to stand up and be heard. To stay here was her decision, even if it was Hannah that helped her to make it. That was all right too. Her sisters needed to see that she was capable of making decisions and keeping them regardless of whether they were aligned to their way of thinking or not.

That was one drawback of living a cloistered lifestyle. It was normal, minding each others' business, opinions given freely, and this *right* to assert authority to an adult sister. To move away with this alarming amount of miles between them was new and rather frightening. So perhaps that was the reason Emma and Lydia had come in the first place. Perhaps they too felt the separation and wanted to come to see the devastation, and then, having seen it, were alarmed by it.

Sarah vowed to try to push away the comment that she would not get a penny to rebuild. If she acknowledged those words, she would have to accept their greediness. Instead, she chose to banish it, turn it away, and she felt much better.

Hannah sloshed around in the black mud, handing lumber and nails to the men. She cleaned up, ran errands, and did anything to help the building process along.

They used shingles this time. Hannah was thrilled to see the gray asbestos shingles nailed into place, hammers rising and falling with a speed she hadn't thought possible. In less than a day, the roof was on.

The following day, the men placed long slabs of German siding horizontally outside and covered the inside with sturdy wallboard. Then they installed the windows—six in all. The house was an icon of luxury. Seven windows! Two in the front room— the living room, it was called—two in the kitchen, and two long, low windows that allowed them to see the prairie on every side.

After two days, Emma and Lydia left on the train after two days, and, as usual, their willing husbands left with them. "Obedient puppies," Hannah said.

Sarah reprimanded her sharply and said the West was making her uncouth. "Whatever that means," Hannah muttered to herself, then went to find Manny.

The barn began to take shape, another long, low building. Hay would be stored in an adjacent lean-to, allowing easier access, all Manny's planning. He said here on the level grasslands, with no hillsides to build into, there were no bank barns. So why stack hay upstairs?

Jerry found Hannah, standing tall with her arms wrapped around her waist, viewing the barn's beginning. He walked over without hesitation. "So, what do you think?"

She nodded.

"Look okay?"

She nodded again.

"Do you like the house?"

Another nod.

Jerry laughed, a true, uninhibited sound. "You know, if you keep nodding like that, your head might fall off!"

His sense of humor caught her off guard and she laughed outright, that short, sharp blast of sound that very few people ever heard. He laughed with her.

"You do like the house, don't you? Does it look the way you imagined on paper? You know, you did pretty good, for a girl, making a drawing that precise. We could easily build with what you had drawn up."

Hannah looked at him, her mistrust rising to the surface like foam. "You're just saying that."

"What do you mean, 'I'm just saying that'? I meant it. I was impressed. You did a good job."

Only for a moment he saw her lower lip tremble, a second of transparent vulnerability. Jerry tore his eyes away from the perfection of her mouth, steadied himself, and asked about the fire, his quiet voice drawing the story from her.

Yes, the gas engine was the culprit. Unbelievable, still. He stood and listened, tried to stay calm and composed, but took in every flash of her dark eyes, every movement of her mouth. He could read her fear, sensing her determination, and could only guess at the cost of giving up the fight. For Hannah, the price must have been an awfully high.

Suddenly her story was finished. She glared at him with all the old animosity back in place. "Why did you come out here?"

"Same reason everyone else did. To help where there was a need. If I ever saw a need, it was right here. I honestly don't know how you did it. I admire your courage. A lot."

"So you're going back?"

"Yeah."

Unexpected, unexplained, the intense longing for him to stay shook her. It left her feeling unsure of anything that had ever happened in her life and anything that would occur in the future. Why did he do this to her? The first thing she had to do was get her priorities straight, which was to walk away and stop listening to his compliments. As if he was lifting her up to set her on a pedestal that she was bound to fall from. There could be no yielding here, no caving to those compliments.

His ridiculously handsome face. She wished she'd never met him. Wished he'd go home, now, this instant.

The sisters had brought a trunk load of Amish clothing, having decided between themselves that it would be the saving of Sarah's family, keeping them true to the *Ordnung*. Who else would see to it? Sarah waved and bowed down like an obedient white flag of defeat where that Hannah was concerned. So they took the matter upon themselves.

Sarah was grateful. She knelt by the trunk and lifted out one freshly sewn garment after another, examined the sturdy broadfall trousers and cotton button down shirts, the dresses and aprons without hems in a brilliant array of blue, purple, and green. She almost wept to see the amount of stiff white organdy coverings, a necessity for living out the faith.

Without the head covering, she felt undressed, exposed, as if the covering completed the obedience to her Mose, now deceased, taken away, leaving only his gentle words and strict adherence to the way of life described as Amish. The least she could do was carry on the traditions and stay true to his teaching.

Gladly, then, Manny wore the new Amish clothing, complete with the straw hat pressed down on his dark hair. With Hannah, however, and her prickliness, her hidden rebellion, there came a myriad of questions. Why? What was the difference? Dat was dead and gone. Who was there to see what she wore?

Patiently, Sarah explained. "You were born to this, Hannah. It is your duty to remain obedient."

In the too-small drafty tar-paper shanty, Sarah sat on a chair, trying to keep the new clothing off the ever-present smears of black soot that the men perpetually tracked through the door, covering the floor like a remembered curse. She plied her needle in and out of a hem so fast it made Hannah dizzy to watch.

"You may not understand now, Hannah, but later in life you will realize the value of it more than you do now. To separate ourselves from the world does not mean that we feel superior, or that we flaunt our righteousness. We are only trying to live simple lives in order to please God, to abstain from worldly pleasures that often lead to sins of the flesh."

Hannah interrupted. "There's no difference, Mam. These folks that you label worldly are not nearly as worldly in their attitudes as Emma and Lydia. You call them good, God-fearing women, with all their greed and jealousy?"

To this, Sarah had nothing to say. She bit her lip, but knew that Hannah spoke the truth. The danger of dressing plain to hide a cauldron of hidden sins rose before her, and she trembled in its presence. Her sisters meant well, she knew, but to tell Hannah this would only infuriate her.

"Hannah, listen. We cannot look on the mistakes of other people to justify our own lives. What Emma and Lydia say or do does not give you license to desert the teachings of our forefathers. That is like pushing them down to lift yourself up, which only results in a hard fall. They are only trying to preserve their own homestead and their own way of life. Think, Hannah, how you strive to manage these three hundred and twenty acres of land. Think of your hopes and dreams. So too they are trying to keep their farms, pay their mortgages, to hand them down to their children, and their children's children.

"Look at us. Off on a wild goose chase, in their opinion, robbing them of what is rightfully theirs. You can't blame them.

Now, the worldly thing to do would be to become angry, to separate ourselves and not speak to them; to think ourselves mistreated, the victims, if you will. When, in truth, you know your father had his shortcomings, his wandering ways. Godly wisdom is easy to be entreated; it tries to see both sides, and this we have to follow if we don't want to create a family rift."

Hannah snorted with her customary derision. "I can't believe you're acknowledging any wrongdoing on Dat's part."

"I didn't say it was wrong. I only said he was . . ." Her voice fell away, the needle held between her thumb and forefinger stilled. Her hands lay in her lap, loose, the strength leeched from them by the vast, open, uncharted void between the two of them.

How was one parent to uphold the virtues of the other, when his whole walk in life had reflected his unwise choices, which bordered on insanity? Hannah was no longer a child. That time of budding acceptance and worship, looking to a father as the one who does no wrong, was past. She well knew of Mose's failures, and even made up a few of her own, feeling him inferior to her own choices.

"Well, Hannah, let's just say we're taking on the challenge of your father's journey. That was your choice. So are you different from him? Better? Your dream of the Bar S and the better herd of cattle? Is this not so much like your father and his dreaming?"

The second she finished talking, Sarah knew she had wandered into a territory where she should not have gone. Blind anger clouded Hannah's dark brown eyes and her face contorted with rage.

"You think I'm as dumb as Dat, then, huh? That's all you think of me? I can't believe what you just said!" Hannah rose to her feet, grabbed her coat and scarf and let herself out of the thin, tar-paper door, closing it with a quick flick of her wrist. The whole shanty shook with its impact.

Sarah took up her needle and jabbed it through the blue fabric straight into the tip of her finger underneath, drawing a drop of crimson blood, staining the new dress. She did not weep at her daughter's outburst but merely looked at the bloodstain on the fabric, taking it as an omen.

Our blood runs thick, she thought, with the ways of our fore-fathers who looked on their path of life through eyes of humility, eyes filled with the wisdom of the simple lifestyle, the denying of the flesh. All of this is the secret to a lasting inner peace, a happiness that cannot be explained, like Jesus said.

The job of raising Hannah rose before her like an insur-mountable cliff yet again. She could not become idle, noncha-lant. She must stay alert, seek guidance, and warn Hannah of the follies of the world. She would no longer allow Hannah's perception of life to shut her out, the willing, passive mother who had no backbone, no strength to meet the strong words of rebellion. She needed to take Hannah in hand, firmly, but with love, and likely with a thousand gifts of patience.

Hannah stormed out of the house, blinded by her own outburst and the unbelief that curdled her blood. Her own mother! She was not one bit like her father. He would never have acquired the windmill, these cattle, and now, this house. This wonderful house that sustained her battered spirits. He would not have pressed on in the face of so much adversity. Then she remem-bered the hunger, the impossibility of their situation, and how he had pressed on until he bordered on losing his mind.

Hannah stood in the cold air, the sky the color of a bat-tered tin pail. She knew another storm was brewing somewhere above the plains. She felt sick with the realization of her moth-er's words, which pounded into her.

She threw a saddle on Pete, jerking the cinch until his ears lay flat and he shifted uncomfortably from side to side. She hit his teeth hard with the bit and flattened his ears as she yanked the bridle over them. "Hold still, you old nag!" she shouted.

She rode past the house, kicking the stirrups against Pete's side, leaning forward as if she was on a fast racer coming into the finish line. She galloped past the house and the workers who lifted their straw hats and stared after her in bewilderment.

Hannah rode hard past the windmill, through the burned area, throwing up little puffs of black ash, until Pete had worked up a good lather. She was breathing hard, her face numb from the cold, her hands like frozen claws. Should have worn gloves, she thought.

She held a hand to her forehead, palm down, searching for the familiar huddle of black cattle. Turning from right to left, she surveyed the level prairie. There were swells, hidden hollows, gentle bowls of earth that weren't visible to the human eye, so sometimes they weren't easy to spot.

She urged Pete on, then pulled abruptly on the reins. There they were. Breathless, she counted each black cow. Thirteen. One big mean one with bowed horns and the audacity to use them. Two cows that would be dropping calves in the spring, and ten young heifers. The bull. There he was, wide-shouldered and magnificent. They were all there. Every last one.

A few of them lifted their heads, observed her, then bent to tear mouthfuls of grass, wrapping their powerful, rough tongues around the tufts of dry grass, never stopping to chew or swallow, as far as Hannah could tell.

They didn't appear to be losing weight, in spite of the cold and the surprise snowstorm. She figured they would, though, till winter was over. All she asked was that they survive. They needed every cow, every calf, to repay her grandfather's loan.

A fleeting thought ran through her mind. How long till the wolves became hungrier? She knew they were always hungry, always on the move, dark denizens of death to anything weakened or alone. It was only when the snows of winter drove them to a bold desperation that the cows' lives were in actual danger.

She planned on borrowing more than one rifle from Clay. She'd teach herself to become a sharpshooter, able to hit a running target from yards away. She'd teach Manny, too, and together they'd keep an eye on their cows.

She glanced up at the mottled clouds that hung like moldy cottage cheese, dark clumps among lumpy gray and white ones. She wondered what that meant. She'd become fairly skilled at predicting the weather on these plains but she'd never seen anything quite like this. Her eyes roamed the level land, the endless swell of cold, rasping grass like hay that met the gray horizon, the sky cold and mysterious above it.

The sense that there was something much greater than herself washed over her, giving her a cold chill. When things ran amok, and everything seemed out of control, propelled by wheels of fear and doubt, it all came together out here, alone, without anyone's interference.

It was the vast earth and the sky with nothing in between that caused bewilderment. Was that another trait of her father? He'd spoken of the babble of voices, the constant debates that gave him so much grief. Had he been unhinged then, as he was before he died? Was she so like her father that she needed vast amounts of empty space, muddled dreams, and unrealistic ventures to stay sane? Her mother's words lay like lead in her chest.

Quickly she justified her motive for keeping the homestead, knowing her father would never have stoop to asking for a loan to better himself. Never. That was the difference. She wasn't afraid to forge ahead, to look to the future, to plan.

That was where he went wrong, muddling along without a plan, dreaming about miracles that didn't happen. And yet, here she was with the small herd, winter storms, wolves, lack of feed, which added up to nothing short of a miracle if they all survived.

She lifted her shoulders and shook her head, a small grin playing across her mouth. One day at a time. She had Manny. They'd try their best. Heartened, she rode home, unsaddled

Pete, and went to see how many days before the men would leave. They had been laying the floor, and working on the doors and trim. The chimney was finished.

Ben Miller acknowledged her with a smile. "One more day!" he shouted.

Hannah gasped. "Really?"

He nodded proudly.

The house had all come together in the last few days. A new cookstove stood against one kitchen wall, the stovepipe entering the stone chimney between the two windows. A row of store bought cupboards housed a real porcelain sink with running water and a drain like they had back home. A large living room with plenty of space for a table and chairs. A hallway with bedrooms on either side. An indoor bathroom with a bathtub.

Ben Miller said there were only a few families who had dared install a bathtub back in Lancaster County. The bishops discouraged every new form of luxury, but this was only good hygiene and common sense. The bathroom contained a commode and a sink to wash hands and brush teeth—things Hannah thought the homestead would never have.

It was all charity, though. People had given away their hard-earned money so the family could gain a new foothold out here in this no-man's land. Well, so be it. That was another of her father's weaknesses. He had been too proud to accept charity.

Hannah and Sarah followed on the heels of the builders, polishing windows, washing walls and scrubbing floors.

The day came when they carried in and placed all donated furniture. The end result brought tears to Sarah's eyes and a deep sigh of happiness. Oh, this house. She could never have imagined a house half as big or as cozy or as handy or as filled with lovely furniture, even if it was other peoples' cast-offs. No matter. Every piece was a pure luxury. It may as well have been plated in gold, so precious it was.

What did anything matter? The arm of the brown sofa was worn smooth and faded in spots, but it was a sofa. A couch. A soft spot to enjoy, to sit down and relax with her knitting or mending.

What if the kitchen rugs were mismatched? They were rugs much better than anything they had ever owned. They unpacked dishes and marveled at the smooth pots and pans. Like a loving caress they wiped the plates and cupped their hands around tea cups and tumblers like a warm embrace. They lined drawers with leftover wallpaper and glued down the edges.

The pantry was stocked with food, staples that would sustain them long after winter was gone. Dried peas, flour, cornmeal, brown sugar, dried navy beans, oatmeal, lard and white sugar, baking powder and salt. Jars of canned tomatoes and cucumbers, mixed pickle and applesauce.

Sarah wiped the dust from her forehead yet again, her eyes red with fatigue, a smile on her face as she told Ben and Elam where to set the corner cupboard. They would have dishes to put in there too.

Ben surveyed his handiwork, narrowed his eyes, and told Sarah that he'd love to build his wife a house like this.

"Maybe we'll just have to sell out and move out here. There'd be plenty of work for the windmill installing, that's for sure. I can't tell you how many of these ranchers asked about your windmill. But I don't know what the wife would say. She'd be out of fix, for sure. Davey here, he's thinking along the same lines. Why not? Grab on to that pioneer spirit and run with it. Break the mold. Get away and try something new. See what the wife says."

Hannah thought, Oh boy, Davey. He'll want to get a wife out here, which means me. Set her mind like cement.

They slept in the house that night. Mary snuggled beside Hannah on thick flannel sheets and covered with heavy quilts, breathed heavily and was asleep. Hannah lay thinking at the miracle of this house. All because people shared their money, their possessions. She hoped every person who donated even one item, no matter how small, would be rewarded ten times over. She remembered that passage from the Bible. She hoped it was true.

She thought of all the electric lamps and irons and appliances the local townsfolk had contributed. She felt sorry for them, not realizing they'd never be used, and she hoped her mother would have the good sense not to return them to the kind-hearted people.

So what was so terrible about electricity? It would certainly be nice to pull a string and be illuminated with bright light on demand, instead of straining to see by the light of a smelly old kerosene lamp. Or, the way it used to be before coal oil—candles. She heard the wind moan around the eaves and wondered when the storm would arrive.

Across the hallway, Sarah lay holding Abby until she slept, then slid out of bed and down onto her knees. She folded her hands, bent her head, and prayed. Over and over she thanked God for the generous giving and asked Him to bless each individual for their kindness?

She wished Doris Rocher abundant happiness and many customers for Harry. She prayed that Betsy from the café would have a thriving business and Leonard Heel from the feed store a healed back. She mentioned all her acquaintances by name, and when she finished, she simply laid her head on her folded hands and softly wept with pure gratitude until the flannel sheets were wet.

Outside, from the curdled black clouds, the first winds of December brought snowflakes the size of a quarter, flung them against the sturdy ranch house and whirled them down along the good German siding, where they began to accumulate in a hour's time, just when Sarah lay her head on a pillow made of blessings.

CHAPTER 5

Hannah was down at the barn checking to see what remained to be done, the snow coming down steadily, a world of white around them, when Jerry found her.

"Hannah."

She turned, wide eyed.

"We're leaving."

"Are you?"

"Yes."

She stepped back, afraid he would hear the impossibly loud banging of her heart.

"I want to wish you the best." His voice quivered. He shook his head. "You're a brave girl. I admire you, honestly. A part of me wants to stay here, protect you, watch over you."

Her eyes became hooded, the old bitterness a curtain of anger. "You sound like God."

"You know I'm not."

"Yeah, well, I can take care of myself."

"Can you?"

"Of course. Manny's here. My mother. Clay."

Jerry couldn't help himself. "What does he mean to you? Clay."

"Nothing. You should understand that I'm never getting married. He wants me to marry him, but that . . . well, you know."

The silence stretched out. The interior of the barn was lit by a dim gray light, the new yellow lumber permeating the air with the acrid smell of pine. Through the door, a rectangle of white swirled in restless little arcs of wind tumbling the snow around.

"What?" Hannah couldn't take the silence, so static with unspoken words it was like the air during a prairie thunderstorm.

"Hannah." Jerry moved toward her, holding out both arms. "Just let me hold you. Something to remember me by."

"No!" Hannah stepped away, her back against the sweet-smelling lumber.

"What would you say if I decided to move here if Ben Miller and Davey do? I don't mean to be rude, but you could use a few good horses here in cow country. Not to mention a farrier."

"I don't want you out here." Blunt, the sharp edges like a serrated knife. From a distance they heard Davey's high-pitched yell announcing the driver's arrival.

Another moment of her heart hammering against her ribs and then he stepped closer, gripped her shoulders in his large, calloused hands, gently drawing her toward himself, speaking her name as his eyes searched hers.

"I know, Hannah. I know you don't." His lips closed over hers in a gentle kiss of goodbye, and then he released her.

"I don't know why you think you have the right to do that, Jerry Riehl. Go home to Lancaster County and find some Susie or Becky and marry her. Stay away from me!" She ran the back of her hand roughly across her mouth, her eyes bright with frustration and unshed tears.

"Jerry! Get out of here!"

But he held her again, with a hold like a vice. Crushing her to him, he bent his head and kissed her again. This time, he meant it. "Remember me, Hannah." And then he was gone.

Hannah had never been so angry, or so thoroughly shook up. She fell back against the wall, her chest heaving with agitation. In case he didn't know it, he had just lost his last chance. That was a serious breach of good manners, or Amish *Ordnung*, or whatever you wanted to call it. If he moved out here, she would move to Utah, or California. She'd get a job picking tomatoes in some fertile valley. Oh, he had just now ruined his chances forever! But she moved stealthily to the side of the doorway, watched the two cars, her mother and Manny waving, dark figures standing alone on the prairie, the cars moving steadily away, through the gray white world of burnt earth and falling snow.

Hannah breathed out, a long sigh of spent emotion. So now the men were gone. They were alone, her and Mam and Manny. She expected a rush of euphoria, an intense feeling of joy, but all she could manage was a weak smile that wouldn't stay in place before sobs caught her unprepared. She stifled them with a balled up fist and swiped viciously at her streaming eyes with the corner of her scarf. But nothing could stop her feeling of desolation as she watched those two cars lumbering through the snow.

She stamped her foot in frustration, blew her nose into a wadded handkerchief, and then took a fist and slammed it against the door frame, resulting in bruised knuckles that throbbed painfully through the remainder of the day.

Sarah was in high spirits, humming a song as she cooked their dinner, rushing to the window to exclaim about the falling snow. A gift from God, this snow. Imagine the dried-out earth receiving this moisture that would give new life to the grass around them. She reveled in the wonders of the new cookstove.

Abby discovered the water in the commode, threw wooden blocks into it, delighting in the splash, her high shrieks a signal that ended all her fun. "No, no," Sarah scolded. Abby wailed in protest, hiding her face in Sarah's skirts.

There were so many new and useful things. The pantry contained many shelves, a corner that Sarah declared was the best idea any man had ever thought of.

"You're *grosfeelich*, Mam," Eli chirped.

Sarah laughed, a trilling, happy sound of the heady joy she felt. "Then I guess I will just have to be boastful for awhile, won't I?" she said lightly, whirling from stove to table with the grace of a much younger woman.

Mary watched her mother, put a hand over her mouth and giggled. This was a new Mam, one she had seldom known. Hannah gave away her bad mood by frowning, her eyebrows heavy above dull eyes. "Hope the food lasts, is all I can say."

Sarah chose to ignore this, knowing it would only bring out the worst in her if she chose to answer the endless, senseless argument that was Hannah's style, caught in the net of her own dark mood.

"Think Ben will move out?" Manny asked, sitting at the table, lifting lids and sniffing the delicious aromas.

"I hope so. Davey Stoltzfus too. Jerry Riehl even spoke of it."

"Yeah, and he's a horseman. Imagine the Jenkinses and the Klassermans when they see his horses!"

"When," Hannah spat out. "You don't even know if he's going to move out."

Manny eyed her levelly and thought, so that's what's wrong. Must have gotten tangled in some upsetting conversation with him.

"I hope he does," Sarah said, easily.

"Why?" Hannah wanted to know.

"For the same reason Manny says. The horses."

Hannah snorted.

They ate the good hot vegetable stew and bread with apple butter, silently chewing their food in the bright new kitchen with the patterned linoleum like a rug in the middle of the room. The tablecloth was checkered in red and white squares, the snow casting a white, winter light over everything.

A sturdy house, food in the pantry, the windmill churning away not far from the buildings, the cows out on the prairie finding grass, the unfinished barn housing their two old horses and aging wagon, the neighbors living close enough to help in an emergency. God was above all and they were blessed beyond measure.

All day the snow fell steadily. It was a beautiful snow, not a storm. The wind whirled it playfully, as if God was smiling down on them, presenting them with the clean white beauty of a winter barely begun. It piled on the good shingled roof and slid off with a sound like falling water, a dull whump as it hit the snow below.

Down at the barn Hannah and Manny were hunched over a rough drawing of the interior of the unfinished barn. "If we have two stables on each side with a wide enough walkway, we can push a manure spreader back there and clean out slick as a whistle," Hannah said.

"As if we'll ever own a manure spreader," Manny muttered.

"Sure we will. Maybe not next year or the year after, but sometime." Hannah straightened her back and viewed the dim interior of the barn. She began to whistle, then hum, and then went back to whistling.

Manny set up two sawhorses, flopped a wide piece of lumber on top and began to measure. Hannah grabbed a handsaw, ready to cut the board after it was marked correctly, still whistling, nodding her head to the internal beat only she could hear.

Manny stood up, watched her with narrowed eyes. "You're happy," he said dryly, thinking it didn't happen too often.

"Oh, skip, skip, skip to my Lou,
    Skip, skip, skip to my Lou,
    Skip, skip, skip to my Lou,
    Skip to my Lou, my darlin'."

Manny frowned. "That song is senseless."

"Not if you're dancing."

Alarmed, Manny stared at his sister. "You never did."

"I certainly did. That's where I was the other week—well, months, weeks, how long ago was it? I danced with Clay. It was the best thing I ever did. I could dance all day, every day. I'm good at it. You wouldn't believe it." Hannah grinned, lifted her arms, and did a quick two-step, leaving poor Manny blushing, shaking his head in embarrassment.

"Stop it, Hannah. What would Dat say?"

Hannah shrugged and did another two-step, then another. "I'm never getting married, Manny. I hope you know there is no one who I will love enough to be his slave and be tied to a house like a common goat and have a bunch of kids. Nope. Not for me. It's easier to flirt and be happy and see how many men want you to be their wife, and you know you're never going to be."

Manny lifted another board, carried it back to the far end, and bent to position it before pulling out a handful of nails. Lifting his hammer, he began to pound in the nails.

"Nothing to say to that, huh, Manny? That's because you don't know what to say. I'm right. I control my destiny. If I choose not to marry, that means I can be the rightful owner of the Bar S, make my own money, make all my own choices, do what I want with no whining man to cook for or wash his dirty socks. *Nein. Nein.*"

Hannah laughed out loud, that short, raucous sound that came from deep within. Manny kept hammering away without giving her the satisfaction of a reply.

"Aren't you going to say anything?"

Manny finished nailing the board, looked Hannah straight in the eye, and said, "Then you'd better not let Jerry Riehl do what he just did."

Hannah dropped her hammer. It landed on the toe of her boot and bounced off, unnoticed. She coughed, choked, and cleared her throat as her eyes widened and a deep flush spread across her cheeks. "What are you talking about?"

"Next time he wants to say goodbye, you'd better make sure there is no one else in the barn."

"You weren't! You were standing right out there with Mam. I saw you!"

"I was in here. What do you think the back stall door's for? A fast escape when . . ." He couldn't bring himself to say *kiss*, so he stopped.

"When what?"

"Nothing." Angrily, Manny pushed past her and began sawing another board, the movement of his arm jerky and his face hidden.

"That wasn't my fault, you know. He thinks he likes me and has the right to do that. He's bold and despicable, and I can't stand him!"

"Didn't appear like that to me."

That remark was a battering ram to Hannah's wall of protective pride. She flew into a volley of angry words, telling him that he knew nothing about anything, and he couldn't tell how she felt, no matter what he saw. "Snooping, nosy little brother. You ought to be ashamed of yourself!"

"Oh, I'm not ashamed. You're the one that should be. Stringing two of them along the way you are."

"I'm not stringing anyone along!" Hannah shouted, her dark eyes snapping with denial.

"What did you just say? You were dancing with Clay, and Jerry just kissed you this morning."

"It wasn't my fault!"

"Wasn't entirely his, either."

Hannah balled her fists, her head thrust forward as she stalked out of the barn, sizzling with wounded pride. Her feet stamped down hard in the ever-deepening snow as she walked blindly, without thinking, heading toward the tar-paper shanty that had been their home for the past weeks.

How could her own beloved Manny turn against her like that? What did he mean by that last sentence? The one about it not appearing to him as if . . . As if what? As if she wasn't willing? Well, she wasn't.

Like tangled yarn her thoughts knotted and folded in over themselves until she yanked on the door handle of the makeshift dwelling and heard a man's cough.

Her attention was brought up sharply when the cough was repeated. Peering through the gray gloom of the near windowless dwelling, she thought someone had left a pile of clothes or quilts in the corner. Then she heard another cough, raspy, like gravel tumbled in a creek bed.

"Hey!" she called out, bold and unafraid.

Immediately the pile of rags shifted, shoulders appeared, a head covered with an old cap, a gray blue scarf tied over the top. Two eyes like raisins in a flushed face etched like a map with blue and dark red veins crisscrossing the cheeks.

"S'cuse me, ma'am. Beg pardon." The breathing came in irregular puffs, labored. "Musta got sick. Come down with the flu." More harsh, short breaths.

"Well, tell me who you are," Hannah demanded, short on patience and still holding onto the residue of her outrage.

"Lemuel. Lemuel Short from over by Crock's Landing." A series of short, harsh barks followed.

"Well, that doesn't help. Never heard of a Lemuel. You sure it isn't Benuel? Lots of Benuels where I come from."

"No, ma'am."

"What am I supposed to do with you?"

"Just let me rest a minute, ma'am."

"You'll freeze."

"No, no, I'm out of the snow. Thank you kindly, ma'am."

"I can't just let you lay there."

He coughed so violently that Hannah became alarmed, closed the door, and waded through the deepening snow to the house.

She clattered up on the porch, stomped her boots to rid them of the clinging snow, opened the door, and yelled loudly for her mother, who looked up with frightened eyes as she opened the oven door. "Hannah! What is wrong?"

"There's a man in the shack."

Sarah straightened up, her eyes wide in the white, snowy atmosphere. "What man?"

"Come and see for yourself."

Sarah grabbed her heavy black coat, a hand-me-down from her sister, Emma, and shrugged into it. A scarf on her head, boots on her feet, she followed Hannah across the yard to the shanty and let herself inside, more timid than Hannah had been.

"His name is Lemuel Short," Hannah hissed.

"Mr. Short?" Sarah called softly.

Immediately a head wrapped in the old blue gray scarf with small black eyes appeared.

"Beg pardon, ma'am. Just resting awhile then I'll be gone. Just let me rest and I'll be on my way."

Sarah heard the harsh cough and instantly recognized Lemuel Short as a test from God, who had given, shaken, pressed down, and running over. Now it was her turn to give back by ministering to this angel in disguise. Not a trace of doubt. Clear-eyed, strong, the banner of her faith rippled in the soft wind of her voice. "Good afternoon, Mr. Short."

"Ma'am. Thank you."

"You will come to the house. We'll get you better. I have a pot of *ponhaus* cooking, and we'll make you a hot toddy. My name is Sarah and this is my daughter, Hannah."

Sarah reached down to help him up. He reached out a hand and tried, but fell back, then tried again. Hannah met Sarah's eyes, a question answered by the lifting of Sarah's chin to the left.

Together each inserted a hand under his armpits and lifted gently until he stood on his feet. He was of average height, clothed in ordinary country outerwear, smelling of wood smoke, kerosene, and tar. His denim trousers were soaked from walking in the snow, his knees trembling.

"Ready?"

He nodded.

Awkwardly, they maneuvered him through the small doorway, across the snowy yard, and up onto the porch, where he stood gasping and coughing, retching horribly while managing to mutter weak apologies.

Manny came wading through the snow, plowing through at a half run, billows of loose snow like a wake behind him, his eyes dark questions in his face.

"Help," Hannah mouthed.

They got him to the sofa where he collapsed and lay gasping amid his apologies. Sarah worked quickly. First she unlaced and removed his boots and then the gray wet socks. His toes were as white as if there was no blood circulating at all.

Softly Sarah said, "The large agate tub with warm water." Hannah obeyed promptly for once. Eli and Mary stood wide-eyed, Abby sitting with her fat little legs thrust straight out, her thumb in her mouth, watching every move.

Tenderly Sarah rolled up the sodden denim of his trousers and unbuttoned his coat. Lemuel sat up and helped Sarah remove all his outer garments, his hands shaking like spring leaves, his jaw wobbling until his teeth clacked together.

When she removed his scarf, Sarah could feel the heat. His face was flushed, his small brown eyes red-rimmed, shimmering with fever. Sarah realized the strength of his sickness. He may already have pneumonia or worse. Well, there were onions. She made a tincture paregoric. She would see what she could do, with God's help.

She brought a clean sheet, made up the sofa while he sat on the chair with his feet in warm water. Hannah came over and told Sarah in a hiss that he smelled awful. Why couldn't he bathe and wear some of Manny's clothes?

"He's too sick," Sarah whispered back.

"He stinks! He smells like a billy goat!"

"Shh."

Hannah moved off in a huff. What a predicament. Now they weren't more than settled in their nice new house and here comes this sick, smelly old man to mess everything up. He was probably a thief. Or worse. They'd probably all be dead by morning. She was going to sleep with Dat's rifle under her pillow. All that coughing and carrying on could well be a bluff, and as soon as they went to bed, he'd sneak around stealing stuff and . . . Oh, it gave her the creeps.

The house smelled of cooking onions and paregoric, chamomile tea, and *ponhaus*. It was enough to make her lose her supper, especially with the rank odor that steamed off his soaked clothes. Like a wet dog. Fleas and lice, she guaranteed.

He coughed all night. Spat and honked and wheezed like a goose caught in a trap. Hannah knew because she heard every sound as she sat on the side of her bed with Dat's rifle across her lap, figuring he might get the others, but he was not getting her. She had a ranch to operate. The Bar S.

Mam had the fuzziest soul. She was all love and compassion and tenderness, treating Lemuel Short as if he was royalty. She could just see the Bible verses Mam had before her. "Inasmuch as ye have done it to the least of these my brethren, ye have done it unto me." She probably thought she was entertaining angels unawares. Well, that was all right as far as it went, but Hannah was not taking any chances.

In the morning, Hannah was in bed, the gun clutched in her hands. Lemuel Short had fallen into a deep sleep, his mouth open, all manner of wheezes, whistles, and sawing sounds coming from his dark, toothless cavity.

Sarah drew her dress tightly around her shivering form, lifted the lid on the cookstove and threw a match onto the prepared paper and kindling. The sun had not yet risen, but the sky was a vast dome of reflected white light from the level snow-filled land that nestled right up to the horizon. She stood at the window, shivered again, the comforting sound of the popping, crackling fire filling her with peace.

They were so well *fa-sarked*. Taken care of. Every need had been supplied. If she praised God for the remainder of her life, she would never have thanked Him enough. She folded her hands, bowed her head, and, thanked her Heavenly Father for sending Lemuel Short and allowing her to be His servant. She prayed for Lemuel's well-being and for guidance.

Hannah was summoned to the breakfast table, flopped in her chair with a sour expression, and stuck a thumb out in the general direction of Lemuel Short, raising an eyebrow at Sarah.

"Sick," Sarah mouthed.

They ate fried *ponhaus* and buttered toast, then relaxed around the table with mugs of tea sweetened with a dollop of honey. The sun burst above the plains, filling the house with strong yellow light till the red horizon gave way to winter's icy blue sky.

Sarah remarked about not being able to get used to the light. So many windows. It spoiled her, being able to see out across the prairie. Manny smiled at Sarah, told her she deserved every window, and hoped she'd enjoy them for a long time.

Hannah choked on her tea. So much sugary talk. It was enough to gag her. Plus, that man on the couch was going to have to move along. She didn't want to spend one more night in this house with him and his life-threatening noises. She'd even caught herself holding her breath, waiting until he exhaled safely, his rattling intake of air enough to make her imagine he was dying.

The whole thing was unsettling, to put it mildly. She wished she'd never gone into that tar-paper shack. He would have moved on by now. He would have made it as far as the Klassermans. Sylvia could keep him.

That brought the first smile of the day, thinking of meticulous Sylvia ministering to poor, smelly Mr. Short. She'd probably get Owen to take him to the livery stable in town. Well, he was here now, and by the looks of her angelic mother, he'd be here awhile longer.

CHAPTER 6

Hannah was right.

Lemuel Short stayed on the couch, smelling the same as the day he arrived, Sarah ministering to him like a most devoted nurse. With the snow piled up to two feet and no telephone nearby, there was no use summoning the doctor. Stranded on the prairie, miles from the nearest neighbor, there had been no sense of isolation until the sick wanderer had arrived.

Sarah realized his situation was grave. She used up half her store of onions, vinegar, paregoric, tea and mustard poultices, and still his fever would not break.

The morning after, the snow was still coming down but thinner and slower. A weak sun showed its face in the gray clouds and the wind slammed into the north side of the house with such force that Sarah straightened from her job tending to Lemuel, her eyes wide with alarm.

It was indeed fortunate that everyone was in the house when the wind sprang up. Manny said he didn't know how they would have made it back to the house, the wind whipping the loose snow to a blinding, stinging frenzy, obliterating anything and everything in its path. A wall of moving snow driven by the hissing, humming wind scoured the top layer of it, then the snow beneath, leaving jagged patches of bare, brown grass, a jigsaw of high, impenetrable drifts like jagged little mountain ranges as far as the eye could see, which wasn't any great distance.

Hannah paced and muttered to herself, a caged lion sick with anxiety. She worried about the cows, wondering if they could survive. She wanted to ride out and see for herself, but that was impossible.

Lemuel Short sat up for a short time, his small raisin eyes watching the oldest daughter's agitation. He could tell she was of a different nature than her mother but kept his observations to himself.

It didn't help Hannah's short temper that she sat up every night with the rifle on her lab, robbing herself of restful sleep, priding herself that she was the only one who remained vigilant.

Mr. Short was not to be trusted no matter how sick he was. Her lack of sleep, coupled with the anxiety and frustration of listening to the howling wind and blowing snow, almost drove her mad. She took to chewing her fingernails down to the quick and drinking black coffee that made her so jittery she spilled everything, slopping soup on the tablecloth and dumping tea on the floor. She yelled at Eli when he crawled underfoot with Abby astride his back, yanked her off and smacked her bottom, till she set up a red-faced howl of protest. Eli pinched her leg, a firm pinch between his thumb and forefinger, resulting in a cat-like yowl from Hannah. Poor Eli was promptly cuffed on the ear by his tightly wound sister, whereupon he slunk away and folded himself up in the corner of the couch opposite Lemuel, his knees drawn up to his face, the forbidden thumb finding its way to his mouth.

Sarah sighed, her eyes snapping with impatience. Eli heard a "Psst." He sat very still, rolled his eyes in Lemuel's direction and quickly removed the disobedient thumb.

"Little boy," Lemuel whispered.

Out came the thumb again, only to be quickly hidden from sight in his trouser pocket. A smile, quick and furtive, appeared as quickly as it disappeared.

"Your sister bigger than you?" Lemuel whispered.

Eli nodded, his dark eyes slanted toward the sick man.

"Not to worry, Son. You'll outgrow her one day." Lemuel winked, one raisin eye disappearing beneath a blue veined eyelid. Eli laughed outright. Hannah glared in his direction.

The following day, Lemuel's fever broke. He spent a long time soaking in the new claw foot tub, dressed in Mose's clothes — clean, wrinkled, taken from the small bundle Sarah had thrown on the wagon the night of the fire.

He was so thin that the shirt and trousers hung on his gaunt frame. He was bald across most of his head but had a wealth of gray hair hanging to his shoulders in the back. After he had shaved, he appeared to have shrunken in size, his weathered face revealing a life of hardship.

Hannah guessed he was close to seventy years old, but he said he was only fifty-nine. In his quiet, breathy voice, there was an underlying rasp, an unsettling timbre that rattled Hannah.

He began to sit up at the table to eat, didn't even know enough to bow his head when Sarah told him there was always silent grace before a meal. He didn't put his hands below the table, either. Just sat there with a foolish expression in his small eyes nearly hidden in flaps of loose skin.

Hannah knew because she watched him when he thought her head was bowed. So, right there, that told you a lot, she thought. No teaching about God, which meant he would think nothing of holding them all hostage after he had his strength back. Rob them probably, take everything and perhaps leave them all dead.

Manny strongly disagreed and said he had none of those mannerisms. Sarah plied him with more food, more soup, but he ate very little. Finally, he turned his attention to Hannah.

"Miss," he said softly.

Hannah didn't reply, the soft-spoken word left her floundering, unsure.

"Miss, I can see you're anxious about something. Do you care to tell me?"

Hannah left his sentence hanging in the air. He gave her the willies, those dark, unblinking eyes watching her like a squirrel's.

Manny answered for her, his face flushing at her outward lack of good manners. "We're all worried about the cows."

"You have cows?"

"Yes."

"Ah, so did I, so did I. At one time. Do you care to hear my story?"

Sarah nodded eagerly, Manny a mirror of his trusting mother. Hannah sat back, folded her arms and glowered. Likely the yarn he would spin would be filled with lies, a colorful pack of fabrications he told to everyone he met, spreading words of untruth thick as flies across the table, lies only she could decipher.

"I had a spread in Montana," he began. "A wife and two children. I was young."

"Where in Montana?" Hannah asked.

"Just across the border. The North Dakota border. It was called the Sun River Range. Good grasslands. I was building up my herd. It was a lonely life—but a good one. I loved my days, my herd of cattle, and the isolation. I guess that's what Mae couldn't take. She left me and took the children, in the fall before the winter came. Went back to her parents in the East, where we both come from."

Here his voice slowed, faltered. In spite of herself, Hannah found herself listening, her eyes downcast, the palm of each hand wrapped around an elbow.

"I followed, left my heard of cows. I found her, but all my pleading didn't do any good. Her parents wouldn't allow her to return even if she wanted to. The children, Jack and Rory, cried and wanted their daddy. But they were like stone—the parents and Mae.

"So I came back, had plans to sell out, give it up. Could hardly do it, but knew it had to be done. All my hopes was wrapped up in my homestead."

Hannah blinked and swallowed.

"In the end, the whiskey got me. I started to drink to dull the edge of the pain. Guess it was a rebellion, an inner anger that burned slow and mean, pitying myself. Never stopped drinking.

"It was my homestead, my ranch, my wife, and my children. It consumed my life, glass by glass. I lived for the dull numbing it brought, the bottom of the emptied glass the fulfillment I needed. It erased most of my sense of failure, but never all of it. As long as I live, I'll hear my boys crying as I turned and walked away. A sound I'll never get rid of. Or the sight of Mae and her parents. Like hawks, they were."

He shook his head, the veined lids falling over the small black eyes. "I wandered, held different jobs, always got into fights, was fired more times than I can say. Rode the rails."

Manny broke in, "What's that?"

"Hitched a ride in a boxcar. On the train. Hundreds do it."

"Like real hobos? Tramps?" Manny asked, his eyes alight.

Sarah smiled, "We used to have them come by our place back in Pennsylvania. *Vaek-laufa*. Road walkers, in English."

Lemuel nodded. "You speak two languages?"

"Yes. We are raised speaking Pennsylvania Dutch first, then we learn English as we grow older."

Lemuel nodded again. He seemed satisfied to drop the subject of who they were, or why they spoke Pennsylvania Dutch.

"I got away from God. Don't hold to no religion. Figured if there was a God, He was right cruel taking away everything I had."

There it was! Hannah sat up sharply, an intake of breath hissing between her teeth. "If you don't believe in God, what would keep you from . . . from, you know, getting rid of all of us and keeping our homestead? Claim jumpers will do that. How do we know all this sickness was only to fool us?"

"Hannah!" Sarah said sharply, her disapproval obvious in her tone.

Lemuel held up a hand. "It's all right. The girl's only being careful. I didn't say I don't believe in God. I said I got away from Him. I done wrong. Now I don't know how God will have me back. I done a heap of sinning. Not sure I didn't leave a man to die once. Among other things."

Well, here they were. Sitting ducks. Hannah was disgusted and began chewing the corner of her thumbnail, her eyes dark and hot with an inner light.

Eli and Manny slid off the bench, began to play with their wooden spools and fences. Silence shrouded the table, a prickly quiet.

Sarah sighed, toyed with her coffee cup, obviously at a loss for words.

"You think the cows will survive this?" Manny asked finally.

"They'll survive the storm better than the wolves that will soon be starving, hungry and powerful mean. Got a bull out there?"

"Oh, yes. And a cow that's meaner than him." Without thinking, Hannah spoke ahead of Manny. Manny looked at her, blinked, but kept quiet.

"If I were you, I'd soon be riding out. I saw you have a right good windmill. They'll be in, if they're thirsty. Best thing would be a lean-to, stored hay. Don't know if you have either one."

Quickly, Hannah shook her head. That was the hard part. The part that kept her up at night.

Lemuel spoke again. "They should be all right. They might need a little help here and there. Riding out, starting a good strong fire at night, all these things will help repel them wolves. Have you heard them?"

"More coyotes than wolves."

Lemuel nodded. "They'll be the enemy once calving begins."

Fear shot through Hannah. "They tell us purebred Angus have trouble calving." She spoke quickly, the words tumbling out of her mouth, her mistrust pushed to the background.

"No. Someone had it all wrong. Them little Angus calves are small in the head. Delicate. Most ranchers have part Angus for that reason. They drop calves better than some breeds."

Hannah's eyes shone. She leaned forward. "How do you know?"

Lemuel shrugged. "Common knowledge."

Hannah clasped her hands together beneath the table, like a child, she was so delighted.

They rode out. Manny took the lead on Goat. The sun shone with a weak light through the gray veil of the sky, obscuring the brilliant winter blue. The wind had calmed but was still fickle, little spirals of snow puffing up unexpectedly to fling the flakes in stinging whirls against their faces. The horses walked in a few inches of snow, brown grass sticking up like strubbly hair, then plunged into drifts that came up to their chests. All around them the prairie looked level, the snow an even blanket of white, gray shadows swirling a pattern like cold marble. It was all a fine deception. The drifts arose, then faded away, the horses stumbling on clumps of frozen grass.

The air was frigid. Hannah's teeth chattered uncontrollably. Her fingers were like ice picks. She had no idea the cold was so intense. The fabric of her coat was like a window screen, letting in the icy drafts that swirled around her. She watched Manny, hunched in his saddle ahead of her, Goat's sturdy legs breaking a path through yet another drift.

She was shivering violently now, her teeth chattering like pebbles. "Manny!" she shouted.

He stopped Goat and turned to listen, his face wind whipped and raw.

"I can hardly keep going. I'm so cold!" For Hannah to admit anything quite like this must mean it was serious.

"We haven't found the cows yet!" he yelled.

"I know, but I can't go on."

Undecided, Manny gazed across the unforgiving white prairie. To find the cows was necessary for their peace of mind and worth the cold that penetrated like thousands of needles. Hannah was always the one who knew everything, who goaded him and tried him to his limit. So now it was his turn.

"You have to," he shouted back.

"No, Manny. I'm too cold." Hannah bit back her plea for mercy.

Manny goaded Goat without looking back. Hannah had no choice but to follow. She bit her lower lip to keep her teeth from chattering and tasted blood. She couldn't feel her fingers or her toes. Like dead chunks of ice, they were encased in her hard leather boots, stuck in the creaking, frozen stirrups.

Riding above the snow, the cold like sharp needles against her skin, they continued without sighting even one black cow. Impossibly cold, fraught with anxiety and lack of a good night's sleep, Hannah stopped Pete, dismounted, and began to scream at Manny, flailing her arms in circles and stomping her feet against the frozen earth. She felt as small and insignificant as a pinhead in the center of a tilting white orbit that was eventually going to swallow her alive.

Stupid cows. Dumb bovine creatures that couldn't even think for themselves. Let Manny ride on and get lost. She had to help herself or turn into a frozen lump of ice and snow.

Manny stopped Goat, turned in his saddle to watch his sister dismount. Without emotion, he watched her wild motions, stuck his gloved hands beneath his armpits, and waited, squinting his eyes against the stark white light and stinging snow.

When a section of the snowdrift on his right broke away, he blinked. Shading his eyes with his gloved hand, he squinted and blinked again.

Voss in die velt?

The cows!

They had not seen them because they were looking for black objects. Here they were, backed into a snowdrift and, by all appearances, alive and well.

As Hannah continued to flail and scream, chunks of snowdrift continued to break away, black legs carrying the snow until it broke into pieces and slid down the animals' sides, revealing the thick, black hair on their backs covered with powdered snow—like salt on burnt toast.

Manny yelled, twisted in his saddle and pointed. Hannah continued her wild pounding and arm swinging, until her feet stung with returning circulation.

She stopped and heard Manny's voice, saw his outstretched arm.

"What?" He didn't hear her question, and Hannah saw nothing. Quickly she mounted her horse, looked in the direction he was pointing.

"There they are! Manny! Manny!"

Cold and almost hysterical at the sight of the emerging cows, Hannah came undone, crying and laughing intermittently. There was no one to see, no one to hear, except Manny and the crazy old snow-covered cows that ran mooing and bawling over the frozen ground, frightened by the sound of Hannah's screams.

She rode up to Manny. "How many?" she yelled.

"They're all here," he yelled back.

"The bull?"

"Yep, every one of them. That old one, the mean cow, she looks to be calving soon. In a month or two—maybe before that."

"Should we keep her in the barn?"

"What would we feed her? We have barely enough hay for the horses."

Hannah nodded.

Supper that evening was a cozy affair. Sarah was in good spirits and some of Hannah's anxiety had lessened, now that they knew the cows had survived the storm and would likely continue to survive in the coming months. Manny was tall and manly, pleased with his ability to lead Hannah, finding the cows while she mostly cried and floundered around.

He wouldn't always be the follower, which was new knowledge that caused him to hold his head high and his shoulders wide. Hannah wasn't as mighty as she wanted him to believe.

Sarah had put the agate roaster filled with navy beans and tomatoes, cane syrup and salt pork, in the oven hours ago, filling the house with a mouth-watering aroma. She roasted potatoes, and fried slabs of beef, sliced thin and salted and peppered to perfection. She had made warm cracker pudding with canned milk and she had thickened canned peaches, a treat in the middle of winter.

Lemuel Short stayed all that week. Not that Hannah was interested in having him stay that long. He simply had nowhere else to go and no means of transportation.

"What's the harm in it?" Sarah questioned in a whisper, washing dishes with Hannah in the afterglow of their warm and wondrous meal.

"He's bold and old and his eyes look like raisins," Hannah hissed back to her mother, wiping a plate with a corner of the tea towel she was holding.

"It's all right," Sarah said softly.

Lemuel must have heard, opening the subject of his leaving less than an hour later. "I must be on my way," he stated simply.

"But how will you go?" Sarah asked.

"On foot. The way I always go," he answered.

"You can't. It's too cold. The closest neighbor is miles away. I'm not sure that Sylvia Klasserman would appreciate visitors at all. She's pretty meticulous."

Lemuel Short chuckled. "Nothing wrong with that. My Mae, she was no housekeeper. The house was crawling with flies over unwashed dishes. Never swept the floor. Baby rabbits, ducklings, chickens ate the crumbs from our table. Wandered in and out of the house like children. They were her children. She took better care of them chickens than her own babies."

His soft voice rolled to a stop, turning into a sigh of regret tinged with remembrance colored in shame. "It was not good. Seems now I could have done more. Mae wasn't happy. She didn't care."

Hannah thought of Doris Rocher and felt an intense longing to see her. She wondered how she was surviving the winter. She hadn't realized the winter storms would isolate them quite like this.

Were there any happy women in the West? Surely not, now that hard times had come in what history would call the Great Depression. Things weren't so good in the big cities back East, either. Her grandfather had spoken of businessmen committing suicide in New York City, wealthy men who lost their fortunes overnight, and folks migrating to California to the fertile valleys for work picking fruits and vegetables. It was hard luck for countless people.

Perhaps here on the prairie, what was considered hardship back East was only normal, resulting in an easy slide through lean years. But then, not everyone had a grandfather with money laid by and no mortgage on his farm. Already, young men from Pennsylvania were moving to Ohio and Indiana. Would they move even farther west?

Nope. Didn't have to, as far as Hannah was concerned. Certainly not the dashing Jeremiah Riehl. Didn't he think he was quite the fellow, though? Going around kissing girls like it meant nothing. He ought to be ashamed of himself, considering everything. He probably told a dozen girls in Lancaster County the exact same thing. She conjured a picture of Jerry marching along blowing a brass horn and a gaggle of silly girls following him like goslings.

How could Manny accuse her of wanting Jerry? Hadn't he heard her biting words of refusal? She had meant it too. Just a trick of one's mind, thinking about the Great Depression, followed by young men moving west, followed by thoughts of Jerry. Just the way a person's thoughts flowed along, as uncontrollable as a river. It wasn't that she'd tried to think of him.

Actually, if she ever did decide to get married, she'd pick someone who wasn't handsome. Someone who was much too humble and kind to go around thinking he could win her over. Look at Clay. He was every bit as conceited as Jerry. Nothing humble about him either.

Take Lemuel Short, this rail thin, wizened little man who drowned his sorrows in whiskey. He likely kissed Mae, wooed her, lured her to the West, without a humble thought in his head. Look where it had gotten him. He should have stayed humble and asked a girl who was common-looking, with eyes like raisins, just like him. With a large nose maybe, or stick-thin figure.

He hadn't said, though, what Mae looked like. Later that evening, she asked him and then regretted it instantly.

Poor Lemuel's voice shook, his small eyes seeming to take on a life of their own, lids fluttering like a trapped butterfly, working furiously to keep back the tears.

"She was like a fairy princess. Hair like spun gold and eyes so blue the sky was only a reflection. Lips like a rose."

His deep sighs were like the roaring of a bull to Hannah. She wanted to clap her hands over her ears and leave the room. Simple, doddering old man. Quite his own fault.

There, she had love figured out again. Best to stay away from it if you weren't humble. If you thought too much of yourself, you were bound to be attracted to the same kind of man. Handsome. Good looking. Swaggering and thinking himself a real winner.

That's where most girls went wrong. For the thousandth time, she knew she wasn't like most girls. She wondered how Jerry figured, saying that he wanted to bring horses to the West. Didn't he know horses wouldn't always be in demand?

Look at all the automobiles and tractors popping up like thistles. Not to mention electricity, railroads, and about every modern new thing you could think of. The only thing was, there would always have to be cows, rodeos, show horses, and the need for a good farrier. He could probably make a go of it. Word got around surprisingly fast out here on the plains, especially if you had a telephone.

Jerry had some outstanding horses in that barn in Lancaster. Her hands went to her cheeks, hiding the flush that gave away her thoughts. That day still rattled her as helplessly as it ever had.

Enough now!

She was not going to make the same mistake Lemuel Short had made. What kind of a name was Lemuel Short anyway? Honestly. She shrugged her shoulders, worried the hangnail on the side of her thumb with her teeth, and watched from beneath hooded eyes the little man seated there on the couch with Eli on one side, Mary on the other leaning against him. Baby Abby sat on his lap. He held the Little Golden Book of Hansel and Gretel high so that everyone could see, reading in a good, steady voice punctuated with sighs and squeaks and harrumphs until they were so involved in the story they were oblivious to everything around them.

The children with no father, the father with no children, both supplying what the other longed for. Sarah stood by the kitchen table, the balding, stoop-shouldered man dressed in her dead husband's clothes, a bewildering, mysterious sight that she could not begin to unravel.

CHAPTER 7

THE HIGH, UNDULATING CRY OF WOLVES REMOVED HANNAH FROM her curtain of sleep. Her bedroom was cold, but the sound sent a frigid chill up her spine. Her open mouth was dry and her tongue stuck to the roof of her mouth, her breath coming in short, quick gasps. Her heartbeat accelerated at the sound of their howls.

They had come, then. She pictured them, high-backed, long-legged, bony, the ragged hair along their backs like the teeth of a saw, bad-tempered, their driving hunger propelling them toward the rich smell of cows.

It was more than she could bear lying there helplessly, a mere dot on the endless white expanse that was their home, their acquired portion of prairie, their homestead. For a fleeting instant, she grasped a vision of herself sleeping soundly in the winter wonderland that was Lancaster County, a job secured in some little dry-goods store, unaware of the appalling dangers of the West. She regretted the move—almost.

She jumped out of bed and made her way along the hall, startled at the soft voice from the couch asking, "You heard?"

Too frightened to speak properly, she nodded. Lemuel Short sat up, quilts wrapped securely around his legs, her father's nightshirt sliding to the side, exposing the veins on his thin neck. The candle in her hand flickered.

"If I was younger, I'd ride out with a lantern," he stated.

"Should we?" Hannah asked, like a child.

"If you have good horses. Be foolish to try it on middling ones." Pete and Goat were definitely middling.

"Will they be able to defend themselves?" she asked in a quivering voice.

"If you have a bull and one ornery cow with horns, they'll give it a good shot. What worries me is how hungry the wolves are."

Hannah nodded. She sat in the chair facing him and set the candle on the oak table, twisting her hands in her lap, her eyes large and dark.

"Should I wake Manny?" she asked.

"I'd let him sleep. You can't ride out if your horses are middling."

"I can't go back to bed, either."

"You don't have to." Sarah appeared, a heavy flannel wrapper secured about her waist, her hair loosened, worry lines creasing her delicate mouth like parentheses. "Surely it is the worst sound a rancher could hear at night." Her words were soft, gravelly with sleep, but devoid of Hannah's panicky tones. "You won't ride out?" she asked.

"Lemuel thinks I shouldn't with the horses we have."

"A wise choice, Hannah. I couldn't bear to see you and Manny ride out." Sarah shuddered, a small involuntary movement, then seemed to shrink in on herself.

Lemuel threw aside the quilts, drew his trousers up over his flannel long johns, hitched up the nightshirt and scratched his stomach. Hannah hurried out to the kitchen, where her mother was putting the kettle on, lighting the kerosene lamp—automatic movements she made many times without thinking.

Lemuel followed, sat down at the table, coughing into his red handkerchief, apologizing, begging their pardon.

The long drawn-out wail sounded again, mournful, primal calls of hunger and loneliness. Hannah's eyes showed the terror she felt, the despair following on its heels. "Could they attack a year-old heifer, bring her down successfully, do you think?"

Lemuel watched the flame in the lamp, his wrinkled face like unironed linen, etched and crisscrossed with blue and red veins, his raisin eyes glittering like wet river pebbles.

"I'll just tell you that if the cows are smart, they'll stick tight, and the bull and the mean cow should be able to protect them. If they spread out, face the pack separately, you'll lose some."

"We can't afford to lose any!" Hannah burst out.

"Sometimes life on the range teaches you what you can afford and what you can't," Lemuel stated. "It's not always up to us. Nature throws us some punches, you know. You gotta go with it."

Real appreciation shone in Sarah's eyes while Hannah resisted his easy speech. No wonder he didn't make it and took to the bottle. You had to fight for everything you got. You had to be smart and cunning, no matter what Lemuel said.

They rode out in the crisp, biting morning, the sun on the snow blinding them as they set off. Hannah's teeth chattered from fear, the dreaded unknown, the pit of her stomach like a stone. She didn't feel the cold, only the specter of possible death before her.

Manny was grim but composed, riding Goat like a true knight, his face toward the sun, courageous. They rode into deep snow, the force of the horses' churning legs sending it spraying, instantly slowing them down. Out to windswept high places, and they could increase their speed.

Their eyes searched the snowing plains, longing to see the familiar salt-and-pepper cows sprinkled with frosty snow. There was nothing. They rode to the east for miles, turned north in a sweeping arc, the horses' breath coming in short, white puffs. A thin dark line appeared below Pete's bridle, the sweat staining the light brown hairs of his face.

Manny shouted and pointed a gloved hand. A tight bundle of cows. Hannah rose up in her saddle and strained to see, her eyes squinting against the early morning sun.

At the horses' approach, the herd scattered and ran off in their awkward hump-backed gallop, snorting and wild-eyed. There was no evidence of a struggle, the snow around them smooth and windblown.

There was the bull, and the mean, horned cow. Quickly Hannah counted. Only counted eleven; there should be twelve yearling cows.

They came upon the grisly scene before they could brace themselves. Snow trampled into the consistency of cottage cheese, deep hoof marks, huge paw prints, then the awful pink color of blood mixed with snow.

The bones protruded, a rib cage with bits of hair, meat, and gristle, the empty eyes staring and wild-eyed, horribly panicked from the ripping, clawing feet and slavering mouths that brought her down.

Half eaten, the cloven hooves barely attached to the devoured leg portion, snow and old dried grass mingled with the remains of the yearling heifer. The struggle to save herself must have been fearsome, the cow and smaller bull trying to stave off the wolves.

Hannah dismounted after Manny. They stood together, heads bent, unable to grasp what the wolves had accomplished.

"I hate those big brutes. They'll kill anything just to kill," she yelled, angry and needing to avenge herself. She wanted to ride home, get the rifle and hunt down the bloodthirsty pack and kill them all.

She would.

She turned with swift, jerky movements, placed her foot in the stirrup, and flung herself astride her horse.

"Where are you going?"

"For the rifle. I'm going to hunt down this pack of wolves until I've killed every last one!"

"You can't do that!" Manny yelled after her, then mounted his horse and tore off after her.

They shouted at each other the whole way home. Manny tried to talk sense, tell her the wolf pack roamed for miles on end, much farther than old Pete could manage even if she rode hard for most of the day.

"Shut up! I don't believe you!" Hannah shouted over her shoulder.

In the end, it took hours of reasoning by Lemuel with Sarah's tearful pleas and Manny's words injected at opportune moments, until Hannah relented.

The cows had to come in. They had to be brought into the corral, today. No matter that they had nothing to feed them. They'd starve out there anyway. In their weakened state, the wolves would finish off the whole herd.

Lemuel told her the horses were spent. She could go nowhere now, likely not all week, unless they had a warm spell. The wolves would be back to finish their kill, but they would not necessarily be able to kill another one. The cows would not starve on the prairie. Better to leave them. They'd be in for water from the tank.

Break up the ice, make sure they had access to water. In spite of giving in to Lemuel's advice, Hannah took matters into her own hands after dinner. She saddled Pete and rode off to the Klassermans against Lemuel and Manny's advice.

They'd drive the herd to the Klasserman ranch. Hannah was crazy with fear, obsessed with the possibility of dead yearling carcasses dotting the prairie, a ruined mess of blood and man-gled flesh, protruding bones that were an open invitation to the golden eagles and buzzards from the sky.

She couldn't bear to think of their ability to pay back the loan taken away by the ruthless hunger of scavengers in winter. Nature wasn't that cruel, and God surely wasn't, either. So that left only the devil and his unclean mischief.

Half-frozen, she barely clung to the saddle as Pete stumbled into the Klassermans' barnyard, exhausted from wading through deep drifts of snow.

Red-faced Owen Klasserman lumbered through the snow wearing so many clothes he resembled a human snowman, lifting a fat, gloved finger and wagging it as he spoke.

"You dumb voman. Vott iss wrong mitt you? Ei-ya-yi-yi-yi. You easy freeze. You kill dat horse."

Hannah threw herself off the saddle, her feet like blocks of ice, her knees crumpled so that she sat down hard in the snow, Pete heaving, his head hanging straight out, the way horses do when they are beyond reasonably tired.

"Get up, Hannah. Get up!" Owen shouted, disgusted that she had had the gall to ride that old horse through the drifts. She could have become lost or disoriented, lost on the prairie, frozen to death. The plains in winter were not to be taken lightly. Owen knew this well.

Nearly crying, Hannah stumbled into the barn after Owen. He removed Pete's saddle with excessive grunts, scolding and lamenting in between.

"Dis horse too oldt for your dumbheit," he scolded.

"We don't have a better one."

"Den you must stay home."

"I can't." Almost losing control and giving way to little-girl tears of rage and frustration, Hannah told Owen between shivers and chattering teeth that the wolves had killed a yearling heifer.

Owen's blue eyes popped open. "I told Sylvia. I told her I hear them volves."

Hannah followed Owen to the house, past the swept porch and the broom hanging from a nail by a short length of rawhide.

Sylvia threw up her hands, a glad light in her blue eyes, her apron stretched tight across her doughy hips, waggling a red, plumpish finger and scolding just the way Owen had.

Hannah removed her boots, carefully staying on the colorful rag rug, setting them neatly side by side. They led her to the table, where a steaming cup of Dutch cocoa waited along with a variety of cookies, sweet rolls, and breads.

The kitchen gleamed in the winter sunlight. The gas range shone like a mirror, the curtains above the sink so white they shone blue. African violets were blooming in an array of colors, lined up in coffee cans like a harbinger of spring. The patterned linoleum floor was waxed to a high sheen, not a crumb or scuff mark anywhere.

Hannah resolved to be a housekeeper just like Sylvia if she ever had her own house. It would not include a husband to clump through the kitchen with bits of manure clinging to the soles of his shoes.

"The wolves got one of our heifers," Hannah explained. "We have no lean-to, no shelter of any kind, and no hay stored because of the fire." She took a deep breath. "So, the reason I'm here is to ask if there's a possibility of driving our cows to your ranch where they could be taken care of."

Owen drummed his fingertips on the oilcloth table top. "You can't drive them over. Likely dese cows is already hungry and not so strong. To keep volves away iss not easy unless you camp out on the prairie." He shook his head. "Too hard. Too hard. How you gonna keep firewood? How you gonna take it dere?"

Hannah's eyes widened. "You mean there's nothing to be done?"

"Without stored hay, no. Especially not without goot horses. Do you vant me to call Jenkins on the telephone? See vhat Hod says?"

Hannah nodded, grateful.

So a yelling into the telephone mouthpiece ensued, punctuated by many "Vot's? Vot you say? Huh?" Finally he handed the phone to Hannah, who took it with trembling fingers. Hope was slipping away too fast, the awful prospect of letting those cows out to fend for themselves beyond her comprehension.

"Hello?"

"Hannah?"

"Yes."

"Hod here."

"Yes."

"You crazy?"

"Owen says I am."

His deep, relaxed chuckle came through the line. "Believe me, you are." That deep, automatic chuckle again that seemed to iron out every hopeless obstacle in her way. "So you lost a heifer, Owen tells me."

"Yes." She hated the tears she felt were forming.

"Well, there ain't a whole lot you can do if this snow keeps up. Them cows might do good on their own. Learn to stay tight. You got that mean one and the bull. But, tell you what. Pickin's are gonna get pretty slim so what we'll do is watch the weather. If'n we git a warm spell, we'll take the tractor and try to haul some hay over there to yer windmill. Yer biggest problem is no hay. Them cows won't starve, but they might not do too good, either. You might lose a few more heifers to them wolves. Boys and I might ride out, see what we can find. Wouldn't suggest it now, the way the snow's piled around. You get yerself home now, Hannah. Sit tight and see what the weather does."

"But I can't wait to see if it will warm up," Hannah said. "It will seem like every day and night is a week long, sitting there while the wolves chew up our whole herd."

Hod laughed outright. Abby pestered Hod to give her the telephone and he handed it over to her.

"Hannah!"

"How are you, Abby?"

"Doin' all right. How's them little ones? And your ma?"

"We're cozy and warm. We have plenty to eat. We're blessed." Now she sounded just like her father.

"You shore are."

"We have a man staying at our house, Lemuel Short. He's homeless and wandered into the shack. He almost died."

"Mercy sakes, Child. You can't trust them people." Abby let loose a hailstorm of warnings about folks helping those vagabonds and how badly it turned out. "Best send him on his way," she admonished.

The very next morning, late, a posse of men arrived on horseback. Hod and all his boys and two men neither Sarah nor Hannah had ever seen before. They rode in, their horses well lathered, nostrils expanded, breathing rapidly, their necks stretched out after the men dismounted.

The boys hung back and led the horses into the barn as Clay led the way to the porch. Sarah became alarmed, watching Lemuel, whose small, kind eyes turned hard as glittering pieces of coal. He sat on a kitchen chair like a bound animal, straining against unseen forces, twisting his hands and leaning forward, his elbows on his knees. Then he sat up straight, breathing rapidly.

There was an insistent rapping. Hannah opened the door and stepped back to allow the men to enter. Sarah stood off to the side observing. Manny came out of the wash house door, clearly surprised, then alarmed.

The teakettle's low humming was the only sound after the men had all filed through the door, standing at attention as they watched the tallest of the two strangers. He was dressed just like Hod, heavy denim overcoat, jeans, a woolen scarf, his black Stetson jammed down halfway over his ears, face brick red from the cold, a mustache like a dark brush, stiff, as if each hair had been frozen.

"Mornin', ma'am," he said to Sarah, who smiled politely and nodded. He looked at Mr. Short, who sat upright, one palm on the table, his face white and without expression.

"Lemuel? Lemuel Short?"

Features etched in stone. No reply.

The man reached into a pocket of his overcoat, produced a badge, the gold star of his profession. The sheriff. Lemuel's expression remained unchanged.

"We've been lookin' for you, Mr. Short. You need to accompany us back to Pine."

Lemuel remained mute, as still as a carved statue. The accompanying sheriff told him he was under arrest, quietly, as solemn as a minister. It was only when he produced the silver handcuffs that Lemuel reacted, leaping sideways, rocketing from his chair with the speed and agility of a much younger man. There was no evidence of his cough, his weakness eclipsed by his desperation.

Chairs overturned as a scuffle broke out. Sarah, standing by the stove, lifted both hands to cover her face. It was only a matter of seconds until Lemuel was subdued, the cold metal of the handcuffs clicked into place. His head was bent, the skin on top shining from beneath his thin, gray hair, as vulnerable as a child. For a fleeting instant Hannah wanted to believe he was innocent of whatever wrong he had done in the past. Or *was* it the past?

"Sorry, ma'am, for the inconvenience," the tall, burly sheriff said. "But I don't believe you want Mr. Short in your care any longer. He's wanted for killing a man in a bar fight in Lacoma, about a hundred miles west of here."

Sarah nodded, wide-eyed, a hand to her mouth.

"You need some heavy clothing," the sheriff ordered brusquely. Lemuel could not raise his head. It was as if there was a rock on his shoulders weighing him down. He did not resist as they loosened the handcuffs, standing patiently as he put on his overcoat, one of Mose's homemade denim ones, and wound the old scarf around his head.

Hannah carried the look of his eyes with her for days. When he lifted his head, his eyes reminded her of a wounded animal caught in a trap. The desperation gave way to a sad acceptance of his fate, his words soft and filled with sincerity.

"Ma'am," he said to Sarah, "if I die in prison, your face will get me through until the end. You're one of those rare people that shine with an inner light. Your prayers alone is all I need. Pray for me every morning and evening so that God can accept my repentance. I deserve to burn in hell forever, but with your prayers opening the way for my own feeble begging, I just might make it."

Hannah straightened her shoulders and bit her lips to keep the weakness at bay.

"I'm ready," he told the sheriff, then walked through the door into the blinding world of sun on snow, his head held high.

Sarah sank into a chair, a shuddering breath releasing the tension in the room. She shook her head. "At a time when I should have spoken to him about salvation, words wouldn't come. Now he'll go to prison without hearing about Jesus Christ, and all I have is my German Bible. And Mose's . . . "

Manny broke in. "He wants to be forgiven, Mam. He'll find the way. I believe his story about his past. I do. He was just a bitter man. I'll help you pray for him."

"Thank you, Manny."

"He could have killed us all," Hannah said with conviction.

"But he didn't," Sarah said softly.

"We have to stop trusting people, Mam. We're such ignorant, greenhorns from the East. We lived in a cloistered society. Being raised Amish to live in peace and forbearance might be all right as long as you stay in Lancaster County. But we're here in the West now, where tramps are murderers and wolves destroy cattle, snowstorms can threaten your life, and drought shrivels anything you plant. We need to become smarter, wiser, or we're not going to make it."

"God will take care of us," Sarah said quietly.

"And what if He doesn't?" Hannah burst out. "We have no guarantee on this earth that He'll magically turn everything in our favor. That's how Dat thought. He lived by those principles and dreamed his way into poverty and starvation."

Sarah watched the heated passion in her daughter's face. She sighed, a weary sound of resignation. "Perhaps if we were as smart as we should be, we'd realize homesteading is folly and return to our native land. Perhaps God is allowing all these frightening things to show us we are not living according to His will."

Hannah didn't consider her mother's words, just tossed them aside like apple peels, keeping what she wanted to believe.

"So you're saying it wasn't God's will that Dat traveled out here?"

Miserably, Sarah shook her head. "I don't know, Hannah. I don't know."

Manny sat up. "Well, Mam, we're here now. We're in debt. We're blessed to have a sturdy house and our health. We have sound minds to think this through. I think we'll get through the winter and, to my way of thinking, the cows will learn to fend for themselves. To try and put everyone else in danger by bringing the cows in, providing hay, is foolish. I don't care what you say, Hannah."

"It will be a setback to lose more heifers, but it would be worse to lose our lives or cause our neighbors to lose theirs. I don't believe the weather will warm up, according to Hod and the boys. Clay says it'll likely keep snowing. He knows more about the prairie weather than we do, so I think we need to take his advice."

Instant rebellion rose in Hannah. "It's just dumb, Manny!"

"What?"

"Letting those cows out there to weaken."

"What is better? Bring them in and let them starve around the water tank?"

"Hod and the boys will bring over hay."

"How?"

"The tractor. They said they would."

"Well, if it's possible, they will. It might not be possible and you know it. For once in your life, Hannah, consider someone else's opinion and let go of your own."

Hannah met Manny's gaze, direct, calm, filled with conviction. She hated for him to tell her what to do, but she knew there was no choice. Even as she watched his face, the brilliance of the blinding sun on snow faded, casting shadows beneath his dark eyes.

Sarah looked up, then turned her head to watch the sun's disappearance, the mountain of gray clouds swelling and inflating even as they sat there together.

"Is there plenty of firewood in?" she asked softly.

Chapter 8

THE LIGHT GREW DIM AND FALTERED. THE KITCHEN TURNED OMInous, dark shadows appearing in corners that had been filled with sunshine.

Hannah's dark eyes flickered with fear. Manny's face paled as the light was erased, turning the house even darker.

Sarah rose, lifted the glass chimney on the coal-oil lamp, struck a match with her thumbnail, lighted the wick, and watched the steady yellow flame before replacing the chimney.

Hannah stood and went to the west-facing windows, meeting her adversary head-on, arms crossed around her waist like steel armor. As far as she could see, the level snow-covered land stretched before her, pure white, indented by blue gray shadows. The horizon was smeared into the land, as if the boiling gray clouds were gobbling up the earth, destroying it as the winter storm approached.

There was no wind, only a threatening calm, a quiet portent. The hairs on her forearms rose with the quick chills along them. The urge to fling herself on a horse and round up the cold, hungry cattle was overpowering, followed by a helplessness and loss of ability she could not name.

No one could prepare a person for this all-encompassing force of nature. It sent you whimpering into yourself. As she stood there, the clouds shifted, steely gray and flat, as dark as a moonlit night, the snow on the prairie brighter than the sky itself.

Had all the rain that did not fall during the summer packed itself into a vast cloud that stayed above them in the gentle, drought stricken days of autumn? How did one go about understanding the weather patterns in this God-forsaken land?

There! She had finally thought the unthinkable. Had not God forsaken them in their hour of need? Hannah felt alone, isolated, punished by forces beyond anything she could control, like a tiny vessel pummeled by the seas, hundreds of miles out away from the security of the land.

So then, ultimately, God did what He wanted to do, leaving His mortals to flounder around for themselves. There was no mercy in the face of this fast approaching storm.

What about the sheriffs and Lemuel Short? If they were caught in what appeared to be a maelstrom of wind and snow, they'd lose their way and freeze to death. It might be just as well for poor Mr. Short.

Sarah busied herself building up the fire. She jumped back as the cookstove lids rattled, followed by a puff of white smoke that belched from the fire pit. Alarmed, she raised questioning eyes to Manny. "You think the chimney is clogged with soot?"

Quickly, Manny threw on his coat and boots, pulled himself up the porch posts and onto the roof, as agile as a cat, Hannah watching from below. He waded through the snow on the roof of the porch, but the wind had blown most of it off the house roof, allowing him to reach the stone chimney. He lowered a long pole, wiggled it around to test for a buildup of soot, then shook his head, perplexed.

"There's nothing there!" he yelled.

There was a cry from the kitchen as the cookstove puffed out more billows of gray wood smoke. Manny slid off the roof, landing in deep snow, then shook himself, his face and hands already red with the cold.

"Must be the air," he said. "A downdraft. Before the storm."

Hannah watched the pewter gray sky worriedly. "Think we'd better find a rope to attach from the house to the barn?" she asked.

"Might be a good idea."

They found pieces of rope and knotted them together until a long line could be attached to the barn, propped up here and there by pieces of wood as high as a clothesline. Sarah continued to deal with the cranky stove, waving her apron to dispel the onslaught of wood smoke that coughed out of every crack at regular intervals.

The children coughed and wiped their streaming eyes. Abby began to cry, rubbing her eyes as she tried to rid herself of the bothersome fumes.

When the storm hit, it sucked up the smoke and spewed it out of the chimney, raising the red-hot coals underneath into leaping flames and heating the stove top to a cherry red glow. It was as if the stove had no controls, no levers to open and shut the draft, leaving the fire to burn hotter and hotter.

Sarah realized she could only throw on a few sticks of wood at a time. It would be better to be cold than let the fire rage out of control and threaten them with the loss of their house and perhaps their lives.

The wind shook the well-built house in its teeth. Snow scoured the windows like gravel flung by a giant hand, rattled against the window panes, and bounced off to form a drift against the walls. There was nothing to see except a dizzying whirl of snow and ice, the sky and the prairie blending into one.

Hannah wrapped herself into an old quilt, the edges frayed by many washings, and pouted. She picked at loose threads, loosening thin patches of worn fabric, and pitied herself with a deep and abiding sympathy. She refused to answer her mother's worried inquiries, turned her face away, closed her eyes, and shut out the whole business of life that included storms and wolves and cattle and deceased fathers who had made insane choices to move their family to a land that was simply unlivable. She railed against her mother's subservient demeanor and was angered by Manny's disobedience.

Why hadn't someone stood up for them when her father had made poor choices and lost the farm? Why had they all followed him like docile sheep out to this—there it was again—this God-forsaken, impossible land?

The drought and the fire had been one thing, but these awful blizzards were a new and terrible thing.

A metallic sensation welled up in her mouth; a stone settled in her stomach. Real fear had a physical taste, like moldy bread served on a rusted plate.

Sarah cooked a fine vegetable stew seasoned with scraps of canned beef. Above the roar of the wind, the metal spoon clanking against the glass jar brought an intense homesickness, as she remembered her mother opening a jar of beef chunks, dumping them into the heated browned butter in the pan, the fragrant meat simmering in its own juice before she thickened it with a heavy white mixture of flour and water.

Beef gravy over mounds of mashed potatoes eaten with fresh hull peas from the garden, homemade white bread with freshly churned butter and raspberry jam.

Had they taken it all for granted? *Undankbar.* Unthankfulness, one of the deadliest sins. Was that why God had sent the Great Depression, forcing them into the unreasonable slide of unmet payments, unpaid bills, and collectors like wolves slavering on the porch? Surely Mose had not seen where they were headed. Or had he?

Chunks of canned beef had not been available for many Amish families. Some smart housewives learned to cook bacon or bologna rinds, frying them into a deep, dark gel, adding milk and thickening it with flour like gravy.

Blooney dunkas. Bologna gravy. And it was good. Turnips had taken the place of potatoes after they were gone toward the end of winter. A stronger flavor, one many children disliked, but what Elam King's Salome had said was true: "A child who is hungry enough will eat almost anything."

Who could have foreseen it, this Great Depression? Money, as the stalwart Amish had come to know it, suddenly became worthless. Uncountable debt. Land without value. Unthinkable. The old, white-bearded men shook their heads and blamed the president. The crooked politicians who would bring down the greatest country on earth.

They argued, their words circling among themselves, but no one really understood the root of the problem or how to fix it. So they always circled back to the president. They tightened their suspenders, pulled their straw hats low and went to work. They did without, made do with what they had, and were more thankful for leaner rations than they'd been in fatter times.

Wasn't it something how you could make dresses from feed sacks? Housewives repeatedly devised ways of dyeing the letters and objects printed on the rough cotton material. The children owned three shirts or dresses, one for Sunday, one for school, and one for *voddogs*, usually the everyday one patched and patched again, then handed down to a younger child and held together by still more patches.

Well, they'd certainly been prepared for the lean times here in the West. Real poverty was something the housewives of Lancaster County could not have understood, even in the grip of the Great Depression. Turnips and bologna gravy was one thing; but to go to bed with a yawning pit that hurt from being empty, a stomach shriveled and aching for lack of food, was quite another.

The aroma of the fragrant vegetable stew filled the cold, dark house. Sarah dished it up, bowls of thickly cut potatoes and carrots seasoned with beef and onion and parsley. She cut wedges of sourdough bread and spread it with dark molasses from the barrel.

Hannah refused to leave her self-inflicted cocoon of quilts, turning her face away and keeping her eyes closed, her mouth a hard line of determination. Manny glanced her way, shrugged his shoulders, and began to eat hungrily. Sarah lifted her eyebrows and was met with a shrug of Manny's wide, young shoulders. Let her pout.

"Hannah, come on. Aren't you hungry?" Mary called before she lifted her spoon to begin eating the stew.

"She probably doesn't feel good," was Eli's verdict.

Abby waved her spoon and gurgled happily, as Sarah tied the cloth bib around her neck.

The wind roared like a freight train. The snow hissed against the window. A death song for the cattle, Hannah thought, allowing bitter thoughts to hold her in their grip. They would never survive this. The ones that didn't starve would be eaten by ravenous wolves, specters of death descending on them through the ever deepening snow.

Manny could not rouse her to help feed the horses. Little Eli accompanied him along the rope to the barn, red-faced and gasping, his chest expanding by his sense of being one with his brother. Sarah fussed over him, saying he was a right young man, and made him strong hot tea flavored with molasses.

Mary sang a little German school song in her sweet, low voice as she played on the floor, building a tower with wooden spools for Abby.

Kommt liebe Kindlein,
Kommt zu dem Vater.

Abby squealed when the tower fell over, wooden spools rolling in every direction. Eli dove after them, reaching beneath the oak cupboard, the couch, and pushing aside the roll of quilts that encased Hannah's legs.

"Move. I need those spools," he directed.

Angrily, Hannah kicked out, hitting the side of his head, sending him from a good-natured crawl to a sprawling, indignant roll on his back. He gave a loud, insulted yell, which brought Sarah from the bedroom where she had been putting more covers on the beds.

"She kicked me!" Eli howled.

Sarah stood there, quietly taking in the situation. The storm shook the house, rattled the windowpanes, moaned and whistled around the edges of the roof, setting her teeth on edge and allowing no great amount of patience where her eldest daughter was concerned.

With brisk steps she strode over to the couch. Without a word, she gripped the corners of the quilt in both hands, threw her weight backward and heaved, rolling Hannah out of the quilts onto her stomach, leaving her sprawled in an ungainly position across the couch.

"Get up! Get out of these quilts and go to your room. If you're going to act like a six-year-old, then I'll treat you like one." With each word her temper increased, until she reached out and gave Hannah a hard cuff on the shoulder.

Hannah was shocked into obedience. She sent a desultory glance in her mother's direction, got herself onto her feet, and slunk into her room, closing the door with a firm slam.

Sarah reached down, grabbed the quilts, opened Hannah's bedroom door, and tossed them inside before closing the door with a decided click.

Sarah didn't speak for a long time after that. She washed dishes, dried them, and put them away. She cleaned the stove top with an emery board, piled on more wood than she should have, swept the floor, and got the children ready for bed.

Night came early, and with the darkness, the sound of the storm seemed to grow louder. Tension already ran high and taut, a tight rope that none of them had the skill to navigate, so they may as well go to bed. Things would be better in the morning light.

Hannah finally undressed, put on her long flannel nightgown and crawled beneath the heavy covers. Her teeth chattered and she was ravenously hungry. She wasn't about to set foot out her room to eat cold, congealed vegetable stew. Or face her mother's wrath. What in the world had come over her? She should have displayed some of that gumption to her husband! Likely he wouldn't have dared to even think about moving out West.

That certainly was a put down, your own mother treating you to a solid smack on the shoulder. At her age. She cringed in embarrassment.

What in the world? Her meek and quiet mother. Well, she'd seen that side of her before, and it was a scary spectacle. Her large dark eyes, that solid, tall body made of muscle. She could be tough if she wanted to be. Most times, though, meekness and goodness covered the tough side, , like fluffy frosting on a layer cake.

The cold burned her nose. She should get up and open the door to allow some of the heat from the wood stove to circulate, but there was no way she was going to let her mother know she was cold.

She dreamed a long, unsettling dream that night, one that set her eyelids to fluttering, small squeaks coming from her throat until her eyes flew open and she was fully awake, staring wide-eyed into the roaring, snow-scoured night that was as cold as an icicle.

She thought about the dream, reliving her feelings of desperation. The wolves were devouring the cattle, one by one, the great horned cow the only one remaining alive. She had devised a plan—she couldn't say what it was—to save the cattle's lives, but she was hampered by her mother constantly slapping her shoulder.

Manny was nowhere around in her dream. Well, that was certainly frightening! Perhaps her dream meant something. Maybe it was God's way of speaking to her. Who knew? Very likely it meant that she could have ridden out and saved the cattle if her mother had only allowed it.

That might not be the case, though. She knew she could very well have been caught in this deadly blizzard if she had disobeyed.

She didn't go back to sleep for a long time, partly because she was so cold and partly because she thought she would surely lose her mind listening to the wind and the snow. Anxious about being in debt, and about the cows, she wondered what they would do when the snow melted and uncovered fourteen carcasses half-eaten by wolves or starved to death.

That blizzard was only the second in a series of winter storms unlike anything the local folks had ever seen. Some of the older men and women remembered worse winters, when the bitter winds drove the snow into ten-foot drifts that dotted the prairie like mountain ranges.

It was in late March that the snow began to become soft and heavy. The edge of the roof was lined with shimmering, glassy icicles. It became a dangerous route to pass beneath them when they dripped icy water or let loose entirely, crashing to the snow with a grand display of shattered ice.

The sun shone with varying degrees of warmth, but eventually the day came when the snow was shallow enough to attempt navigating. Still, Sarah would not allow it, saying the storms could raise their heads and arrive in less than an hour, which wouldn't allow a sufficient amount of time to ride home safely.

Only after the Jenkins boys rode over did she allow it. Hannah found herself feeling awkward and tongue-tied, her feet clumsy when confronted by the young men—Clay, Hank and

Ken. All of them were attractive, curious, eager to know how the family had fared during three months of winter.

How was Hannah expected to tell them the truth? The endless dark hours of anxiety, the dread of another approaching storm, the certainty of finding only cattle remains, her night sweats and attacks of panic?

To her own sense of pride, she had never cried. She refused to do that. She had battled her own inner demons, to be sure, the determination to survive unaided while she bitterly railed against the storms and doubted God's mercy.

Sarah remained the firm foundation for all of them after that evening when she sent Hannah to her room. It was Sarah who rallied valiantly when Hannah fell into another swamp of despair, wallowing in her lethal self-pity, covering herself in the muddy slime of blaming her father for all of her woes, unwilling and unable to see that it was she who had orchestrated the move back, who had goaded the remainder of the family into the pioneer spirit.

Clearly, it had been Hannah's choice. But the price was unforeseen, and the toll it took on her emotional health uncalculated. So now, standing before the Jenkins boys, she found herself ill at east, unsure, incapable of hiding her terror at having lived so isolated and alone.

Clay was pale, blond, clean cut, as lean and handsome as she'd ever seen him. Clean shaven, his gray Stetson pulled to his eyebrows, his eyes shone like blue ice. Hank was a mirror of his brother; Ken was even taller than his siblings.

Their eyes bore into Hannah's face, curious, alive with interest. Hannah was thinner, dark circles under her huge, brown eyes. There was an intensity about her that seemed unsettling somehow. Manny was good natured, saying they'd come through okay. Really. A large affable grin sealed his sincerity, and the Jenkinses believed him.

Tight-lipped, Hannah suggested they all ride out together to check on the cows. A nervous tic at the corner of her eye, her lips twitching, her voice hoarse, her fingers restlessly easing out of her gloves and stretching back into them.

Clay watched her silently. She hadn't taken the winter well. He noticed the too-wide eyes, the blue veins that showed at her temples, the cold blisters that lined her upper lip, appearing painful.

"Horses need to rest awhile before we ride farther," Clay suggested to his brothers.

Manny invited them in for coffee, gladly brought them through the door to his welcoming mother, who met the three boys with hands extended, her dark eyes alight.

"Oh, it's just a pleasure to see your faces!" she beamed. Gladly she served them mugs of hot coffee and brought out the sourdough bread and the jam she kept for special occasions.

She asked so many questions that Clay finally laughed and said he couldn't find all the answers for her soon enough. Yes, Hod and Abby were both in good health. Abby had had a bit of pleurisy, a cough, but got herself over it without seeing a doctor. "Not as if'n the doctor could have done a whole lot, stuck in town the way he was."

Amid all the talk and slurping of hot coffee, Hannah remained stone faced, one thumb and forefinger picking constantly at her cold sores until they bled.

Clay cringed as he watched her apply a clean handkerchief, watched as she tried to conceal the spots of red blood. No, he decided, she had not come through the winter well. An ordeal is what it had been.

It was only when he stretched and suggested they ride out that she came to life, springing up with cat-like energy and grace, yanking at the sleeves of her coat to tear it off the wooden peg on the wall. Her fingers shook as she tightened the cinch on her saddle. The bit rattled against Pete's teeth as she tried to insert it into his mouth.

They rode out in single file, Hannah falling behind, old Pete working to lift his wide hooves through the wet snow. The sodden earth, a quagmire of mud, rotting roots, decaying grass and, where the fire had burned it off, a black, slimy mush of soot, ashes, and snow, sucked at the horses' hooves.

"You go west, Clay!" Hank shouted, jerking a thumb in the spoken direction. Clay turned in his saddle, looking for Hannah. "Go with me?" he called to her.

"She can ride with me," Hank offered.

"Naw. You go east. Take Manny and Ken with you." Hank gave his brother an exasperated look, but was too proud to object. He knew well enough that Clay was sweet on Hannah. Good luck with that one!

Clay sat astride his horse, relaxed and waiting for her to catch up. Hannah's pale face was pinched, wan, and much too thin.

"You musta forgot to eat most of the winter," he said, watching her dark eyes focus anywhere but on his.

"Yeah, well. It was a long winter," Hannah snapped.

"That's when most people enjoy their food. You know, hibernate like bears and get fat!"

"I got sick of sourdough bread."

Clay laughed. Hannah's eyes scanned the prairie with a furtive look, almost like a person obsessed. She bit her lower lip, her gloved hand went to her mouth repeatedly until she remembered the gloves, lowering her hands to fiddle with the buttons on her coat.

"You're more nervous than a cat on a hot tin roof," Clay observed.

"You would be too if your whole life depended on these cows."

"Now, Hannah. There's more to life than makin' a livin'. You won't starve."

Soberly, Hannah nodded. "We almost did one time. Probably will again if these cows didn't survive. You know that."

"I told Hank to shoot if they see 'em, so listen for a gunshot." They rode on. Clay produced a pair of black binoculars that he put to his eyes to scan the white prairie. Once, Hannah thought she saw a dark lump but it passed from her vision.

The sky was blue, studded with small gray clouds like sheep's wool, dirty and thick. The air was cold but the sun shone on their faces, not warm but with a softness of promised spring. A dark line appeared on the horizon. Hannah shouted, pointing a shaking gloved finger.

Clay shook his head. "It's them cottonwoods north of the Klassermans. Doubt if yer cattle stuck that close."

"Think not?"

"They had a wide area to travel if they wanted to find food."

Hannah could not have answered if she had wanted to, with the hard knot of fear forming in her chest. Clay probably knew they would never find their cattle and was only humoring her.

"Let's ride to those cottonwoods anyway. Maybe they went there for some kind of shelter."

"Sure. We can check." Clay goaded his horse, leaving a weary, mud-splattered Pete behind.

CHAPTER 9

The cottonwood trees were much farther away than they appeared. Clay had to halt his horse repeatedly, waiting until Hannah caught up. They rode together, Pete's sides heaving, a good lather of sweat appearing beneath the cinch and around the saddle blanket. He walked faithfully on, his head bobbing, his ears flicking, listening for commands.

There. Wasn't that line of trees too dark? Hannah lifted a hand to her forehead, shading her eyes from the sunlight. There was a band of black, irregular shapes too thick to be trunks of trees.

Was it a ravine, or a bank behind the trees? Did the prairie have a drop-off point? She tried to call out to Clay, her eyes riveted to the dark objects beneath the cottonwood trees.

The cows!

Clay yelled. He whooped and hollered, raised a fist and pumped the air.

Cows exploded from beneath the bare branches of the trees. Thin, long-haired, spindly looking things, every last one.

Hannah wasn't aware of Pete or Clay or the fact that he was shouting hoarsely. She was counting, babbling numbers to herself through eyes that blurred with tears running down her cheeks of their own accord, down her cheeks and dripping off the end of her nose, running into her cold blisters, the salty tears stinging and hurting.

Twelve. Thirteen. A dog? Two dogs. What were dogs doing among the herd?

Hannah screamed at the same time Clay shot his rifle into the air. The small ones were not dogs. They were calves! Healthy little black calves. Two of them!

Hannah screamed again, then slumped in her saddle, crying with great, uncontrollable sobs that wrenched hoarse sounds from her throat and mucus from her nose running down into her cold sores. She didn't care about anything. Nothing.

There was the bull, still wide in the chest, but definitely gaunt, his ribs showing beneath his ragged coat. There was the mean cow, looking more belligerent and wild-eyed than ever.

The herd scattered and came together to watch warily, the new young mothers bawling for their spindly calves.

Clay shook his head as he dismounted. "Look at this!"

Hannah was afraid to dismount, afraid her legs would not support her, so she followed Clay from her perch on the saddle.

"I'd say that old cow gets the credit for saving your herd. Look at this." He held up a bleached ribcage, the frozen tattered paw of a wolf.

Hannah nodded. She swiped at her streaming eyes, her chest heaving.

"Once them wolves know whose boss, they don't hang around. Once these cows could back up to these cottonwoods, that ornery old cow let 'em have it. The bull, too. Look at this. Here's another one. That pack of wolves took a lickin'."

Hannah nodded, swallowed. She tried to laugh, pointed at the crazy antics of the wobbly, long-legged calves, then began crying hysterically again.

Clay looked up at her and then dug in his coat pocket for a handkerchief, producing a well-used and rumpled red one. Han-

nah honked and snorted, wiped her eyes and took a deep breath
to steady herself.

"Wal, Hannah, I'd say the Bar S is off and running," Clay
said, accepting the red handkerchief as she handed it back to
him. "It won't be long until those cows is sleek and fat, munch-
ing grass like you ain't ever seen," he laughed.

Hannah laughed too, a hoarse sound bordering on a sob.
"It was a long winter, Clay. I was so worried. I had bad dreams.
One day just blurred into the next until I thought the storms
would never stop and we'd die, all of us together out on this
homestead in the middle of the prairie."

He caught her hands, hauled her off the saddle, pulled her
against him and cradled her head against his chest, swaying
lightly, the way he might comfort a child.

"It's been rough for you, Hannah. Too rough. I could see it in
your eyes. I wanted to come to you, to see how you were doing.
But it would have been foolish. I still have feelings for you, Hannah. I'm still waiting."

Hannah nodded. "I know. Let's just be friends for now. You
know I'm different than most girls. I don't want a husband or
a boyfriend right now. And there's this Amish-English thing to
consider."

"I'll wait. It's all right." He pulled back to look into her dark
eyes. "I'd love to kiss you, Hannah, but that mouth . . . "

Hannah laughed and slapped him with her gloves. "I need to
keep these cold sores. Scares you away."

She thought of the other person she needed to scare away.
Now there was a brazen one! That Jerry Riehl. The dark horse.
The one who was impossible to forget.

Hadn't she tried on so many sleepless nights when yet another
storm ravaged the prairie, the house on the homestead a black
dot in a vast land, scoured and pummeled by forces they could
not predict or control? Hadn't she tried to push thoughts of him
from her mind?

Why now, here in Clay's arms, thankful and filled with an emotion she herself could not fully understand, did Jerry's face, no, his . . . It was too humiliating how much she wanted him. She needed to stop all thoughts of love and romance or any entanglement with Jerry or Clay. Either one distracted her from the business at hand, which was to keep the cows alive and healthy, gather hay for the winter, keep the windmill working, help her mother plant and harvest a garden, and hope for the best.

Sighing, she stepped away from Clay. They stood apart, watching the cattle. It almost scared her how thin a few of them were. She noticed the swelling of udders, a few more calves would soon be born.

"Them mothers are gonna need grass to nurse them young 'uns," Clay observed. Hannah nodded.

When Manny, Hank, and Ken found them, another celebration broke out with Indian whoops and raised fists pumping the air above their heads.

The herd was here, they had survived the worst winter. Manny's face was a mixture of awe and deep reverence—so much like his father—and little-boy tears, all strengthened by his own will to appear grownup and nonchalant in the presence of the Jenkins boys.

They rode home, threw themselves off their horses, and ran toward the porch to announce the good news to Sarah.

As soon as the weather, permitted, Sarah cooked a celebratory meal and invited the Jenkinses and the Klassermans. The arrival of sighing breezes, running water that formed joyful little puddles that eddied and swirled from banks of melting snow, was enough to call for a gathering of friends and good food.

The wind was still harsh, as if it was reluctant to announce its defeat, but that was all right. What was a bit of dashing cold if you could feel the sunlight on your face and listen to the sound of melting snowbanks?

Sarah baked an entire ham, basting it with molasses and brown sugar mixed with hard cider. The whole house smelled of sweet, baking ham, an aroma that always took Hannah back to her grandparents' kitchen at Christmas time.

They peeled potatoes, breaking off the long white sprouts before they could apply their paring knives, the potatoes wrinkled and dusty from having lain in the cold cellar, which was attached to the wash house.

Sarah laughed at the long white sprouts. She laughed at the wrinkled carrots and smiled as she peeled onions. The winter's dark anxiety was being erased now as the warm sun melted the snow banks, a sign of hope, of survival. The grasses would spring up and cover the prairie in verdant waves of thick, hardy growth that would sustain every cow and calf.

The kitchen was filled with brilliant sunlight that cut rectangles of yellow light on the scrubbed and polished floor. The aroma of baking ham mixed with the earth smells of cooking potatoes and carrots.

Sarah wore a gray dress with a black apron, her hair, like the wings of a raven, parted neatly in the center. Her crisp, white covering had been washed in soapy water with a few shavings of paraffin thrown in to starch and stiffen the fabric. Her cheeks glowed, her large eyes turned gray with that certain hint of sadness that had darkened them the day Mose had died. It seemed they had never regained their original luster.

Hannah never wore a white head covering anymore, choosing to pin a diagonal half of a man's handkerchief as far back on her head as possible, her own black hair arranged loosely with decided tendrils framing her face. She was especially attractive in a dress of deep purple, a black apron tied around her slim waist. Her face glowed with a wellspring of renewed hope and energy, her step quick and light, every shadow of anxiety gone.

Manny's dark hair was neatly trimmed in the traditional Amish bowl cut, his face pale from the months of winter, his jaw square and clean shaven. The children were dressed in their best clothes, Baby Abby as cute as a button in a pink dress with a row of tucks sewed into the hem, to be lengthened as she grew. She crawled, pulled herself up, took tottering steps, her fat little hands clinging to furniture as she babbled excitedly to herself.

Sarah, however, could only dream of the desserts she would have liked to make, choosing instead to ration the scant amounts of flour and sugar that remained after the long winter. She knew another year would go by without income, the calves needing time to grow before being sent to auction. Her father was more than generous, but in spite of this, she remained frugal, guiltily aware of using anything to excess.

The Jenkinses were the first to arrive, clattering into the barnyard in the rusted old pickup truck that had once been blue but now was striped with gray, speckled with brown rust, and splattered with snow and dark mud.

Abby alighted with the eagerness of a young girl, beat Hod to the porch, and stepped inside without bothering to knock or announce her arrival. She scooped up Baby Abigail and plunked her bony little frame in the armless rocker.

The baby set up a desperate howl, lunged, and wriggled away from her until she gave up and set her down. She raced on all fours to her mother who picked her up, nestling her head on Sarah's shoulder before lifting it to peek at Abby.

"Oh now, come on. It's me, little one. It's only me. You know who I am. Come on." She reached out both arms, her fingers wiggling, beckoning, but Abby merely bent her head and hid her face in Sarah's neck.

Sarah laughed. "She'll warm up to you, Abby. It's just been so long."

"Hasn't it though? Oh, it's been a long one. Terrible. Thought I'd go crazy with them winds a' howlin'. Pure miracle yer herd made it, ain't it? Beginnin' to think God's favorin' you."

Sarah shook her head. "Oh, please don't think that. God just knew we couldn't get along without the herd. We wouldn't be here if it wasn't for my father back in Pennsylvania, you know that. Or you and Hod. We would have starved that first year without your kindness."

"Oh now, don't go makin' up stuff. We never did nothin' 'cept loan you some food. Anyone else woulda done the same."

Sarah smiled and looked into Abby's eyes. The two women had been thrown together on this bleak prairie, and they were grateful for the friendship, the companionship, that grew and flourished in spite of their differences.

Sarah frowned, concern drawing a line between her eyes, when Abby began to cough, a deep-seated, rasping sound from low in her too-thin chest. To hide her alarm, she bent to open the oven door, lifting the lid on the roaster, inserting a fork, and then replacing the lid.

"Ah."

Abby thumped her chest with a fist, tears forming in her brilliant blue eyes. "Got myself a real cough a coupla weeks ago. Don't nothin' seem to help. Cooked enougha onions to steam the men clear outa the house. Tried mustard till I blistered my chest. Guess with the warm weather it'll go away."

"I would hope so. Get Hod to take you to the doctor in Pine."

"I wouldn't take a half-starved cat to that joker. He don't know a thing 'bout nothin'. Mind you, Sarah, you know that Rocher woman? Her husband owns the hardware? I forget her name. She's sort of spindly, looks like a washrag someone left floatin' in the dish water too long. She doesn't like it out here in the West. Somepin' wrong in her head. Doc Brinter tol' her she got TB. Tuberculosis. Now you know that ain't true. Them TB people turn lemon yellow, so they do. Ain't nothin' wrong with her, otherin' she needs to quit pityin' herself. That Roger knew what was good for her, he'd take her back home. Land sakes, she's a pain in everybody's life, not jes' her own. Isn't Hannah goin' back?" She fixed her blue eyes on Hannah.

"I don't know," Hannah announced.

"Wal, you should. Everybody said you was doin' her some good, keepin' that house in order, keepin' her spirits up."

Hod and the boys stomped up on the porch, ridding their boots of slush and snow, tracking mud up the steps and onto the rug, unaware of having done anything out of the ordinary.

The boys had ridden their horses, racing along the way they always did, smelling of horse sweat and that vague rancher's scent of cows and mud and manure, their coats and hats slick with saddle grease and leather. Their faces were ruddy from the cold, their hair smashed to their foreheads by their tight hat bands, then billowing loosely down the back of their necks and around their ears.

Clay was growing a mustache, Hank the beginnings of a full beard. The youngest, Ken, looked stubbly and pimple faced, as if he needed a good face washing and a shave.

Why had Hannah never noticed this before? She never realized these boys lived their days in happy oblivion to how they appeared, with yellowed teeth and unwashed faces, hair that was much too long and separated into clumps, never being washed often enough.

Perhaps they had never been in this new sun-filled house in the middle of the day, either. Without meaning to, Hannah's dark eyes measured the Jenkins boys with the fastidious yardstick she used to appraise all men.

Those white, white foreheads! They'd grow old like that. The lower part of their faces would become lined and wrinkled, actually deeply crevassed, the way Hod's was from exposure to sun and rain, sweltering summer temperatures and blasting winter winds. Their hair would always be glued to their heads by those greasy Stetsons. They'd hardly ever take a decent all-over bath, or brush their teeth with baking soda. They'd always clump through the house with whatever clung to the thick soles of their boots, and never know the difference. This is how they were raised by Hod and Abby. Hannah tried hard to measure them in a new and better light, but she knew there was no use.

She was who she was. For a moment, the thought took the light from her eyes. This was not the first, nor the only time, she had felt this aversion to men. Today, though, it was sobering, this knowledge of why she was never seriously attracted to anyone.

Look at Lemuel Short. She'd been right about him for sure. But the Jenkinses were here now, and she needed to do her best to make the dinner a success.

The Klassermans arrival caused quite a stir, with Owen yelling across the room, followed by his pink, exclaiming spouse. If anything, they had increased in size, the long winter whiled away with many culinary forays, no doubt.

Sylvia seemed almost shy, a tad apologetic, but soon realized all was forgiven. Her meticulous housekeeping and lack of endurance when the Detweiler's house went up in flames had been forgotten. Oh, she had tried to be the good Samaritan and house them all, but in the end, her nerves wouldn't take it. Owen supported her to this day, thank God.

Sarah served up the meal with Hannah's help, Abby and Sylvia shooed out of the way. Talk rose in lively spurts as Owen, Hod, and the boys discussed the winter, the cattle market and the local news, everything swirling and tumbling about like a creek in springtime. Hannah strained to hear, but it was useless. She was unable to decipher much at all with two or three of them talking at once.

The table was stretched out to accommodate them all, spread with a freshly washed and ironed white cotton tablecloth. The plates were flowered china, a design of pink roses and blue forget-me-nots entwined with green ivy, the gift of an anonymous donor back in Pennsylvania.

There were small cut glass dishes of sweet pickles and red beets, saved for an occasion such as this. The applesauce was a bit dark in color but tasted just wonderful all the same.

They enjoyed the thick sourdough bread without butter, but with plenty of jam, red and shimmering in tiny glass dishes. The potatoes were mashed with salt and one precious tin of canned milk, covered liberally with thick, salty ham gravy, rich and dark. Stewed carrots and onions, *knepp*, those tiny little white flour dumplings simmered on top of sauerkraut, an old Amish favorite that Hod and the boys ate until every bit was scraped from the serving bowl.

There were noodles too. Rachel's homemade noodles, cut thick and wide, simmered in chicken and parsley broth, flavored with small amounts of hard cheese. Browned butter would have been perfect, but without milk, this was simply impossible. So they did without.

Hannah filled water glasses and coffee cups, refilled serving bowls, laughed and talked and smiled, aware of Clay's hungry eyes and Hank's near worshipping looks, never responding fully, always aloof, always on the outer edge of any warm conversations.

She glowed when talk turned to the near miraculous survival of the herd, but spoke very little, still loathing the amount of tears she had allowed Clay to witness, and him pulling her into his arms at every opportunity.

It irked her, these men doing things like that. Why couldn't he have walked away and allowed her to have her moment of bawling when her eyes were red and her nose ran like a child's? But no, he had to pull her into his arms again. She reached a hand up to tentatively feel the healing cold sores, suddenly grateful for their awful appearance. She should try to sprout them on a regular basis!

Sylvia ended the meal by disappearing into the washhouse and reappearing with a stack of homemade pies, carrying them triumphantly, like a torch, to the table where she set them down with a flourish, her face as red as a cherry, amid yells and thumps of boots and claps that fell on her shoulders.

"Apple pie!" she trilled, her cheeks bunched up around her eyes like fresh, pink bread dough.

"Cherry pie!" she shouted, unveiling a huge pie baked in a monstrous blue agate pie plate as big as a frying pan.

Wedges of pie disappeared like snow in summer. Forkfuls of flaky crust bursting with sweet, thickened fruit disappeared into hungry mouths, Sarah and Hannah no different from the rest of them.

"Deprived too long," Hod said, chuckling, his face creased in smiles of pleasure.

"Now don't you go making as if'n I never bake you a pie," Abby said, shaking her fork at him.

"You don't!" Hank yelled, good naturedly teasing his mother.

"Wal young feller, if that's how you 'preciate my hard work slavin' over that there stove, wal, you kin bake yer own pie next time!"

Hod laughed outright, reached over and patted Abby's thin shoulder. "Now, Ma. We're only funnin' you, is all."

They shared the same look Hannah had often seen between Mose and Sarah, her parents who were closer than anyone she knew. So here was another couple who had been married even longer, living together with that mysterious harmony, that bewildering sharing of thoughts and emotions that Hannah could never understand.

She had no longing to be patted on the shoulder as if she was a dog who had obeyed. She would never see that kind of appreciation by a man for having baked him a pie. For one thing, she hated the thought of pie baking. For another, a man could survive real good without pie. He could eat cake or, if she didn't feel like baking him a cake, he could eat bread with molasses on it!

That's what married women turned into the minute they sealed their fate with that innocent "Ya" in answer to the minister's questions about promising to love, honor, and obey. All that stuff. Dutifully being turned into a slave of sorts. No, not really a slave, but . . .

Hannah sat drinking black coffee, the taste of pie like a sweet afterthought, contemplating this thing called marriage, her eyes dark and brooding, her mouth compressed, listening to Sylvia's high, breathless voice as she gave out instructions for successful pie baking.

Hanna snorted inwardly. Sylvia had probably eaten half a pie and had no room for air, so she had to take helpless little breaths. She was huge! Hannah watched the rise and fall of her bosom, the lifting of her fork, a skinny, tiny utensil held by the thick, fleshy fingers. She marveled at the ability of an insignificant fork entering a normal sized mouth with enough food to build up this pyramid of a woman.

Owen was no different, discretely loosening the top button of his too-tight trousers beneath the table, but she'd seen him and looked away quickly when his bright eyes met hers.

Hannah decided she didn't like people who ate too much, and all men who went through life without washing or brushing their teeth. In fact, she didn't care a whole lot for hardly anyone. She wished they'd all stop talking now and go home. They'd said everything that was important and a whole pile of things that weren't important, so now it was time to go home.

Abby coughed and coughed. She left the table to go out to the washhouse to hack and gag, bringing up phlegm and mucous, sounding like she wasn't able to get her breath.

Hannah spoke without thinking. "Hod, why don't you take your wife to see a doctor?"

"She won't go."

"Well, she needs to."

"I know."

She met Hod's blue gaze and what passed between them was definitely not even close to the glances of understanding that Hannah had witnessed between him and Abby. He doesn't care enough about her, she thought.

She's about as tactful as a wire brush, that one, Hod thought, with a look so vinegary it could sour mile. She needs to be taken down a notch, sittin' there like the queen of Sheba and all his boys moonin' around, and she knows it. Don't care. Clay was the worst. He needed to talk to him right soon. No use wasting is time and breath on that bad-tempered filly.

CHAPTER 10

ONE DAY IN LATE APRIL, THE COLD WINDS SUBSIDED, SHUDDERED, and gave up, allowing the warm sunshine to turn the playful breezes into mellow, friendly little puffs of air that tugged at skirts and sent hats, untied kerchiefs, and bonnets flying.

They hitched Pete to the plow, tilled the garden, planted left-over wrinkled potatoes and seeds of beans, squash, and tomatoes they had saved. Seeds were dropped in the furrows with painstaking precision, careful to let not one seed go to waste.

Calves were born and frolicked with the herd of cows as the grass shot up from the blackened earth.

Cold rain seeped into the soil and replenished the already snow-soaked earth. Prairie dogs sat on their skinny haunches, their front feet dangling as if waiting to pray, then shot into their burrows with the speed of lightning. Prairie hens ran without direction, squawking like alarmed old women, necks outstretched, running simply for the sake of leaving one spot for another. Butterflies hovered, took off in their dizzying flight, leaving a trail that was impossible for birds to follow. So they survived, flitting from clumps of columbines to low-lying bunches of purple violets, their wings lifted then lowered, as they guzzled the nectar.

Hannah worked from sunup to sundown. Her bare feet walked across stubbles of new growth, slimy black ashes, and new grass shooting up from beneath winter's brown growth.

She learned the ways of birthing calves. She knew when to spot trouble and when the time of birth was near. She was not one to be overly religious but her heart lifted to God of its own accord every time she came upon a mother licking her newborn calf, a healthy, black calf with a wide chest and sturdy, knobby knees, the cleft hooves splayed as delicately as toenails on a newborn baby.

The milk cow gave birth to a brown calf and what the calf did not drink found its way into the house. They all enjoyed glasses of creamy, sweet milk, the top cream turned into butter and cheese.

Haymaking time came, sending all of them into the fields. Manny raked the hay with Pete and Goat hitched up to the mower. Everyone helped fork it onto the wooden wagon. The haymaking never stopped. It was the one single thing that would keep the anxious nightmares at bay on those awful dark nights of winter.

No matter that Mam said prayers were more trustworthy. Prayer was what triumphed over anxiety. Hannah listened half-heartedly, refusing to allow what she knew was her own version of security to be ridiculed by her devout mother. Hay in the haymow. Stacks of hay in the barnyard, by the windmill, hay in every corner they could find. It was certain to keep the cows fed, ensuring survival and, ultimately, the success of the ranch.

Hannah's face turned dark, browned by the sun. Her arms became muscular, her hands calloused, the soles of her feet as tough as the cows' hooves.

A new concern raised its head in spite of things going so well. Pete was wearing out, and Goat was running on his last legs. Something had to be done about dependable horsepower, and Hannah had no idea how to procure another decent horse.

The calves they would sell before winter would barely tide them over this first year. She refused to ask her grandfather yet again for a loan. But something would have to be done.

She talked it over with Manny, who had no real solution except to ask the Jenkinses, which, Hannah felt sure, would result in the generous gift of another pitiful creature like Goat.

"I mean, Goat's all right. We couldn't have managed without him. He helped us through lots of haying. I'm sure the Jenkinses have half a dozen horses like Goat that they'd be glad to get rid of."

"I'm not going to the Jenkinses."

"We could get a tractor."

Hannah laughed. "Mam would never allow it. She's so Amish it isn't even funny."

"We all are."

"Not me."

"Oh, come on, Hannah. You're always bluffing and blustering. You'd never hurt Mam by disobeying her."

Hannah shrugged and changed the subject back to the problem of a horse. "For now, we're going to have to let it go and hope Goat holds up for another year or so."

The letter arrived with the Klassermans driving in and waving a handful of letters as their impeccably clean station wagon came to a halt. "Ve're back from a visit to the dentist. Picked these up at the post office for you."

Sarah wiped her hands on her apron, leaving streaks of brown dirt from weeding the onions. She used the back of her hand to push back the windblown strands of hair that had blown loose around her face.

"Oh, good! Thank you so much. I was starting to wonder if everyone in Lancaster County forgot about us. Not that I could blame them."

"Ya. Ya. But they didn't. Relatives don't forget," Owen smiled.

"Yer garden looks beautiful," Sylvia observed, hitching her bulk to a more comfortable position.

"Lots of horse manure. We spread it on throughout the fall when we cleaned out the stable and plowed it in before we planted. Nothing better."

"Ya, ya. Vell, ve must be on our vay. Haf you heard? Abby Jenkins finally vent to a doctor. She has the double pneumonia. Stubborn voman."

"Oh, dear." Sarah's dark eyes filled with quick tears. "I must go visit her. Take her some food or offer to do the washing or cleaning. Maybe I'll send Hannah."

The Klassermans took their leave, leaving Sarah to stand in the driveway by the porch as she riffled through four letters before sitting on the edge of the porch to rip open one long white envelope, gripping the white paper with both hands and moving slightly back and forth as she read.

"Oh my. Oh my," she repeated, her lips moving silently. Elam and Ben had agreed to give up the farm. "Lord willing, we are making plans to begin our move west," her father wrote. "The pioneering bug has bitten us hard."

Sarah lifted her face to the sun, her eyes closed, absorbing every word, the vast open sky and the waves of grass etched into her heart and soul. This was her home, this unfettered land. And now her father and two brothers were planning to come and begin a new life on the prairie with them.

She lowered her head and red on. "Ben Miller's and Ike Lapp's see great opportunity in building windmills, so they are in the planning stages, same as we are. I believe the two young bachelors will be accompanying them. Word is getting around that a young horse dealer by the name of Jeremiah Riehl has shown interest in moving his horse trade to North Dakota. He is also a farrier.

"Your sisters remain of the same mind. I pray to God they will yet repent of their overbearing ways, but for now, we are on good terms. I have not dared mention our future plans to them. Rachel's health is not the best. I'm afraid if she's confronted by these sudden goings on, she may fall victim to a stroke."

Here, Sarah lifted her face to the sky, propped herself up with two palms facing outward. Kicking both feet in the air, she howled with abandon, a most unladylike move and not like her at all.

It brought a concerned Eli and Mary from around the back of the house where they were playing horse, a rope tied around Eli's waist. "Mam! What is wrong with you?" Mary asked worriedly.

"Oh, nothing, Mary. I'm just reading a letter from Daudy. And just think, Daudy and Ben and Elam and Ben Millers—a whole bunch of Amish people—are moving here. Here! Here to North Dakota with us! We won't be alone anymore! We can have church services and we can have people like us to share our Sundays."

Eli looked at his mother and frowned. "We don't need those people."

"We don't," Mary echoed.

Sarah laughed aloud, reached out to grab the rope around Eli's waist and hauled him in for a tight hug and a resounding kiss. "Your hair smells like a cow," she said, nuzzling his cheek.

"Ah. Ah," he grunted, trying to squirm out of his mother's arms.

"You need a head washing," Sarah said.

"Not now. He's a horse," Mary reminded her before pulling on the rope to lead him away. Eli whinnied and kicked one leg out to show his mother that he was a horse to be reckoned with.

Sarah watched them, smiled, and went back to her letter reading. Emma had a boil on her back. My goodness! That should be treated by a doctor for sure. Amos King's Naomi was published to be married to the widower, Jacob King.

My, my. Naomi was going on forty years of age. Jacob King *sei* Becky passed away only a year before. He had nine or ten children. Just wait until Hannah hears this!

She read and reread each precious letter. She laughed and cried, then took a deep, cleansing breath of pure unadulterated joy, allowing the wonderful news to sink in, to spread through her limbs and give them new life.

Oh, wonder, blessed, benevolent Father, the Giver of all good things. Her heart sang praises, her soul was lifted to the heights of the unending sky and rode the prairie breezes like the notes of a song.

Every bit of hardship had been worth this moment. Every dark night of suffering and indecision. She had eaten the food of despair and tasted the bitter cup of sorrow. Many times she had drunk thirstily from the cup of grace and was able to go on.

She wished her mother was alive, and then realized as quickly that her father would not be moving here to the prairie if she were. Her mother would never have allowed it.

She got up, went into the house, put the precious letters in a cupboard drawer, and then came back out to finish weeding the onions. She worked as if in a dream; she caught herself talking, murmuring things out loud, making plans, the future full of possibilities, full of security from shared responsibilities.

Sarah adjusted her covering and listened to the sighing of the wind in the prairie grass. The rustling was now so dear and familiar; it was like her own heartbeat. Without it, her life would be devoid of a certain endless rhythm, a breathing of earth and sky, a oneness with nature, with God. This experience she could never have found in Lancaster County amid the hustle and bustle of life.

The realization dawned like the parting of storm clouds to reveal the sun. Here was her destiny. Here the land would shape and form her into a being created for God. Humbled, Sarah wept.

Hannah grasped the letters with white-knuckled fingers, her lips moving as she read, her eyebrows drawing down in irritation.

Sarah cast silent glances in her direction, busying herself with warming a pan full of ham noodle soup for their evening meal.

Was it only her imagination or did Hannah's face lose its ruddy brown color? She watched Hannah lay the letter aside and stare stone faced out of the window without comment.

"What do you think, Hannah?" she asked, quietly.

"I don't know." Her words were flat, lifeless, as if all the air had been taken from her. Without another word she got up and let herself out through the door. Sarah went to the window, watching her daughter's long strides as she went to the barn, disappearing behind a stack of hay.

She'd never understand Hannah if she lived to be ninety years old. Didn't she want her grandfather and her two uncles to come? Surely she would be happy to have them come out and start their own homestead.

She shook her head, lifted a scalding spoonful of soup to her mouth, tasted it, grimaced. Too salty. She peeled a wrinkled potato, threw it in, added more water, toasted bread in the oven and went to the door to call the children.

Supper was a silent affair, after Manny's joyful whooping, which was struck down immediately by Hannah's scathing words, sharp like daggers.

"If we'd want all of Lancaster County to live with us, we'd move back to Pennsylvania where it's jammed full of all sorts and shapes of Amish and Mennonites, Dunkards, and whatever else in the world exists there. What does that long-nosed Ike Lapp want out here? I can't stand him. He'll probably bring a whining, long-nosed wife and a brood of sniveling kids!"

Here Sarah broke in, shaking her spoon in Hannah's direction. "The world does not turn only for you, Hannah. God loves us all. He made us all, and He must be saddened by your blasphemy."

"I'm not blaspheming. I'm just saying it the way I see it. I don't want people crawling all over the prairie like lice. Those two bachelors will be like that, as unwelcome in my opinion. You know they're going to want a wife. Guess who'll be available?"

"Do you realize how much you are like your father?"

Hannah snorted, the trademark of her derision. "Not much. I'm not wailing and fasting."

Sarah realized the futility of the endless sparring of words, a contest she was certain to lose. Unwise, this volley of regrettable words. So she resigned herself to allowing Hannah the upper hand—sometimes she had to—and said no, she did not do that, and let it go, thinking bitterly that Hannah had nothing to worry about with her attitude, as prickly as a cactus. No man would dare get close to her.

Manny said the homesteads would be miles apart and no one would likely be closer than the Klassermans, which did nothing to change Hannah's foul mood. She washed dishes, banging them against the granite dish pan till Sarah thought they would fly into dozens of pieces, like falling icicles. But she said nothing.

Sometimes she almost despised her own daughter. When those eyebrows came down and spread across those brown eyes, she wanted to physically slap her. Why, when a mother and daughter's heartstrings were so interwoven? Often she wondered if she was a bad mother, if, somewhere along the way, she had missed some element of child-rearing, or some giving of love.

Hannah stalked out of the door, stiff-legged, her large feet slapping against the porch boards, and disappeared, a tall figure becoming smaller and smaller until she appeared as only a dot on the prairie. Sarah turned away and whispered a prayer for her safety.

Hannah was furious! How dare they invade her privacy? This land was their homestead. Theirs. Hers and Mam's and Manny's. She didn't want the prairie dotted with Amish homes, Amish folks sticking their noses into her business, giving advice, superior voices clanging against her own particular way of doing things.

She knew how to start the ranch. Was well on her way. Hadn't Clay said so? This is exactly what would happen. They'd all move out here, figure out a way to grow corn, feed their cattle better, moving ahead and leaving her and the Bar S scrounging in the dust. They'd end up with inferior cattle poorly fed, insufficient horse power, and no modern equipment to cut and rake hay.

She sat down in the fast-growing grass, yanked out a flat stem, aligned it between two thumbs and blew vehemently. A sharp, high whistle split the air. She did it again and again. It satisfied a deep longing to assert herself.

Let the clouds in the west and the sky know that I am Hannah. I can be a homesteader. I can run a successful ranch without dozens of other folks telling me what to do. Perhaps the trains that would bring them would all run off the tracks, a regular train wreck. The scared Amish would take it as a bad omen, a sign from God that they should all go back to Pennsylvania and stay there!

Grandfather Stoltzfus hadn't written that Jerry Riehl was coming with the rest of the herd, just that there was a rumor that he was interested. Well, he could send a few good horses out, but he may as well stay in Lancaster County if he thought he had a remote chance with all his kissy romance. He was about the last one she wanted to see, that was for sure.

Hannah sighed and threw the blade of grass aside. A whole shower of troubles had rained down on her head in the form of a bunch of letters, leaving a sour taste on her tongue.

She had a notion to whack off her hair and go English! She could tell Clay she'd marry him just to get away, but that would open another can of worms, no different from her original troubles. She groaned, threw herself on her back, and watched the puffy cloud formations to the west. The sun's light was already casting a pink glow, the rustling grasses changing color as it sank lower, turning the undersides of the puffy clouds to a lavender hue.

Birds wheeled silently without so much as the flap of a wing, gliding along effortlessly, little black etches against the evening sky. A lark called its plaintive cry, another answered. Hannah pictured the bird clinging to a tall grass stalk, tiny feet clenched perfectly as it opened its beak to begin its song. She knew which insects they preferred, and which jays lived in the rotten branches of the old cottonwood trees.

She often sighted herds of antelope, the leader with his black, two-pronged horns, running like music, the strains of perfect symmetry, beauty in motion. She always hoped fervently that they would not encounter barbed wire, knowing they sometimes became entangled, dying a long, slow, torturous death. It was almost more than she could bear.

Hannah knew that many of the local ranchers considered them pests, but to her way of thinking, they were the most beautiful creatures of the plains, even if their meat was often unfit to eat, tasting of a bitter goat flavor. They would have been more than happy with the strong-smelling meat before the loan from Daudy, when starvation lurked in every corner of the old log house.

She watched the shadows play along the every-moving surface of grass, clouds playing with the wind, teasing the sun. If those ambitious Amish men came out here to live, would they notice or appreciate the endless wonders of this land? Would they use common sense, or would they look on the fertile earth beneath the grass and, ambitious and eager to turn the prairie into a profitable landscape, go crazy with dollar signs?

Well, there was nothing she could do about it. Let them come, let them face a drought, winter storms, and whatever else God chose to send them. They'd learn.

Back at the house, Sarah's thoughts ran along an opposite line. She could hardly grasp the fact that her life would resume in the ways of her childhood, the beloved closeness of a group of like-minded people, who understood the importance of *Ordnung*, were obedient to church doctrine, forming an invisible protective fence around the family, making choices and decisions for her, and abiding by a discipline they believed came from God.

It was a way of life that allowed one to walk in the footsteps of Jesus. It was what she had been born into, raised as a child to accept the manner of dressing, the church services held in homes every two weeks, the strict adherence to using the horse and buggy, and the shunning of electricity and the automobile.

Oh, it wasn't that it set them apart as elite members of God's family. She never wavered in her attitude that all like-minded Christians who believed in God's Son, Jesus Christ, and who lived as they had been taught, would enter into the same rest with other good and faithful servants.

The Amish way of life was her lot, and a beloved one. Even a few families, those of her own father and brothers, living within a distance she could travel with a horse and wagon, were a gift. A rare and precious gift she would never take for granted.

They would hold an Amish church service, even without an ordained minister. Tears sprang to her eyes as she hummed the slow melody of the *"Lob Sang."* Page 770 in the thick black *Ausbund*, the book containing the verses written by men of faith while incarcerated in the damp, stone-walled prisons in Passau, Germany. *Unser fore eldern.* Our forefathers, who chose persecution over the doctrines they found questionable and forged a way of life they preferred.

She giggled, a maudlin, hysterical little sound, as tears ran unchecked down her face. She had no pickles or red beets. She had served the last jars to her neighbors. What were church services without the pickles and red beets served with traditional bread and cheese and pies?

How gladly she would spread the white tablecloth! With a song in her heart she would clean and polish, sweep and mop, rearrange the furniture to make room for benches forming a line of people seated facing the minister.

Evening shadows lurked in the corners of the house after the sun disappeared below the horizon. Sarah lifted the glass chimney, struck a match, and lit the oil lamp. She called the children in from their play, set a basin of warm water and soap on the porch, and washed their hands and faces by turns. They washed their feet until the water turned black from the dust and dirt they had accumulated.

"Now, into your nightclothes," she announced.

"I'm hungry."

"I don't want to go bed. It's not dark yet."

Sarah smiled at Eli and Mary as she spread slices of sourdough bread with new butter and molasses. They drank cold well water, then became droopy with sleepiness, their eyes taking on that certain dull, half-alert look, until she shooed them off to bed.

Together they knelt by the side of their small, single beds, clasped their hands, bowed their heads, and recited the same German prayer Sarah had prayed as a child. Then she tucked them in, kissed them goodnight, and softly left the room, the door slightly ajar.

She found Manny on the front porch removing his shoes, his wide shoulders slumped with weariness.

"Where's Hannah?"

Sarah shrugged her shoulders, picked up the dish pan of dirty water, and threw it out over the yard before wiping it with the washcloth.

"She went for a walk," she said quietly.

"She's upset, isn't she?"

"Yes. She read Father's letter."

"She'll get over it."

"I'm not so sure. Oh, Manny. Life would be so perfect if only Hannah would . . ." she almost said, "Be like you," but she caught herself. How, she wondered, could two children, raised the best she and Mose knew how, be so different from each other?

Sarah sat on the rough-hewn bench, her hands in her lap and sighed. "She's so hard to figure out."

"She's a loner, Mam. She simply doesn't like people. She loves this land and has no desire to see if filling up, especially not with our people. Plus, she has a real problem with Jerry Riehl, the horseman."

Sarah looked at Manny sharply. "What do you mean?"

Manny shook his head. "I can't tell on her, Mam. But he is certainly interested in her. Seriously interested."

"How do you know?"

"I just do. They all want her. Everyone who lives around here would like to have her for a girlfriend, a wife, and she knows it. Look at the Jenkins boys. They fall over their feet to please her. She couldn't care less. She's downright mean to Clay sometimes.

"It's why they all want her: they know they can't have her. She presents a challenge to them. I guarantee you, Mam, Hannah will never marry. Pity her husband if she ever does."

They sat together in the gathering darkness, mother and son, a companionable silence between them, the night easing itself softly around them, folding the dark, low-lying house in its whispering embrace.

A quarter moon sliced its way up through the blanket of night clouds on the horizon, the stars arranging themselves in their age-old positions, twinkling and blinking.

From out of the night, a lone, dark figure appeared, silently stepping into the yard, wordlessly, as if part of the night, a being devised from the earth and sky and vast stillness around her. Without speaking, she stepped up on the porch, opened the screen door, and let herself inside.

"Good-night, Hannah." There was no answer, but then, Sarah didn't expect one.

CHAPTER 11

HANNAH DECIDED EARLY ON THAT GOD MUST NOT HAVE HEARD HER begging for a train wreck.

The spring rains ran their course, then stopped as if all the rain clouds had been cut from the sky with a giant scissors, leaving the yellowish, copper tone that spoke of drought and dust, the sky cloudless and sizzling with white heat. Everywhere Hannah looked, from one horizon to the other, there were ripples of heat above the waving grass, the sun a fiery ball that saturated the earth and sky with heat. The wind dried out the heavy new growth. Dust rolled from wagons and horses, trucks and tractors, anything that moved across a road, leaving an imprint in the inches of loose dust that clung to everything.

By the middle of July, Ben Miller and his brood arrived, settling into a tent, of sorts, while the building began on his 1200 acres. Ike Lapp and his wife and children chugged in on the back of a flatbed truck, the wooden sides flapping and creaking dangerously, threatening to spill all of them out over the side.

Hannah stood by the door frame, her arms crossed, watching the clattering apparatus rumble up to the porch. She stayed right where she was, letting her eyes convey her disapproval.

Of course, they all climbed down, the six offspring of various sizes, the lean and hungry wife who couldn't have weighed more than a hundred pounds.

Sarah received them warmly, her eyes wet with unshed tears of welcome. Manny stood by her side, pumped Ike's hand with enthusiasm that seemed genuine, inquired about the children, always mannerly, always proper and polite, pleasing his mother.

Hannah turned away, went inside, out through the back door and across the prairie to the windmill. Likely Mam would cook them a good dinner while she listened to news from home. Well, she'd do it alone. They didn't need to feel like this was a celebration with everybody fussing and fawning over them, as if they were important moving out here where they probably wouldn't make it anyway. Hannah vowed to have nothing to do with them. Ben Millers either. Talk about shunning! They hadn't seen anything!

When Sarah told her that Ike Lapps were moving on a claim only six miles east of them, Hannah was furious. Sarah listened to her displeasure until it ran itself out, then told her she didn't have to be neighborly, if that's how she felt, but she herself would do as she pleased. "They're poor, Hannah. They have only 320 acres. You know how hard it was for us."

"Yeah, well, the summer's turning out dry, so we may not have enough for ourselves, let alone peddling everything to that Ike Lapp family."

Sarah set her mouth in a firm line and turned away.

The calves arrived one by one, little, wet and black, their long, spindly legs knobby kneed and wobbly, their tails whacking at flies only hours after they were born. Their eyes were large and liquid, with slanted lids and heavy lashes, the prettiest animals Hannah had ever seen.

One after another, the mothers dropped their calves that nursed successfully without any serious complications, which was a miracle of sorts, Hannah knew. Thirteen cows and now there were eleven calves. The herd was swelling in size, the calves capering among their mothers, exact little replicas of the Black Angus breed.

Hannah was never happier than when she was sitting astride Pete, out by the cows, milling around with them, checking on the health of the babies and the mothers who had not yet calved. She knew them all apart by small differences, a whorl of hair on a forehead, a longer neck, a heavy tail, or a peculiar set of nostrils. Some small difference was always there, and she named each calf to match their oddity.

She hoped they could have at least seven or eight of the calves weighing close to eight hundred pounds till late fall or early winter, make a successful drive to Pine, and meet the cattle truck that would take them to the large auction in Dorchester.

She believed that with Manny's help, they could accomplish this, if certain new and nosy neighbors would stay out of it.

Oh, it irked her! Here was Mam, cooking and baking, riding off with Manny in the wagon like two saints, leaving her alone, uninvited and never letting her know what they were doing. They could at least tell her which family they were visiting.

Fueled by a strong dose of anger, she yanked the old, brittle saddle with the cracked wooden stirrup off Pete's back and hurled it into a dark corner of the barn.

She hadn't bargained for this. She had battled, even anticipated drought and winter storms. They'd survived the awful fire, the long winter, met Lemuel Short, acted like greenhorns and took in the poor man.

This, now, this wave of Amish people migrating out here, thinking it was all one big lark, wealth hidden everywhere they looked, was going to be a tough load to shoulder. Nosy, judgmental, deciding right from wrong for themselves as well as everyone around them, it was enough to make her yank off the *dichly* and go cut her hair. That would give them something to talk about!

You just watch. Mam would give half of her garden produce away. That wife of Ike Lapp, whatever her name was, looked as mean and hungry as a wolf in winter. The children picked their noses and examined whatever they had dug out.

Hannah shuddered. She picked up the saddle, hoisted it on to the wooden rack, hung up the bridle, then leaned on the fence, one foot hooked on the bottom board, her arms crossed on the top rail, watching Pete walk out to meet his only companion, Goat.

They possessed two of the oldest, most battered and worn horses she had ever seen. Ribs like washboards, skinny and distended necks, scrapes and cuts and swollen knees.

Hannah shook her head and wondered if they'd last another year. That Goat was as worthless a horse as she'd ever seen. He had no eye for cutting cattle from the herd, just ran pell-mell among them like a happy calf. You could yank on the reins, yell directions, and still he simply did not get it. He was stupid. Stupid and loathsome, and constantly dropping loose green bowels that made a mess wherever he went.

It never stopped. But, it was all they had and Hannah would never mistreat poor Goat. Manny had more patience, so he rode him among the cattle more than Hannah did, mostly to save the poor horse from Hannah's frustration.

They practiced their roping skills on the calves, making them wild-eyed and skittish. Clay told them it was not a good idea, but Hannah told him that a bit of chasing wouldn't hurt them. He narrowed his eyes and set his jaw and thought—wait until you try and drive them to Pine—but didn't say it aloud.

Two half-dead horses and saddles that were falling apart, bridles held together by rivets and pieces of twine. Comfortable, serviceable buildings, a windmill, the start of a good herd of cattle. Hannah guessed they weren't doing too badly. With a satisfied nod, she turned away.

What was that? Dust rolling out toward Pine? Someone was approaching. Hannah fought the urge to hide, stayed where she was, squinting, the wind tugging her black hair out from under the flapping men's handkerchief that served as her head covering. A loose brown dress, one sleeve torn, pinned haphazardly down the front, the skirt, well below her knees, blowing in the ceaseless wind that caressed the plains all day long.

A pickup truck hauling a cattle trailer. Nothing new or different, it resembled the Klassermans' rig.

Her bare feet were planted apart, brown and strong, and she stood there unwavering as she watched the truck draw the trailer up to the barn, followed by a cloud of brown dust and grit that rolled over everything as it came to a halt.

Hannah didn't recognize the driver or the two passengers. She crossed her arms and glared, hoping to convey the message she felt inside: Move on. Don't bother me.

Her squinting eyes tightened, the lids drooped and closed momentarily as a long sigh escaped through her lips, a whoosh of air expelled by the jumping craziness in her chest.

It was him!

He walked up to her, at ease and unselfconscious, lifted his straw hat, the wind picking up the dark hair underneath, the light in his eyes meant for her.

"How are you, Hannah?"

She nodded.

"I need a place to keep three horses until I get a lean-to built. I bought the old Perthing place out past the slough. What is it called? Swamp . . . or something?"

Another young man joined them, tall and thin, straw hat pulled low, thumbs hooked in his suspenders. Hannah met his dark, curious gaze with her usual coldness and her flat, unwelcoming stare that usually froze the friendliest person.

"This is Jake. Jake Fisher."

Hannah nodded, lifted her chin a few inches and kept it there. Jerry Riehl and Jake Fisher. Sounded like horse thieves or something.

"I don't want your horses."

Jake looked at her, startled.

Jerry said, "Well, you're going to get them. I don't know where else to put them.

"There's the Klassermans. The Jenkinses too."

"I don't know them."

"So?"

Jerry stepped closer, stared at her, his eyes bright with anger. He was here now, and he had a plan firmly in place. This obstinate girl was not going to stop him.

"I'm leaving them here, Hannah. I want to keep them in your barn. I have salt blocks and grain, so feed them until I can come and get them."

"No."

Jake looked at his friend, a small smile playing around his mouth.

"Manny will do it. So will your mother. If you want to be so bull-headed, go right ahead. It's not going to make any difference."

Hannah's eyes blazed. "Yeah, well, I'm not my mother. Or Manny. So don't come here expecting a bunch of favors because you're not getting them. I don't want a gaggle of bossy Amish folks as neighbors. We were doing just fine on our own, so don't expect me to be of any help."

"If I remember correctly, your whole family was not doing so great after the fire. You would not have been able to stay on your homestead without your grandfather's help, and you know it." Jerry's face had gone white, his nostrils flared.

For once in her life, Hannah did not know what to say. Any smart retort that came to her mind fizzled and died before the blaze in his eyes, a reflection of her own.

With that, he stalked off, yanked the bar on the trailer door, let down the wooden ramp, and walked up, calling to his horses.

Hannah stayed where she was, her tanned face suffused with anger.

She had never seen horses like the ones he led down that ramp. Sleek, well-fed, their necks arched and thick, rippling manes and tails like poetry. Their eyes were calm, without the whites showing, well-trained by the way Jerry led them down easily, without any coaxing or commanding.

A black one and a dark brown one with a beautiful mane and tail as black as a crow.

The third horse he led down made her draw in a sharp breath. Golden! A golden horse with a mane the color of molasses in milk. Or oatmeal. The tail was arched and flowing almost to the ground. A groan of longing rose in her throat, and she brought her fist up to her mouth to silence it.

She would never let either of them see what she was feeling. Never.

Her eyes followed the golden horse, taking in the waving mane, the deep, wide chest, the long symmetrical legs, the perfect withers. A white blaze on the forehead. Hooves perfectly trimmed and shod. Likely he had done it.

They led the horses over, Jerry holding the black one and golden one. "Meet my horses, Hannah."

She lifted her chin and stared coldly.

"The black one is Duke. The brown one is King. Haven't named the palomino. You can name her. They're all riding horses, not drivers, so don't go trying anything crazy. Keep them penned. They won't do well turned loose. This is strange country for them. One scoop of grain and plenty of water. Make sure they have hay.

"You ever hear of the Perthing place?"

She shook her head.

"Some old guy hung on to the place at the turn of the century. Wasn't mentally capable and they found him dead in the house. After that, the winds and whatever else got at the buildings and basically destroyed them. But it is actually a ranch of over a thousand acres. I bought it for a song. Figured if I bought it then decided to go back home, I'd probably make a nice profit."

Hannah snorted.

Jerry looked at her. "Think not?"

"Nobody wants swamp land."

Jake Fisher watched Hannah's face. When she spoke in that low, husky voice, he could see the irresistible charm of this girl who sizzled with anger.

"But that swamp land might be all right in dry weather. Does it ever rain here in summer?"

Hannah shook her head. "Hasn't so far."

"Then I should be making heavy hay when the rest of you are traveling pretty far to cut and load some decent hay. So I might not be as dumb as you think I am."

They stabled the horses, Hannah keeping her distance, showing no interest, scuffing her feet in the dust, her hands gripped together behind her back.

Jerry gave her a few more clipped instructions, saying they would need some exercise, so they should be ridden.

Hannah's heart fluttered against her chest, but she gave no sign. Goat stuck his head over the top of the fence, whinnying. Hannah cringed as the men turned to look.

"S' wrong with your horse?"

Before she could catch herself, she laughed. "Nothing. That's a product of the North Dakota plains. They all look like that. They're tough and rangy and full of worms."

Both men laughed genuine laughs that came from finding her blunt, truthful words hilarious. They both eyed her with new appreciation.

She didn't laugh.

"I'm guessing he needs his teeth filed." Jerry climbed over the fence, grabbed Goat's unsuspecting chin, and pried his mouth open with two fingers. He ran his hands along Goat's teeth, whistled and said it's a wonder this horse wasn't dead! Never saw a worse set of molars.

Hannah's defensiveness was back in place. She didn't say anything. This was where it would start. She'd be bossed around and told what to do. They were here ten minutes and already they found fault. Well, she'd have to tell them now so they'd get the hint.

"You can just leave if this is what you're going to do. Come out here to start ranching and thinking you're better than anyone else, telling us what to do. You can just forget it. It's none of your business if that horse's teeth come down all the way to his knees. It's my business and I'd appreciate if you'd go home and stop bothering us."

Jerry nodded once, turned and left, a bewildered Jake in tow. Hannah nodded her head in their direction, then turned and made her way back to the house. Let him think what he wanted. Just wait until he caught sight of the herd. That would give him something to think about.

He had the nerve, not taking no for an answer. She'd distinctly said no. He had brushed her aside like a housefly.

Why had he gone and bought that old ranch? He could easily have gotten all the acres he wanted for free. All he had to do was live on them for ten years.

Out here throwing his authority around! Didn't he know there was a depression and times were hard? Perhaps he thought he was better than them. He lived above most people's standards.

Well, she wasn't touching those horses. That was Manny's job, since they thought Manny and his mother were so sweet and welcoming. Which they were, but that didn't mean *she* needed to be.

The horses stayed in the barn. Manny took responsibility for their care, slavishly feeding them the grain Jerry had provided, leading them out to drink, brushing them, exclaiming about this wonderful horse flesh to anyone who would listen, and always, without fail, at the breakfast table, the dinner table, and the supper table.

Manny knew his own sister well enough to keep her out of the conversation. He knew her refusal to help had nothing to do with the horses themselves but everything to do with their owner.

Sarah stood on the porch, watching Manny lead Duke first, then King, and last the palomino, riding each of them in turn. She felt Hannah's presence beside her. Silence hung between them like a heavy curtain, separating the thoughts and the words that should have flowed so easily.

A waste, Sarah thought. A waste of precious hours lent to us by our Lord. A total, unfruitful waste, to be so miserable with one's own will that it directed foolishness of endless pouting and a bold refusal to comply. It was enough to send a tremor of frustration through her.

Quietly, Sarah asked, "If the brown one is King, and Duke is the black one, what is the name of the light-colored one?"

Hannah stood like a statue, staring straight ahead. Her lips parted but no sound came out until she cleared her throat and said roughly, "Doesn't have one."

Sarah looked at her. "Why not?"

She was rewarded with an offhand shrug.

"Let's think of one."

"I already did. Mistral."

Sarah's eyebrows went up. She gave a short laugh, shook her head. "Never heard of it."

"It's a wind."

Sarah gestured with her hand. "You mean like this wind?"

"No. A master wind. In France."

"Really? You think it fits her?"

"Didn't you see her run? If we raced those three, she'd win."

Ah, here was her chance, Sarah thought. "So, go ahead and race them."

Hannah shook her head.

"Why not?" But a seed had been sown, sprouting in Hannah's mind, although Sarah knew her daughter would do her best to stomp all over it.

When Jerry and Jake showed up with the necessary tools to file Goat's teeth, they greeted Sarah, who sat on the front porch cleaning green and yellow beans, thankful for the fine vegetables, in spite of the drought. Thankful for Manny's expertise in rigging up a long pipe underground to a hydrant close to the garden. The windmill's clanking and whirring powered by the constant wind supplied them with the necessary water for the garden.

Every evening and every morning, Eli and Mary filled blue and white speckled granite buckets, lugged them to the long rows of vegetables, and poured water on the plants, cup by cup. The children never complained. They were too glad to have something to eat when the snow and the cold slammed the house like a battering ram.

Old enough to remember the pinched pain of their empty stomachs, they worked with energy, making a game out of arriving at the hydrant together.

When Jerry and Jake arrived, they stopped watering and stood upright like two curious rabbits, watching quietly as the two men dismounted. They didn't stop at the house or look for Hannah and Manny. They just went ahead, climbed the fence, caught Goat by the halter, yanked open his mouth, and set to work.

To the children, it looked like the work of a serious murderer, sawing away inside a horse's mouth. They looked at each other, nodded, and raced for the house, clattered up on the porch, their eyes wide with alarm.

Eli pointed a shaking finger and said, "Why is he doing that?"

"He's killing him dead!" Mary shouted, agitation making her voice shrill and loud, which brought Hannah from her job at the wash tubs, scrubbing Manny's trousers with lye soap.

She glared at the two men, tucked a few stray hairs under her *dichly* and stalked off, stiff legged, pumping her arms.

"What are you doing?" she demanded.

Jake Fisher stopped, but Jerry kept on going, told Jake to keep his hold on Goat's mouth and not to worry about her.

"Release that poor horse this instant!" Hannah screeched.

Jerry kept working with the file, took his time, and didn't give her so much as a sidelong glance.

"Stop it! You'll kill that horse!"

Jerry finished, told Jake to let Goat go, bent to gather his tools, and turned to face the dark fury in Hannah's eyes.

"He'd die sooner if we didn't do that. Now his grass and hay can be chewed properly and he'll digest his food better. He'll fill out now."

"You don't know a thing, Jerry Riehl."

Jerry didn't bother answering, merely lifted one eyebrow and laughed, a sound that only served to increase Hannah's bad temper. "How's the exercising going?"

"How would I know? I don't touch your horses. I didn't give you permission to bring them here, so it's Manny's chore, not mine."

Jerry busied himself opening the gate and threw back over his shoulder, "Too bad. I was thinking of giving the palomino to you, but I guess you're not interested."

Hannah was so taken aback she had absolutely nothing to say. She forgot herself enough to let her eyes widen and her mouth hang open, clearly showing her shock, followed by disbelief. She caught herself just as Jerry led the palomino out, stopped and lowered his face a mere foot away from hers.

"You know you want her, Hannah," he stated in a husky whisper as he lowered an eyelid over one dark eye and gave just a hint of a smile.

What a self-righteous . . . Hannah ground her teeth, curled her hands into fists, stamped her foot and yelled. She yelled and shouted words that she had no idea she could be capable of using to disparage someone.

She told him to get his horses out of there in a week or she was going to turn them loose with the cattle, and if he never found them again, well, that was just too bad, now wasn't it!

Jerry tightened the cinch on the palomino's saddle, his shoulders shaking, his face well hidden, hiding his laughter from her. "Guess if you did that, it would be more of an invitation to cattle thieves than they already have, with that fine-looking herd of Angus cows you have. Or maybe you haven't heard?"

Hannah's big dark eyes came up and met his immediately.

"They made off with twelve of that Owen's cows. I forget his last name—German guy. Heavy. At night. Hauled them out in a big truck and trailer, they think. Better watch your herd, I'd think. Better be careful, Hannah."

CHAPTER 12

THE DROUGHT WORSENED.

The sun beat down mercilessly. Tin roofs creaked and snapped, grasses swayed and shriveled to a melancholy brown color that spoke of the prairie's desperate need for rain. The creek bed whispered itself to nothing, dry, jagged cracks appearing like dark scabs on the parched earth.

The wind blew hot and dry, laden with brown dust particles and the smell of dying vegetation. Cows moiled around the water tank and wandered far to crop the grass that had turned to hay on the stalk. Wild flowers gave up their glad colors of yellow, pink, and blue, hung their heads and became hot and dry and dusty like everything else.

The newly arrived Amish thought surely the end of the world was nigh. They had never experienced anything like it, these blue skies that refused to send even a spattering of raindrops. Sarah smiled and shook her head, saying, oh no, this was a normal North Dakota summer. The rains would come. That's why we have so many acres, the cows travel far to get their fill of grass.

For awhile, Hannah and Manny rode out to sleep on the prairie, keeping watch like shepherds over their herd after Jerry had told them of cattle thieves. When nothing happened, they figured it was over. The Klassermans were the ones known to be wealthy and were therefore an easy target.

Ike Lapp built a horrible little stick house out of thrown away shingles and corrugated metal, the roof flat and wide and rusted to a deep brown. They moved their belongings and their seven skinny children into it, hung green blinds in the windows and called it home.

Ben Miller, of course, designed a long, low ranch house with dormers in the roof and bought logs from some fancy company in the Northwest. He built a barn the size of two or three ordinary barns put together, maybe four.

His windmill was up and running with orders pouring in from folks for miles around. The Midas touch, he had. Just about everything went well for that man. He even invented a homemade sprinkler for the garden, and chuckled and laughed his way through the dust-filled days. He said the women were blessed, now weren't they, all that laundry that dried in a few minutes flat. No mud to worry about either.

Nothing much was heard from the vicinity of the old Perthing place. After Jerry took his three horses back, Hannah figured he must have built a barn, and didn't care about anything other than that.

They all got together to have church services in the summer before the arrival of Grandfather Stoltzfus, Elam, and Ben. Hannah refused to go. Her excuse was that she didn't know if she was ever going to be Amish, and why should she try to figure it out at her age?

Sarah and the children rode home from services at Ben Millers, renewed and refreshed, their faces alive with smiles and conversation, an invitation to dinner at Ike Lapps the following Sunday.

All of this was like a reviving drink of water to Sarah, a long awaited renewal of her faith, her roots. She was surprised to find herself missing Mose so keenly. It was like an ache that settled into her chest and didn't leave all day. She believed it was the atmosphere of knowing friends he had known, the chattering of the women punctuated by the men's voices rising and falling, peppered with guffaws of laughter that made her curious. Sometimes, when he was alive, she had gone to sit quietly with him, listening to the men's talk, which was often more interesting than the endless pursuit of the best apple pie or child-rearing practices.

But she was blessed. She was thankful to have Manny and the little ones. Baby Abby was asleep on her lap and of course, the blistered Hannah, burned with what God had handed her, preferring to pick out the sour grapes, digest them like vinegar, then blame everyone else for her self-chosen path of prickliness. She guessed this is where you loved without condition; loved, kept your mouth shut, and allowed God to do the work of teaching your daughter.

Sometimes, she found herself watching Mary, looking for signs of determination, unkindness, or a strong, selfish will. She remembered Hannah at Mary's age. She'd had trouble in school, slandering the teachers, repeating uncouth rhymes the boys taught her, and yes, it had always been someone else's fault. The teachers were too strict, they picked on her, girls were stupid, jumping all that rope. And on and on.

It wasn't that she went unpunished. More than once, Mose had taken her to school to apologize. Could a person really determine their fate, born with a nature that rebelled from a young age? Like a mule, Hannah was. Set and determined. Though her caring parents disciplined her, spouted Bible verses to her, and tumbled holy prayers around her head like a waterfall, all of it passed her by, untouched, unimpressed.

Lord, have mercy. Sarah's lips trembled with whispered prayer.

Toward the end of summer, Hannah broke out with a fierce, red rash, followed by a sore throat and a high fever. It was when she was cranky, hot and bed-ridden, her eyes closed against the misery of her days, the heat oppressive like a punishment, that she found out about Clay.

Abby Jenkins came to visit, thinner than ever, still coughing, her eyes rheumy, but shrugging it off as if it was nothing. Her skin was stretched across her cheekbones, her wrinkles like crumpled waxed paper that had been smoothed out again.

She took one long look at Hannah and said she had a bumper crop of German measles, that she'd better stay in bed because she didn't want no lasting effects.

They left the door open, so their voices were heard clearly, sentences spoken between sips of spearmint tea. Abby spoke barely two sentences without coughing, which served to irritate Hannah to the point of clawing at the thin sheet covering her itching legs.

"You heard about Clay, did you?" she asked Sarah.

"No, we haven't heard anything."

"He's takin' the car every Saturday night and goin' to dances with that Judy Harris. She's that redhead from Pine. Says he'll likely ask her to marry him come fall."

Hannah stopped breathing in order to hear every word.

"Always hoped him and Hannah would git hitched but then, I guess yer traditions wouldn't allow it, an' I doubt as Clay would hold too much to some of yours. Afraid Hannah might be better off on her own anyhow, leastways as long as she don't like folks much. But now me? I coulda get along bein' her mother-in-law. I'da let her set. Jus' stayed away. Best thing. She'da been awright."

Sarah smiled as she listened to Abby. She saw the open bedroom door and figured Hannah could hear this. Her own feeling about the whole Clay thing had always been to pray that Clay would stay with his own kind, or recognize early on that Hannah was a peck of trouble.

Now, seated with Abby at her kitchen table, Sarah's smile was bright and genuine and her congratulations heartfelt. To her way of thinking, there had never been a Clay and Hannah. The drama was certainly not over. Hannah did what she wanted, so who was to know the outcome? Marriage might be a small thing, or perhaps there would be no marriage at all.

Oh, Hannah, Hannah. Suffering with measles in this heat, her skin as prickly as her nature, she was only beginning to see all that life would offer.

Sarah smiled at Abby, but felt her mouth tremble as she held back tears. "Yes, Abby, I have no doubt you would have done right by Hannah. You're a genuinely good-hearted soul. I owe you so much. You'll be rewarded some day for all your giving. You were more concerned about us than we were about ourselves."

Abby laughed, then coughed and coughed. "Ah." She cleared her throat, wiped her eyes with a corner of her flowered apron.

Hannah lay in bed absorbing every word between Abby and her mother. So he'd gone and done it, then, what he'd threatened out by the windmill a month ago.

Always after her, a lone wolf circling her, trying to bring her down. He was nice enough and attractive enough by far. But just so everlasting wanting to touch her, hold her, be with her, so that the minute she saw him arrive on horseback, her main intention had been to stay away from him, or at least make it clear she wasn't interested.

Well, so that was that. There he went. Good.

Her throat felt as if she'd swallowed a mousetrap, and her breath tasted like it too. Her skin felt hot and clammy, worse than a dose of poison ivy. Likely the whole family would come down with this contagious thing, and since she had it first, guess who'd be the nurse? She turned her head to the wall and tried to block out the sound of Abby's cough, rasping like sandpaper on a rough board. She sniffed, reached for her used and rumpled white handkerchief, grimaced at the stains, and called for Sarah to bring her a clean one.

When Sarah returned to the kitchen, Abby shook her head. "S' partly what's wrong with that girl."

"What?" Sarah lifted innocent eyes to her neighbor.

"She coulda got her own handkerchief."

"But she's sick."

"I don't care. She's grown up. Let her get her own or use her soiled one."

"Well." Sarah didn't know what to say to this.

"That tone of voice comin' from that bedroom door? Makes me feel like takin' holt of them sheets and rollin' her outta bed!" Abby's eyes glittered, her mouth in a firm line. "She needs to be stood up to, Sarah. Yer ways with Mose was okay, but this girl ain't yer husband. She needs to know you ain't puttin' up with none of her mouth."

After Abby took her leave, Sarah foundered, unsure about anything as far as Hannah was concerned. She'd thought it best to love her and leave the rest to God, but now she wasn't so sure. She respected Abby, loved her, and took her advice seriously. Well, one thing for sure, she had a very irate patient to look after, so perhaps true wisdom would be given her.

As it was, the whole family came down with the German measles, except Sarah, who'd had them when she was thirteen.

Hannah was left with red, flaky skin, the rash driving her wild with its cruel itching, like bugs crawling lightly over her skin. Her fever left, her throat healed, and her appetite returned. She cooked oatmeal and ate huge portions, fried bread in the cast iron pan and ate it with raspberry jam. She ate prairie hen gravy on new potatoes, green beans, and applesauce.

Color bloomed in her cheeks, her dresses became tight across her chest, her teeth shone white when she smiled, which was quite frequent, for Hannah.

Goat grew into a sleeker, fatter version of himself. His thin neck filled out and his ribs became rounded with flesh. The long, miserable hair hanging on his stomach disappeared. His strength rebounded and his stamina returned.

Manny couldn't stop talking about it. He said if teeth made so much difference in horses, why did every ranch for miles around not know this? He'd get Jerry to teach him and they'd supplement their income, at least enough to stock up on supplies before winter.

Hannah turned a deaf ear, pretended she hadn't heard. She'd never once acknowledged any difference in Goat. She ignored it all, including Manny's talk.

She strode around the house caring for Eli and Mary, rocked Abby when she cried with the fever and painful red rash.

They received another letter from their grandfather. They would not arrive until next spring. Complications had risen between Emma, Rachel, and Lydia, although he did not go into detail. Sarah fretted and worried and longed to speak with her father. What had happened? Why hadn't he gone into more detail?

Manny came in for the evening meal, his face blazing with fever, his eyes unnaturally bright. He staggered to the couch and flopped onto his back, one hand thrown across his forehead. "I am so sick," he whispered.

Alarmed, Sarah and Hannah rushed over to him. His face was dry and radiating with heat. His lips were cracked and peeling. His nostrils were distended as he breathed shallow breaths.

They bathed him in vinegar water to bring down his fever. He seemed to be fairly comfortable after that and fell into a deep sleep, allowing them time to care for the little ones.

With the heat during the day and interrupted sleep at night, Sarah and Hannah were exhausted, moving around the house half-awake, perspiring and quick to take offense.

Eli's rash appeared quickly, which seemed to alleviate his fever and sore throat. He was cheerful, propped up on pillows, writing and drawing on his small slate with a piece of broken chalk.

Mary lay in a deep sleep, her fever alarmingly high. But after the red rash appeared, she too felt much better.

Manny, however, seemed to languish in the grip of a fever they could not break. When the red rash did not appear after the fifth day, his tossing and moaning increased. Sarah sent Hannah to the Klassermans to use the telephone to summon Doc Brinter from his office in Pine.

Hannah saddled Pete, obedient for once and seriously alarmed. It was unthinkable that something might happen to Manny. God wouldn't allow it. He was not that cruel.

She knew Pete was slower than Goat would be, but there was no reason for her to accept the new version of him, which would prove Jerry right. She rode Pete hard, lashing him with the ends of the reins, her breath coming in shallow jerks, her mouth dry with fear. They'd been so worried about cattle thieves, which proved to be nothing, and now here they were, stricken with this illness in the middle of another champion drought.

Now, though, she thought along the same lines as everyone else. They were homesteaders, facing things head on. Gladiators of the plains. Fearless. Hadn't they already proved themselves? Already they sounded like Hod and Abby, talking to the new families who'd come to live on their claims.

Hot puffs of wind smacked her face as she rode. All around her the brittle grass rustled, a brown gray mass of dried out vegetation that rolled away to meet the hot sky at the horizon. Hannah loved the dry season now that she knew the cattle would always have something to eat, and the windmill would always pump cold well water for them. She could never get enough of watching the calves turn into sturdy little replicas of their mothers, and she couldn't help but count the pounds they were adding into dollar bills.

She rode up to the Klassermans, summoned the doctor, and after a drink of yeasty, sour-smelling homemade root beer, she was on her way home. She allowed Pete his head and his pace as well. The day was warm, so she'd have to take it easy, after the mad dash to the neighboring ranch.

Doc Brinter's car chugged up to the low ranch house only minutes after she'd unsaddled Pete. This was frightening in a way she herself didn't fully understand. How could he have driven all that way in so short a time?

She let herself in through the wash house door. The smell of soap and vinegar was strong in the stifling heat of the low house. She placed her bare feet carefully, her heart in her throat, listening to low voices from Manny's room. She walked to the door, stopped to listen to the doctor's voice, and then her mother's soft, rasping whisper. She could hear Manny's shallow breathing.

"You do understand, German measles are a virus," the doctor inquired. There was no answer from her mother.

Hannah watched Sarah's face, fearful of her mother's features set like stone, as if her submission had been stretched too far, turning into anger that God would allow this, her oldest son, her sweet Emmanuel, to be taken so sick with this horrible, fiery, skin-altering disease.

The doctor stayed for a long time, working to bring down Manny's fever, talking in quiet tones to Sarah, who remained in that odd realm, as if she could not fully comprehend anything that was happening.

Finally the doctor, kindly though he was, spoke to Sarah sharply. "You are his mother, Mrs. Detweiler. You need to pull yourself together and listen to what I'm trying to tell you. You are responsible for him."

He showed her a small white envelope filled with aspirin, white tablets to be crushed on a spoon and given in pudding or applesauce for the fever. A liquid medicine for pain, in a dark glass bottle with a stopper. To be given every three hours, as long as he can swallow.

Sarah's head jerked up and her eyes widened. "What do you mean, as long as he can swallow? You mean the time will come when he won't be able to? You're trying to tell me my son will die?"

Hannah was frightened to hear her mother's voice rising to a hysterical pitch, her face contorted with something Hannah had never seen.

Doctor Brinter was no longer young. He had seen plenty cases of German measles, and he knew all too well the lingering high fever, the red rash so long awaited that never appeared, followed by a slow, painful end.

"We'll have to wait and see. The rash should have appeared by now. If you want, we can transport him to the hospital in Dorchester."

"Can they help him there?" Sarah asked, her words like ice picks. Hannah looked at her sharply.

"They can keep him comfortable. As I told you, this is a virus."

"Answer my question!" Sarah shrilled in a high, unnatural voice that drove fear into Hannah.

Dr. Brinter turned and beckoned Hannah to follow him, then spoke in quiet tones, left a packed of pills for Sarah, who was showing signs of shock and instability. He told her, kindly, his eyes never leaving her face, that there was a real possibility that Manny would not live if the rash did not appear. Hannah swallowed, blinked, and struggled to remain composed.

"Just keep a constant vigil. There is a possibility of seizures if his temperature goes too high. If the measles, the lesions from the virus itself, do not appear within the next few days, he will probably not survive this. By all appearances, your mother is unfit to accept what I must tell her. So you are the one to keep watch."

He reached out to lay a heavy hand on her shoulder, patted a few times. "You appear to be a strong young woman. Bear up for your mother and the little ones."

"What . . . what about the hospital? Wouldn't it be best to take him there?" Hannah asked, laying a hand on his arm.

The doctor hesitated, then shook his head. "I'm sorry, Miss, but no. With the cost, I doubt it would be best. The hospital in Dorchester is famously understaffed, so it would be better to keep him here."

The overwhelming responsibility lit on Hannah's shoulders with a crushing weight, turning her breathing into shallow gasps. How could she sit by Manny's bedside, waiting for a rash to appear? What if seizures overtook him? What about Mam?

She stood at the window, looking out, watching the doctor leave as he carried his black bag and stowed it in the trunk of his car, opened the door, and slid behind the wheel. He started the car and slowly drove away, a cloud of gray dust swirling up behind him.

Oh, God.

Hannah wasn't aware that she had called on a Higher Power as she groaned under the weight of this heavy calamity that had fallen upon them, just when things were going surprisingly well. If something happened to Manny, she wouldn't be able to go on.

Alone, standing in the heat and dust of the drought-stricken day, Hannah clamped her jaws shut like a vice. Manny would live. He had to. She hadn't come out here only to be flogged and beaten back by circumstances she couldn't control. She would get him better. She had no choice.

The heat shimmered in a rippling haze that spread across the land. Manny's fever would never come down unless they could cool him off. She made her way to the door of his bedroom, where he lay moaning and turning his head from side to side, his tanned face flaming with the elevation of his body temperature.

His hands plucked at the thin sheet covering him, then threw it off as if the light touch burned his skin.

"Manny, don't!" Sarah screamed, her voice high and unnatural. A shot of pure anger coursed through Hannah's veins. There was her mother, the one who should be shepherding them through this, slowly losing control, acting like a child.

Hannah drew back a well-muscled arm and delivered a ringing smack to her mother's face, sending her head to one side, almost knocking her off the low chair on which she was seated.

"Stop it, Mam! Get ahold of yourself!" she shouted. Sarah slid off the chair, a crushed, crumpled heap lying inert, staring at Hannah in disbelief before she curled up in a pitiful fetal position and began to sob.

Hannah had often seen her mother cry, but she had never heard anything like the deep primal wail that tore out of Sarah's throat.

She had survived so much. Now, when she could touch and taste joy again, now to be dealt this blow of Manny's sickness and questionable survival. It was her undoing. It left her battered, exposed, and vulnerable, pushing her to the brink of insanity.

Hannah left the room.

Manny's anguished moans melded with her mother's hoarse sobs, and there wasn't much she could do about either one. A bucket of cold water. Some rags. Vinegar for a fever.

First, she went to speak to Eli and Mary, telling them how sick Manny was. Mam was tired but she would soon feel better. She promised them molasses cookies and milk if they would take care of Abigail and stay quiet.

"Is Manny going to die?" Eli asked, his eyes liquid with fear.

"No. He'll get better."

Mary sighed, "Good."

Hannah pressed a cold cloth to Manny's forehead, but he immediately clawed it away, writhing and calling out, mumbling words that made no sense. Hannah put the cloths back in the bucket, then pulled up a chair by his bed. She reached out to stroke the long, dark hair away from his face, alarmed at the absence of perspiration or tears, his lips hot, chapped, and dry.

He needed water.

After repeated attempts, the white pills and all the water except the small amount that dribbled down his chin, remained in Hannah's hand.

"Manny. Please listen. You have to take these pills." Hannah spoke in soft tones, begging him to drink the water, but his teeth remained clenched.

Hannah sighed, reached out to set everything on the night table and watched her mother's form silently heaving in her agony. She thought this weakness of her mother was unnecessary, walked over and touched her shoulder, said, "Stop it now, Mam."

Sarah pushed herself up with both palms, her white covering sliding sideways, her dark hair pulled away from the severe bun on the back of her head, her eyes swollen from the force of her weeping. She sagged against the wall, ashamed, a creature of despair and lost hope.

"Forgive me, Hannah. Did the doctor leave pills here for me?" Hannah nodded and handed them over, watching as her mother swallowed the pills with the glass of water that should have gone to Manny.

CHAPTER 13

Long into the night, Hannah sat alone. Her mother had taken not one pill, but two, and lay now in a deep sleep, a small figure beneath the thin cotton sheet covering her.

From time to time, Hannah ran her hands lightly across Manny's arms and chest, searching desperately for a sign of the red rash that should be appearing, the one single thing that would ease his pain and misery. His skin remained smooth and dry, the heat so frightening toward morning that she could no longer bear to touch him.

The doctor arrived early, dressed in his immaculate black suit, his tie slipped behind his buttoned vest. Already the sun was hot, the house retaining yesterday's heat. He soon produced his white handkerchief and wiped at the beads of perspiration that formed on his upper lip.

Hannah's dark eyes searched the doctor's. Seeing the hopelessness, her spirit shrank within her, as a promise his regained health folded.

Sarah moved softly, like a ghost, into the room, wringing her hands in anguish, her face without color or expression.

Hannah felt the calm and saw it in her eyes, knowing she had reached out and found the all-seeing, benevolent Father who directed her life and kept her in the palm of His Hand. If this was God's will, she would bear up beneath it.

"Mrs. Detweiler, how are you this morning?" the doctor inquired.

Sarah nodded, "I'm all right."

"Good. Good. I understand you lost your husband in the not too distant past. I extend my condolences."

Sarah nodded again and asked, "Is my son still doing all right?"

"Yes."

"Can we possibly get him to a hospital?" Sarah asked.

"We can do that if you wish. But to move him might be an effort. The ambulance from the hospital would have to transport him. You have no telephone, I gather?"

"No."

"Then I will use one, if you will give me directions to the nearest ranch."

"I can accompany you to the Klassermans," Sarah offered.

Hannah gazed steadily on Manny's face, serene now, in a deep sleep. She agreed to let her mother go, knowing the anguished vigil would be too much for Sarah.

After they left, Hannah cared for Abby, changed her diaper, dressed her, combed Mary's hair and made breakfast for the children. She set the kitchen right, swept the floor, washed dishes, and wiped the countertop and table. She gave Eli and Mary instructions on feeding the milk cow and checking the level at the water tank.

When she returned to Manny's room, he lay as before, his face without color. Panic seized her. She bit down on her lower lip to keep from crying out.

Surely not.

But his face was warm.

Warm? Not as hot as before?

Hannah tore off the sheet and bent to peer at his chest, his stomach, and his legs, with the dark hair growing over them. She rushed to the window, grasped the heavy window blind and yanked with too much force, sending it crashing to the floor. A blaze of hot, morning sunlight illuminated the room. Without attempting to replace the fallen window blind, Hannah retraced her steps to the bed and bent over Manny.

Was that a red welt appearing on his shoulder? Yes! It was!

Without thinking of his pain, she grasped his shoulders in her strong hands and pulled him forward like a limp doll. His head fell sideways. She reached behind him to prop him up, bent her head and saw that his back was covered with red pustules, the scaly, disfiguring rash on his skin like a beautiful, long awaited sign.

Manny's eyes flew open. Irritation crossed his face. "Put me down," he said hoarsely.

But Hannah was crying, her eyes squeezed shut as tears ran down her cheeks. Her lips quivered and a glad cry escaped her lips. "Manny!"

It was all she could manage, before she lowered him, turned away and, with heaving shoulders, fixed the window blind.

Manny lay back, opened his eyes, and croaked like a frog as he told Hannah he would die of thirst if she didn't bring him some water. By the time she brought the glass, his chest was already breaking out in angry spots, the awful virus leaving his body through his skin.

"Look at you, Manny," Hannah quavered.

Manny bent his head, felt the lesions on his skin, asked if he'd been very sick.

"Manny, you were so ill. So terribly sick!" Hannah burst out.

"Measles, huh?" Then he lay back, exhausted, and fell into a deep, restful sleep as the rash continued to grow and spread.

When Dr. Brinter and Sarah returned, Hannah met them at the door with a glad cry. She threw herself into her mother's arms and began to weep hysterically.

They rushed to the room and quietly observed, Sarah weeping now, the tears a flow of healing water.

Dr. Brinter bowed his head and thanked the God of healing. He placed a hand on Sarah's back, and she went weeping into his arms. At once she stepped back, ashamed. To be in a man's arms, to lay her head on a strong chest, no matter how briefly, awakened in her a longing she had forgotten existed. Mose. Mose. If only you could be here to share this moment.

Dr. Brinter told them the Lord had chosen to save Manny's life. He would live. He left an ointment for the itchiness and then left instructions for the ambulance driver when he arrived. Then he let himself out the door before Hannah or Sarah could gather their wits to thank him properly or ask how much they owed him.

They were quarantined now. No visitors until the measles were gone. They thoroughly disinfected house, scouring the walls and floors, washing the bedding and curtains in bleach, wiping down the doors, cupboards, and furniture.

The dust blew in and around them, the sun shone on the dry grass, but a happiness soaked every wall and doorway. The dust could settle in on the freshly washed floors, but what did that matter? Manny would live, would regain his health, ride the plains with Hannah, shoot coyotes, and chase antelope.

Thankfulness had always been a way of life for Sarah, but now it was magnified tenfold. She spent her days hugging her children impulsively, squeezing poor Abby until she struggled to free herself. Eli squealed and wriggled out of her grasp but sat there blinking afterward, a small, silly grin playing around his mouth.

She celebrated Manny's health in song, humming and whistling softly under her breath. She cooked great quantities of stew, thick with chunks of canned beef, carrots, and celery from the late garden. She baked potatoes, fried prairie hen rolled in egg and flour and seasoned with fresh herbs.

Manny gained weight, his cheeks filled out again, his skin healed and tanned under the hot summer sun.

Hannah bloomed, her cheeks reddened, her teeth shone white as her lips parted in smiles about everything, and sometimes, about nothing. To be truly delivered from the awful death of a loved one left a lasting impression on her.

Then one Sunday, without warning, uninvited and unannounced, Ike and Barbara Lapp and their seven children came to visit, driving two surprisingly nice horses hitched to a spring wagon painted black.

Sarah met them on the porch. Manny hurried out to help Ike put away the horses.

"Why, what a surprise!" Sarah exclaimed, throwing up her hands. "Come right in, Barbara."

Hannah sniffed, went to her room, and closed the door firmly. If Mam needed her, she could come get her. No need to visit with Ike Lapp. They had the nerve, uninvited, at that.

The children circled each other shyly, Eli and Mary uncertain how to start a friendship, so they sat with the grownups while Sarah busied herself in the kitchen making coffee.

Manny kept a conversation going with Ike. He rather liked the man. Not too much ambition, but he had a great love of life and a dry sense of humor that sent Manny into peals of mirth.

They had brought along Barbara's sister's daughter, Marybelle. She was a quiet, skinny girl with large feet, hair the color of ripe wheat, slanted eyes so blue they were shocking, and a splattering of freckles like dark sand over her tiny nose.

"She just arrived last week with the Henry Esches."

Sarah called from the kitchen, "Who?"

"Didn't you know? You know, Amos Escha Henrys, from the Gap."

Sarah brought a tray bearing four cups of steaming coffee and placed it on the low table by the couch. She thought, a hand going to her mouth, "Amos Escha? You mean Amos, the one who has the threshing rig?"

"Yep, that's the one. He moved his family out here last week. He's going to try his hand at raising wheat. There's a new seed wheat, an early variety, and he thinks if he gets it in in the fall, he'll be able to grow a good crop before the drought hits. He's sitting on close to a thousand acres right now. In a tent."

Ike Lapp lifted his coffee cup, sipped, grimaced. "His wife is so fat, I don't know how she'll take to prairie life. She takes a lot of feed."

Manny sputtered, choking on his coffee.

Ike laughed heartily, a sound without guile, just pure, light-hearted merriment, the joy of a humorous situation shared with others.

Barbara, pinched and thin, chortled with him. "Marybelle, why don't you take the children to see the windmill? Your Uncle Ike helped erect it, one of the first ones out here."

She looked at Ike, who rewarded her with his smile. "Where is the windmill?" she asked, her voice low.

Manny jumped to his feet. "I'll take you. Come on, Eli. Bring your friends. Sorry, I don't know your children's names."

"Oh, they'll let you know soon enough," Barbara said, waving a hand in dismissal.

They all filed out the door into the heat of the afternoon. Barbara began to talk the minute they were gone. "Yes, well, about the girl. You notice her name is not plain, not truly Amish. Well, her mother, my sister Anna, ran off with the local grocer, and she is the product of that marriage. Anna was only sixteen. Left the Amish, left all her teachings, ended up in Georgia or some such state down South. Just a year or so ago, we got this letter from a mental institution asking us to come and get Marybelle. A horrible place." She said the word "horrible" with a slight shudder.

"Guess Anna took up with a snake hunter who lived in a swamp and raised rats and mice to feed the snakes he captured. It got the best of her and they took her away. I don't know if she'll ever be right again."

Listening to Barbara, Sarah's face went slack as she thought how she'd been to the brink herself, and so recently. A great welling of sympathy for Anna washed over her. Poor girl, making such wrong choices. Who's fault? Sarah felt a deep sadness for the woman, incarcerated now in a place where no human being should ever have to live.

"Anyway, this Marybelle stayed with the snake hunter and lived in his house with him. She kept it clean enough and kept some food on the table. It's hot there. You think it's hot here. This was like liquid heat. Like swimming in humidity. He's a drinker; passed out drunk most of the time. So we took her. She didn't want to go. I believe she had a nice enough life. He was good to her, when he was sober. She seems sensible, no ill effects from her life in the swamp.

"She told me she wasn't afraid of the snakes. They milked them for the venom and sold it, I guess. Alligators and mosquitoes, bugs—the whole place simply buzzed with hundreds of insects. Thousands.

"We're trying to teach her about God, but she doesn't really seem to understand." Barbara stopped for breath.

"How old is she?" Sarah asked.

"Older than she looks. Guess how old."

"Fourteen?"

"Almost fifteen. But immature. Needs discipline. Wants her mother and misses being near the water."

"I bet."

Hannah lay on her stomach, her room like an oven with the door closed and no breeze. The buzz of voices rose and fell. She dozed and woke up sweating, seized by an irritation. You watch, she thought. Mam will invite them to supper. She'll waste all our food on those starving little brats.

Sure enough, she heard the clatter of pots and pans, the sound of water running, footsteps. A knock on her door. She had a notion to crawl out the window. Here, this situation, was precisely why she resisted the Amish migration to North Dakota.

Instead of roaming the prairie on Pete and being left alone on a hot Sunday, she was expected to keep up appearances, help make supper, talk, smile, and go to church, when she'd rather go lose herself on the plains, completely unknown, forgotten by anyone who came from Lancaster County.

Stupid old Ike Lapp with his oversized, hooked nose and yellowed teeth. He looked like a horse!

Her happiness about Manny's regained health was overshadowed by her own dark nature, leaving her annoyed, in no mood to shake hands or make small talk. Meddling old man! Hoping to creep out of her room and sidle down the hallway to the bathroom, Hannah opened her door and slid through noiselessly.

"Hannah!" She sagged against the wall, clapped a hand to her forehead, and rolled her eyes.

"Hannah! Get over here! Didn't know you were home," Ike called. Hannah arranged her features into some semblance of normalcy, her lips in a tight smile that only served to provide an aura of frost around her. If she were a horse, she could buck and kick, break through the door and take off running, but as it was, she was stuck. Strangled by company.

"Well now, Hannah," Ike Lapp chortled, saying her name as if she was the title of a story he was about to write. "Still the same. You don't want anyone around, but they all want you!" He slapped his knee at his own hilarious observation, sending Hannah to the kitchen in a huff, where she greeted Barbara in a voice strung with icicles, resulting in a firm jab in her ribs from her mother's elbow and followed by a dark look of warning.

She mashed potatoes in the torrid kitchen, the steam rising up over her face, listening half-heartedly to Barbara's high-pitched voice, which irritated her worse than a whining mosquito.

Sarah told her to open the table and add at least eight leaves, as there would be fifteen of them. She stood at one end of the table and yanked. Nothing happened. She knew someone would have to pull it apart from the other end, but there was no way she'd ask Ike for help. Of course, watching her like a hawk, he rose to the occasion, helped her pull the table apart, added leaves, chatting all the while like a woman.

"You heard about the new barn? Down on the old Perthing place?"

Hannah shook her head.

"Quite a barn. That Jerry has some excellent horses. Never saw better."

Hannah didn't answer so he continued to ramble on about nothing. She didn't care how many horses Jerry had, or if his barn was covered in gold. She only half listened, wishing he'd go sit down and be quiet.

With a clattering on the porch, Manny and the children came in, windswept and red-faced, the constantly blowing dust powdering their hair and shoulders. Hannah caught sight of Marybelle. Now what? She wasn't one of the Lapp bunch, sure as shooting. Boy, was she a looker. That hair like a palomino.

Hannah blinked. Blinked again. Tucked a strand of hair behind her ear. She couldn't stop looking at her. What was it about that girl? She looked to be about fourteen, but carried herself with a practiced grace, her shoulders back, her head held high. Her eyes were astonishing—slanted, huge, and blue.

No one acted as if there was anything going on that was out of the ordinary. She was too proud to ask, so she remained in a fog of curiosity that only became thicker as the meal went on.

Ike Lapp ate with his usual bad table manners, but Barbara was surprising, holding her fork in a proper manner, speaking quietly to the children, spreading elderberry jelly on their bread and cutting it in half for the little ones, who ate quietly, without speaking.

She watched Marybelle, sitting across from her, cutting the chunks of beef, spearing her carrots. What was it about her eyes. Like a knowing, a telling of something. Was it sadness? Experience? Hannah decided that her eyes were older than her face. And those freckles!

Ike Lapp was rambling on about the need to add onto his house and insulate it a bit. "I could cover the whole thing with mud and call it an adobe house. Isn't that what they do farther south?"

Marybelle looked up from her plate at the same time Hannah did. Their eyes met but neither one acknowledged the other.

After the Lapp family left, Sarah threw herself on the couch, thrust her feet in front of her, and sighed, her eyes half closed. "Wonderful! Just *wunderbar*." She grabbed Abigail and nuzzled her little face, then turned her toward her chest and kissed her all over.

"What a blessing! What an opportunity for good old fellowship. Making Sunday supper for company. Just the way I was raised. And now we can keep up this old tradition of visiting, just showing up at someone's door and being welcomed in. What about that Marybelle?"

Hannah jerked to attention. "Is that her name? Fancy," she said sourly.

Sarah related Marybelle's life story. She was surprised to be met with a snort, a shrug of disinterested shoulders, as Hannah evidently found her story uninteresting. She brought her little story to a close, closed her eyes to relax, and let it go. Typical Hannah. Pessimistic. Always looking on the dark underside of everything.

Suddenly Hannah said, "Well, if she's not lying and *was* raised in a swamp, she should be dried out by now."

No one laughed. They all fastened cold eyes on her face until she felt a prick of humiliation, one eyelid twitching uncomfortably. She got up and walked out of the door into the evening shadows.

Out to the water tank where the grass was trampled until it disappeared, the roots dried out and mashed into the dust by the wide, cloven hooves of the cows that milled around their only source of water in the blazing sun.

They were all there, every one, fat and black and sleek, chewing their cud contentedly, others cropping the short, brown grass. The calves were growing into well-built heifers or steers at an alarming rate. Hannah couldn't believe how well the tough prairie grass fed these cattle, all the feed they needed without a cent paid out.

Haymaking had gone well, but they'd need to resume, starting tomorrow morning. She could never let her guard down, never relax about the amount of hay they'd need.

The calves were growing, but not all of them would be sold. Only enough to make a nice payment on the loan.

She watched them cropping grass, well-built, firm in the front shoulders, wide chests, straight spines and muscular legs. They'd sell well at auction. Compared to the Jenkinses' slat sided, pot-bellied creatures, these heifers would bring a good price.

She loved to smell the dry, trampled earth, the wet smell of mud where the clear cold water ran out over the sides of the tank and mixed with the dust. She could stand for hours, listening to the whine and clanking of the great wheel as it turned, the huge metal paddles taking full advantage of the slightest breeze. The long steel rod that pumped up and down glistened in the late evening twilight, the life of the wind and the water pump.

Manny often climbed to the top, hung by one arm crooked over a metal rung, his eyes shaded with his hand, dark hair blowing in the wind, his trouser legs flapping like a struggling bird. That he had been restored to health still seemed like a miracle. So easily he could have slipped away from them, leaving her to work the homestead by herself.

Well, Mam too, but she couldn't ride and shoot and rope and make hay. She'd have to get a dog. After they sold the cattle, she'd buy a decent dog, teach him to watch the herd; maybe two dogs. Then, if one of them couldn't be there, the dogs could take over. Plus, they'd be good in winter at keeping the wolves away.

A deep satisfaction spread through her, a sense of well-being, like the wearing of a new garment.

Proud. She was proud of her accomplishments. If she hadn't worked in town at Rocher's Hardware, they would have starved or have gone crawling to the Jenkinses, the same thing they always did. Yes, they'd had help after the fire, but so had plenty of other folks. If anyone else had a fire, they would help in return. It was the way they did it.

Hannah knew that pride was squelched down among their people, stepped on, destroyed by acts of humility, half-disguised tut-tuts of, Oh, it isn't so. Go on. A wave of dismissal, turning a scarlet cheek.

But still, it was pride. Perhaps people like Ike Lapp had none. He had no reason to have any, never amounting to a hill of beans. Happy as a pig in mud, though.

Take Ben Miller. In the middle of the Great Depression, when times were unbelievably hard for most ordinary folks, here he comes, raking in opportunities by the handful. 'Cause he was smart, that's what it was. He saw things, took life by the horns, and ran with it.

She had one big obstacle coming up, and soon. They had to do something about better horses. That teeth filing, or floating, as Jerry called it—why did she always imagine large yellow molars floating out of a horse's mouth? It did make Goat appear to be a better horse, but he was still the same lazy, winded old bag with the jounciest gallop God ever gave a horse.

Pete was also on his last legs. The long journey from the East, coupled with her father's insane plowing of the prairie grass. It still made her sick to think about Pete standing with his neck outstretched, sweat running from his belly, his withers.

They had no money until they sold the calves, and then, all of what they made at auction should go to pay back her grandfather's loan.

Pete and Goat would never manage the round up or the long drive into Pine, perhaps Dorchester, or father. The summer's drought would produce fewer cattle than usual, which meant the small town of Pine might not have an auction this year.

They could have them trucked, but Hannah didn't want that. Ever since she had set foot on this prairie, she'd wanted to join in a real cattle drive, and she was going to do it.

A thrill shot through her. All she needed was a good horse for herself and one for Manny. So if that meant being nice to Jerry Riehl and Jake Fisher, then she'd do it. Yessir. She would.

CHAPTER 14

WHEN THE HOT WINDS FADED TO A LUKEWARM JOSTLING OF GRASSES, and the house cooled off at night, Hannah knew the worst of the summer was behind them.

They redoubled their haymaking efforts, teaching Mary to drive the horses hitched double to the creaking old wagon, so that both she and Manny could fork hay, one on either side, expertly trampling it so that they could stack it high before returning to the barn.

Manny would mow one day, they'd load it the next. There was an urgency to their work now, knowing how soon the mellow winds could turn sharp as a knife blade.

They loved their work. Alone on the high plains with nothing but the sky and the land, flocks of wheeling birds bursting from the waving grasses like hurled stones, exploding into the sky until they formed a perfectly synchronized turn and settling again in a whirr of sturdy little wings.

The hay smelled sweet, dusty, and earthy. The sun was sizzling on their faces. Dust settled in the cracks of their arms, between their fingers and toes, and behind their ears where the sweat trickled down. The wagon groaned and creaked; the horses' harnesses squeaked and flapped against their backsides. The wind blew and blew, raking across their faces, flapping dress skirts and handkerchiefs tied in a double triangle around their heads.

Rabbits were unafraid, hopping in front of the horses like lead dogs, escorting them along the flat rows of mown hay. Prairie dogs eyed them with undisguised curiosity before popping into their holes, allowing the wagon to rumble across, only to reappear moments after, sitting upright, their eyes like marbles bulging from their heads.

Occasionally, a small herd of rust-colored, white and black antelope appeared on the horizon, the sight of the haymakers spurring them into a headlong flight, seeming to float above the prairie on wings. So smooth was their running they could have been on wheels. Shy deer emerged from hollows, bounding away on stick legs.

Hannah felt good about the hay storage. There would be no anxiety this winter, no appetite-seizing panic that left her wild-eyed with fear. No Lemuel Short, either.

Hannah burst out laughing, thinking of poor misguided Lemuel. He had been quite an actor, though. Very good at his craft.

"What's so funny?" Manny grinned.

"Oh, nothing. Thinking of last winter. Poor Mr. Short."

"We were fooled. Thoroughly taken across."

"We sure were!" Hannah shook her head.

"We learn." Manny laughed, a happy sound Hannah often heard these days. He was alive, ripe with youth and good health, his arms muscled from the constant hard work, his long dark hair swinging almost to his shoulders. He never wore a hat. Devout in his faith, Amish to the core, there were no homemade straw hats available. Sarah never bothered ordering one from Lancaster County, so, his old one in shreds, he went without.

It became a family joke, Manny without a hat. In winter, he wore the serviceable black felt hat with the wide brim, but never took to wearing one in the summer.

Forking hay furiously to get the load done, by dinnertime they were ravenous. Sitting atop a load of hay, the sun directly overhead, her stomach hollow, saliva collecting in her mouth as she thought of fried bread and *schmear kase*, Hannah chewed on a strand of hay and, without telling Manny, plotted her trip to the old Perthing place.

He'd try and persuade her to stay.

On the day she was prepared to go, a car, a red convertible with the white top down and a white stripe of along the side, came chugging up the road.

Hannah stood to the side of the living room window so as not to be seen and watched the slow approach, trailed by a cloud of the usual brown dust. It was Harry Rocher, and his wife, Doris, her hair piled on top of her head and covered by a white, gauzy headscarf. She was dressed in a pale yellow dress.

She remained in the car, watching with her normal pinched expression as Harry approached the house. Sarah was in the garden, hoeing up the dry soil around the gnarly celery. She laid down the hoe, dusted her hands, wiping them on her patched gray apron as she walked toward Harry Rocher.

"Hello."

Harry Rocher stopped just as he was about to step onto the porch when he spied Sarah and smiled. "Mrs. Detweiler."

"Yes, Mr. Rocher. It's good to see you again. If Doris would like, we can have a cold glass of tea together."

"No, no. I doubt if she would. I came to ask if Hannah would be willing to lend assistance at the store. My wife, Doris, is unwell. She went back East for a time but has returned. Why, I can only guess. Perhaps to make my life miserable. This time, I'd be willing to pay Hannah a small wage, beings as you're fairly well established here."

"Let's go in and ask Hannah, shall we?" Sarah asked. The poor man. Thin as a rail, like a stick man, with that stricken look about him, like a whipped puppy.

Hannah met them at the door. It was all arranged. She would work two whole days, spend the night, for five dollars. She was expected to resume her duties as before, cleaning, organizing at the store, and do some cooking. Mr. Rocher would transport her, if it was allowed.

The cogs on Hannah's brain wheel caught and set her thoughts in motion. Perfect. This would be her biggest need, the most pressing reason for a horse. Her ride to work. Jerry didn't need to know her boss had a perfectly good car. She needed a horse to ride to Pine.

"No, there's no need for you to drive your car. I always enjoy riding my horse to town. Thank you." Harry agreed, grateful for her promise to help out.

Hannah spun in a circle on her tiptoes, arms outspread. "Just perfect, Mam. Five dollars a week till the snow flies will stock our pantry with everything we need—flour, cornmeal, oatmeal, coffee, tea—all of that stuff. We can make our own way this winter. Nobody has to look out for us, not the Klassermans or the Jenkinses, and none of the greenhorn Amish either."

She gave one last exaggerated twirl on one foot. "We are westerners. Real ranchers, planning our cattle drive. Home-steaders who made it pretty good, without our father."

Manny smiled and Sarah laughed outright. She wanted to hug her again, with abandon, the way she'd thrown herself in her mother's arms after Manny's measles rash appeared. Since then, a certain self-consciousness had come between them, as if they were much more aware of each other. That move had been so uncharacteristic of Hannah, exposing a new vulnerability she had never been aware of. And now Sarah knew that beneath Hannah's veneer of disloyalty and unkindness was a profound love of family that she had never displayed with such abandon.

This created a shyness in Hannah, a wariness of her mother's trying to force that vulnerability again and corner her into a sort of submission, into changing and being a better, more unselfish person, when she planned on clapping that veneer firmly back in place, and keep it there.

"Yes, Hannah, we are survivors, aren't we?" Sarah said.

Hannah spread her fingers. "Remember when Eli got lost that time? Dat's death, winter storms, fire, diseases, starving hungry, cold, drought, heat."

"Lemuel Short!" Mary shouted.

Eli giggled and blinked his eyes owlishly. He remembered Mr. Short and had loved every story he told while sitting on his knee.

"He was a good man underneath all of his troubles," Sarah said.

"He was not. He was an actor," Hannah said, forcefully.

"Whatever. I still do feel sorry for him in prison. If we could, we'd go visit him and take him some food."

Then there was nothing left to do but dress in her most brilliantly colored dress, comb her hair becomingly, brush Pete and saddle him, tell Mam and Manny she was going to visit Ben Miller's, and then ride off in that direction.

Summer's end was all around her. The grass looked as it always did after a drought, but the assortment of weeds by the dusty road were bent double, heavy with seed pods and dust. The butterflies had left, except for the dizzy white moths that fluttered over everything. The crickets and katydids set up a racket, undeterred by the long, dry summer.

Hannah wasn't sure exactly where the Perthing place was, so she kept a steady eye on the horizon. The prairie could be tricky when you were searching for something, like the roof of a building or a creek bank or a lone tree. Everything appeared level, but there were deceiving swells, the land rising slightly, and then falling away to a large hollow, like a shallow bowl. The road was straight, disappearing to a point in the distance.

Hmm. Not much as far as she could see.

Pete was acting strangely. His head was lower than usual, and he kept stumbling, as if his feet were too heavy to clear the ground. She tugged on the reins, chirped, making the sound most horses understood as a sign to quicken their pace. His sweat-soaked ears flicked back, then forward, but he did nothing to increase his speed.

She wondered idly whether he had had a drink of water before she left home. He certainly was not in top form but, oh well, he had a lot of miles on him and the day was as hot as the middle of summer. Would this heat never end?

She noticed the swaying, then. The unnatural rhythm, as if Pete couldn't carry his back legs properly. She had just cleared the saddle, her feet hitting the ground, when Pete went down in the back, his legs folding up like a massive accordion.

His front legs stayed stiff, his neck outstretched, the whites of his eyes showing his alarm, as if he did not understand what was happening. Then his front legs buckled, and he went down on his knees, grunting with an expulsion of air. He rolled sideways, his legs bent and the saddle half buried beneath him.

Hannah stood helplessly by. This was a fine pickle. Out in the middle of nowhere with a horse down. Great!

She tugged on one rein and called, "Pete! Come on here! Get up! Pete!" But he never really made an effort. He just lay there as if he planned on taking a long nap.

Why was a horse so large when they were laying there helplessly? He was like a mountain of flesh, and as immovable as one.

The sun beat down on both of them, as if purposely making things worse. Hannah's mouth was dry and perspiration beaded her brow. All around her, the wind kept up its steady, even rustling of the grass, tossing it, and tearing at her perfectly combed hair, flapping the triangle of her *dichly*.

Hannah tried to get Pete back on his feet, lifting, sliding her hands beneath the impossibly large mound of his body. Her face reddened with exertion, her temper steadily becoming shorter, like a length of rope being eaten by fire.

She straightened and took a long breath, folded her hands into fists, and stamped her foot. Now what? Keep walking?

Keep looking for this old place even if she couldn't see a roof or the tip of a windmill for miles in every direction?

She could leave Pete, turn around, and go back home. But who would ever get this horse back on his feet? If she walked the long dusty road home, it would be a few hours, at least, before she could return with Manny and Goat and the spring wagon. Even then, what could they do?

Hannah plunked herself down. She studied the rise and fall of Pete's heaving sides and thought he didn't appear to be in pain or particularly stressed. He had never done anything like this before.

She was thirsty. She wondered if this was how people who were lost in the desert felt. She couldn't sit in the heat and the wind and dry out; she'd have to walk in one direction or the other.

On her feet again, took stock of the situation. Pete lay in the middle of the narrow dirt road. If an automobile or a truck came barreling along, it would plow right into him. She renewed her efforts imploring Pete to stand, tugging on the reins, calling his name, but he only opened his eyes wider and grunted that strange whooshing sound.

Hannah was just about to start walking back toward home when she heard, or rather, felt, the dull clop of hoof beats. Some-one was riding toward her. Help was on the way. Billowing dust clouds preceded a galloping dark horse, his legs pounding the parched earth. The hatless rider, judging by the width of him, looked much like Ben Miller.

Self-conscious now, Hannah raked at her disheveled hair and the wildly flapping *dichly*, which had slid back on her head, tugged by the mischievous wind.

The gladness in her eyes darkened, replaced by a dull sheen of pride.

Jerry Riehl.

Oh, of course, she thought bitterly. Damsel in distress, plunked right down in his path. The chivalrous rescuer—big, bold, and brave!

The magnificent horse slid to a stop with an easy touch on the reins. Hannah could tell it was easy, not the usual western way of the Jenkinses, sawing and pulling on the reins attached to the bit in the iron-mouthed mustangs they rode, half-broke and cranky.

"Whoa! What have we here?" Jerry sat astride his horse with the easy grace of being one with the animal, smiling down at her with his white, even teeth in his dark face.

Why did she think of the scent of toothpaste and aftershave? She glared up at him, figuring that if she could convey all that ill-will, he'd have no idea she remembered ever kissing that grinning mouth, and, even more important, that she was certainly *not* glad to see him.

She just had this bit of a problem with a downed horse.

"You don't have anything here. I do," she stated, flat and hard as a sheet of granite.

His chuckle increased her irritation. Sit there and laugh, she thought bitterly.

"Yeah, you definitely do."

There was no way to answer that so she didn't.

Jerry leaned forward and crossed his arms on the horn of the saddle as his horse snorted, side-stepped, and pranced as if there were springs in his hooves.

She wished he'd fall off. Flat on his righteous backside.

He dismounted, all fluid grace and expertise, swinging the reins to the ground and leaving his horse standing there, still as still, as if he was made of stone. Trained like that, Hannah knew.

Jerry ignored her as he ran his hands across Pete's back, felt his ears and checked his legs, which were now stretched out full length.

"How'd he go down?" he asked, straightening up and running one hand through his dark hair.

"He just went down."

"No, I mean, did he collapse suddenly, or did he act strange? Did his gait change? Did he maybe go down in the back?"

"His walk wasn't right. He swayed. And then his back legs kind of lowered."

"And then they went down?"

Hannah nodded.

Jerry walked around Pete and considered the problem. The wind blew, lashing the grass to a rustling frenzy. It grabbed Hannah's kerchief off her head and sent it spinning away, across the now almost horizontal grass.

Jerry lifted his head and searched the horizon at the same time they heard a pronounced rumble, deep in a bank of roiling clouds to the north.

"Does a storm crop up at midday out here?" Jerry asked.

Hannah shrugged.

"At any rate, there's one on the way," he concluded.

"It won't hit us, coming from the north."

"How do you know?"

"I've lived here a lot longer than you have. I should know."

"You mean to say, in the few years you've been here, it hasn't happened? Doesn't say it couldn't now." His eyes watched the clouds.

In spite of the hot sunlight, there was a decided change in the atmosphere. A prickly kind of feeling, as if each blade of grass now crackled instead of rustling. A boom in the distance rattled the ground beneath their feet.

Jerry said sternly that they'd have to try and get Pete to stand up, then perhaps get him to the ranch, if he could walk. He guessed Pete had kidney problems, going down at the back like he had.

"Are you feeding him corn?" he asked.

Hannah snorted. "Yeah, we raise a lot of corn out here where it never rains."

A quick flicker of irritation rose in his dark eyes. He turned. "Come on, put your hands beneath his withers. When I pull on his head, push. Heave toward the front."

"What does that have to do with it?"

Another boom of thunder sounded in the distance. A split second of jagged white lightning appeared in the steadily darkening north. Jerry stood far too close to her, lowered his face, his dark eyes boring into hers and ground out, "Do as I say for once."

She refused. What were two hands going to amount to? Nothing. That mound of horseflesh could not be moved by any mere human, she was sure. He thought he could come out here from soft little Lancaster County and tell her what was what, the weather and everything. Well, he couldn't.

Jerry urged Pete, lifting his head by his neck and drawing him up and forward, straining, calling his name in a level voice. Hannah stood and watched him, her arms crossed, her skirt blowing wildly in the wind. She hadn't tried to retrieve that *dichly*, he noticed.

Another boom of thunder. The wind increased. Jerry shouted something Hannah didn't understand. Suddenly he loosened his grip on Pete's neck, stalked over to his horse and lifted the reins. He looked at Hannah, his eyes snapping, his dark hair blowing up off his forehead, accentuating the stark wings of his black eyebrows.

"I'm leaving. I don't trust that storm," he shouted against the ever-increasing wind.

"It won't hit us. It'll go to the east. Round by Pine." Her words deterred him, but only momentarily.

"You better leave the horse. Come on, I'll take you home."

Hannah shook her head, crossed her arms tighter, her shoulders hunched forward.

Jerry mounted his horse. "Come on!"

"I'm not going with you."

"You can't stay here."

"I sure can."

Jerry's eyes scanned the north. The prairie appeared yellow, drenched in a strange glow against the backdrop of storm clouds as black as night. As they watched, the sun's heat became weak, losing its power, like the wick on a kerosene lamp when it's turned down.

Another rolling, menacing boom rattled the ground beneath their feet. The air around them crackled.

Hannah watched the light fade and felt a prickle of doubt. She weighed her options: stay here, in the middle of nowhere, unprotected, a sitting duck for the wind and the probable hail, or get up on that saddle with Jerry.

The choice was easy. She'd stay right here. Storms always— usually—followed a pattern. The wind was roaring in her ears. She turned to watch the storm and braced herself against it. She had never seen cloud formations quite like these. The dark-as-night wall, which was the storm, she figured, preceded by a writhing gray mass of either rain or wind, she couldn't be sure which. Hod had warned them of cyclones, the twisting, turning whirlpools of monstrous wind and destruction.

Hannah screamed as she felt a grip around her waist; she screamed again when she felt herself being lifted and hauled like a sack of feed across Jerry's lap. She yelled and kicked, but his arm was like a vice and held her fast, pressing the breath out of her until she was fortunate to be able to take small, desperate intakes of air.

She could only grasp at air, her hands flying down the side of the now galloping horse. She was completely at Jerry's mercy. The ground was so close she could have touched the tall weeds on the side of the road, whizzing by in waves of dark grass, streaks of brown dust, and parched, cracked earth.

Hanging by her waist like that, blood rushed to her face, and her head began to pound. The horse increased his speed into a headlong, mad gallop, his hooves flailing and pounding, the neck by her left side moving in rhythmic lunges. She felt as if her life was in danger.

Her anger dissipated, replaced by a sick fear she had never known. He didn't care about her. The truth was worse than the hard, cutting slice of pain that tore into the side of her face, her outstretched arms, and her bare feet. The pain was indescribable, like thousands of knife points stabbing her skin. She cried out in a choked, pleading voice, but all that emerged from her throat was a guttural sound like a choking animal.

Determined to endure this and stay alive, she hung on, resigned to whatever happened next.

What did happen was that hail assaulted every exposed inch of her body, and the vice-like grip around her waist tightened. She could not breathe. She tasted blood in her mouth and realized the hail was cutting through her skin.

Booms like falling timbers. Weird flashes of blue light. She couldn't breathe. She couldn't breathe. Then, the hail ceased and gave way to a cold, drenching deluge that soaked them. It was like being under a waterfall.

She struggled to stay conscious. The world turned into movement, a pinwheel of sound and color, of wet and cold and pain, always choked by the grasp around her middle.

The horse's hooves no longer pounded; they splashed, plopping through rivers of water and flying brown grass that blew loose from the weakened dry roots and hurled itself against them by the storm's force.

She heard a shout, struggled to stay conscious. Waves of pain and cold set her teeth to chattering, jouncing around as if they were no longer a part of her.

Another shout. Then they crashed headlong into the smell of dirt and hay and manure and blessed stillness.

She felt his hands around her waist, pulling her off the horse and lifting her to the ground, helping her to stand against the rough lumber of a stall, where she slid down, the barn floor solid and unyielding beneath her.

She was as soaked as if they'd dragged her through the watering trough. She pulled at her skirt, too weak to make much difference.

Rain pummeled the metal roof like bullets. Lightning flashed, followed by rolling crashes of thunder that spoke of the bottled-up fury contained in the summer clouds that had refused to give their rain.

Hannah had read of sailors who were weeks at sea, kissing the earth beneath their feet after arriving safely on shore. She now knew exactly how they felt. Never had she blessed a metal roof like she did this one.

CHAPTER 15

Conversation was useless, as the storm hung over the old Perthing place and pounded the metal roof with a wind-lashed deluge that sounded as if buckets of water were being thrown against the metal.

There wasn't much light. Only a grayish dark world and the smell of leather, horse sweat, manure, and dry hay. The black horse's nostrils quivered as they moved in rhythm to the heaving of his flanks, sweat dripping on the floor of the barn.

Hannah's chest rose and fell as she breathed, each intake of breath a sucking of air driven by desperation. She shivered, wrapped her arms around her waist, puddles of dirty water mixed with hay and straw pooling beneath and around her.

She was aware of Jake Fisher and Jerry dragging off the soaked saddle then rubbing down the magnificent horse. There was no other word to describe him, this massive black animal made of powerful muscle and tendon. Hannah marveled at his incredible ability to almost outrun a fast-moving storm, keeping his hooves pounding through mud and water at a pace that never slowed, staying on his feet in the slimy muck made of dust and dry, parched earth pasted to the falling rain.

"She all right?" Hannah heard the words, not meant for her ears.

There was no answer, only the sound of the lashing rain and wind.

The care of the horse went on for too long, in Hannah's opinion. Evidently the horse's comfort was far more important than her own well-being, as they busied themselves without so much as a glance in her direction, which, she finally decided, she wouldn't have seen anyway because of the dark interior of the barn.

She was cold. Her middle hurt, right across the top of her stomach, where she'd been flung over the horse like a dead calf. Exactly the way Clay slung a dead calf across his saddle.

Hannah was unaccustomed to humiliation. Now she couldn't bear to think of herself sprawled across Jerry's saddle. She couldn't think of it. Let him mention it once and he'd be sorry.

She was wet. Wet? She was soaked! She was as wet as if she'd stayed right there with Pete. Likely the poor old horse had died, alone on the prairie in a pounding storm that hurled hailstones on his faithful, fallen body. She had meant to stay, meant to stay right there with him.

When the rectangular shapes of the barn windows appeared to be turning from dark gray to a lighter color, the rasping, hissing sound of driven rain turned to a softer, whispering sound. Jerry walked over and stood above her. He said nothing, just stared down at her.

Then, "Cold?" he asked.

She didn't raise her head. All she could think of was being slung across that saddle and the headlong dash through the hail and wind and rain.

"Your face is bleeding."

She didn't lift her face or bother answering. Just sat there like a log.

"Can you hear me, Hannah?" Not a trace of tenderness. Nothing.

"I can hear you," she said, low and harsh.

He loved her voice. It was so low, almost like a man's, and husky. Well, she was angry now, so he'd better be careful.

"You can come inside with Jake and me."

"For what?"

"To take care of the bleeding and get you into some dry clothes."

"You should have left me alone. I'm as wet now as if I'd have stayed with Pete."

"You think?"

When there was no answer and the silence dragged out, Jake walked over and said he was making a run for the house.

Jerry nodded, "Go ahead."

When Hannah refused to look at him or answer his questions, he plunked down beside her, raised one knee and laid an arm across it. With the other hand he touched the dirty, sodden fabric of her dress. She slid away from him, leaving a wet trail through the dirt.

"What if a cyclone would have touched down? You'd have had no protection whatsoever. None. I couldn't leave you out there."

"Pete's probably dead."

"He's an old horse. He has kidney problems."

"You don't know how old he is. Or if he has kidney problems."

Touchy. Testy. He could never say the right thing. "Come on, Hannah. Let's go inside."

"No."

Jerry sighed. "Don't you ever do as you're told?"

"Hardly ever."

"Why?"

"People are dumb."

He bit off the words that came to his mouth and asked instead, "What were you doing out riding so far away from home?"

"Nothing."

"Just riding?"

"Yes."

"Well, if you won't come inside, can I take you home after the rain quits?"

"I can walk."

"No, you can't. I'll ride King, and you can take the palomino."

Hannah turned suspicious eyes in his direction. Still trying to see that she got that horse, although he knew perfectly well she wasn't going to take him. Sly, slick, and deceiving, that's what he was.

"I'm not taking the palomino."

"Why not?"

She shrugged. Jerry got to his feet, stood looking down at her. In the half-light of the storm she was so hauntingly beautiful. Dark lashes on a firm, beautifully contoured cheek. That petulant mouth, just enough of a pout to intrigue him, wondering what had ever happened in her life to make her so obstinate, so hard-hearted.

He had never met a girl—no, any person—quite like Hannah. Nothing suited her, nothing pleased her. Everybody annoyed or irritated her. If he had a lick of common sense, he'd stay far away from the Detweiler ranch. But a challenge like Hannah was intriguing and captured his interest the way the plains of North Dakota had.

"Well, if you won't come inside to dry out, and you won't ride the palomino, then I suggest we ride King double."

"Don't you have a buggy?" she asked, picking at the bits of hay clinging to her skirt.

"It's tore apart right now." Partly true. He was replacing one dry wheel, oiling it.

The rain was still whispering across the roof, the day was turning steadily lighter, as Jerry remained standing, hands on his hips, looking down at Hannah, marveling at her sodden, rain-washed beauty. Not one other girl could sit in the middle of a barn littered with dirt and hay and straw, soaking wet, her hair plastered to her head like a shining dark cap, its tendrils drying out, framing her face, and be the most attractive thing he'd ever seen.

What he wanted to do and what he did were very different things. He walked away, opened a gate, led King and the brown gelding out to the watering trough, and then began to brush King's sleek sides with long strokes of the grooming tool. He could learn as he went along, what worked and what didn't with Hannah.

Obviously, holding her close, certainly as close as he had before he really knew her, was off limits. He wasn't the kind of person that would cringe about past mistakes, but he acknowledged that there was definitely a learning curve.

Like an untamed horse, she had never been taught to listen, due either to an absent father or a weak mother, or perhaps through no one's fault. Perhaps she had been born with this irritation. Who knew?

King saddled and bridled, he brought out the palomino and began to brush him in the same easy manner, ignoring Hannah. When he was finished, he turned to her.

"Ready?"

"I told you, I'm not taking the palomino."

Jerry counted to ten, then said it was still raining anyway, they may as well go into the house, dry out a bit, and get something to eat.

"No."

So, he left her there, sitting on the dirt floor of the barn and went into the house. He opened drawers and slammed them shut like the bang of a rifle. He made a sandwich with quick, jerky movements of frustration, wolfed it down with bitter swallows of hot coffee, grabbed his old felt hat and swung out the door.

Jake Fisher went on with his carving of a wolf and didn't say a word. Jerry better be careful, he thought, or he'd be in over his head with that one.

Jerry noticed the storm clouds passing on, leaving the northwest washed blue through rents in the residue of black storm clouds. He'd risk it then. He opened the barn door wide, allowing afternoon light to stream in along with the smell of parched earth reawakened by the rain.

Hannah blinked, turned back to threading a piece of straw through her fingers.

"Look, I'm busy. We're working on the house. Get up on the palomino and follow me. I won't ride the whole way. We've got work to do." He raised his eyebrows, waiting.

She got to her feet—she was so tall—and pulled at her damp skirt, smoothed her hands across the front of her dress to rid herself of any clinging straw and hay.

He watched as she walked over to the palomino and without a word, swung up into the saddle and walked him through the barn door, ducking her head slightly to clear the overhead beam. There was nothing for Jerry to do but follow.

The earth had changed to a washed brown. Everything shimmered with raindrops, like jewels, clinging precariously to brittle brown grass that had been softened by the deluge. It was a joy to breathe in and absorb the scents of the settled dust, the wet grass, and the rivulets that still trickled beside the road, vanishing shyly into the moistened roots.

The horses felt the change and tugged on the reins, wanting to run. Hannah felt the tugging, the step sideways, the dancing, as if the palomino was walking on air. She felt the tightening of his muscles, the gathering of unleashed power beneath her, the golden horse waiting for her command to run.

Ahead of her, Jerry was up on King, looking as if he was having difficulty holding him back. Excitement welled up in Hannah, but she knew she could not let it show and allow Jerry to see any willingness to accept his horse. If she did, she'd be indebted to him, the last thing on earth she wanted.

Jerry brought King to a stop. Hannah caught up. "He wants to run. I'm going to give him his head for a few miles to settle him down. We'll go slow and look for your horse afterward."

Nothing could have prepared Hannah for the surge of speed, the clean, flowing gait of a well-bred horse. The comparison to their old horses was like night and day.

She had never known such speed existed on horseback. She became frightened, realizing that she was hurtling along on the back of a lunging animal that reveled in this breakneck speed and had no intention of slowing down. Quite simply, this horse loved to run, loved to race with the brown horse well ahead of her.

The distance was closing in. She could see King's flailing hooves as Jerry bent low, his hat pulled down over his forehead, the gathering of the horse's withers, loosened when hooves dug into the earth, sending mud and water and bits of grass flying up to hit the palomino's chest. His nose was close to the bobbing flanks. Hannah ceased to think. There was nothing in her mind, just getting past Jerry to show off her riding skills.

She leaned forward, loosened the reins, shook them the slightest bit, and was rewarded by another, stronger gathering of hoof, tendon, and muscle.

Now to Jerry's side, to his horse's neck. A shout from Jerry. On they went, thundering across the wet, muddy road with the remnants of the storm hanging like banners to cheer them on.

Nose to nose, and Jerry reined in, laughing and throwing his hat on the ground, his dark eyes shining into hers. In the exulting of the moment, Hannah forgot her pride, all her foolish refusal to cooperate, everything. She stood up in the stirrups, pumped an arm upward and yelled across the wide, rain-washed prairie that she had won! If they had been neck and neck in the beginning, the palomino would have won effortlessly.

"I held King back," Jerry stated, slanting his eyes at her. Hannah laughed and shook her head, then laughed deeper and more genuinely. Jerry had heard that sound only once before.

They both turned to look at the same moment, taking in the sight of an old bay horse, his neck outstretched, his ears lifted in welcome, alive and, by all appearances, quite recovered.

"Pete!" Hannah flung herself off the palomino's back, reached Pete with a few quick steps, gathered up the reins that dragged on the ground, and held on to them. She rubbed the scruffy head, sliding a hand beneath his mane where his coat was as smooth as silk.

She forgot Jerry, who sat in his saddle taking it all in and wondering at this girl, this Hannah Detweiler, with a hard, impenetrable crust covering her like a burr on a chestnut. But what, really, was on the inside?

The palomino followed Jerry home, and no decision was made. Hannah rode Pete home and arrived to loud acclaim from the porch, Sarah and Manny having been quite beside themselves with worry.

Jerry went home to the place they called a house, although it wasn't a house by anyone's imagination. It was merely a leaking old board shack they'd cleaned out and planned to insulate against winter's arrival. The barn had taken up more time than they'd planned, and here was summer on the way out with nothing much else done.

He had to put the thought of Hannah behind him. She addled his wits, making a mess out of his common sense. He needed to focus on the work at hand.

Jake fried steaks rolled in flour in the cast iron skillet. He thickened the pan juices and poured the hot gravy over biscuits that were so hard, you couldn't eat them unless they were softened with it. He was the worst cook ever, but Jerry never said anything, knowing full well he could do no better and would probably do worse.

"Supper," Jake announced.

Jerry pulled up a chair, ate the salty gravy marbled with streaks of fat and dotted with white lumps of flour. The biscuits had to be cut with a serrated bread knife; a table knife couldn't dent them. But after the gravy soaked through, they were edible.

Jake was younger than Jerry by a few years. They'd gone to school together and attended the same church service. They liked the same girls and drove the same kind of horses. They were more than impressed with North Dakota. The wide open spaces got into their blood, and they lived for the day when they could move out here and stay.

Unlike Jerry, Jake came from a family that was as tight as a ball of yarn. Jerry teased his friend, saying that if he accompanied him out West, the whole family was sure to follow.

At night, Jerry detected homesickness when Jake became quiet, a faraway look in his eyes, not answering when Jerry spoke to him. Jerry knew he was back with his family, the sisters and brothers he loves, the kindly father who spoiled him just a bit, and the mother who doted on his every whim.

Poor as church mice they were. Especially now, with the value of land falling, the cash flow cut off by plummeting sales and the stagnant exchange of everything.

But he loved horses, Jake did, taking an avid interest in all the work of shoeing, filing teeth, and, especially, breaking a young colt. So the partnership worked well, for now. But Jerry knew the time would come when Jake would return to his family, the ties that bind as tight as glue for him.

Jerry had brought these three horses, but he had eight more being sent as soon as he wanted. Hi problem now was to complete the fence-making before winter. He couldn't imagine letting the horses run wild with no boundaries, slapping a brand on their backsides, and hoping for the best.

He wanted fences with boundaries for his horses, grain from the local feed mill in town, salt blocks, and minerals. His goal was to start up a horse auction. To get the locals involved, he thought maybe he'd have a barbeque to introduce himself. Observing how these old ranchers kept their horses, he knew he'd have to settle for some inferior ones in the beginning. Not all of them. The Klassermans had a few horses that equaled some of his.

Jerry loved the solitude, the days on end without encountering another human being, the wide open spaces, the unexpected, uncontrolled scenery of waving grass, and a sky so immense it was all right to feel insignificant.

The way he had felt most of his life. His father was a harsh, exacting man, ensuring none of his boys would turn out *grosfeelich*. His way of raising children was to work them hard, give them no money to spend, and then they'd stay out of trouble, especially if they were put in their place frequently enough.

Jerry had been his mother's favorite, for some reason, which only increased his father's dislike and jealousy. After he turned eighteen, he left home, but his sister and her husband took him in. There he learned what a normal family was like.

To love without judging, to be able to please someone, anyone. It was a different life. After his introduction to horse training, he had found his vocation, his meaning in life. But as he grew older, the horses were not enough. He wanted to have a companion by his side, someone to love and build a future with.

He'd dated plenty of girls, but all of them left him empty and bewildered. He thought something might be wrong with him; maybe he was not able to love a woman because of his upbringing, his anger toward his sniveling, spoiled mother as solid as his rebellion toward his father.

So he let go of girls, as the years came and went. Until Hannah showed up, soaking wet and angry. She had grasped his interest in those two strong brown hands of his and taken over his thoughts, his waking hours, his whole life, the way God was supposed to.

Of late, things had gotten worse. He felt as if he was running out of time. Would he actually have to go through life without her? She had no interest in him, absolutely none. All that girl thought about was her herd of black cows.

What was she doing riding out in his direction anyway? She'd never made herself clear. Visiting Ben Millers? Highly unlikely. At any rate, old Pete was on his last legs, whether she admitted it or not. He couldn't see how her and her brother did all that hay-making with those two worn out horses. They had enough hay to feed twice as many cattle as they had. Someone had worked hard, all summer long.

So, there she was again, soaking wet in his barn, years later. A very different set of circumstances this time—a different barn, a different place. Who would have thought they'd end up in North Dakota?

Life was strange. He wondered if she'd ever forgive him for the mad dash to the barn. He had never been quite so irritated with anyone in his whole life, except his father, of course. You simply couldn't tell that girl anything. She knew everything and wasn't afraid to let you know it. Why did he even think of her?

By all outward appearances, she was unfit to be anyone's wife, hard-headed, often rude, and ignorant. Likely the best path for her would be the life of a single cattle queen. A bar-oness of the West. Or that was what she imagined herself to be. There was no doubt about it, she was a dreamer. He could see the resemblance between her and her father.

And yet, here she was, by all appearances her Bar S well on the way. It was only a stroke of luck that the fire ruined the house. That, and God's Almighty wisdom, His ways. All that help they'd received was all to their good.

But Jerry also knew that they had a well-to-do parent some-where. Someone had to give them their start with those cattle. Someday, he hoped to be close enough to her to hear her story, which, he supposed, contained a lot more fear and trials than she would ever let on. That was exactly the reason she intrigued him and kept him always wondering about her. What made her say and do the things she did?

He looked at Jake, who stood over him with another biscuit and question marks in his eyes. He nodded and the biscuit clattered onto his plate. Jerry raised his chin in the bread knife's direction. Jake handed him the salt shaker instead. Jerry shook his head and said, "Knife."

Jake handed it over with one hand and cut off a bite of steak with the other. Feeling the shanty shake in the teeth of the wind that sprang up after the storm, they both looked up from their gravy-soaked biscuits and shook their heads.

"I have a feeling we're in for quite a few surprises living out here on these plains," Jake observed. "It seems like the wind and the heat and the rain all have a mind of their own."

Jerry nodded and tried to sop up gravy with his biscuit. Giving up, he stuck it in his mouth, chewing it like a pretzel. "We'd better worry about this little pile of sticks we live in." They both winced as a piece of metal flapped wildly, making a steady buzzing sound like a giant angry wasp. There was a decided breeze coming from between the rotting logs, flapping the towel that hung beside the wash basin setting on a bench.

"We need to come up with a plan. We don't know how to go about procuring lumber here in the booming town of Pine. Or roofing, or windows, not to mention door handles and plumbing supplies. We may have to keep our deluxe plumbing system we have now," Jerry said, smiling broadly.

"Won't hurt us," Jake said dryly.

"What if we get company?"

"No one will bother us. That . . ." Jake jerked a thumb in the general direction in which Hannah had arrived.

"Hannah?"

"Yeah, her. She could come calling."

Jerry shook his head. "She won't be back anytime soon, I have a hunch."

Jake chose to keep his curiosity to himself.

After they washed the dishes, wiped out the frying pan and hung it back on its nail on the wall, they went outside to see how cheaply they could get by winter-proofing the old, falling-down remainder of a half log, half sod house that had stood for a century or more, attacked by all kinds of rain, hail, snowstorms, and extreme temperatures.

The wind scoured the rusting metal, bent the tired, brown weeds and grass up against the old logs, swung the door back against the wall on its hinges with a loud clap.

Somewhere in the distance, coyotes set up their high, yipping bark, answered by another set of yelps close by. Jake said they needed a dog if they were planning on raising horses successfully.

"They wouldn't touch a colt with the mother nearby."

"Think not?"

Jerry nodded. "Think about Hannah Detweiler's cattle. They were out all winter, with no hay for them at all. That was nothing short of a miracle."

Jake thought it would take another miracle to get Jerry back to normal.

Chapter 16

The whole thing was bad timing.

Stuck behind the counter at Harry Rocher's hardware store, to look up and find that Jerry Riehl was the one that had set that annoying little bell to tinkling. If he hadn't already spied her, she'd have ducked behind the cash register and crawled away, which, for one panicked moment, she almost did.

Her practiced glare firmly in place, she looked at him standing tall, slim, and wide in the shoulders, her faded purple dress too tight in the sleeves.

When his dark face broke into a welcoming smile, his white teeth gleaming and looking ridiculously handsome, her glare intensified.

"What are you doing here, Hannah?"

"What does it look like?"

"Well, since you're standing behind the counter, I'm guessing you're employed here."

"Smart of you."

A flicker of irritation passed through him. Why did she always make him feel like a bumbling second grader? "I need doorknobs and hinges," he said, brusque now, turning away to inspect a bin of bolts.

She came out from behind the counter and led him to the section where all sorts of hinges were displayed, along with a variety of door handles. Standing back, she turned on her heel and left him to decide. No use trying to help him out.

When he had chosen the hinges and doorknobs he wanted, she was involved with another customer, a small boy who silently handed her a slip of white paper.

Jerry stood patiently, watching as she bent over the counter, propped her elbows, her too tight sleeves revealing her muscular arms. For an instant, something like fear of her wafted across his vision. Definitely someone to be reckoned with.

But when she spoke to the thin, wide-eyed little boy, her smile brought one to his face as well.

"You're mama had no time to come get her own thread and buttons? So you had to come the whole way here by yourself?" she asked.

The boy nodded, whispered, and bent his head.

Hannah came out from behind the counter, got down on her knees and placed her hands on his shoulders, squeezing gently. "Can't hear you."

"My bike. I rode my bike."

Feigning astonishment, Hannah said, "My, you are little to be riding a bike. You deserve a piece of candy for that."

The boy's face lit up as if an internal light switch had been flipped on, watching every move she made until the bit of wrapped chocolate was in his hand.

Jerry stood, without realizing his own soft expression, his eyebrows slightly raise and his mouth open. So she had a tender heart for children, a well-buried kindness that rose to the surface on occasion. Somehow, to witness this scene balanced the muscular arms and her glare. He knew he'd continue his pursuit, but this was certainly a boost.

Hannah helped the boy first and left Jerry standing there holding his armload of doorknobs and hinges. No apology for keeping him waiting when he unloaded them on the counter, she merely pecked the keys on the cash register, a hidden face, presenting only her profile, the perfect contours of cheekbone and jaw, the small, flat nose. Oh, she was beautiful!

His heart set up a sweet pounding, like an ache. To begin a conversation, he mentioned the little boy. When there was no response, he tried the weather; no response then either. As she bagged his purchase, he became desperate and asked when she'd be ready to race horses again.

A flicker of interest, the lifting of her eyes and looking straight into his. "We'll be driving part of our herd and part of the Klassermans' to Dorchester the last week in October before the snows come. We need horses. Pete is . . ." The slightest tremble of the firm lips. "Not strong enough," she finished, her voice husky.

"It's his kidneys."

She nodded and held his gaze.

Suddenly, it was as if they were conversing with their eyes. The interior of the store with its yellow light bulbs overhead illuminating the shelves and dark walls, the shadowed objects, disappeared, leaving them both in a world where only the depths of their eyes existed.

Help me.

You know I would give my life for you.

Ride with me. I'm scared.

I'll be there for you.

And then it was over, the moment broken by the jarring sound of the bell above the door. Jerry cleared his throat, ran a hand across his eyes, and left. There were no words, and if there had been, they would have ruined what he had just experienced.

He rode home, bouncing high on the saddle, flinging himself into the wind, a song like the high notes of a wailing bugle in his chest, an exhilaration of his spirit that rode high in the heights of the prairie sky.

Hannah rode home with Harry Rocher in the red car, a scarf tied over her head, black and warm.

The day was too cool to have the top down, but that was what he liked, so she crossed her arms, pulled the light denim jacket tighter, and didn't say anything.

Harry talked nonstop, his considerate face thinner, pulled down, as if the years had not been kind. His hair had thinned and turned white at the temples. His hands were long and lined with heavy blue veins across the backs.

Old hands. An old face, long before it was time. Curious, Hannah asked about Doris. It was strange that she had worked in the store all day without being asked to do one chore for Doris in the house.

Harry talked then, his voice rising well above the rushing air and the sound of the motor. "She's going downhill, fast. I don't know what to do. She says if I don't accompany her home to Baltimore, where her folks are, she's going to file for a divorce. I don't want that. It would be a public scandal. But I don't want to live in Baltimore, in the city, with the heat and gut-wrenching smell of saltwater, the humidity that is so stifling you can't breathe in the summer.

"Her parents are aging. They need our help. I don't want to go, and I don't want a divorce. She's beyond miserable. I'm afraid if I don't consent, she'll lose her mind, and I'll have to put her away. I can't do that, either."

Hannah considered his words that were peppered with self-pity. Hadn't he promised to care for her in sickness and in health, or any other circumstances presented by God? Perhaps English vows were unlike the Amish vows.

"I hate Baltimore," he said, his grip tightening on the steering wheel. "She hates it here. I love it. I love the people, the open sky, the land, snow, drought, dust—all of it. This is where my heart is."

Hannah thought of her mother. Lancaster County was where her heart was. But she had followed Hannah's father withersoever—as the Bible said. His God had been her God, or rather,

her father's version of God, his own translation of dreams and miracles and high-mindedness.

Call it what you wanted. Straight into near starvation they had gone. Hannah realized again that the reason for having survived that winter were both sitting here in this car. It wasn't a miracle. You simply went out and did what you had to do, whatever came your way.

"Well, seems your choice is pretty clear. You need to go home to Baltimore if you want to do the right thing. You're supposed to give your life for your wife."

"And she's supposed to submit to my will," Harry said, the kindness in his face vanishing, leaving him looking old and thin, his face papery with wrinkles, his eyes hard.

Hmm. Here was a side of Mr. Rocher she hadn't seen. When they pulled up to the door, the dust following them, blowing across the open car, the porch, seeping into the house and away across the prairie, Harry turned to her.

"Next week, same day?"

"Till the end of October. Then we drive the cattle."

Harry nodded. He hesitated, ran the tip of one finger around the smooth rim of the steering wheel. He straightened his back, reached into his pocket for a rumpled, red handkerchief and busily dusted the glass of the gas and speedometer gauges.

"What do you think I should do, Hannah?" he asked.

"I told you."

"But you have no idea. The smell of fish hangs over that city like a plague. The noise, the stench, the ships in the harbor, smelling of rust and oil and old saltwater. I can't tell you how much I loathe that place."

"Then get a divorce."

"I can't."

"You mean, you can't give up to take Doris home."

Harry gazed off in the opposite direction. Finally, he thumped the steering wheel with his clenched fist and said he never should have married her. Hannah shrugged, got out of the car, and went into the house without watching him drive away.

Big baby. She had no sympathy. Grow up. Do what it takes to face life. You're married to a squeamish little woman who is afraid of her own shadow, so get over it. She didn't blame Doris.

Her face clouded over with her disgust of Harry's indecision. She stormed into the house to find her mother bent over the open oven door, poking a fork into the aluminum roaster filled with a steaming mound of *roasht*.

The house smelled like Christmas dinners and weddings. Sarah straightened and smiled at Hannah but her smile faded as she saw her dark countenance.

"You're upset, Hannah."

Hannah gave a quick snort of derision, then gave her mother an account of Harry's life. Sarah nodded, feelings chasing over her features like light and shadow. She could not judge Mr. Rocher harshly. No. Buoyed as she was by the foundation of her upbringing, it still had not been easy. After she had ridden away from her home on the hard seat of that covered wagon, resentment had crept up and rode on her shoulders like a heavy burden, more times than she could tell. The private and bitter struggle, so much more than her daughter would ever know.

English hardware-store owner, Amish wife of a dreamer. Was there a difference, when the hardest task for all members of the human race was to relinquish the hold on your own will and allow someone else to present you with their will, expecting the nearly impossible?

No! It was called life. Living here on earth, giving your life, if not to your spouse, then for the sake of Christ alone.

Christ, who had bled and died, tortured by Roman soldiers, for her, for all of mankind. Without this belief, the bedrock of her faith, she would not have done it, and now, prospering here on this bleak and unforgiving land.

Or was it? She had come to love it. She had come to love her home, her neighbors, the vast realm of prairie, the magnificence of an ever-changing sky, a kaleidoscope of times and seasons, the hard work of producing vegetables from a garden that, except for their efforts, would remain unwatered.

The dust and the heat, the storms of winter, were all a part of her life, her love. This is where the children were, where Mose lay beneath the soil of the homestead.

All of this went through her mind in a second, as she listened to her daughter. The judgment of the young, the inexperienced. Sarah knew well the time would come for Hannah's own test, the times when God would send her an unannounced quiz, when she was least prepared.

But she smiled, nodded, listened to Hannah's words swirling through the kitchen like hard, pecking birds. Birds that needed to be avoided and chased out the back door.

She lifted the lid on the boiling potatoes, inserted a fork, poured off the water, called to Mary to set the table, turning her head to avoid the cloud of steam that rose above the pan.

The gravy was made, the green beans from the garden boiling in their buttered water. She applied the potato masher, pounding the potatoes with a strong arm, inhaling the rich, earthy smell of them.

She could never cook a good meal without gratitude, ever. The lean times were forever stamped on her memory.

Sarah dished up the steaming *roasht*—bread cubes, celery and onion, bits of cooked chicken, butter, salt and pepper, mixed well and baked in a roaster. Every edible part of the chicken had been used—the liver, gizzard and heart, neck meat and bits of skin, the rich broth simmered for yellow gravy.

"I am so hungry." Hannah elaborated each word before bowing her head, or slightly inclining it, actually. More often than not she'd be gazing off somewhere above everyone's head, her thoughts anywhere but giving thanks, while the rest of the family bent their heads, closed their eyes and actually gave thanks.

Everyone ate the evening meal with a healthy appetite. Sarah had to refill the serving bowls more than once, especially the *roasht*.

"You keep butchering these chickens and we're going to be without eggs," Hannah said, laying down her fork.

"This one was caught in the fence by her foot. She was unable to free herself without breaking it. I figured she'd never be able to escape the night varmints."

"Varmints?"

"Sorry. A word borrowed from Hod and Abby."

"I guess if we start to say varmints, we're genuine western folks, huh?"

Summer waned, like a brilliant full moon that steadily lost its light, until only a delicate sliver of light hung in the night sky.

The sun was warm, but only at midday, the mornings as crisp and dry as crumpled toast, the evenings laid bare with encroaching cold.

The moisture from the infrequent thunderstorms had long evaporated or soaked into the bone-dry soil like an inadequate whisper. The prairie grass looked thin and beaten, as if it had given up hope, knowing winter would whip the remaining life from it.

Hannah watched the sky, tested the direction of the wind, her eyes clouded over with worry. The cattle drive would not be possible without rain. The cows needed water to make the long trek to Dorchester.

Manny spoke of trucking them. Why not hire a local truck with a cattle trailer? It was by far the most logical thing to do.

Hannah would hear nothing of it. She knew well the times she had dreamed of doing a real cattle drive. The thrill of roping, chasing, and branding, doubled by the excitement of sleeping out on the prairie under the stars, the cattle watched by vigilant riders. Besides, it would take a big chunk out of her profit to hire a truck and trailer. They'd do it the old way.

Hod Jenkins didn't think it was a good idea. He hung out of the door of his rusted old pickup, squinted at Hannah and her mother as they stood on the porch steps. The motor idled, a low, rumbling sound, so they both moved off the steps and went to talk to him, standing in the dry, chilly air.

"You and that brother of yours better brush up on them ropin' skills. Them cattle's wilder 'n deer."

Hannah shook her head, her mouth set in a stubborn line. "Our cattle aren't like yours." She had a notion to add, "skinny-ribbed, horned old horrors." He should be ashamed to drive those long-haired skeletons to market.

Hod wagged his head. "You'll find out."

Hannah gave him a black look. "Yours would never make it, as skinny as they are."

Sarah winced, looked at the bed of the pickup where an old gate was stacked to one side, a roll of rusted barbed wire and a digging iron leaning crazily against it.

"Longhorns is supposed to be skinny, Miss High and Mighty." His blue eyes shone with an unusual glint of anger.

"Yeah, well, all right then. If Clay doesn't want to join the drive, will Hank and Ken do it?"

"I couldn't tell you." Hod opened the door of his pickup, climbed out and stepped away a few paces before sending a stream of tobacco juice like pressurized water from a hose. The ill-smelling brown liquid landed with a dull splat in the dust, raising a small cloud that settled quickly over it.

Hannah swallowed and felt the bile rise in her throat. She watched as he settled the wad of liquid-sounding tobacco strands further in his cheek, wiped his mouth with his forefinger, then dragged it along the side of his jeans, which appeared to have been the recipient of many tobacco juice encounters.

Dust covered his greasy hat, settled in black granules around the band surrounding the crown, and lay in the creases and pocket flaps of his vest. His shirt had been blue at one time, but resembled the color of stagnant water now. His boots were cracked, the heels both worn down until he walked on the outside, the too-long legs of his jeans frayed and brown from dragging along in the dust.

Hannah swallowed again and imagined the odor of his unwashed socks, if he wore any at all.

Sarah, however, was blind to all of Hannah's magnified scrutiny. She seemed to think Mr. Hod was the most important visitor of the month. She fired questions about Abby's cough, listened to Hod's words that became increasingly garbled with emotion, his head bent as he said that all the pills from the doctor hadn't eased her cough. He was afraid she'd have to accept the inevitable hospital stay.

Immediately, Sarah offered to go to Abby. She'd ride back with him and take Baby Abby along, knowing how much Abby loved her. She hurried back into the house to change, leaving Hannah standing with Hod, who was leaning against the rusted sides of the pickup, the motor still rumbling in small, muffled chugs.

Hod turned to look at Hannah. "So yer pretty set on doin' this cattle drive?" he asked.

"Yes."

"How come?"

"I don't want to pay a fee to have them hauled."

"You know it'll cost you, the way them cows will lose weight on their long walk. If I was you, I wouldn't do it. How come old man Klasserman don't know any better? You sure he's sendin' em?"

Hannah nodded. "He said he was."

"His cattle's ornery."

Hannah frowned. "You have no idea what his cattle are like."

Hod squinted, his blue eyes slits of light, gazing off across the plains. He hooked two thumbs into his belt loops, wagged his elbows and gave a sound between a snort and a laugh.

"You are one determined young lady. You have no idea how hard it can be, keepin' them cattle on the move, all in the right direction. You'll have cars, mebbe a coupla trucks. They'll scare 'em straight across the prairie. So then when one of you tries to turn 'em back, the rest will be hightailin' it somewhere else. You better pick good men."

"Manny's going."

"He can't rope worth a toot."

Hannah bristled. "Sure he can."

Hod shook his head, then faced her, lowered his frame closer to her and said forcefully, "You think you know everything. You ain't seen nothin'. I'm only warnin' you once. It'll be tougher than you think. And when you get there, they'll all have lost weight. So don't come cryin' to me iffen you don't get nothin' for them black cows."

Hannah looked away from him, off across the garden.

"You got any spare horses?"

"No. You going to let the boys go?"

"That's up to them."

"I need a horse."

"Wal, git your own. Them Amish have some fancy lookin' horse flesh paradin' around."

Hannah wanted to stamp her foot in frustration. Instead, she watched her mother emerge from the house wearing a purple dress with a black apron pinned around her waist, the stiff black bonnet on her head. She always dress according to the *Ordnung*, the laws branded into her, giving her life.

"All right. We're ready." She smiled at Hod, who pulled himself away from the side of the truck, opened the door for Sarah, then went around to the opposite side and closed his door before leaning out the window and wagging a finger. Probably the one he'd used to wipe his mouth, thought Hannah.

"Mind what I said. You need to think about it."

Hannah didn't give him the benefit of an answer. Filthy, arrogant old coot. Seriously, who did he think he was?

Well, she'd show him. She would brush up on her roping skills, her riding, everything. She'd have Manny, Jerry, and probably Jake. So those Jenkinses could just stay home, then.

As she stalked off to find Manny, she yelled to Mary and Eli to stay close to the house because they were going to work cattle.

Pete was stiff and slow, loose and wobbly in the hind legs. Goat was more interested in the occasional mouthful of grass than anything else. Manny wasn't being very enthused, Hannah interrupting his harness mending, but he did what she asked, his nature far too dutiful to resist.

The cows had multiplied in number, of course, with twelve healthy new calves grown into young cattle and probably weighing six or seven hundred pounds. Manny guessed a few of them would tip the scales at closer to eight hundred. In spite of the drought, they'd had plenty of thick, dry prairie grass and fresh water from the tank, all sufficient to produce twelve half-grown cows.

The young cattle were well-rounded, filled out nicely in the chest and shoulder area, their heads well shaped at the top, with square, black mouths that moved constantly, ripping at the grass or laying contentedly, chewing their cud.

Hannah's eyes shone as she sat in the saddle surveying her herd. "What do you think, Manny?"

He nodded and smiled.

They practiced riding and roping, chased cattle, missed many more times than they actually roped one. The horses were soon winded, Pete sagging in the back, Goat snacking on yet another mouthful of grass.

Hannah dismounted, sat in the grass, and told Manny that unless they had better horses, they couldn't make the drive, that was all there was to it.

Manny nodded, agreed. "We'll ask the Jenkinses."

"I already did." Manny looked at her, his eyebrows raised. Hannah shook her head.

Manny straightened his shoulders and sighed. "Guess I'll have to make a trip over to Jerry Riehl. He'll let us use a few of his, likely."

Hannah tried to hide the exhilaration she felt at his suggestion.

CHAPTER 17

THE RAIN DID NOT COME.

The days grew shorter, the air around them containing only a dry, bone-chilling cold, especially at night.

Manny split and stacked wood from the fallen cottonwoods in the creek bottom, shoring up the supply leftover from the year before, the thought of the previous winter's blizzards goading him on.

Hannah continued to watch the skies, biting her lower lip in anxiety, knowing if the rains held off, there could be no cattle drive. With Manny's help, Jerry had given his consent to bring two extra horses, which only served to double Hannah's anxious watching of the empty sky.

They set the date for separating and branding the cattle. They would be sending eight of the heaviest ones, along with ten of the Klassermans, which brought the total to eighteen head of unruly young cattle, a fact Hannah could no longer dismiss.

The well-attended, most important cattle auction was to be held at the fairgrounds in Dorchester, about thirty-five miles away.

Hannah allowed a week for the branding and separating, the preparation of the food, depending on the fact that the rain would come. She forged ahead with her plans, in spite of Hod

Jenkins's warnings, Sarah having joined forces with him, advising Hannah to call it off, in spite of risking her anger which, inevitably, came thundering down around her ears.

Frustrated by the lack of rain and unwilling to give up her plans, Hannah railed against her mother, accusing her of siding with Hod just to go against her, that she didn't know a thing about cattle drives.

Whereupon Sarah informed her daughter that no, she didn't, but anytime you went against an experienced person's advice, you were setting yourself up for failure. It was too dry, too risky.

Undeterred, Hannah forged ahead with her plans, until one afternoon Sarah had a glimpse of her deceased husband in the glittering determination in Hannah's eyes and the set of her mouth. In the way her head jutted forward on her neck, as if her goal was closer as long as she kept her face forward. Well, Hannah hadn't taken to fasting and praying, but that was the only difference.

Sarah was drying strips of beef in the oven for jerky, to be taken on the drive, a labor of love, and one she enjoyed. It was just so unsettling, this dealing with her daughter's determination.

How can we go through life running parallel with the one we most disdain? It was uncanny, the likeness to her father, holding on to a dream with an iron grip, regardless of the circumstances that warned against it. But to face Hannah and throw this fact in her face would be unwise, like throwing gasoline on hot coals, an inevitable explosion.

She lifted the limp strips of beef from the herbal mixture, patted them in place on the thin aluminum sheet, and placed it in the oven. All she could do was place her trust in God and pray that He would keep the riders safe and the cattle healthy, somehow.

On the day of the branding, Jerry and Jake met the Jenkins boys for the first time. Loquacious as always, the Jenkinses were quick to make new friends and easy to talk to, giving easily understood instructions. They spent a good half-hour inspecting the horses, asking questions, circling them, whistling in admiration, then bargaining for a horse just like these.

Jerry didn't say much; he was watching Hannah. She had been a puzzle ever since she'd watched them ride in. She had not acknowledged his presence, or the palomino, and refused to touch the horse, acting as if he didn't exist.

So, that was the way of it. Jerry ignored her, took to the Jenkinses like a magnet, then sat back and watched Clay and Hank go to work. They rode as if there were no horse and rider, just one animal that thought and moved together.

In spite of the belligerent cows savage advances, the bellowing, pawing, dust-throwing of the bull, they showed no hesitance, merely rode among the cows with authority, packing them into a moving, black mass, trundling them across the prairie to the water tank where the rest of the crew was expected to hold them.

Jerry watched, eyes alight. When he wasn't watching her, Hannah untied the palomino's reins, mounted quickly without looking at Jerry, and rode out to the tank. He went on talking to Manny, who was astride the roan, an older horse, but a large one, well-formed, clean in his limbs, and sweet tempered. She felt sadness for Pete and Goat standing by the barnyard fence watching the goings on, Pete offering a gentle nicker occasionally. Goat was too busy taking chomps out of the top board of the fence, eating splinters like hay.

The Jenkins boys rode back, leaving instructions on holding the cattle, then started a roaring fire which soon burned down to a bed of red hot coals.

Out at the tank, however, things took a decided turn for the worse. The ill-tempered, outsized cow suddenly displayed an unwillingness to be ordered about, charging with all the weight and fury of a great buffalo and scattering the two men, who had no experience with being sidelined by a horned monster the size of that one.

Jerry yelled, wheeled the black in the direction of the barn, the cow intent on chasing them all, followed by whinnying horses, and the bawling, excited cattle. A few of them ran across the bed of hot coals, scattering them and igniting the bone-dry grass, which only added to the melee of animals and riders. Panicked, half-grown cattle stuck their tails up like broomsticks and thundered off across the prairie.

Hannah was mad. She saw red. What a coward, she thought. She stayed by the water tank and watched all of it, holding the prancing palomino in check and snorting inwardly. So much for those two helping on the cattle drive. It couldn't be done with those creampuffs. And Manny was no better. She lost no time in loping off in their direction, after everything was controlled, including the fire.

From her perch on the palomino, she told them all how unbelievably unnecessary that whole pile of chaos had been, and if they couldn't do any better than that, they may as well all stay home.

Even Manny's face turned red with indignation after the tirade from his sister, thoroughly embarrassed by his unlikely display of cowardice, then feeling bad for Jerry who was being good enough to lend them the use of the two horses.

He had just opened his mouth to tell Hannah a thing or two, when there was a combination of shouts and hoarse yelling, followed by a spray of dust and the sound of hooves, as the fiercely determined cow streaked toward Hannah on the palomino, who twisted his body in a flash to avoid the red-eyed, crazed old cow, unseating Hannah in the process.

She felt the horse turn away from under her, felt herself sliding off the saddle, airborne for a split second before her shoulder hit the ground, her head snapping back, the rest of her body following with a bone jarring expulsion of breath, a folding in, as if she did a slow somersault, which she was never sure if she did or not.

The palomino was off in a wild flight, the stirrups slapping his sides, the reins flying of their own accord. The belligerent cow stopped, turned and eyed Hannah who was up on one elbow, faced with the enraged, pawing cow that had killed her father.

With no thought for anything other than getting away, she scrambled to her feet, running like the wind, yelling and shouting, horses wheeling, the cow lumbering off amid the galloping of horses' hooves, all one big chaotic explosion of movement and noise around her.

She slumped against the barnyard fence, gasping for breath, one half-breath after another, turning into a painful tearing in her chest. She slowed her breathing, tried to get out from under the terrifying weight on her chest and around her middle.

The first one to reach her side was Clay, his face ashen.

"Hannah!" His voice was terrible.

She remained calm, kept herself level-headed, fought for breath and nodded, watching Clay's face.

"You all right?"

She nodded again.

Surrounded now by the rest of the crew, Manny's face hardly recognizable as he worked hard to keep his emotions in check, Hannah was soon able to assure them that she was all right.

Clay felt her shoulder and asked her to turn her head both ways, then checked her arms and knees, asking her to bend and straighten them.

"I will be okay," Hannah said, soft and low.

The cattle were sorted and branded that day, but not without a sensible and serious discussion about the upcoming cattle drive.

When the air turned brittle with cold, they stood around the coals left over from the branding, Clay holding court.

"This thing of drivin' these cattle ain't gonna work. You saw what happened today. None of you is experienced. You gotta give it up."

He didn't spare any feelings or try to decorate the facts with flowery praise. He just kept talking, building his case, counting the reasons that stacked up to a considerable height.

The most important thing was water. "There ain't none," he stated, bluntly.

Hannah broke in, "It will rain, soon."

"What if it don't?"

"We'll go anyhow."

"How you gonna keep these cows alive? How?"

"It will rain, I said."

"You ain't God. You don't know whether it will rain!" Clay shouted, clearly upset with her stubborn refusal to accept his advice.

Jerry suggested they wait out the next three days, and if it rained a significant amount, they'd go. If not, they'd truck them.

"We're not trucking these cattle."

Sure enough, the following evening, a dark gray mountain of clouds blew in from the northwest. Hannah could smell the rain long before it arrived. The smell of wet dust, a raw, earthy smell that set her senses quivering. She stood on the porch, exulting, clapped Manny's shoulder and did a little dance of "What did I tell you?"

He grinned, always good-natured, always glad to give Hannah the top rung of the ladder, the best spot on the totem pole.

There was only one thing wrong with the cold rain that rode in on the wings of a genuine deluge, driving cold needles of wet, sluicing raindrops into every crack and crevice where it could possibly go.

Sarah shook her head and said no, they had better not attempt it. The dusty path that led to the house turned into a slippery bowl of pudding—like brown sugar cornstarch pudding. The creek filled, the yellowing willow leaves swayed, let loose, and were hurled across the prairie, leaving some bare, dark branches, whipping and glistening in the wind and rain.

The roof of the house was shining wet, like polished metal, the wooden sides of the house turned dark yellow, like maize, rivulets of water splashing down from the roof and across the windows.

Hannah thought the rain would surely quit after the downpour, but it only let up for an hour or so, with walls of soft, gray fog like sheep's wool hovering between the sky and the horizon, before it began again, a fresh shower of rain driven by a whining wind.

The Klassermans rode through the wet night, the headlights of their truck piercing the dark like glaring white eyes. They splashed up onto the porch, their pink faces like wet ceramic, chortling, laughing, pulling off their rubber boots with red-faced effort.

"Ach, de rain, de rain. When she finally arrive, she arrive full force," Owen said loudly, his pink gums showing above a row of even, white teeth.

Sylvia whooshed and blew through her nose, shaking her head like a dog, drops of water flying every which way.

Sarah laughed and ushered them in, happy as she always was to receive visitors. Long gone was the memory of Sylvia's meticulous behavior. She had *schenked und fagevva.*

"Come in, come in, out of the rain. How unfortunate for you to be out in this weather at night," she said, holding out a hand for their wet outerwear.

Owen rolled his eyes with importance. "Oh, but very necessary. I decided it is far too foolhardy to attempt to drive my cattle to market. We will truck them. I will drive it mineself. My wife will not hear of me allowing your children to drive them on foot."

Sylvia rose to the occasion, patting her massive bosom with one hand, flapping it like a large, startled bird. "Oh, *nein, nein*. I say to mine Owen, *ach du lieber. Vot iss diss?* Such dumbheit. Ve cannot ride dis horse, chase dis cattle, so vy allow some young ones to do it? No. No. We use the truck. The truck iss only sensible choice."

Hannah sat at the kitchen table, her ears heating to a deep, dull red, her eyes sparking with frustration. How many things had gone against this long-awaited cattle drive? Drought, too much rain, uncooperative neighbors, Jerry and his willy-nilly partner, Jake, who were afraid of cows. Honestly. Now what?

"Hannah?" A large, glistening pink face was thrust into her own personal territory, the kitchen table and a perimeter of ten feet around it. "Hannah, mine darlink girl. Haf you been well?"

Hannah wanted to say no, I had measles and was almost killed by a cow yesterday, but what she said was, "Yes."

"Yes? You are well? Oh, goot, goot." Again, the fluttering of that large pink hand. Sylvia was breathing hard as she lowered her flowery bulk into a groaning kitchen chair and proceeded to give Hannah an hour by hour account of her lost barn cat.

Why didn't you just shoot her? Hannah thought sourly. She couldn't stand cats. Mewly things, rubbing themselves up against your leg when both hands were occupied pegging wash to the line, until you became fuzzy all over, finally reaching out with a backward heave of your foot that sent the sniveling thing out of reach.

"So you vill also truck your cows, I presume?" Sylvia asked now, reaching gratefully for the soothing cup of peppermint tea Sarah brought to her.

"I don't know." Well, she didn't. See what the morning brought.

What it did bring was more rain. Slanting, steady sheets of rain that didn't give any indication of letting up. The creek rose, full and muddy, churning with dead grass and dead roots, the banks swallowed by the ever increasing water.

She heard nothing from Jerry Riehl, but the Jenkinses waded through the brown slop to let them know they'd haul their two trailer loads of cattle, then come back for hers tomorrow around noon. If they wanted, they could all ride along. Clay was hauling the cattle, and Hod was taking the car.

Sarah didn't ask Hannah's opinion, just nodded her assent happily and said she'd look forward to the auction. Manny nodded, smiled and said yes, that would be great. Eli and Mary bounced up and down, clapping their hands.

As soon as Hod left, Hannah informed her family that no one had asked her opinion. Sarah searched Hannah's face and said kindly, "But, surely, Hannah, you wouldn't attempt anything as dangerous . . ."

Hannah broke in. "We could have done it. In the rain. No one gave me a chance." And then she pouted. She walked around the house with her nose in the air and wouldn't speak to anyone, stalking from room to room, window to window, scowling bitterly at the bad timing of all this rain, this endless pouring that soaked into the earth, puddling around the house, and destroyed her long-awaited plans.

It wasn't so much about the profit. It was the novelty of the whole thing. Range riders. Cattle drivers. Western horsemen. Dust and rain and cold and hail. Eating beef jerky around a roaring campfire, the cows bedded down close by, strong coffee as the sun tipped the edge of the earth.

Perhaps they'd just have to move farther west, to Wyoming or Colorado, where there were even less people and cars and ranches. If you could truck your cattle to market, it was far too close, too civilized, too full of other people sticking their noses in your business.

That Clay and his high opinion of himself! At least Jerry had the right idea. Even if he didn't know anything about cattle drives, he kept his mouth shut.

She refused to load the eight head of cattle. The Jenkins boys and Manny did it by themselves, in the pouring rain. Hannah stood behind the curtain in the kitchen and watched, the mass of glistening wet cows being separated, moiling around as if they knew this was the first step to a serious departure from all they'd ever known.

When they clattered into the house for dry clothes and a cup of steaming coffee, Hannah went to her room and stayed there until Manny knocked and said that Hod was here with the car. If she wanted to see her cattle sold, she'd best get her clothes changed.

She rode in the back seat, her head turned to the window on her left, the dismal landscape jarring to her senses, the way there was no letup in the clouds, even now.

Her mother sat in the front seat with Abby on her lap, talking in quiet tones, difficult to hear above the sound of the steady chugging of the engine. The windshield wipers' hypnotic rhythm made Hannah feel slightly crazy, not wanting to watch the movement, but quite unable to tear her eyes away.

Eli and Mary fidgeted until Hannah delivered an ill-tempered pinch on Eli's trouser leg, resulting in a shocked silence, followed by peace and quiet.

Hannah's mood worsened to see a tear in the dark rain clouds, as if a hole had been cut with a giant knife, allowing a glimpse of blue, then a shaft of yellow sunlight pierced the parted clouds, and the rain was over.

The town of Dorchester was large, a rain-washed sprawling cluster of businesses and house, trees, paved roads, slippery mud, people, and cars. The fairgrounds were a cluster of long, low buildings, trees, and acres of dead grass awash in more mud.

Trucks and cattle trailers were everywhere, engines grinding, steel cables squealing as gates were lowered, black cattle, long-horn steers, baldy-faced bulls, all bellowing or mooing or dodging men with cattle prods.

Children ran wild. Their clothes plastered with mud, their hair damp with the last of the raindrops. Automobile horns blew warnings as another trailer wedged itself like a giant digging iron between two trailers, men standing by the open gate in the back and giving the driver calculated stares.

There were a few horses tied by an ancient hitching post under the dripping foliage of a tree, but mostly there were old, bent Ford trucks, and all manner of trailers, some expensive looking, built of steel and painted white or blue, with the insignia of the owner's ranch inscribed on the side. Other trailers were merely wooden racks fastened to a metal flatbed with screws, baler twine, and good fortune.

Hod let them out at the entrance to the auction barn, a building made mostly of gray corrugated tin and rust, a few splintered doors with paint peeling like molting chickens. The smell of food was powerful, and Hannah swallowed.

The interior of the building was higher than it appeared from the outside, with an oblong center, the floor strewn with sawdust. On two sides, seats were built one behind the other, stacked toward the ceiling, so that folks were in layers and everyone could see over the heads of the people in front.

About half the seats were filled with what appeared to be farmers or ranchers, perhaps all ranchers. Various colors of Stetson hats bent in all sorts of shapes and silhouettes adorned most men's heads. Their women were like weathered flowers, brittle and creased, their faces pounded into crevices of flesh by the harsh winters and blazing heat of the summers, riding the herds with their men.

Keenly aware of their Amish dress, Hannah walked with her back straight, shoulders squared, a fierce scowl on her face, her brown eyes looking straight ahead, unwavering. Sarah carried Abby and held on to Eli and Mary, hurrying after Hannah's long strides until they were seated, somewhere above the third row.

Glad to find a spot to rest, her arms aching, Sarah smiled at the children, breathed deeply, then dared a peek at her oldest daughter, who sat like a stone, unmoving.

"Hannah?" she breathed.

Hannah glowered at her mother, held a finger to her lips. "Hush. Everyone is looking at us. I hate my clothes. So Amish."

Sarah looked around. She did not see anyone looking at them. All eyes were glued to the ring below them, where a heavy-set man in a red shirt was picking up a sheaf of papers, riffling through them, bending to speak to another even bigger fellow endowed with a face as red as his shirt, crowned with a white Stetson set back on his head like framework for the brilliance of his visage.

Hannah watched the two men, decided she'd never seen anyone as ugly as they were. What in the world caused their faces to be so red? They looked boiled, like a piece of liver.

She jumped with a squawking sound that came from the ceiling. Eli began to cry, and Mary grabbed Hannah's hand with both of hers. "Testing. Testing. One, two three."

Hannah decided the men's faces were red from bellowing, if that was the way their voices were expected to carry. But Sarah pointed to a black box hanging from the ceiling, said it was something electrical to carry the man's voice. Mose had described them for her in New Holland at the sales stables.

The sale began with a roan colored steer with horns like curved swords entering the rung, a huge growth protruding from his lower abdomen, his massive head shaking the horns from side to side, the large hooves stirring the sawdust.

Two men held evil-looking black whips, cracking them repeatedly over the bewildered animal's head. Confused, the

roan steer dashed first in one direction, than another, the grotesque growth swinging as he moved.

"Here's one for the killer!" shouted the auctioneer. "Nothin'
but ground been for this one. Yup! Who'll give me ten? Twenty?
Five dollars, now five dollars, five, five, five. Yup!"

The bidding didn't last long enough to even make sense.
Hannah had no idea if the price was per pound or if that was
the amount for the whole steer. If they got that amount for eight
heifers, they'd be paying their grandfather's loan back for a long
time.

Hod came up the aisle, smiled at Sarah, and sat beside her,
taking Abby on his lap. He handed a candy bar to Eli and one to
Mary. A Mallo Cup. Chocolate covered marshmallow. Hannah's
mouth watered but she didn't let on, bent to help them unwrap
the candy, told them to remember to thank Hod, who was too
busy watching the cattle being sold to notice their thank you's.

He better be worried, Hannah thought. That sickly wife of
his was coughing her lungs into pieces. He was going to have
some hospital bill to pay if he didn't get the poor woman some
help soon.

Or perhaps it was Abby herself, refusing to be treated. She
turned in her seat, the smell of chocolate so powerful she asked
Eli for a bite, and looked straight into the eyes of Jerry Riehl!

CHAPTER 18

"How'd you get here?" It was the only thing she knew to say, her mind going blank the way it did.

"I rode King."

"In the rain?"

"Yeah. I brought the palomino for you."

Hannah blinked, had no comprehension.

"You mean . . . ?"

"I felt bad for you. I knew you had your heart set on that drive, so I thought I'd risk it, hope the weather cleared, and we'd get the cattle sold and ride back together. You know, camp out, take our time."

"You mean . . . ?"

"Yeah, if you want to."

Hannah licked chocolate from her fingertip, swallowed, and blinked.

"Only us two?"

"Us."

Well, now what? What was she supposed to say? She didn't trust him. Not at all. He'd get her out on that wild prairie and start getting all sweet on her again. Huh. Uh . . . but he'd brought that horse the whole way. What was wrong with him, thinking she'd go back with him? Alone. The two of them. She couldn't.

"Sorry. I don't want to."

Jerry looked comfortable with her answer, shrugged, said all right or okay, something like that, and began his descent.

Hannah opened her mouth and then closed it again. Well, he had more nerve than common sense thinking, no, assuming, she'd go. His appearance and offer of riding home ruined the whole sale. She knew how badly she wanted to go. Knew, too, that her pride would never allow it. Or should it?

If that black box from the ceiling kept up that squawking all day, she would personally shoot the stupid thing down. She craned her neck, peered at it with half closed eyes, then down at the crimson-faced auctioneer. She wanted to stand up and tell him to shut up, wave her arms and get his attention good and solid, but she'd end up buying some cows, and Lord knows, these cows were nothing to look at, long-haired, skinny-necked creatures with wild red eyes.

The afternoon dragged on, with bunches of cows in various sizes and colors being sold for different prices, some high, some low.

Hannah had not seen any cattle that looked as nice as hers, but she figured they'd keep the good ones till last. She didn't know.

She watched as they prodded four black Angus heifers into the ring. The auctioneer's tone took on an excitement, yelling about the Klasserman ranch. Immediately, the bidding began at a brisk pace, the price escalating beyond anything she'd heard all day.

Sure enough. The bidding rounded out at almost a dollar a pound. Unbelievable! Hannah's heart raced, her tongue felt like sandpaper in her dry mouth as she drew in her breath in short puffs. If they got that price, they'd be able to pay back more than half of the loan from her grandfather.

Another group of the Klassermans' cattle was sold at an even higher price. Immediately afterward, all eight of her own cattle were herded in, looking every bit as good as the Klassermans', calm, doe-eyed, beautiful young cattle with nicely rounded bodies, sleek hair, and short muscular legs, spaced well.

The auctioneer's face took on a purple hue. "Here we have a new group of cattle. Young, good-looking stuff that'll increase the likability of your own herd. Says here they're from the Bar S. I'd say them folks know a thing or two about cattle raising."

Hannah's hands went to her mouth to stop its trembling. She was ashamed of the quick tears that rose to her eyes. Knew a thing or two about cattle raising? She thought of all the mistakes, all they'd been through to get started, the harsh winter, the anxiety, the wolves. No, they didn't know much at all.

"Whaddaya gimme for these excellent, top o' the line cattle?"

Hannah held her breath as the bidding floundered, slow to start. Folks buying cattle knew the Klassermans but were unsure about the Bar S.

Down to twenty-five cents a pound.

Hannah couldn't breathe. She felt as if she was suffocating.

And then it started. Yup! Yup!

The man taking the bids yelled out, waved his arms and hopped like a banty rooster.

All the way up over a dollar a pound. A dollar ten. Fifteen. Hannah was crying now, she could do nothing about the emotions that came from good fortune, from relief after having suffered so much.

The cattle were sold for the unbelievable sum of a dollar thirty-nine, way over anything Hannah had expected.

She swiped fiercely at her eyes, looked at Sarah, who gave her a wide smile through misty eyes. "We're on our way, Hannah," she mouthed.

Hannah didn't know what love felt like, one way or another, but she figured this was about the closest thing to it.

She wouldn't have gone with Jerry if Clay wouldn't have made her so angry, parading around with the red-haired Jennifer in jeans. Imagine! Right in front of her, he tried to buy that palomino horse from Jerry for Jennifer, his girlfriend. He knew full well how that would rankle, bargaining with an arm draped across Jennifer's shoulders.

So, after that scene played out, she looked straight at Jerry and told him she'd changed her mind. She'd ride home with him, even smiled into his astonished eyes, for Clay's benefit.

The rest of her family rode home with Hod. Manny looked puzzled, but then shrugged his shoulders, having given up a long time ago trying to figure Hannah out.

When it was time to go, Jerry silently handed her a pair of his old trousers. She took them, turned her back, and pulled them on. She looked over the amount of items tied on the horses' backs. Bedrolls, knapsacks, everything looked in order.

Well, this was something, now wasn't it?

Jerry asked if she wanted to go someplace to eat before they started off. Hannah didn't know what he meant, so she said no, not wanting to enter some stranger's house and sit at their table.

"Well, there's a great place to eat just outside of town. Their steaks and potatoes are unlike anything I've ever eaten. You sure you won't come?"

"If it's a café or restaurant, then yes, I will."

So that was how she found herself in that intimate setting with Jerry, his dark eyes watching her beneath the canopy of dark hair, cut exactly right, not too long and not too short.

She had never eaten inside a restaurant before except for her humiliating encounter with the fiery-haired Betsy, an episode she'd just as soon forget.

She looked around, took in the boards with dark knotholes, the red Formica-topped tables, the scattering of ranchers and wives or girlfriends decked out in gaily printed dresses, some of them dressed like men, in shirts and jeans. The trousers for women that Sylvia Klasserman called dungarees.

Instinctively, she pulled her own legs under her chair, hoping no one would notice the men's trouser legs sticking out from beneath her skirt.

She hated being in public dressed in her Amish clothes. Half-Amish, the way she refused to wear the required white head covering. The thing about adhering to a belief, being born into a way of life, wearing clothes meant to convey modesty, a conservative lifestyle, was that people stared.

The ordinary, English people. They looked at you, a certain changing of the eyes, an expression of surprise, another look, the rearranging of their features, usually followed by a half-smile or a sliding away from any eye contact.

So often, Hannah only wanted to fit into the mainstream, be out in public looking like everyone else, unnoticed, unseen. The blending in she longed for.

If she was going to cross over, forget about obedience, now would be the time to do it, before her grandfather arrived, before more people flocked in like unwanted crows, and they ordained the inevitable minister.

As if Jerry was reading her mind, those intent brown eyes on her face, he asked, "Why don't you wear your covering?"

Hannah shrugged, lowered her eyes. When she looked up, he was still waiting for her answer.

"It's unhandy. Gets awfully dirty working at the hay and in the barn."

Evidently that answer didn't suit him, the way the corners of his mouth dipped down.

"You're still thinking of leaving the Amish? I know you were seriously considering it at one time. Why?"

Hannah's eyes flashed. "You know, if you're going to sit there asking me all these nosy questions, I'm not riding home with you."

Jerry realized his mistake the minute he saw the irritation flicker in those large, secretive pools of black. So much like a colt. So much like an unbroken horse. He could be patient, but if he was wasting his time and would only be hurt in the end, there was no sense in putting himself through this.

When the food arrived, Hannah ate very little, too preoccupied with the daunting reality of having someone seated across the table who possessed the backbone to bark out those personal questions like that.

She was in no position to take his questions into consideration, the truth being that she simply didn't know the answers. To admit this would be a serious failure on her part, like walking ahead of him on a narrow trail above a precipice, losing her footing and hurling down the side, complete with pebbles rattling and dust rolling. She had to be very careful, always alert, so he would never be able to decipher the code to her locked away fears and insecurities.

They rode along, side by side, Hannah astride the palomino, pensively mulling over the idea of a name for this beautiful creature.

Goldie?

Honey?

Creamy?

All of them feminine, childish. This was a gelding, after all, one that needed a strong name like "Buck" or "Freedom" or maybe "Roger."

The late evening air held the promise of frost, the sun sliding toward the horizon, painting the prairie with reddish hues. Hannah loved this time of year, the autumnal splendor, the invigorating wind that played among the grasses, so she was content riding along on the smooth-gaited palomino, sneaking furtive glances at her companion, who rode along as quiet and unobtrusive as if he was alone.

When dusk fell with the softness of the plains, Hannah glanced at the twin bedrolls, then felt a warm blush suffuse her face. She certainly hoped that one thin roll of blanket would be enough to keep the chill of night away.

Suddenly, she wanted to be at home, safe in her bedroom, with Mam banking the fire, getting the little ones off to bed.

What was she doing out here in the middle of nowhere with the arrogant Jerry Riehl?

She sniffed, blinked, and looked long and hard at the thin blanket. Then she said that she hoped that blanket was warmer than it looked.

Jerry reached back to adjust it, as if to reassure himself. "You'll be warm."

"Well, just so you know that if I get cold, I don't expect to sleep anywhere near you. You'll have to keep the fire going, because I won't do it." She figured that would put him in his place.

He acted as if he never heard what she said, just pointed across the waving grass and said that bunch of cottonwoods looked suitable and would she be willing to stop for the night?

"You heard what I said about that thin bedroll."

"I heard."

He expertly tethered the horses, the hobbles keeping them close, cropping grass with a satisfying sound of their teeth tearing at the wet growth, grinding it in their back molars.

Jerry started a fire, just as expertly as he did everything else, his movements calculated, sparse. When the dry grass and twigs were cheerfully burning, he added heavier dead growth from the trees, filled a small granite coffee pot with water from a metal flask, threw in a scoop of coffee, arranged it on an iron grate, then stretched out with his back to his bedroll, his hands crossed in front of his stomach.

All this time Hannah stood like an unnecessary fence post, feeling about as useful and attractive, wishing he'd ask her to help, to do something with her hands.

He looked up at her as if remembering her presence. "Sit down, Hannah."

"I will if I want to."

He grinned unexpectedly. "Or, you can stand there all night. Do whatever you want. Makes no difference to me."

Hannah's face flamed. "You know, if you wanted my company, you're not very appreciative."

"Sure I am. I appreciate the fact that you're standing there." He laughed, a short, hard sound.

"I won't sit with you until you promise not to ask me any questions that are none of your business."

He didn't reply, just took the toe of his boot and stirred up the fire, sending a spray of sparks up toward the gray, early night sky.

"Sit down," he said, finally. She sat.

"Look, I meant well in asking you to accompany me, thinking you'd be happy to go on this adventure since having to give up the cattle drive. But if you're going to be as soft and welcoming as a cactus, you may as well get on that horse and ride on home."

Hannah didn't say anything, merely drew up her knees, smoothed her skirt down over her feet, rested her chin on her knees, her arms around her legs, and stared darkly into the fire.

A night owl screeched its high trilling note, sending shivers up and down her spine. The grass around them waved, rattling the night song of the plains, a constant rustling, like waves of water.

"So stop asking me stuff I don't like to answer."

"All right. What do you want to talk about?"

"Nothing. Drink coffee. Listen to the owls."

He poured her a cup of bitter, boiling hot coffee, strong enough to make her splutter. "This stuff is horrible!"

"You think?"

"I can't drink it."

"Sure you can. Want me to add some water?"

When she nodded, he got to his feet, tipped the metal flask and dribbled a few splashes of cooling water into her cup. She watched his hands, brown and calloused, the nails rounded and clean, the fingers long and tapered. He had nice hands. They were very close to her own. She'd just have to lift a finger to touch his knuckle.

For a wild instant, she wanted to do just that.

He moved away. She felt his absence like an ever-widening chasm.

"Tell me about you, Hannah. Tell me about your life. What makes you the way you are?" He settled back against the cushioning of his bedroll, his eyes squinting in the firelight. "I was hoping if I'd be alone with you, I could uncover some of the barriers, the many layers of protection you seem to wear."

"What for?"

He grimaced, swallowed his anger. So blunt, so forthright, always jousting, her sword of defense held aloft. He decided to meet her with a sword of his own.

"You fascinate me."

"What is that supposed to mean?"

"What I said."

"How could I fascinate anyone?"

Jerry believed this statement was real. Had she no idea of her own beauty, her own allure, the captivating eyes and the mouth that smiled only on occasion, like a rare flower that only showed its face for a day, then wilted away? The fiery temperament, the joy she had shown at her success today?

He sighed and watched her face. "Well for one thing, not too many girls would have returned to North Dakota after all you experienced. You rose from the ashes, literally. You made it through the worst winter in a decade, your cows intact."

"We lost one."

"Right. But today you showed your dreams are now reality. Your cows are on the way to turning a profit. It's quite amazing."

"You think? Mam says it was the grace of God alone."

"You believe that?"

"Of course. I was raised a God-fearing young Amish child."

"You will remain?"

"Why are you so intent on my answering that question?"

"Your . . ." Here Jerry waved a hand along the back of his head, his eyes squinting, as if trying to gauge her response before he aired his opinion. "Your covering, or absence of it."

"You want to know why I never wear one? I'll tell you. It's because the strings get in the way. It gets dirty, it wasn't made for ranch work, and there is no bishop or minister to come tell me what I can do and what I can't. This little triangle of a handkerchief suits me just fine."

Jerry nodded. "Okay."

"I'm Amish."

"Then come to church."

"If I come to church, everyone will think I approve of them. It will be like telling them it's all right that they rode that train out here to our North Dakota, our prairie. They're going to keep coming until we have a regular old settlement like the one we left. We'll be right back into it—neighbors, gossip, scrambling to make money, all of it. I don't like people. They give me a headache."

Jerry listened, said, "Like your father."

Hannah nodded, then shook her head back and forth, correcting the nod. "I'm not like him. You should know that."

"You're a loner like he was."

"Well, maybe. But there it stops."

"Tell me about your childhood."

"Why would I? There's nothing to tell." But she did. She told him about the farm causing her father's worry, the money never quite reaching to cover the bills, her mother's absolute devotion, her backbone like jelly, always submitting.

"Dat could do no wrong," Hannah said. "That was nice, for us as children. Our home was secure, a warm place filled with the smell of baking bread, the odor of ironed linen and cotton, wooden spools to make towers, cracked linoleum, and the smell of Lava soap. Mam was an excellent housekeeper, taught us well, allowed us to have baby kittens and piglets, lambs and baby goats in cardboard boxes behind the stove when they were newborn.

Hannah hesitated. "The hard part began when we lost the farm. My father did a very foolish, untrustworthy thing, and we left. We left amid horrible rumors and shame on our heads like rain. It hurt a lot. I was about ready to start my *rumschpringa*, so naturally I felt the cruelty of our downfall. I resented my father a lot. Anger built up inside of me, I suppose."

She spread her hands, shrugged, her face pale in the glowing coals of the fire. "So now you know why I'm, well . . . the way I am."

"It was your father's downfall," Jerry said quietly.

"I don't know. I guess. I didn't like the men who came to our house to help. They made Mam cry. Dat was quiet, brooding. Everything, my whole world, changed after we lost the farm."

"You weren't the only ones. Many families lost everything. City people, English businessmen, thousands of ordinary wage workers. It was not unusual to not meet your mortgage payments."

"I know. But when it happens to your own family, it doesn't make it any easier."

Jerry nodded. "You know, I came out here with my horses to get away from Lancaster County, just like you. I loved the idea of starting a new settlement. The thrill of trying to make it. You should see what we did to that old wreck of a house. We're just getting started, and we're doing it as cheaply as possible, but you should absolutely come over and look at it."

Why was she disappointed that he didn't say he came out here for her? Hadn't he said that once?

She should not think these thoughts, ever. She was failing her own resolve to stay single, untroubled by thoughts of love, a genuine slippery slope into unhappiness and betrayal.

But his face had an arresting quality. She couldn't seem to stop herself from watching him, the way his chin jutted a bit, the cleft in it just made for a fingertip to touch. His dark eyes, so often half-closed with his heavy eyelids, or squinting in the firelight or sunlight. His nose was wide at the top, stubby at the bottom, with perfectly formed nostrils.

Well, she could think these thoughts, then hide them away. He'd never have to know.

Jerry admired her ability to remain quiet, to spend long minutes in restful silence. The first time he met her, this had caught his attention. He would pursue her further, unafraid, if it wouldn't be for the fact that she was not devoted to her faith, her birthright, her culture.

His peace lay in the love of the brotherhood, the rightness of it. How could he love God if he could not love the brethren? He was steadfast in his baptismal vows, living his life as defined by the will of God and the acceptance of the blood of the Lord Jesus.

He could not be certain that Hannah wanted to share his beliefs. But this, this evening by the fire, on the prairie, was something. She had spoken far more than he had allowed himself to hope.

Suddenly, she got to her feet, turned her back and rid herself of the cumbersome trousers, kicked them into the grass, returned to the fire, and began to unroll her blanket. She stood, hands on her hips, her head to one side, considering. "No pillow?" she asked.

"Your saddle."

"It's getting awful cold."

"That blanket is one hundred percent wool. You won't be cold." He got to his feet, brought her saddle over, and stood by her bedroll with a question in his eyes.

"Two people together are much warmer than one," he said, his eyes warm with humor.

All she said, with the coolness of an icicle was, "You think?" Then promptly wrapped her coat tighter around her slim form, slid into her blanket and, knocking her head up and down on the saddle a few times, grimaced, and complained, "I won't sleep a wink. To use a saddle for a pillow can only be comfortable for giraffes. My neck should be about three times longer. It stinks. It smells like horses. Why couldn't you bring at least a small pillow?

"I never slept with a girl in North Dakota," he said dryly.

Chapter 19

THE NIGHT TURNED EVEN COLDER. THE FIRE DIED DOWN TO A SMALL circle of red coals, an ominous red eye that kept Hannah awake. To relax and fall asleep meant the coals would die to gray ashes and she would certainly freeze.

At first, the woolen blanket was sufficient, its heavy weight like a comforting arm the entire length of her body. But when the frost settled in, the temperature dropped even further. Shivers began to ripple along her shoulders and the backs of her legs. Her face was so cold she curled up even tighter, pulled the odorous blanket up over her head and tried to concentrate on the pockets of warmth she could find.

She wondered vaguely if your nose could crack right off your face, if it was frozen solid, or if the tissue and blood vessels kept it warm enough to stay fastened to the rest of your face.

Repeatedly, she opened one eye to peer at the glowing coals. When the call of the wolves sounded through the woolen blanket she clutched around her head and became rigid with fear. The long drawn-out wails rose to a hair-raising crescendo, floating above the prairie like ghosts of the wolves who howled before them, a long drawn-out cry that jangled Hannah's resolve, ruined her pride, and goaded her into action.

Flinging aside the useless thing he called a blanket, she scrambled to her feet, scavenged around in the pitch black night, her back bent, her hands scouring the campsite for more wood. Sticks, logs, anything. She was slowly turning into a human icicle, about to be eaten by wolves, and if her judgment was right, he was the same as dead, sleeping so soundly the only thing that would wake him would be a shotgun or a herd of buffalo, not necessarily in that order.

What if there was no wood? She wasn't about to wade through the frosty grass to the group of ash and cottonwood trees. Not with the wolves running in packs, howling their heads off.

She could see them. Huge, long-legged brutes, black or gray, some brownish gray, silver-tipped hair on the darker ones, their long powerful legs efficient machines that propelled them easily over the roughest terrain, their wide foreheads and large, pointed ears, and red eyes that saw everything, like the devil.

No wood anywhere. The fire out. Her teeth rattling together like strung beads in the wind.

Then, instead of feeling despaired, or helpless, Hannah got mad! She stomped over to the sleeping mound called Jerry, drew back her foot and gave him a solid kick, then another.

Immediately, his dark head appeared, followed by his hands clawing at the blanket, muttered words of confusion cutting through the night air, all unintelligible, which did nothing to assuage Hannah's temper.

"Get up! Where's the wood? I'm freezing!" she yelled.

"Wood? What wood?" he asked stupidly, running a hand through his hair.

"Wood for the fire."

"Oh, here. Right here."

Jerry picked up a few small sections of a dead branch, scattered the dead ashes into a few glowing red coals, and soon had a crackling flame that ate away at the dead wood, sending light and warmth into the dark like a promise.

"You're shivering," he observed.

"Yeah. What do you think? It's zero degrees and there's a pack of wolves howling. Very restful."

"Why didn't you wake me before now?"

Hannah didn't answer, mostly because of the clacking activity of her teeth.

A high, ripping howl began, rising higher and higher, until it turned into a cacophony of intermittent yelps and mournful cadences that could only be described as ghostly.

Hannah hated the wolves ever since the previous winter when that sound was like a dagger, attempting to slice away her hope for the future, slavering jowls of primal beasts devouring her cattle.

"They aren't close," Jerry observed.

"So what? Get this fire going." But she was glad he'd said they were at a distance.

He did get the fire roaring, loading the small flames with carefully placed wood, until the heat toasted her face and hands. He brought her blanket and wrapped it around her shoulders, then set her saddle at her back to lean on.

"It's much colder than I thought possible," he said gruffly.

"You have a lot to learn yet," she answered.

He chose to ignore that comment, poured water into the pot, and set it on the grate, than stood over her, his hands balled into fists and propped on his hips.

"Will you share your blanket?" She could hear the mockery in his voice.

"Get your own."

"You sure? I could warm you up just sitting beside you."

"No."

"All right," he said cheerfully, retrieving his blanket, wearing it like a shawl, lowering himself so close to her, their shoulders touched.

Hannah moved away but put only inches between them. The truth was, she was still shivering all along her back, even if her face was roasted.

"Still cold?"

"No," she lied.

"Good. You'll warm up. Sorry I slept so soundly. I sure didn't want you to be miserable, but I guess girls sleep colder than men do. I don't know much about girls, never had sisters, you know."

Nice of him to be all chatty in the middle of the night. She stared into the fire and thought if he was all nice and apologizing for every little thing it was likely because he wanted to kiss her again. She'd thwart that before it started.

She tugged at the blanket and said sourly, "You don't have to apologize. And you better not think of kissing me, either, if that's why you're being so nice."

Hannah was startled when a loud guffaw came from his mouth, followed by rolling peals of laughter rising into the night sky.

She ended all this by saying, "That's not funny."

"Sure it's funny. You must be thinking of when I kissed you before. You never forgot that, did you?"

"I forgot. Of course I don't remember." But her face felt on fire.

"Then why did you say that?"

"I don't want you to try it again."

"You sure?" He laughed again, all good humor and benevolence in the middle of the night on the freezing prairie with one small fire and wolves loping off somewhere in the distance.

After that was out in the open, there was an awkward silence, as if each one knew what the other was thinking, but trying to be calm and nonchalant, as if nothing had ever happened between them. Yet the memory of it lay there like a rock, an unmovable object that grew as the minutes ticked away.

Hannah stirred, crossed her arms, crossed her ankles and uncrossed them. She cleared her throat.

"I'm never getting married. I have no plans of falling in love or allowing a man into my life. I can run the Bar S by myself, with Manny's help. And, if too many Amish arrive, we'll move on, to Wyoming or Colorado. So you know that now."

Jerry shifted his weight so his shoulder hit hers. He turned his face to look at her, just watched her brooding, dark eyes for a long minute, before saying, "You know, Hannah, that is the saddest thing I have ever heard. Why would you want to be like that? Wouldn't it be better to share your life with someone? Someone who would cherish you, treat you with love and respect? Don't you want the companionship of a good husband?"

"Never met one that I liked well enough to want to marry him. Husbands are nothing but trouble. Like dogs. They get crazy ideas in their heads and away they go, leaving their wives to stumble along behind them happily ever after."

"Your father did that. Not all men are like that. You can't measure every man by the past mistakes your father made."

Hannah considered this. She looked over at Jerry, who was watching the orange flames dancing in the mirror of her dark eyes. He wondered how many other fears and secrets were well-hidden in the depths of those dark pools.

Many girls had dark eyes, but hers were so dark you could hardly tell where the pupils began or ended. Hers were the darkest eyes he'd ever seen. His eyes moved to her mouth, the swelling of her perfect lips that made him turn away and wrap his blanket tightly around himself, like a woolen armor against what he knew would be an act of poor judgment.

To have kissed her before was one thing, done in an offhand, "see if I can get Hannah to like me" sort of thing. He'd kissed lots of girls; they all fell for him. Sometimes he'd had to be rude just to get them to lose interest.

Hannah was a thing apart. The more time he spent with her, the more the truth wrapped itself around his heart, like a giant elastic band that pulled so tight it hurt, only to be released again, but always there.

He often asked himself the question—was it the thrill of the chase? Longing for something he could not have, like the foolish fox jumping for the out-of-reach grapes in his reading book in school?

Was it the fascination of her cold heart? Or was it a love that was alive in the spirit of God? The thing so many folks sense, notice, and follow? Feeling the obedience of God's will.

All he knew for sure was that he wanted Hannah. He wanted to stand by her side for the rest of his life. How lightly the phrase was tossed about—"If it's meant to be, it will be." He could not take it as lightly as that, like a dandelion seed blown by a puff of air.

She surprised him by speaking in a husky voice. "He was just so, I don't know, unstable. Carried away with thinking himself to be a prophet, a person set aside to receive special favors from God, while the reality of it was, we were starving. Jerry, do you have any idea what it's like to be so ravenously hungry your stomach hurts and you give your bowl of cornmeal mush to your little brother because you see the hunger in his eyes? And your father, the husband and leader of the weaker vessels, is flailing around, and praying in the bedroom, thinking that God will send manna, or something?"

He could hear the resentment in her grating voice. What had she gone through? He grasped the idea of a husband that had been planted in her brain like a virus. She was afraid to trust. Afraid to live the life her mother had lived.

"See, that's why I haven't made the decision to be Amish. If I stay with our people, I'll be expected to marry, and mar-riage is forever. No separation, no divorce. I am not my mother with her sweet temperament. I couldn't handle being tied to a no-good dreamer leading me with a rope tied around my neck like a nanny goat. Most men just irritate me."

"Most men? Does that 'most' mean there is still a chance that I'm not among the ones that irritate you? Or, wait a minute. You gave me a few good solid kicks awhile ago, caused, no doubt, by irritation."

Jerry laughed, the easy sound that rolled from the depths of his chest. Far away, the wolves' lament turned into shivers, raising the hair on Hannah's forearms. The fire leapt into the night sky, sending sparks to share the darkness with the stars.

Hannah's head drooped onto her chest, her eyelids fell as the heat suffused her body. Jerry shrugged out of his blanket, draped an arm around her shoulders and drew her close as he would comfort a child.

"Thanks for sharing, Hannah. It gives me a lot to think about. And I promise not to kiss you, okay?"

They rode home together in the gathering cold, the clouds bunched together like heaps of dirty wool, puffing away across the prairie sky, changing the light as they thinned out and stretched, allowing a few shy rays of sun to slant through, then disappear.

The powerful gait of the palomino made her heart sing. Sometimes, for no reason, chills chased themselves up and down her spine, quick tears springing to her eyes. The sizable check would be put in the bank, the full amount paid on the debt to their grandfather, leaving no money to buy golden horses. But she was here, now, up on this horse that was like something she could only dream about on this breezy autumn day with the air crisp and invigorating, breathing new life into the parched, arid earth.

And she had to admit, the person riding with her was like a magnet to her sight, her eyes constantly turning to the denim jacket across the wide shoulders, the way he rode so easily, as if he was one with his horse. Both knew what was required of the other, a thoughtless unity that was as graceful as the dance of wildflowers hidden among the lush grass in spring.

She was sorry to see the homestead, knowing this was the end of the ride on the palomino, and yes, the end of his company as well as Jerry's.

They both dismounted and stood by the horses, unsure now, a silence stretching between them.

"You want to feed and water the horses?" Hannah asked quietly.

"I should, I suppose," he answered.

In the barn, she stayed a safe distance away, watching as the horses lowered their heads and drank thirstily, the gulps of water passing up through their long bent necks with a quiet glugging sound.

"You can stable them, if you want. We can see if my mother has something to eat."

She didn't tell him that the dried, over-peppered meat he'd supplied for breakfast was barely enough to tide her over. She was starving, positively light-headed with hunger. That awful coffee he made was so strong it was almost like syrup, with a bunch of bitter grounds in huddled on the bottom and clinging to the sides of the cup like fleas.

Together, they walked to the low ranch house, welcomed warmly by Sarah. Manny was out checking the herd; he'd noticed a limp on the old cow last night.

Sarah served them leftover vegetable stew with a layer of fluffy white dumplings covering the fragrant chunks of potato, carrot and onion, a broth made of tomatoes and beef. She apologized about the lack of butter, but there was plenty of plum jam.

They had discovered a gnarled old plum tree hidden behind two big oak trees down along the creek, about a mile away. The fruit had already begun to ripen and fall, staining the brown, trampled grass purple, flies and hornets zig-zagging drunkenly, sated with too much sugar and the flesh of the rotting, fermented plums.

It was like a windfall, a blessing to be able to preserve this fruit for the winter months. They'd gorged themselves on the sweet fruit for days, until stomachs rumbled and trips to the new commode became hasty affairs. But now they had this jam, the promise of the old plum tree once again laden with fruit.

Jerry seemed hesitant to leave, sitting back in his chair, his eyes half-hidden by his lowered lids, his hands crossed on his stomach.

Sarah's cheeks were flushed, her eyes large and sparkling with good humor. Why not? Here was an attractive young man in the company of her daughter, so could any mother be free of thinking thoughts of love and romance? She saw no signs of either one in the bristly Hannah, who lowered her head and slurped the stew, stuffed her mouth with dumpling and bread and jam until she could hardly swallow fast enough, without her cheeks bulging.

Had she simply no social skills, even? Most girls would react to Jerry in a normal fashion, eating daintily, smiling, trying to be attractive, perhaps batting eyelashes on occasion.

Sarah turned to the stove with sinking heart. She wanted to shake Hannah! Hair disheveled, *dichly* discarded the minute she walked into the house, her apron knotted around her waist instead of being pinned neatly, in the Amish fashion. Men's trousers—whose?—protruding from her skirt, worn boots, castoffs from the Jenkinses.

Didn't she care, ever, about the impact she made, going through life so unhandily, so unconcerned about her appearance?

"You're still wearing my trousers. I'd let you have them, but with two bachelors, laundry is something we don't look forward to."

"Oh, that's right. I forgot I was wearing them."

Sarah was horrified to see her turn her back, hike up her skirt in front, shimmy out of the denims, and kick them across the room.

Jerry didn't seem to be embarrassed, so Sarah bit back the dismayed "Hannah!" and busied herself at the sink.

"Well," Jerry said, stretching his arms above his head. "I'd better get going. This isn't working on the house. I figure Jake is about tired of working alone. Thank you for the good dinner. I usually don't drop in a lunch time unannounced."

He smiled at Sarah with his white teeth, so evenly spaced in his tanned face and, to her shame, she felt herself blush.

She answered quickly that it was nothing, there had been plenty left over, glanced at Hannah, hoping she had missed the obviousness of her girlish response.

Nothing to worry about there. She'd picked up one of her boots and was picking loose pieces of the heel with a table knife. "I need a new pair of boots," she stated flatly.

"Well, perhaps it will be possible with the money from the sale of the cattle," Sarah said, kindly.

"Huh-uh, Mam. Not one cent of that money will be spent. We can repay Doddy Stoltzfus up to half the loan. No new boots."

"What about stocking up on winter supplies? There's the doctor bill to pay."

"I'll go to work. I am working."

Jerry thought, Ah-ha. So there was a reason or her being at Mr. Rocher's hardware store. She was being paid wages to survive the long winter. In a flash, he realized the futility of offering the palomino to Hannah. If this was the tight ship she ran, she would never accept the horse without being in debt, the thought of more debt hounding her like a pack of dogs.

He was relaxed now, ready to leave, without the daunting task of trying to get her to accept the palomino. He would be surprised if old Pete made it through the winter, so maybe her pride would be flattened out of necessity.

He thanked Sarah again, looked at Hannah, who was still worrying the heel of her boot with the knife.

"Hannah."

She looked up.

"Thanks for riding home with me. If you need anything, let me know."

Hannah nodded, her gaze dropping to her boot.

He smiled at Sarah, then let himself out the door, walking to the barn where he saddled King, took up the palomino's reins, and rode home, acknowledging wearily that he had gained absolutely nothing where Hannah Detweiler was concerned.

She was like a mist, or a vapor, a puff of smoke, someone you could see but could never really hold. The closer you came, the more unsure you were.

Back in the kitchen of the ranch house, Sarah frowned, her brows lowered in concentration as she scraped the dishes, and asked Mary to take the scraps to the chickens.

She spoke sharply when she addressed her daughter. "Hannah, should you be using that table knife to scrape manure and what-not off that boot? You weren't very polite to Jerry Riehl, working on that heel and ignoring him when he left."

Hannah gave her mother a weary look. "What was I supposed to do? Stand up and gush over him the way you did?"

Her anger slow to rise, Sarah had time to release a breath, take another one in, before turning away to finish the dishes.

Hannah's behavior was forgotten when a cloud of dust heralded the arrival of two sheriffs from the town of Pine, who wasted no time getting out of their gray, dust-covered vehicle and striding up on the porch.

They were tall, formidable looking men, their faces weathered like old saddles left in the sun, the rain, and the scouring wind. Their serious expressions brought instant fear. Manny appeared in the doorway of the barn before making his way to the house, coming in through the wash house and standing quietly by his mother's side, as if his presence would support her.

Sarah's hand went to her mouth, her dark eyes widened as alarming thoughts crashed through her head. Were they conveyors of bad news this time? Wasn't that the way you were contacted if there was a death or an accident?

But when the older of the two began to speak, there was a moment when she realized this was not about news of home.

"We're asking you to be alert, perhaps keep a rifle or shotgun handy. That Luke Short. . ."

"Lemuel," the other sheriff corrected him.

"That Mr. Short that stayed here. He broke out of prison with another inmate. They're believed to be between this area and west of Dorchester. He knows you're good people, having helped him before, but don't let him close. Don't allow him into your house. They are both armed and dangerous. It might be a good idea to get a dog. All ranchers have them. Be very careful going out to your cattle, on the road, at night. Just be reasonable and don't take risks."

Sarah nodded, took a deep breath to steady herself. "All right. We'll do our best."

Hannah heard her light words, as if all hope and conviction had been abandoned, only a shell of herself remaining.

After they left, Sarah sat down on a kitchen chair, put her elbows on the table, and placed her head in her hands.

Hannah looked out of the window to avoid seeing her mother's distress, thinking that perhaps the sheriff was wrong. Manny went over to his mother and put a hand on her shoulder.

"We'll be all right, Mam. I'll keep the rifle handy."

Sarah lifted her head. "It's not that," she said to the opposite wall. "Do we really have to live like barbarians? Plain old shooting a rifle to protect ourselves? This wild land will be my undoing, at times like this. Mr. Lemuel Short was a nice man, and I believed every word he said. If he comes around, we can't just up and shoot him like savages."

Hannah tried not to snort, but she did anyway. "What did I tell you?"

"Oh, hush. Just hush. For once in your life stay quiet, Hannah. You don't know everything."

Hannah stalked out of the door and out to the barn, took up the pitch fork and threw hay around blindly, not caring where it landed or who ate it. Why couldn't her mother be strong? Why this caving in at the slightest adversity? So what if old Lemuel came around with his chronic cough and his craziness? She wasn't a bit afraid of him, and she couldn't imagine his consort would be too awesome, either. Get a dog, the sheriff had said. As if it was so easy to find a grown dog to haul home and get to barking obediently. She wasn't about to get a dog.

Here they were, well on their way, a sizable amount of money to put on her grandfather's loan, Amish neighbors to keep her content, and now this little man to upset her. Sometimes she just wearied of her mother's collapsing at the slightest provocation.

Hannah jabbed the pitch fork into the haystack, turned and left the barn, then stalked back to the house and went to her room without speaking.

When her mother knocked on her door, asking what was the matter, that she shouldn't worry about Lemuel Short, they'd be all right—Hannah didn't give her the satisfaction of an answer.

And when Manny took things into his own hands and brought home a skinny, mean-looking German shepherd dog, half-grown and rambunctious, an ugly dog that barked incessantly at nothing, or anything, she told him that dog would end up chasing young calves, and then what?

Manny smiled in his good-natured way and told her that's what dogs were for, to train and teach them how to work for you.

CHAPTER 20

On a dry, bitter cold afternoon, Abby Jenkins passed away, leaving Hod and the boys bereft, like floating debris on a flooded river, carried along by the churning wake of their grief, unraveling to an extent that they forgot everything else—their ranch, the cows, or how to go about living their lives without her.

Sarah divided her time between the Jenkins' place and her own, driving Goat in the spring wagon, with Eli and Mary beside her, Baby Abby on her lap, alone and unprotected. She did their washing, cooked meals, and cleaned the house until she became gaunt and weary, the work load being too much for her.

Hannah offered to help and took her turn, allowing her mother to rest. She hated going to that sad, empty house, but she bit her lip and went anyway. The boys stayed out of her way, slinking out to the barn like feral cats, as if it was an embarrassment that Abby had left them alone.

Hod talked to Hannah, though, showing her the wooden cross he'd made to put on her grave. Together, they walked out on the brittle prairie, where a sad pile of soil had been dug, her casket lowered, the soil replaced, an oblong mound of testimony to the truth of her death.

Hannah stood in the blowing wind, her skirts whipping about, her gloved hands clutching the lapel of her denim overcoat, watching as Hod slowly tapped the cross into the ground at the head of the grave.

He straightened and looked off across the land, his old, greasy Stetson smashed down on his head, his blue eyes holding the most desolate light Hannah had ever seen.

There were no tears, only the captured grief that lay in his eyes, a sadness so deep it seemed to change the color of blue to a deeper shade, like early twilight, after the sun is gone.

He spoke gruffly, as if the pain was like gravel in his throat. "It's been a good run, Hannah girl. Every year I spent with this woman was like a minute. I loved her with the kind of love I could only wish for all my boys. I know she had her times. She didn't always love the land the way me and the boys did. But that was beside the point. She gave her life for us, for me and them boys. Nothin' can measure the worth of a good woman. She appeared rough around the edges, but didn't have a mean bone in her body."

He shuddered slightly, the imprisoned emotion shaking his empty hands. "I can see her, crossin' over to that there other side, findin' her baby girl. They say there's thousands an' thousands a' angels up there, but she'll find her. She'll scoop her right up and be happier'n she's ever been."

Hannah felt the sting of tears and blinked furiously.

"Wal, we'll be goin' back now, Hannah." He placed a hand on her shoulder, and they both turned to go back to the house. Hannah wanted to say something, anything, words of comfort, words of remembering Abby, but they wouldn't come. There was no way to force words out if they stick in your head and stay there. Or her heart, she wasn't sure where.

At the house, the boys watched their return, seated around the old oak kitchen table with the blue checked tablecloth, drinking coffee that was strong like a fortress, cup after cup.

Hod went to the stove, poured himself a cup, sat with the boys, motioned Hannah to sit.

"Coffee?"

Hannah shook her head. Ever since she'd downed that slop Jerry called campfire coffee, she hadn't touched it. Those coffee grounds still reminded her of dead, black fleas.

"Now, I want you and yer' mother to go through Abby's things. Take what you kin use. No use lettin' it all go to waste. She ain't got no relatives hereabouts, an' the few she does have back where she come from wouldn't want it. I got her Bible, her weddin' ring and her dress. The rest you kin go through. The boys'll git the furniture after I'm gone. I'm thinkin' that'll be enough."

Hannah surveyed the somber faces, the downcast eyes, wondering where the red-haired Jennifer was. She couldn't remember seeing her at the funeral, when the church in Pine was filled with sober-colored dresses and ill-fitting dark suits that were worn without comfort, bared white foreheads hidden beneath slouched Stetsons, the faces below the white foreheads sunburned and weather-beaten.

The mourning and support of the mourners was much like every funeral Hannah had ever attended. These hardy ranchers were linked by deep bonds forged from survival on the plains, an ingrained love of this high, vast, empty land, and the unpredictable weather the subject of so many neighborhood get-togethers.

"I'm gittin' hitched."

At first, Hannah had a mental picture of Clay being hitched to a spring wagon, till it dawned on her what he meant.

Hod looked at his eldest son, his face blank, his eyes fogged, until he shook himself, and the beginning of a smile played around the corners of his mouth.

"Wal, I'll be."

"That all you got to say?"

"No. I ain't done yet."

There were smiles on every face, even Hannah's.

"First off, it comes a bit sudden, this announcement. I'm guessin' it comes at a good time, without yer Ma to do fer you. I wish you the best, son. Give you my blessin'. Hope yer little Jenny will be everything fer you that yer mother was to me."

Was that a light of revenge in Clay's eyes as they met Hannah's? She looked away immediately, left soon after, bringing down the reins on Goat's flapping haunches, chilled to the bone, one thought chasing another through her head until she felt as numb from the cold as she was from those words that became weary sentences.

He had loved me.

He wanted me to be his wife.

I should have left and gone with Clay.

He's still the best looking man. Well, almost.

I hope he's happy. But she knew that wasn't true.

Before the snow came, Lemuel Short pounded on the door, a stringy-looking individual in tow.

Sarah was alone with the little ones, Hannah and Manny had ridden off with the German shepherd, now named Shep by Manny. Hannah ignored the dog like a virus, wouldn't touch him or talk to him, so he had learned to keep his distance, and he wouldn't wag his tail at the sight of her.

Sarah stood by her bread making, slowly wiping bits of dough and flour from each finger before putting her hands in the dishwater to finish cleaning them. She licked her lips as the dryness of her mouth alternated with the pounding of her heart. Yes, she was afraid.

God, help me. Stay with me now.

The pounding erupted again, the latch rattling like chains. Eli and Mary stopped their schoolwork, their eyes wide, as they looked to their mother for assurance.

Wiping her hands on her apron, she scooped up Abby, told them to continue their work before going to the window, peering sideways, then drawing back, her eyes darkening with fear.

It was him. Both of them.

It was useless to try and hide; they'd heard the children.

She opened the door, blinked in the strong sunlight. "Mr. Short?"

"Don't Mr. Short me. I need food."

He drew his revolver, a small, evil-looking handgun that gleamed with a dull, gray sheen, matching the gray pallor of the little man's face.

His companion, or the man who accompanied him—companion seemed too nice a word—glared over his shoulder, his white face twisted into a leering snarl, a face Sarah could have never imagined.

It was a face absent of any human warmth, decency, or kindness. It took her breath away, leaving her mouth open with shallow rushes of air expelled and inhaled, her nostrils dilated, her limbs weak with terror.

Sarah did not speak. She didn't have the strength. Turning, she went to the pantry.

Eli and Mary recognized their friend, Lemuel, their eyes warm as they opened their mouths to speak, saw the handgun, blinked, then lowered their faces to their lessons, their hands holding the yellow lead pencils, without moving.

Abby toddled after Sarah, beginning to whimper. When Sarah didn't respond, she began to cry.

"Get the baby!" Lemuel yelled, a maniacal note creeping into the end of his sentence.

Sarah obeyed.

The pantry was not well stocked. There was very little she could give them, except cornmeal or oatmeal, flour, other dry staples meant to be used in cooking and baking.

There were canned vegetables and the plums. A few jars of applesauce, but all the canned meat and most of the potatoes had been used up.

Sarah harbored a secret concern, one she had not confided to the children, about the amount of food left for the coming winter months. And now this.

She found a paper sack on a high shelf. Carefully, she placed a jar of plums, one of green beans, and one of small potatoes.

"You better hurry!" Lemuel shouted.

"I don't have a lot to give you," she said hoarsely, returning with the three mason jars of canned goods.

"Where's the bread?"

Sarah turned, pointed with shaking fingers. "It's all gone. I was making bread when you arrived."

"You're holding back. You had more than enough when I was here before. Sit down."

Lemuel Short pushed her roughly into a chair, where she sprawled, struggling to regain her balance, clutching Abby to her chest.

The revolver was within inches of her face now, a cold, gleaming weapon that made her throat constrict with horror. She tasted bile in her mouth, and fought rising nausea.

It was then that she found the leering face of the second man pushed into hers, his cruel, white hands on her shoulders pushing her back into the chair. Abby screamed and struggled to get away. Sarah held on to her.

"I can see you won't do as we say, which means we'll have to use other measures," the man said, his voice as slick and oily as bacon grease.

He drew back a hand and swung, hitting the side of Sarah's face, sending her head sideways, the slap like an explosion through her head. There was only blackness before a blinding burst of light. The kitchen floor came up to meet her, then tilted at an awful angle, steep and slippery.

She heard the cupboard doors slamming, Lemuel muttering. Abby screamed and went on crying until he shouted at her to cut that out. Eli and Mary put their heads on their folded arms, crying quietly at their desk in the living room.

"There ain't nothin' cept these canned vegetables," Lemuel mocked. The second man whipped out a length of rope, ordered Sarah to get up and get back on the chair.

"What you doin' that for?" Lemuel asked, then shrugged his shoulders as he tied Sarah's hands to the ladder-back chair.

She knew struggling would only cause her situation to be more difficult, so she sat quietly as the rope cut deep into her wrists, shutting off the circulation to her hands.

"You get smart with us, you'll get worse," the second man snarled.

Sarah had never been in the presence of anything this cold and calculating. She had often heard the word evil. She read it in her Bible and knew it meant something bad. But it came down to this cold-hearted invasion of her own self-worth, this treatment of her that smashed all her rights to the fringes of human dignity.

She now saw that evil was the absence of basic human emotion—kindness, caring, empathy, the will to do good. These men were shells. Empty, crumbling wasted men without a residue of common humanity.

She had always believed in the good of every human heart. She couldn't think of any person as evil. Now she could.

The second man eyed Mary, holding her with a malicious glint in his eyes. When he walked toward her, Sarah let out a piercing scream.

"No! No! Mary, run! Run! Oh go! Eli, run!"

Immediately he whirled and turned his face to Sarah, allowing the children time to get to the door, slip through like ghosts, clatter across the porch, and down the steps.

To the barn. To the barn. Sarah's mind screamed direction. Burrow in the hay. It's cold, Eli. Mary, hide in the hay.

"Shut up, lady! Just shut that mouth!"

Lemuel Short had opened a jar of the beans, spilled them into a bowl, eating greedily, smacking his sips as he stuffed them into his mouth with his hands.

The second man found a scarf hanging from a nail on the wall. He grabbed it, approached Sarah with a mocking smile, and tied it like a vice around her mouth, knotting it in the back, jerking her head like a doll, until it rolled and wobbled on her shoulders.

He smacked his hands together, dusting them off, and said they could eat in peace now. Shut her up good.

They were well into the third jar of beans, the revolver lying on the table between them, Sarah bound to the chair, her eyes watching every move. Abigail came to stand by her mother's knee, crying quietly, gazing up into Sarah's face, before she laid her head on her lap, inserted her thumb in her mouth, and bravely quieted.

That was so much. God was with her here in the presence of evil. A Psalm of David entered her mind as a softness, a mere powder puff of comfort, but it was enough. "Yea, though I walk through the valley of the shadow of death, I will fear no evil." She sat without terror now.

The two men became relaxed and got up to search for more food, leaving the revolver on the table surrounded by empty bean jars.

"Make her bake the bread dough. Man, I could use a loaf of bread. Some bacon. Butter. She always had that stuff before."

Suddenly, the door was flung open!

Sarah screamed, but the sound was muffled by the scarf around her mouth. Only the bulging of her eyes and the veins in her neck gave away the fact that she had made any sound at all.

Shep! Dear God, the dog! Then there was Manny, shouting commands, his face white and terrible, followed by Hannah entering with a pitch fork.

The dog barked, growled, and latched onto Lemuel Short's leg and would not let go. Glass mason jars went flying across the room, shattering in the corners, the sound of breaking glass mixed with hoarse curses and shouts as Hannah knocked the revolver off the table with the pitch fork.

The second man lunged after it, but Hannah was too quick, dropping the pitch fork and grabbing it up, holding it in two hands, as steady as a rock.

"You want a bullet or the pitch fork?" she asked, her voice calm.

"Leggo! Leggo!" Lemuel Short writhed in the dog's grip. Manny loosened his mother's hands and used the rope to tie Lemuel's hands before ordering Shep to let go. The scarf was used to tie the second man's hands.

"Sit," Manny ordered, pushing them both into chairs.

Sarah grabbed Abby, held her sobbing in her arms.

The second man lunged for the back door. A short command from Manny and the dog was all over him, jaws locking on an arm, a shoulder, a leg, amid piercing screams.

Manny bound them together with many lengths of rope, tied them to chairs. They were bound and restrained far too well to think of getting loose.

It was Hannah who rode to the Klassermans, whipping Goat into an uneven trot that drained every ounce of strength from his already weary body.

She found no one at home, the doors locked firmly, the only sound the milling around of a few cattle around the haystacks, the wind whistling along the ornate eaves of the house.

There was nothing else to be done. Hannah grabbed the straw broom, turned the handle toward the closest window, and shoved, cracking the pane into splinters. Risking cuts on the palms of her hands, she reached through until she found the metal clasp on top of the wooden sash, turned it to the left, and pushed up with both hands.

"Thank you," she whispered, as she extended one leg through the opening, bent her back, and slid through. She found the black telephone, the sheriff's number, and dialed carefully, holding her breath with concentration.

It was soon over after the telephone call to the sheriff's office, although Hannah had to leave a winded Goat in the Klassermans' barn and ride home on one of their mean-tempered broncos, which almost unseated her before the ride home started.

The house was filled with men, the yard jammed with automobiles. Hannah opened the barn door to lead the horse through, was calmly sliding the saddle off his wet back, when she heard her name whispered. Chills slid up her back. Her eyes opened wide.

"Hannah! Hannah!"

She turned, tried to locate the whispers. One dark head appeared from the loft, followed by another.

"Eli! Mary!"

"Can we come down?"

"Of course. It's over. The sheriff is here."

"We watched you leave on Goat, and we thought we'd better stay here. Do they . . . are they still here? Those men?"

"Get down. Come on. I'll tell you about it."

Two pairs of legs appeared, one after another they scrambled down, threw themselves at Hannah, who hunkered down and held them as if she would never let them go.

She found Sarah seated on the rocking chair inside the living room door, rubbing the bruises on her wrists, a red, ugly welt appearing on her right cheekbone, dark bruises on each side of her mouth where the scarf had dug into her tender flesh.

Hannah stood, unsure. The words that should have been spoken were all jammed up inside of her, so she said nothing.

Sarah nodded, held her gaze. "I'll be all right."

Manny stood in the kitchen, a hand on Shep's head, the only restraint the dog required. Jealousy flickered through Hannah, the one thing Manny had done that out-maneuvered his sister, and it didn't sit well with her.

Shep was the undoubted hero. She eyed him. Looked into those yellowish brown dog eyes. He stared back at her intently, and his tail did not move an inch.

I know you don't like me, you dumb dog. I don't like you either. But maybe I should.

Hannah never watched them untie the two men, or escort them to the car. She could hardly stand to look at their wrinkled, sullen faces. Baggy old trousers with holes in them from the dog's teeth. Blood all over everything. Green bean juice on their coat fronts. Greasy long hair and yellow teeth like a mule's. She had no mercy on them. She didn't pity either one, not even a thin slice of sympathy.

Sarah and Manny talked with the sheriff and the investigators who asked questions and wrote reports.

Hannah didn't talk, mostly for the fact that she didn't like these men, either. Why did they have to ask all these nosy questions? They could stick them into the jailhouse without knowing every tiny piece of information. It was a wonder they didn't ask what kind of bean seeds they'd planted, and what type of jars they used to preserve them.

They should all leave now, go home or to the sheriff's office in Pine, or wherever it was that they all belonged.

The man asking all the questions had a congested nose, speaking with a nasal twang, the way your voice came out if you put a clothespin on top of it. He kept sniffing, drawing air through his thin nostrils, until Hannah wanted to give him a handkerchief and tell him to use it! Blow as hard as he could. She bet it would be wondrous!

His sideburns were so long she couldn't tell if he has thought about growing a beard along the side of his face, then changed his mind but didn't finish shaving it off. Maybe he couldn't grow anything on his chin.

Sarah was unfailing in her kindness, speaking clearly, trying to remember to the best of her ability, Manny helping her over the difficult places.

Hannah glared at the dog, then at the sheriff, sniffed back at the investigator until she'd had enough. She told them all that her mother needed to rest and would they please finish up.

Of course, they were the law, so they only raised their eyebrows in her direction and stayed on course.

It was only after everyone had finally driven out the gravelly road and the last bit of dust had settled that they realized the fire had gone out. The house was cold, the floor littered with broken glass and splotches of blood, and Abby was hungry and needed her diaper changed.

They all worked together, setting things to rights. They spoke very little until the kitchen floor was swept, Hannah had scrubbed it on her hands and knees, Sarah set the bread to baking, and Manny and Shep fed the livestock.

No one except Abby was hungry, a sense of shock permeating the house like a sour odor. They tried to talk about the incident, but the horror was too real, so their voices stilled and became quiet.

Sarah wondered if it wasn't the same for all of them. The disbelief cut through their comfort level like the ragged edge of a saw. How could a nice man like Lemuel Short, a sweet, fatherly type, turn from his humanity into this animal? Which one was the real Lemuel Short?

For Sarah, the hardest part had not been the physical abuse. It was when the children recognized him, the gladness in their eyes as they looked up, only to have their trust so horribly shattered.

As was her own. Would she ever be able to look on strangers with the same kind of trust as before?

After she finally laid her head on her pillow, sighing deeply, she held her throbbing wrists, then switched to the opposite side, the side of her face that had not been smacked.

He just plowed his fist into the side of my face, she thought wryly. Well, just add this one to the long list of new experiences on the plains, this hateful, unforgiving land of drought and cold and sweltering heat and now thieving men turned into monsters.

She shivered involuntarily. She tried, bravely, to fight these thoughts. How many days had she put on a fresh, new face to begin another day, the rest of her life projected on a screen by the move to North Dakota?

How many battles had she won with goodness, faith, and trust in God and mankind? But now, it was time to face the dark visage of reality. She was afraid. So horribly afraid.

What would keep this incident from being repeated? Couldn't you blame this endless expanse of dried-out land for producing people like Lemuel? He had told her his story and she had believed him. Not every woman could survive, no matter how deep her faith.

Allowing these thoughts to inhabit her mind made her feel like a traitor, like someone who betrays their country.

Somehow, in her heart, admitted to no one and seen by no one, she raised the white flag of surrender. Just go home, return to civilization as we have always known it. But then, there was Ben Millers and Ike Lapps, the new Stoltzfuses, and the bachelors. Her father and brothers would be coming in spring. Safety in numbers. Or was there?

She saw only the expression of trust on her children's faces when she closed her eyes, so she kept them open, watched the stars winking through the gap in the bedroom curtain, rubbed her wrists, and fought the negative thoughts with prayer, until God seemed to be in the room with her, comforting her in her time of greatest need.

And yet, she wept far into the night, the heaving of her quiet sobs the sound of so many high-plains women before her.

CHAPTER 21

THE BITING WINDS OF WINTER SEEMED TO INTENSIFY EVERY WEEK, A dry cold, as harsh as a saw's teeth. Into November, December, past Christmas, and there was no snow, only the endless gale winds that swept from the north, scouring the land with their harsh moaning sounds, bending the dry, brittle vegetation, boiling up clouds of cold gray dust that covered every available surface with a fine and cumbersome grit.

Hands and faces were chapped, dried out with the strength of the arid cold. The cows tore at the haystacks and drank water from the holes Manny chopped in the frozen water tank. The windmill spun and creaked in the cold, forming a swollen river of ice where the tank overflowed.

Many days were bleak, sunless, without cheer. Mary and Eli hunched over their school work, their heads in their hands propped up by one elbow. The provisions in the pantry ran low, supplemented only by Hannah's wages from Rocher's Hardware.

Wolves howled at night, and the terrifying ripples of sound kept Hannah from restful sleep. She trusted the cows to defend themselves, but the high, primal pitch of the wolves baying sent shivers of unease up her spine.

They dressed in coats, scarves, worn gloves and boots, rode out past the tank, across the windswept plains, their guns held across their saddle horns. When they came upon the wandering herd, Hannah knew before they counted that they weren't all present.

Surely they had defended themselves this winter, if they were capable of defending themselves in the deep snows of the preceding winter.

They came upon the grisly scene of mutilated calves and cows, not a few, but six carcasses in various stages of mutilation. Hannah's face showed no emotion, pale as the gray sky, her eyes black daggers of hardened resolve.

Manny picked up his gun, dismounted, and stood looking down at the remains of a calf, not believing the amount of destruction.

"Why? Why?" he asked finally.

Hannah shrugged coldly.

"Why didn't they stay around the buildings? Shep would have alerted us to any wolves."

He turned away and poked the flopping leg of a dead yearling, his face a mask of pain and anxiety.

"Wolves couldn't run in the snow," Hannah said, her words hard and clipped.

"You mean last winter?"

Hannah nodded.

They counted the cattle. The large, oversized cow, the bull, and three remaining young cows. Five head of cattle.

"Not much left," Manny remarked, shaking his head.

"Enough. I have my job. You'll have to get one. We have enough. As long as we're able to keep food on the table, we'll keep the homestead. We have others, now, Amish brethren to help us through."

Manny looked at Hannah. "You said that?" he asked, a small smile on his face.

"It's true. They won't let us starve."

They rode back slowly and talked of penning the remaining cows. Wild as deer, especially that old, oversized one. They'd need better horsepower to round them up, then there was no promise they'd stay within the confines of the posts and few strands of barbed wire that enclosed most of the barnyard.

"It will snow soon," Manny said, trying to bolster his spirits as well as Hannah's.

"Yeah, I think so."

"Will you tell Mam, or shall I?" Manny asked, always thinking of his mother's well-being.

"You can."

Manny told Sarah. Her face registered no surprise, no alarm, nothing. Manny wasn't sure his mother had heard him correctly, and repeated his words.

When she looked at him, it was like looking into someone's eyes where there was no emotion, no feeling, a barren place calloused by too much suffering.

"Man!" he said sharply.

Sarah started, blinked, said yes, the wolves had done them a nasty turn, but perhaps they'd move on, God willing. Words spoken without caring or conviction, only spoken out of necessity.

The winter months came and went, days marching in slow succession. Firewood was becoming scarce, vegetables rolling around in the bottom of the bin, an ominous sound portending tight, empty stomachs that struck fear in Sarah's heart.

She wrote letters questioning her father's and brothers' reluctance to commit themselves to a date—sometime in April or May.

The letter Hannah brought back from town deepened a gnawing unease, almost like an excitement at the idea of surrender.

Dear Daughter,

I hope you are all well.

This letter is written in Jesus' Name, hoping you can take this news as it is written, in love, to all of you.

I regret to inform you that our move to North Dakota has been cancelled for the present time. I have other daughters who think it unwise, and since Ben and Elam have taken up a farrier business from Jeremiah Riehl, we have chosen to stay.

Snow is abundant this year, but milk prices are holding steady, so it is a joy to load the milk cans on the bobsled and take them to town.

Sarah's hands shook. She gripped the paper until her knuckles whitened, her dark eyes boring into the words from her thin, white face, her mind refusing to accept this monumental disappointment. She read on.

I thank you for the check you wrote and sent to me. It is a generous repayment,

and I'm glad you are doing well, the cattle thriving.

Sarah blinked, tried to collect her scattered thoughts, as they raced in paranoid circles. Dat, we aren't thriving. The cows are dead, torn apart by long, lean wolves of the prairie. Thin, hungry animals that live from day to day on what they can kill, running across a lean and hungry land that shows no mercy to homesteaders.

She put down the letter, grasped the thin remnants of her old coat around her body, leaned forward, and rocked from side to side, her eyes closed, dry, the absence of tears a testament to the hardened spirit within.

Snow. Milk. So much rich, creamy milk they hauled it away on a bobsled with Belgians, huge, healthy animals that ate oats and corn and were stabled in a barn made of stone and heavy lumber, painted white, a row of cupolas marching across the peak in perfect symmetry. It was all she had ever known.

She could smell the heavy cream, feel the smooth sides of the glass butter churn, the slow creak of the iron handle that turned the wooden paddles, the schlomp, schlomp of the agitated cream that solidified into butter.

A physical longing stabbed through her stomach, but she only clutched her arms more tightly. It was little Abby coming to rest her head on her mother's knee, that shook her from her reverie. She lifted her head, smiled wanly, gathered Abby in her arms and bent her head over the cold little form.

The house was so cold. She was trying to stretch the firewood, hoping to make it last till spring, but without snow, the foundation and the cracks around windows and doors would seep cold and dust particles that moved about the house like a physical discomfort. Woolen socks and cracked leather shoes were not enough to keep toes from numbing and chills from racing across thin shoulders.

She added a stick of wood to the stove, closing the damper to make it last longer. She longed to open the draft, hear the roaring of the fire, the crackling, leaping flames that devoured the wood and turned the stove top cherry red.

Hannah spent her days stalking from the house to the barn, a tall, thin cold-wracked pack of anxiety, her dark eyes lifted to the sky, searching for snow, the elusive white moisture that would warm the foundation of the house and replenish the grasses that fed her few remaining cattle.

Manny rode the old horse, Goat, trying to keep the cows as close to the haystacks as possible, the mean-natured cow, always a threat without a better horse to dodge her belligerent advances. The bull was more stoic, enduring a bit of prodding with aplomb, until the old cow became too agitated, and he'd begin bellowing low and mean, throwing dust up over his shoulder with the strength of a mighty cloven hoof.

The cold intensified, a strange, dry sub-zero temperature that blackened fingers and toes without warning. Hank Jenkins landed in the hospital in Dorchester, two of his toes partially amputated, they were so badly frozen. Hod said in all his days on the plains, he'd never seen anything like this, as if the clouds withheld every snowflake, every bit of ice that needed to fall.

There were the church services to look forward to, the fellowship with Ben Millers and Ike Lapps, but all that cold, dry winter Sarah could not put her heart into the fledgling community.

The sermons were preached by the new Elam Stoltzfus, who was not an ordained minister, but since they needed a speaker, he had plenty to say concerning the Bible and the Plain way of life.

Somehow, the weak singing led by Ben Miller seemed a spinoff of the real thing, that two-toned swell of song that rolled to the ceiling of an Amish house and rolled out the window on the beauty of the notes. It seemed unholy, somehow, the person's words, thinking himself a gifted speaker when, in reality, he was not.

Ike Lapp's children were thin and riddled with cold sores, hacking coughs, and mucus that ran in an endless yellow stream from their poor, red, chapped noses.

Houses were cold, even Ben Miller's, the one with the best stove among the Amish.

There just weren't very many trees for firewood. The feed mill sold coal, but there was no extra money for Ike Lapps or the Detweilers. Ike said he was experimenting with twisted hay. It didn't last long, but made a hot fire. His wife shot him a look of reproach, and Sarah could not blame her.

But twisting hay is what it came to toward the end of February when the cold became unbearable. They shivered through their scant breakfast, the hot cornmeal mush steaming in the cold air, burning their tongues in their haste to fill their stomachs.

When had it come to this? How like a thief in the night this cold crept in and left them with scarce provisions. Hannah still traveled to the Rochers' store two days a week, one for items they needed to keep real hunger at bay and one to help buy seeds and raise some money for other necessities or to repay their grandfather.

Doris Rocher was wasting away, thin as a stick, refusing food, whispering words to Hannah, words of homesickness and irritation, saying she was going home on the train by herself for the second time, and seemingly proud of this fact.

Hannah had no patience for this self-absorbed woman. Her husband ran a hardware store, perhaps only minimally successful, but then, weren't many places of business just that in these years of hardship? Doris had a nice warm house, heated with coal, snug and cozy, plenty to eat, a telephone, and electricity.

Hannah worked all day, rearranging shelves, dusting, making signs, and then she was sent to the kitchen to clean for Doris. Harry gave her a pleading look, one she knew well, the same hangdog look he displayed every time he looked at his wife.

Don't go looking for pity from her, Hannah thought. There is none. It's gone.

"All right," she said brusquely, brushing him off like a whining fly.

"Try and lift her spirits, would you, Hannah?" he asked, his eyes like a Basset hound.

Hannah turned away, sickened, kept a straight face, and set to work, ignoring Doris who sat propped on a chair with a pile of pillows holding her up like a sagging rag doll.

The kitchen was pleasant, or as pleasant as any room could be on a gray wintry day with the wind buffeting the wooden siding, rasping around the cracks in the window like teeth on a comb. The bulbs on the ceiling cast a yellow haze over everything, the corners illuminated with reading lamps.

White lace doilies hung over the backs of the chairs, over the stuffed arms of davenports and the Queen Anne chairs, which were upholstered in flowered prints. China cabinets displayed ceramic dogs, cats, ladies with parasols, teapots, rabbits, horses, men in top hats, and row upon row of glass objects.

Doris lifted a hand, crooked one finger to beckon Hannah closer.

"What?" Hannah asked loudly. Talk to me, she thought. You can speak.

"I want the ceramics washed," Doris whispered.

"All of them?" Hannah asked loudly, raising one eyebrow. Doris nodded.

"Shall I put them back after they're clean?"

"No. No. In a trunk. Upstairs in the blue guest room there's a small wooden trunk. Newspapers are in the washroom. Wash and dry them and pack them in the trunk."

Hannah did as she was told. She enjoyed washing the odd little glass and ceramic creatures, rinsing and drying them, rolling them in newspaper and packing them away.

Halfway through, Harry walked into the room, stood and watched Hannah with an odd expression before asking Doris what was going on.

"I'm packing." The curt words were loaded with malice and ill will. Like a concealed weapon, she showed him the gleaming barrel of her mental and emotional revolver.

She received the response she was hoping for. Harry fell on his knees, took his wife's hands in his visibly trembling ones, and begged her over and over to reconsider.

The longer the theatrics continued, the faster Hannah worked, slamming the newspaper wrapped objects into the yawning trunk.

"Careful there!"

If Hannah would not have to depend on the wages from this man, she'd break every one of those piddling ceramics and make him drive her home. What was wrong with these people? He obviously would have a nicer life without her, so why not let her go? And if she wanted to go home so badly, then go! Leave already. What a bunch of malarkey! Like two children that needed disciplining.

She thought of her own mother, the adaptation she had made, the grace in which she had accepted the ranch, never complaining, always cheerful. Well, Manny's illness had been rough. Even the experience with old Lemuel Short had been hard for her. But still she was stoic and accepting. She was here in North Dakota for the long haul, supporting Hannah's dream of the Bar S.

Superiority flapped its wings and settled on Hannah's shoulder, making her oblivious to the intense struggles her patient mother suffered still.

"Oh, Harry! Sell the store. Sell out, I implore you. Return to Baltimore with me. If you don't, I must go alone. I will die in my hometown without the support of my betrothed."

"Oh, my darling woman, we are more than betrothed. We are united in marriage. We are as one flesh. We cannot separate!" Harry's voice rose to a strident crescendo.

Hannah fled to the back room. Her hands over her ears, she hunkered down, determined to shut out the sound of those falsely sticky-sweet voices.

What an absolute farce! It sickened her. If one cared for the other even half of what their mouths uttered, they would reside in peace, either in Baltimore, Maryland, or in Pine, North Dakota.

She was going to march in there and let them have it. She carried a few more newspapers to the table, plunked them down, took a deep breath, and asked them to stop.

Harry looked at her. Doris narrowed her eyes. "If either one of you loved the other as much as you say, then you'd be happy together, it doesn't matter where."

And that was only the beginning. In the end, she was fired by an irate Harry Rocher and his indignant, resurrected wife. Hannah collected her pay and Harry drove her home in stone cold silence. He ushered her out car door with a curt, "Goodbye," leaving Hannah standing in front of the ranch house in the raw wind, watching the car disappear into a cloud of dust that rolled across the brown plains.

Sarah reacted to Hannah's news with consternation. "Hannah, how will we survive? It's our only hope, now that the herd is depleted."

"We still have some. It's not depleted."

"But we need to have a way to get provisions until the herd is built back up, which could be two years. Jobs are scarce. If it doesn't snow, when spring comes the drought will continue. And how will we live?"

"I'll get a job. Didn't Manny find anything yet?"

"Not yet."

Hannah went to feed the horses, stomped angrily around the barn, yelled at Manny for dumping saddles and bridles in the corner instead of hanging them on the nails provided for that purpose.

She found Pete lying down, was not surprised to touch his neck and find it stiff and cold, his eyes glazed over with the dull look of death.

So, that was that, she thought. Dead. Finally, the poor old thing. Well, they were down to one scrawny horse, five head of cattle, a long year of drought, clouds that refused to send rain, and, very likely, God Himself had forgot about them. Bitter thoughts, but better than no thoughts at all.

They dragged Pete out using a bewildered Goat, left him lying on the prairie, figured the coyotes, vultures, eagles, crows, and whatever other hungry scavengers would find him and have a square meal.

Manny didn't think the wolves would come so close to the buildings, and, if they did, well, the dead horse would be easier than bringing down a cow.

They came in from completing the task, twisted a wagonload of hay to supplement the firewood supply, then pulled it to the stoop of the wash house, covered it with a piece of canvas, and let themselves in the back door, stomping their boots to keep their feet from becoming numb.

The house was not warm, but it was more comfortable than outside. Sarah had used one turnip and two potatoes, cut them in chunks and stewed them with prairie hens, simmering the pot on the stove until the rich broth permeated the whole house with its savory aroma.

The news of Pete's death was taken without surprise, the poor horse unable to rid his body of any liquid matter. They knew it would only be a matter of time.

Hannah was strangely quiet while they ate. The good stew was sopped up with crusty bread, turning the children's cheeks red, giving them renewed vigor to talk and laugh, punch each other, lift their faces, and giggle at their own silliness.

Baby Abby looked at the ceiling, squeezed her eyes, and opened her mouth, howling like a coyote, trying to be silly and get her share of attention from everyone else.

They laughed. Outside, the wind scoured the house with dust that it picked up and flung against the walls, crackling against the windows, then roaring away into the night.

Hannah brooded beside the cookstove, her legs thrust out in front of her like two slim saplings, her eyes black with too much thinking.

"The hay really helps with the cooking," Sarah said, out of a need to raise Hannah's spirits.

"Yeah, that's good. We don't have many cows to eat our store of hay."

"Is it serious again?" Sarah asked.

"What do you think? Pete's gone, I was fired. If this drought continues, there's only one thing to do. Get another job, both Manny and I. I don't know what we'll do if it doesn't rain in the spring."

"God will provide," Sarah said softly.

Manny nodded, a reverence showing in his soft brown eyes.

"Yeah. Well, it's good you can say that. What if He doesn't? What if this is the beginning of a three- or four-year drought?

Would you stay?" The question was like barbed wire hurled at Sarah by Hannah's hands.

Sarah winced, hoped it didn't show. Firmly, she sat on a kitchen chair and turned to face Hannah with a steady gaze.

"No one would. Not even the town of Pine would stay."

"You don't know. You're just saying."

"Hannah." That lilt at the end of her name, a sweet, soft warning. So, the divide was beginning again. She was thinking of giving up. Panic mounted in Hannah's chest as she watched her mother's face.

"We can make it. I can get another horse. From Jerry."

Manny raised his eyebrows, looking at his mother over the uncovered head of his sister.

They both rode to Pine on Goat. An embarrassment to be seen on the back of the poor, scrawny creature, so Hannah walked after the buildings came into view.

Faces red with the sweep of raw air, hands and feet numb with the cold, they walked through the feed-mill door, accosted by the stares of a group of grimy men peering out from under their stained, battered hats. The owner behind the counter was lean and wrinkled, his eyes bulging out of his head like egg yolks.

"What kin' I do fer ye young 'uns?"

Manny straightened his shoulders, spoke in a clear tone, asking for work.

"You them Detweilers?"

"Yessir."

He stroked his beardless chin, chewed on the eraser of his yellow pencil, picked a piece of it off his tongue, examined it, wiped the tips of his fingers on his trousers, squinted, coughed, wiped his mouth with a filthy brown handkerchief and shook his head.

"Wish I could. Times is hard. You got your cattle yet?"

"Yessir." This from Hannah.

"Wolves ain't got any? Yer lucky. Most folks lost quite a few. Easy for them with no snow."

"We lost five, sir," Manny said, providing the truth.

Hannah glared at the mill owner, swept the onlookers with her proud stare, pulled Manny away by the shoulder and clomped across the creaking wooden floor and out the door, banging it shut behind her.

"Hoity-toity," remarked Abram Jacobs.

The sewing and alterations place was stuffy, a small room blue with cigarette smoke, acrid with the smell of human perspiration.

The owner shook her head, the ashes tumbling from the cigarette she held between thin lips. "Have a waiting list," was all she said.

Manny did no better at the garage, the mechanic telling him he had enough to do without training a young 'un.

They stood together on the lee side of the driving wind. Hannah said there was one more place, but she'd rather go hungry than work for her.

"Who?" Manny asked.

"That Betsy at the café."

"What's wrong with her?"

"She reminds me of the old cow. The one that killed our father."

Manny smiled, shrugged his shoulders.

That was where Hannah found employment. Three days a week. Had to find her own way there and back. Goat. The only available form of transportation.

But she lifted her chin, squared her thin shoulders, and told Betsy she'd take it. She had no other choice. It was that or allow the long, bony fingers of starvation to clench all of them in the grip they had known before.

She could do it. She could go ask Jerry Riehl for the palomino, still uncertain which job would be most difficult.

CHAPTER 22

Hannah thought God must have remembered them when Jerry Riehl arrived in his light buggy, driving a horse she had never seen. Now she would not need to ride over on Goat, that poor thing had enough to do pulling the work load around the ranch without Pete.

Jerry was not the same, open, friendly person he had been. His face seemed pale, set.

When Hannah followed Manny out to greet him, he smiled at both of them, but it was a pinched smile. Tension played around his mouth, his eyes turned often to the leaden sky.

"Is this usual, the normal way, to have no snow?" he asked.

"First winter we've seen like this," Manny replied.

"There will be no planting in the spring if we get no snow or rain. Jake wants to go back. Ben Miller says it's foolish to stay if we don't get any moisture. Wolves got a bunch of Ike Lapp's heifers. His kids are going hungry."

His words raked themselves across Hannah's mind, inflicting a deep and awful hurt.

"It'll soon snow!" she burst out, to hide the pain. "One of these days the blizzards of March and April will arrive and the grass will spring up like never before."

Jerry found her eyes with his. Their gazes held. He saw the feverish determination in hers, she saw the doubt in his. Each one knew the clash of wills with the other.

"Come on in, Jerry. We'll find us a cup of coffee," Manny said, cheerfully.

Hannah followed them to the barn, watched them unhitch. Here was a real buggy horse. Sturdy, long and lean, built for stamina, the miles eaten away by the tireless hooves placed on the road. This horse could easily run ten or twelve miles without exertion, the light buggy pulled along like an afterthought.

"Nice horse," she said amiably.

Jerry nodded. "No relation to King or Duke."

"Doesn't surprise me."

"Where's Pete?"

"Well, between the coyotes, vultures, and whatever other hungry creature roaming these plains, he's pretty much eaten up," Manny said, shaking his head at the thought.

"So, he didn't make it then?"

"No."

"Poor old coot. He was a good one."

"Yes, he was. My father drove a double team of those Haflingers' all the way out here. Hundreds of miles," Manny said, proudly.

Jerry shook his head.

Hannah fought down her rising sense of irritation. How could he be proud? The thought of that journey was a memory she would like to erase, a humiliation.

"You have to admire the pioneer spirit of the man," Jerry said, giving Manny a wry smile.

Manny grinned back. "Yeah, he had that. His faith too. He was a big believer in God's generosity, always looking for miracles and blessings along the way."

Hannah glared and said, "He was a dreamer. He lived in a world of unreality where things were made of fluff. Like a dandelion seed on the wind. That was our father."

"Hannah!" Manny stopped, suddenly knowing that to press his point would only bring the eruption of the volcano of bad memories Hannah harbored within herself.

"It's true."

Sarah was glad to see them come in out of the cold. She set steaming cups of coffee before them, apologized for the lack of food, pie, or small cakes to set out.

"I can't imagine the pantry has come to be so low so quickly," she said softly.

"You have enough, though?" Jerry asked, his voice tinged with so much kindness that Hannah felt a lump rising in her throat.

They spoke of the weather, the drought, the cold, and the dust. Hannah did not join in.

Did they ever speak of anything else? It would snow and rain. Spring always brought moisture.

Tension mounted as Jerry spoke reluctantly of Jake Fisher's thoughts about returning to Lancaster County, and Ike Lapp's inability to keep his family fed comfortably.

Sarah's eyes turned involuntarily to the pantry.

Hannah spoke then, her words hard, falling like metallic objects. They were hard to listen to, rife with disgust at anyone who even thought of returning. Pioneers lived through drought, worse than this. Amish in Lancaster County were the wrong people to settle the West, living in ease and comfort all their lives, cloistered, their sense of community stronger than the slightest sense of adventure.

Jerry's eyes snapped, his suppressed anger rising like steam. "Hannah, you do realize if this drought does continue, we will be forced to leave. It has nothing to do with what we want. Think of our horses, our cattle. Your cattle. No rain, no grass."

"You are only settling on a future, surmising it will not rain. Of course it will. Spring always brings moisture," she said tartly.

Jerry left that day with no idea that Hannah was in need of a horse. Hannah was so angry she decided to walk to the café in Pine if she had to. She'd never ask that arrogant man for so much as a stick.

Manny took it on himself to ride over to the Jenkinses to ask for a horse, telling them of Hannah's need. Of course, Hod provided.

A brown horse with a black mane and tail, an evil glint in his bulging eyes, large yellow teeth he bared repeatedly, as if the sight of them would buy him instant control over any human being.

He took a strong dislike to Hannah, who promptly named him Buck, knowing half of North Dakota's wild-eyed, half-broke mustangs were called Buck.

Hannah was as determined to ride him as Buck was determined she wouldn't. Dust flew from the area surrounding the barn as he shied, crow hopped, and kicked his way across the dead grass and dirt.

After one especially bad hopping, he arched his back and leaped like a grasshopper, unseating Hannah, who slid sideways off the saddle, landing on one shoulder, her legs folding like a piece of fabric beneath her.

She got to her feet, grasped her stomach and gasped in pain, every gulping breath a shooting pain in her ribs.

Manny caught Buck, then came to stand by her, watching quietly, knowing his sister well. Any word of condolence would be batted to the ground like a whining insect, her pride so thoroughly battered that no could help.

She was bent over, taking small painful breaths, her eyes wide as if she was astonished. After a while, she straightened slowly, ran a hand across her left side, grimaced, flopped a hand on her shoulder, and squeezed. She gave a small laugh, almost a sob.

"Give me the reins."

"You can't, Hannah. You can't."

"I can, and I will."

Manny stood helplessly, as Hannah, white-faced, her mouth contorted with pain, grabbed the reins, swung herself into the

saddle with obvious effort, and kept her seat as the horse immediately began his maneuvers to unseat her.

Sarah came from the house, shouting, waving her arms. This
was too much for her, so she tried to put a stop to the horrible
spectacle of Hannah's life being in danger.

"Manny, you must stop this!" she pleaded.

"You know she won't stop, Mam."

They watched as she kept her seat, a firm hand on the reins.
She goaded the unruly horse with the stirrups, kicking her legs
to the side to bring them crashing against his sides, which only
served the purpose of antagonizing him further.

The horse hunched his back, hopped, kicked, and shied
sideways, but Hannah remained seated, grim with pain and
single-mindedness. She was staying on this cranky horse, there
were no two ways to look at it.

Unseated again, she landed hard on her backside. Her chin
flopped onto her chest, and her teeth gouged a formidable hole
in her tongue, blood pouring from the wound and forming a
grotesque appearance of serious injury, when in truth, the worse
abuse was to her pride.

Sarah cried out, grabbed Hannah's arm, her face terrible
with fear and outrage. "Hannah! You must stop! You have to
stop this nonsense and come to the house. That horse will do
you serious harm."

Hannah took up her skirt hem to staunch the flow of blood,
refused her mother's pleading, grabbed the reins from Manny,
and got back on the horse, who eyed her with belligerence, and
began his antics all over again.

When she flew through the air a third time, coming down
hard on one knee, her head flopping forward like a rag doll,
Sarah cried out and ran to her, crying in earnest as she tried to
pick her daughter up.

This time, Hannah followed her mother to the house, hob-
bling on one good leg, dragging the other, blood running from

her mouth, splattered with dust and dirt, sniffing back the blood and mucus that poured from her nose.

She was spitting and gagging on the porch, so Sarah stayed with her, watching to make sure she wouldn't be sick, or faint from the pain.

They went inside as Eli and Mary watched wide-eyed, their pencils poised above the tablets they were writing on.

"What happened?" Mary quavered.

"Oh my, children. Weren't you watching from the window?" Sarah asked, applying a cold washcloth to Hannah's mouth.

"Ouch!" Hannah yelled, flinging the washcloth across the room.

"She was trying to ride a new horse," Sarah called back over her shoulder as she bent to retrieve the washcloth.

So be it, then, she thought. Let her suffer. She rinsed the cloth, put in the washtub with the other soiled laundry, and set to punching down her bread dough.

Hannah hobbled to the bathroom, bent to peer into the mirror. The painful throbbing in her mouth had to be more than a cut in her tongue. It was. She'd knocked a tooth out, a bleeding black spot where the tooth should have been. At least it was on the bottom. No one would notice. Must have gone clear through her tongue.

No cold washcloth was going to do a bit of good. She'd have pain for days, so she may as well get used to it. She opened a drawer, got out a clean rag, and applied it, then sat on the wooden rocking chair and closed her eyes.

The sound of Sarah punching bread dough, working it, kneading with her hands, was strangely comforting. It told Hannah that her mother would let her alone to handle her wounds in her own way, that she was capable of doing just that, and life would go on the way it had before.

The scratch of the children's pencils on paper, Abby's soft guttural baby talk, the crackle of the fire in the firebox of the kitchen range, were all comforting, normal sounds of everyday life. She'd heal. No use telling anyone she had a missing tooth. It was no one's business.

But her knee was on fire, shooting pains that went from her ankle to her thigh. Tentatively, she moved her foot from left to right. Then she lifted her heel off the floor, resulting in more stinging pain. She could bend it all right, so nothing was broken. Her ribs, she couldn't say. There was a tender spot so sore she could barely place the tip of one finger on it. Likely she had cracked or broken ribs, but that wasn't anyone's business either. She could hide that, as well.

But that night when she went to lie down, she cried out with the sharp sensation in her back, bringing Sarah to the door of her bedroom. Hannah told her she believed there was a mouse under her dresser; it had scared her, running over her foot.

"We'll have to set a trap," Sarah said, and left the room.

There was only one way Hannah could rest, and that was gently rolling on her left side, drawing her knees up to help balance the weight on what she now believed to be a broken rib. Probably more than one.

Luckily, her job at the café started the following Tuesday, which allowed her almost a week to heal. There was no question of getting back on that unruly horse's back until she had healed.

As it was, she rode painfully into Pine on Goat, white-faced, perspiring beneath her layer of heavy coats, the pain almost more than she could bear. Her family needed to eat, so she had to do this. There was no turning back, no self-pity. It was an obstacle that she needed to face, and she did.

Betsy greeted her at the back door with words that were less than kind or caring. "You look washed out, girl. Like you seen a ghost. Well, come on. Git going here. We're on behind. Got a special going. Seems like folks are dirt poor, but these men can come up with a dollar for a cup of coffee and eggs and home fries.

She yelled at Bernice, the sallow, pimply-faced young woman who was shoving a mound of fried potatoes into a huge, black, cast iron skillet.

"Show this one around. Name's Hannah. And watch yer mouth. She ain't used to the kind of language comes from your mouth."

Bernice didn't say hello, offer a hand, not even a nod. "Call me Bernie. This here's the egg pan. Lard up here on the shelf. Them's the eggs. We got sausage, bacon, or steak, but don't use a lot. Folks ain't got the money. Sometimes, the judge from the courthouse comes by and he gits steak. Eats the bloody thing half raw.

"This here's the deep fryer, potato cutter. Hamburgers made in the same pan as the potatoes. Fry 'em hot and crispy. Bread here on the shelf. We hafta make the soups yet. Bean soup, vegetable soup, and rivvel soup with milk. Saltines on a plate. I'm the cook. You're the helper. You do whatever I say, and we'll git along great."

Hannah nodded and thought Bernice was like Buck, all eyes and yellow teeth. Hannah disliked Betsy, Bernice, and every customer she was forced to serve. She hated the way the men ogled her way of dressing, waiting quietly without saying a friendly word while she set down platters of potatoes and eggs, filled coffee cups, her mouth throbbing, her ribs stinging with pain.

If Betsy or Bernice brought their food, there was instant banter, loud laughter, jokes thrown across the room, but the minute Hannah appeared, the silence was stifling.

Well, nothing to do for it. Her mouth hurt too much to talk anyway, so let them gawk at her Amish dress and the *dichly* pinned to her head.

Bernice said her appearance at least shut them up. "Can't stand that Roger Atkins," she said. "He thinks he can come in here and eat like a . . ." She caught herself, then continued, "Like a hog, then leave me or Betsy no tip. Not a penny. Complains about the price of a dollar for his coffee and eggs. I told him the other day if he don't wanna pay it, he can go home to his old lady and eat hers. That made him mad!"

Hannah moved fast, learned what needed to be done, and went ahead and did it without asking. Weak with pain and hunger, she almost cried when Bernice told her they were allowed a half-hour break after the lunch rush.

They were only allowed to eat breakfast leftovers, soup, or bread. Meat was too expensive, and it cost too much to drink the sodas, but they were allowed one cup of coffee or a glass of tea.

Hannah sank gratefully into a rickety old chair in the corner, balanced a bowl of bean soup with one hand and two thick slices of buttered toast on the other. She ate carefully, out of anyone's sight, soaking the toast in the hot broth, eating and savoring every mouthful in spite of the pain.

Surely she had never been so grateful for a hot bowl of soup. Her outlook and energy revived, her cheeks blooming with an attractive blush, she carried out the legendary steak to the judge from the courthouse, the one Bernice had mentioned.

Gray hair lined his temples, but he was younger and far more attractive than Bernice had let on. The judge looked up from the paper he was reading, his brown eyes kindly taking in the strange appearance of this tall girl who brought him breakfast.

The courthouse was in Dorchester, but there was a small, squalid room behind the garage in Pine that served as a sheriff's office. When he came to the dusty little town of Pine with paperwork, or he needed to pick up reports, he liked to stop at Betsy's café for a steak with his eggs.

No one could fire up a grill as hot as Betsy, producing legendary steaks, perfect eggs every time, and biscuits as big as saucers with the consistency of a pillow. Spread with homemade plum jam, it kept him coming back at least once a week.

He had no interest in any of the women who worked at Betsy's, but he enjoyed the easy banter with which he could joust verbally, always giving Betsy a good argument. She knew he was smart—all judges were brilliant—so it was a challenge to voice her strong opinions on any subject. All these farmers and ranchers knew in these parts was the weather, hay, and cows, always in that order.

His name was Dale Jones, in his forties, more or less, never married, never met a girl he couldn't live without. He enjoyed his work, kept a neat house on Ridge Street in Dorchester with the help of the Widow Mary Billing, who was at least sixty and as thin and wrinkled as a strip of beef jerky.

Dale Jones's life was predictable and well-ordered. He presided over the small country courthouse, sending mischief-makers and miscreants to jail, sentencing thieves and drunks and murderers, which were rare but frequent enough to keep him riffling through the occasional law book.

Hannah walked out as if she owned the place, tall, thin, and disdainful, carrying the tray as if she was queen for the day. She placed it in front of him with the long, tapered fingers on her well-shaped hands, stepped back, and glared at him, then turned on her heel and left.

Dale Jones blinked twice. He felt an ill-timed flush suffuse his face, the need to follow her to apologize for being here at the café, in fact, to make amends for his existence, and for the fact that it didn't snow this winter. He watched the swinging door until it was still, then shivered with the sensation of a cold winter wind swirling over his table.

He picked up his fork, broke the yolk of an egg, lifted his head to look at the swinging door to the kitchen again. He was afraid she would return; afraid she would not.

The judge picked up his serrated steak knife, proceeded with his usual sawing motion, severing a nice mouthful, the crispy outer edge falling away as he worked. He used his fork to spike a piece and thrust it into his mouth.

Back in the kitchen, Betsy ordered Hannah back out to his table. "The first rule is, serve the food, let him eat, then go see if he needs a refill of his drink, or if he wants anything else."

Hannah eyed her boss, cold-eyed, her arms crossed, fingers gripping her elbows. "He can ask."

Betsy stepped closer, shoved her face into Hannah's startled one. "You wanna work for me, you do as you're told. I run the show here. You don't. Go!"

Hannah went. She had never felt so silly, so unnecessary. How do you ask someone if their meal is to their liking? What if it wasn't? What if he didn't want a refill? What if he wished she didn't exist?

She reached his table. He looked up.

Hannah arched a perfect eyebrow, decided to tell it like it is. "Look, I'm not comfortable asking you if your food is good, or if you need more water. I'm new at this, so if you want something, you'll have to ask."

Dale Jones sat back in his chair, arched an eyebrow back at her, and asked what she meant by that?

"I don't like to serve someone."

"Then you had better look for another job."

"There is none."

"Hard times?"

Hannah nodded and left.

Betsy returned, immediately began her garrulous queries, whereupon Dale immediately changed the subject, asking who the new girl was, with just the right amount of nonchalance.

"Oh, they're homesteaders. Buncha Amish came out here thinkin' to git rich with horses and windmills and whatever else they got goin'. This Detweiler family's been here awhile. The old man was killed by a crazy cow, wife and kids hangin' on. This is the oldest daughter. Tough as nails. The only reason they stay here. Don't look fer any of 'em to outlast the drought, if it keeps on."

"How do they make a living?" he asked.

"Cows. A herd they started. Gardening. The mother's old man back wherever they come from helps 'em out. S' what folks is sayin', although I can't rightly tell."

Dale Jones nodded, chewed, contemplated the word "Amish." He slanted a look at Betsy.

"What's Amish mean?"

"Beats me. They dress weird. Sloppy-lookin' homemade stuff. Supposed ta be better'n normal folks, but I kin tell you right off, this Hannah ain't. I know lotsa people behave better'n her."

"That's her name? Hannah?"

"Yep."

Betsy changed the subject to the drought, the awful, bone-chilling cold, and if it didn't rain until spring it would fix the ranchers.

"This area's gonna be like the Dead Sea. No life, if'n it don't rain. You think it wouldn't affect you, huh? Sittin' in that court-house, rakin' in the money. Who's gonna go to court if there ain't nobody around to thieve and carry on?"

Dale Jones ate his steak and shrugged his shoulders. He wished Betsy would go back to the kitchen and allow him to finish in peace. He was not in the mood to listen to more of her gloomy prophesies.

But, of course, she drew back a chair and settled herself into it, leaned back and searched his face.

"You hear about the hardware?"

Dale Jones shook his head.

"They say he's sellin' out. To who, I couldn't say. Wife's crazy in the head. Fred Bird says they're moving east. Back to Balti-more. Harry come in here the other day, looked sick, fish out of water, eyes buggin' outta his head. Shoulda seen him. You know Harry? He's a good man. Good man. You watch, she'll take him back to wherever they come from, he'll leave his heart and soul out here on the plains. He won't last long, you mark my words."

"Who's Fred Bird?"

"You know Fred. Tall and skinny. Ranches out your way. Runs a few cattle, some sheep. He owns part of the feed mill."

Dale Jones nodded, pushed his chair back and reached for a toothpick. His eyes slid to the kitchen door. Betsy noticed. A hot jealousy swelled in her chest.

When the door swung open and Hannah appeared with a tray of clean glass tumblers, Betsy saw Hannah through Dale's eyes.

Creamy, tanned skin, huge dark eyes surrounded by long black lashes. How could anyone have lashes like that if they had no cosmetics available? That tall, easy grace. The small straight nose. Her shoulders held high, her head on the slim neck.

Ah, Betsy knew the confidence of youth. She knew too that hers had dissipated over the years. A once-firm waistline had developed soft rolls, like the black rubber tube of a tire. Jowls, a heavy neck.

Betsy sighed, was suddenly grateful for the ebb and flow of her regular customers, the life she lived in her café, serving ordinary folks in ordinary ways. She didn't need Dale Jones.

CHAPTER 23

APRIL CAME AND WENT. THE COLD BLEW ITSELF OUT AND A WARM, DRY wind took its place. The grass bent and rustled, broken and battered by the winds of winter. Some yellow-green color appeared at the base of the buffalo grass, the sedges, and switch grass, all native grasses that made up the tough, hardy winter pastures.

Some of the ranchers, like the Klassermans, had introduced bromegrass, also crested wheat grass that was better for hay. No new growth showed on any of it, only the rattling of hollow stems, bent by the endless gale, covered by the gray brown dust and sand-like grit.

Hod came over, folded himself down on the porch step, and said he needed help going through Abby's things. They could have most of it.

So on a day when Hannah wasn't working at the café, they drove Goat the seven miles to the Jenkinses, the children riding on the back of the spring wagon, glad to be out of the house and away from the homestead for a day.

They found a dusty box of journals, old black and white speckled composition books with crumbling, yellowed pages, scribbled with lead pencil marks like the scratches of chickens.

"Go ahead n' read," Hod urged them. "You won't hurt nobody. She didn't have anything to hide."

Hannah sat and read, spellbound, surrounded by heaps of old dresses, shoes, tablecloths and white china, dresser scarves and faded magazines.

The first entry was July 21, 1913. Hannah strained to read the barely legible scrawls. *Hot. No rain yet. Garden dry. Two calves born. One of 'em got scours.*

July 24, 1913. *Been so hot all day. No rain. Trying to water whenever I got extra water. Clay took his first step. Miss my momma, but don't do no good thinking on it.*

Hannah got up, went to a rocking chair by the window where the light poured in, revealing much more writing than she had thought was there.

Some days the wind makes me crazy, like I'm about to lose my mind. I have to be stronger or I won't make it one more day. Can't let Hod know, he got his heart set on this here place.

August 3, 1914. *Things isn't good. The baby is scrawny and sickly. I don't want to lose another one. God is watching over us. I hate this prairie, the wind, the separation from other folks. Can't tell Hod.*

Hannah caught her breath. She chewed on the inside of her lower lip. Surely Abby wasn't writing the truth. Surely this was not the way she truly felt. And Hod had no idea.

September 10, 1914. *Getting ready to winter in. Got squash and potatoes in. The onions. Beef cows doing good. Baby taking on some weight. The wind makes me wonder how on earth I will survive the winter. God will watch out for me I guess. I get these awful pains in my heart, standing and looking out across the prairie. There is nothing, as far as I can see, except grass and sky. How is a woman supposed to survive without the pleasure of company. My homesickness is like a growth in my stomach, crowding out my breath, barely allowing me enough air to breathe on my own. I feel only half alive.*

Abby! Hannah sucked in a breath. She held her finger at the page she was reading and turned the composition book from left to right, searching for truth, as if there would be an inscription on the cover that labeled it fiction. She read on, incredulous.

November 11, 1914. *Cooked cornmeal mush. Hod brought home a hundred pound sack. Snow came last night. Good thing we got the meal done. Now I can fry mush. Hens all but quit laying. They'll start again in spring. I dread the night coming on. That's when the loneliness is worst. I wake up with my heart pounding, feel like I'm going crazy. I have to get out of bed so Hod don't know. Don't need to worry him.*

November 23, 1914. *I think I need help. Nights getting worse. Fear something terrible. Need to get help. Maybe I can be strong. Hope so.*

"Mam, come and read this," Hannah called, holding out the black and white notebook. Sarah was folding a stained linen dresser scarf, its border crocheted with a colorful variety of threads. She placed it carefully in a cardboard box, smoothing it with her palm, as if it was a caress for Abby herself.

"Let me see," she said, reaching out for the proffered book.

She read quietly, then lifted startled eyes to Hannah. "What?" she whispered. "Not Abby."

"That's what I thought."

"But she was everything a pioneer woman should be. Tough, resilient. Nothing fazed her. Nothing."

"The death of her little girl baby," Hannah corrected her mother.

"But this? This suffering? You can feel it in the composition book." Sarah shook her head.

Together, they read more entries over the course of time. The cold, the heat, the length of time Abby lived without seeing anyone but Hod and the babies, which must have been Clay, Hank, and Ken.

"Listen," Hannah said. *I am like a bottle filled with tears during the day. The stopper comes out at night with Hod sleeping beside me. Tears run out of my eyes and I can't stop them. But I don't wake up fearful no more, so must be these tears are a good thing. Maybe they'll stop soon, then I'll be all right. God is watching over me, I can tell. Especially when Hod is out riding the prairie.*

February 13, 1916. Days are terrible long. Hod confessed his sin to me. Don't want to write in this book what it was but I made a trip to town and had a talk with her. Marcella Brown-leaf, he said. Part Indian. It's going to take me awhile but I'll get over it. He went to the tavern. Otherwise, it wouldn't have happened. Bible says to forgive, so guess I'll follow God's Word.

Hannah lifted her face and shrieked to the ceiling. "Mam!"

"Shh. Hod will hear."

"She's an awfully good Christian woman, Mam. I bet you anything this is the reason she seemed to rule Hod and the boys. I bet he lived the rest of her days trying to make it up to her. You know, it gave her the upper hand over him."

Sarah looked at Hannah. It was moments like these when she loved her daughter. When Hannah forgot herself long enough to be happy, animated, absorbed in something of interest.

"Could be," Sarah nodded, smiling.

"Listen."

December 3, 1916. No Christmas presents, Hod says. Wolves got too many cows. No money. We have food, no empty stomachs. Killed all the old laying hens. Stuck the meat in Mason jars and cold packed it.

"Sounds like it," Hannah said grimly.

When Hod came in, they packed the journals with the things they would take back home with them. Hod waved them away, saying it was just woman stuff written in there.

"I don't need no books to mind the past. Them days was heaven on earth, every day. Me and Abby and the boys, God's green earth, some good horses, and a buncha ornery cows that bucked the tar outta each other.

"We built this here home with hard work and lotsa good luck. Coundn'ta found a better woman, always happy, kept herself busy, never pined for her ma and pa the way some of 'em done. She was a good woman. None better."

A slow anger burned in Hannah. She couldn't look at him sitting there with his blackened hands spread across his denim-clad knees. Unwashed denim, she'd wager. As satisfied with his own past as she'd ever seen anyone. The man had no idea of the sadness poor Abby had dealt with.

"Where are the boys?" Sarah asked. "We'll soon be through here, so Hannah and I can cook supper for you, leave it on the back of the stove."

Hod looked at Sarah, then nodded, shook his head repeatedly, saying now that would be just awful nice of her.

Reluctantly, Hannah placed the books in the boxes, carried them out to the spring wagon, returned to find her mother peeling potatoes, with Hod hovering at her elbow.

Potatoes! Why did the Jenkinses always have food? It seemed as if their pantry and cellar was always well-stocked, even during the days of drought that stretched on and on.

Hannah decided to ask and was given a good enough answer. They had over one hundred fifty cows. Wolves got a few calves, coyotes maybe, but those longhorns were hard to bring down with their horns. "Take a few away, we won't know the difference," Hod said.

Did he know the Detweilers had only five cows remaining? Her pride firmly in place, Hannah decided to keep that bit of information to herself.

"So, how's the winter treating your herd?" he asked, at the moment Hannah decided not to tell.

"We lost five." This from Sarah, who wouldn't think of keeping anything from Hod.

He whistled low. "So you have what, five more? Six?"

They left the Jenkins ranch that day with Hannah refusing to speak to her mother, a dark cloud of outrage riding above her head. It was none of Hod's business how they were faring.

Besides, he didn't have to stand there and give that low whistle, then search Sarah's eyes before looking at the bright blue overhead light, the dry sky that stayed the same throughout the winter months.

Did Hod see something in Sarah's eyes? They acted like, well, almost if there was a secret attraction, the way they could tell what the other was thinking.

Sarah lifted her face to the sky. "You know, Hannah, if the heat arrives, the grass already parched, what will keep the cows alive? How long will the wells continue to give water, if it hasn't rained for a year?"

"It isn't a year."

"Yes, it is. Our last rainfall was in May of last year."

"You're keeping a journal?"

"No."

"Well, then you don't know."

Sarah rode in silence, Abigail like a sleeping rag doll in her arms, jostled by the movement of the wagon, the steady sound of Goat's hooves on the hard packed dirt. Everywhere, as far as they could see, was a kind of defeated springtime. As if the earth gave its best, valiantly trying to produce one green shoot, then gave itself over to the drought.

There was still hay in the barn. The grass cured on the stalk all around them. As long as the windmill turned and the well gave its water, replenishing the tank, they'd be all right. She had to keep her job at the café, no matter what.

Manny still had not found work, but kept busy cutting trees for firewood. Hannah estimated they had enough old windfalls in the creek bottom to last another four years, maybe five. So, according to her way of thinking, their situation was not dire, yet.

Sarah rode beside Hannah, harboring a secret wish that God would shut the clouds from giving rain for awhile longer. She didn't know where these thoughts came from. She just knew that Abby's journals were past echoes of her own nights, and too many days.

With a glad fierceness, she had returned to the homestead, to the plains, to stay with Mose's grave, her beloved, who lay buried beneath the sod, his soul departed to his God. But her fierce desire to survive, to prosper, had begun to sputter, and now she found it hard to find the remnant of a spark.

To go home. To find peace and fellowship with her sisters. Estrangement was real. It was the amputation of a family tree's limb, injuring the entire tree. She could not speak of her waning need to fellowship with those who had moved here—Ben Millers and Ike Lapps, the new Stoltzfuses. Hadn't her heart leapt when Jerry Riehl spoke of their wish to return home? And then, her father, waiting to arrive. Had that been God's will as well?

Her last letter home had been filled with the situation surrounding them, an act of God, circumstances beyond their control. Would they still have failed, in the face of this drought? She glanced sideways at Hannah. Her face was unknowable, set in stone.

What was she thinking? What would she do when confronted with the fact of their failed homesteading? She wouldn't mind at all if the rest of them returned home. She'd be only too glad to watch them leave.

Sarah sighed deeply. Perhaps it would begin to rain, and they would continue on as before. They would build the herd, build their lives, the church would grow. Clearly, she was confronted with two choices. Which one did she truly desire?

And still the rains did not come. There was no point in planting the garden; the seeds would lay in a row of dust.

When the sun took on the shine of summer's heat, the shimmering waves that spoke of midday fierceness, Sarah stood on the porch, a hand turned palm down to her forehead, shading her eyes from the unrelenting glare, watching the brown grass rustling in the wind. She could see no way to survive. She would wait, say nothing. Someone would surely come to speak of these dire conditions.

Manny walked up on the porch, sweat staining the back of his shirt, his hair lined with moisture. Beads of perspiration formed on his upper lip, and for a moment, Sarah thought she could detect a certain desperation in his dark eyes.

"Getting hot, isn't it, Mam?" he asked, always pleasant, always hopeful.

"Yes, it is."

A comfortable silence stretched between them. Both looked out over the arid land and made no comment, as if they knew their words would be like a cloud of small flies, bothersome and useless.

Sarah had just turned to go in to check on her bread dough, when she thought she saw the beginning of a gray cloud in the west. She hesitated, took her stance by the porch post, one hand held to her forehead, squinting out over the expanse of prairie to the horizon.

"Is that what I think it is?" she asked.

"Where?"

Sarah pointed with a shaking finger. "Does that look like a storm cloud to you?"

Manny looked, then squinted, straining his eyes to see what appeared to be a narrow brown mountain ridge.

"I would say it looks like a storm cloud, except it's the wrong color. It's a yellowish gray brown."

They stood, watching. The cloud increased in size. As it approached, the wind picked up, sending tumbleweeds and loose vegetation hurling ahead of it.

Sarah ducked her head, closed her eyes and spit the dust and grit out of her mouth. Dry grass smacked into them.

There were no prairie hens, no rabbits, gophers, or birds running ahead of the storm, the way it sometimes happened when a thunderstorm moved across the prairie.

On it came. The wind whipped the corners of Sarah's apron, slapped her skirt to her legs, and tore at her covering until the pins pulled her hair.

It roared across the prairie, surrounding them with a thick wall of dust and whipped-up dirt, flung along by the force of the ever-increasing wind.

Sarah cried out, remembering the windows. Inside, Eli and Mary stood wide-eyed, pulling down the wooden, paned windows.

"Will it rain now?" Eli asked, his brown eyes hopeful.

The faith of a child, Sarah thought. Abby ran to her, flung herself into her arms, and held tight, her face hidden in Sarah's neck.

Manny came through the door, struggled to close it behind him, his face pale in the disappearing light. The house took on a yellow sheen, a dark aura of weird light, as the wind shrieked and moaned around them. It was as if the whole house was being scoured by buckets of sand, a hissing, rasping sound above the roar of the wind.

Sarah sat down weakly, gazing at Manny in disbelief. He shook his head. It was literally a storm of dust and dry wind, hurling anything loose ahead of it, grass and weeds, loose boards and scattered hay.

They both thought of the windmill at the same time. Manny grasped the arms of the chair, pulled himself, a question in his eyes.

"No. No. You can't go out in this. The windmill will . . ." her voice faded away.

"Mam, this wind will propel the gears to a frantic pace. It will break the mechanism that operates the pump."

"We have Ben Miller."

And still the wind blew, the dirt scoured the house. Dust seeped in between the sash of the windows, beneath the door frame, even drifting down from the ceiling, as if an invisible hand was scraping it down.

The wind increased, the sound like a scream, setting their teeth on edge. They both thought of Hannah, in town, hoping she would be all right, wondering how long the wind would stay.

Eli huddled on the couch, drew his knees up to his chin, his hands to his ears, blocking out the sound. Mary began to cry softly, cradling herself with her thin arms.

"Come, Mary," Sarah said, above the roar of the wind. She crept into her mother's arms, with Abby, her arms stealing around both of them, reaching out for all the security she could find. Manny sat with his mother, pulled Eli into his own arms, huddled together at the mercy of wind and dust.

In town, men raced for their automobiles, tried to beat the storm to their distant homes dotting the outskirts of the small group of homes and businesses. Many became stranded along the roads, careening haphazardly into ditches or mounds of scattered weeds and dirt, unable to leave the small amount of safety their vehicles afforded.

The town hunkered down, prepared to wait out the worst of it. Betsy seemed to take it in stride, shut doors and windows, talking above the roar of the wind and saying this would bring a change now. "It'll blow the drought out. The rains'll come now."

Hannah stood, stiff with fear and disbelief. The battle that raged within her was worse than the storm of wind and dust outside the café. Her mother and Manny were barely managing to have enough will and determination to stay, no matter how hard they tried to convince Hannah otherwise.

Would this send them straight back to Lancaster County, their land of milk and honey?

Manny had attended the meager church service on Sunday, came home to his supper of bread and stiff, salty cornmeal mush, and talked of Ike Lapp's plight. Talked of that Marybelle, mostly, how she was withering away, much too thin, without proper food.

Hannah knew he cared for her; she could tell by the dreaminess in his eyes. She knew too that for a young man harboring thoughts of a rosy future with the doe-eyed Marybelle, there would be only hardship and disappointment on the prairie.

Only rain would save them. Perhaps it would appear after this, in the form of thunderstorms, the way Betsy said it would.

How had it come to this? This grinding down of wills, flattening hope, leveling even the staunchest spirit? Even Sarah turning into a white-faced, grim-lipped ghost of her former self?

Doddy Stoltzfus would come. His brothers, Ben and Elam, would bring renewed hope. Wasn't hope the necessary ingredient for pioneers?

Hannah sat in the darkened café, the electric lights blinking above them at first, then not blinking back on, leaving them in the gray storm-riddled light of midday.

In the afternoon, when the sun would have been slanting in through the tall front windows, a thin light appeared through the blowing dust and grime. The roaring ceased, trickled down to a more manageable gale, the kind of wind that flapped at skirts and sent light objects flying off porches, twirled leaves and bent tall grasses. Betsy said she may as well go home, if she wasn't afraid the wind would start up again.

Hannah shook her head, waded dust to the barn, hopped on Goat's back, and entered a world of brown dust and dirt that clung to every available surface, flattening the already skeletal grasses and whipping the dry earth into drifts like snow. Where the wind had scoured the loose dirt, only a bare, swept area remained, wide, deep cracks like broken glass separating the soil.

Hannah tied her handkerchief across her mouth and nose, to help breathe better. She could not stop turning her head, her eyes searching every surface, hardly able to absorb this world without life.

It was like the end of the world, when there would be nothing left. A sense of foreboding made her shiver. Was there ever a time when it simply did not rain for more than a year? That in itself seemed an impossibility. It always rained, even here in the West, didn't it?

She had no one to ask, no one who could assure her that the rain would come. Well, God, but He wasn't very reliable, so far.

Yes, she did believe in God. Of course she did. It was unthinkable to go through life without acknowledging a Higher Power. It was just difficult to think of asking for rain, then believing it might happen. When, in truth, it might not.

Look at her father. He called it faith. Was it? Or was he merely determined, assuring himself over and over that God would hear him and do what he wanted if he fasted and prayed hard enough.

What was faith? Assuring oneself that God would do what you wanted? Or was it never asking for anything except God's will, not your own, be done? Faith was a mystery to Hannah, elusive as the wind. You were supposed to be able to move mountains with it, if you owned even a tiny bit, like the size of a mustard seed.

No one could ever move mountains, so did that mean no one had any faith? Maybe faith was not ours to have, but it was supplied by God at the exact moment He wanted us to have it.

Well, enough of these thoughts. Hannah shook herself, freeing her mind from the numbness of unreality that lulled her into a stupor. Nothing seemed real. The prairie seemed like an alien land, a barren place without humanity.

Some places on the road were drifted so high with dirt that Goat had to wade through. His head nodded faithfully as he put one foot in front of the other, staying on course, his horse sense taking him home.

Hannah dreaded her arrival. She knew the question of staying or returning to Pennsylvania would have to come up, and soon. What would she do?

Five battered, wind-driven cattle that lived on worthless, dry grass and water in the tank, likely coming from a well that sank steadily deeper and deeper each month.

She would wait to come to a decision until she spoke to the remaining Amish friends. What about the Klassermans? The Jenkinses? Would these sturdy local folks let the drought get the best of them? She wouldn't believe it until she actually saw them leaving.

As she neared the buildings, she saw the weird angle of the wind mill. The blades of the giant wheel, the metal paddles that caught the breeze so efficiently, spinning the great circle that propelled the water pump up and down, bringing gallons of cold water from the underground stream to the surface hung lifeless, at odd angles, completely still.

She heard the high bawling of the thirsty cattle before she saw them.

CHAPTER 24

THE RIDE TO THE HOMESTEAD IN THE FACE OF THE ONSLAUGHT caught Hannah's breath, held it, left her lightheaded, dizzy, her limbs weakened with the force of the windmill's ruin. Always quick to size things up, calculate the cost, deciphering the best plan, Hannah's mind went blank. There were no thoughts, only the black, painful realization that they were ruined, finished.

There were no funds to pay Ben Miller to restore the windmill. Every available source of water had dried up months ago. Underground streams ran quick and full, but with no means of bringing the water to the tank, it was useless. Hannah envisioned a deep, dark flow of life-giving water beneath bedrock, layered with ancient stone and packed, dry soil, dead roots of any growing thing, destroyed from beneath, and pounded to powder by the merciless scourge of hot wind and fiery sun.

She was brought to the present by Buck's nickering, Goat stretching his neck to rid himself of the reins, his nose reaching for water. He pressed his face deep into the brackish hay-strewn moisture in the bottom of the trough, lipped the sides as if it would give him a few more drops.

Hannah peered to the bottom of the galvanized water trough to find only a layer of soggy hay and silt, dust turned to mud, leaving a foul, swampy odor. She straightened, led Goat to his stall, hung up the saddle and bridle, stood in the middle of the barn and gazed blankly at the water trough, her mind refusing to accept the inevitable, unable to focus on a solution.

Her breath came in quick gasps, as panic overtook her, seized her in a cloying grip like tentacles from some alien creature.

She walked to the side of Buck's stall and leaned against the rough boards as she struggled to gain control. She thumped a fist against her chest, licked her lips, swallowed, tried to regain some sense of calm, knowing there was only one solution.

Kneel before Ben Miller's mercy. Cast themselves on someone else's benevolence, the thought nauseating, repulsive. Strutting bantam rooster that he was, he knew everything. Never let her get a word in edgewise.

She found Manny and her mother white-faced with fear. There was no water.

Hannah would not meet their eyes. To protect herself, she did not want to acknowledge the questioning, the defeat, so she sat on a chair and put her head in her hands, unapproachable.

Abby's chatter, the hum of the children's low voices, the sighing of the wind in the eaves, were the only sounds in the room. The house stood, squat and low, the ruined prairie spreading out on every side, falling away to the edge of the horizon, the windmill rising like a battered sentry, fallen by the very power that had brought them life-sustaining water: the wind.

The roiling, eternal wind, that movement of air around them that never ceased, harnessed by the clever windmill, only to be stripped of its power by too much of it.

This homestead. Built by hands of generosity, caring hands that helped them back on their feet after the brutal fire, standing here, a testimony to her father's hopes and dreams, a harbinger of prosperity and peace, the lush grasses feeding the herd as it grew into a vast number of fine, black Angus cattle.

The herd was Hannah's dream. She invested so much of her time in the fledgling herd, nurtured and cared for by hard work and planning.

She saw the vacant buildings, the interior destroyed by wild creatures of the plains, the dust and desperate sadness of failure. The evacuation of men and women who had met the end of their ability, leaving these echoing dwellings containing nothing but the ghosts of what might have been.

Cars would rumble by, the occupants turning their heads idly, viewing the abandoned buildings with disinterest, a vague knowing of another person's collapse. Another victim of drought and the Depression.

The knowing raked across Hannah's body like a physical pain. She clutched her stomach, leaned forward over her crossed arms, spoke to the floor in ragged edged words of defiance.

"We're not giving up, so you and Manny can stop looking at me with all that stupid pity. I'll ride Buck. I'll find Ben Miller and bring him back. He can fix it."

She lifted her head, her eyes black with a dangerous light. Sarah lifted a hand, shook her head. "No, Hannah. No. We are done. Manny and I . . ." her low voice was sliced off by the dagger of Hannah's outcry, a volley of harsh and rebellious words that pressed against Sarah, smashed her down into a chair, and held her there, robbed of an answer.

Manny stepped up, pleaded, spread his hands in supplication. "Come on, Hannah. Can't you see?"

"All I see is your refusal to try," she spat.

Fueled by the force of her anger, she saddled and bridled Buck, who sidestepped every time she tried to place a foot in the stirrups.

There was no help from Manny, so Hannah's determination swelled with every misstep. It was her's or the horse's will, and he was not winning.

She arrived at the Ben Miller homestead, stiff and sore, so thirsty her mouth felt as if it was stuffed with cotton. Buck was lathered with white foam, breathing hard, wild-eyed and cranky. He tried to bite her shoulder when she led him into the barn, so she swatted him with the ends of the leather reins, which only angered him further, resulting in a good strong kick with his left foot.

"Whoa, there!" Ben Miller stood in the barn, short, wide, the same generous grin he always wore creasing his round face. "Some horse you have there."

"Yeah, well, he serves the purpose." She told him of her mission.

Ben raised both eyebrows, then bent his head, wagging it back and forth like a big dog. "Hannah, I don't know how to tell you this."

She froze.

"We're quitting. Going back home. No one can outlast this drought. Senseless. Unwise. We know better. We know where there is a much better land of opportunity. I made a mistake, falling in love with the whole pioneer-spirit idea. Lost a lot of money. But so be it."

Hannah's eyes hardened, her chin raised. "Quitters."

Ben Miller spat with force. Hannah swallowed and looked at the wet spot on the dusty barn floor. Anger sizzled across Ben's friendly blue eyes, reddened his face.

"You best listen to reason, girl. I'd rather be alive and a quitter, then dead and still hanging on."

"I'll stay with my cattle."

"Hannah, listen. It's very serious. If it doesn't rain this summer, there is no possibility of survival."

She knew this to be true, but bucked against it anyway. "Sure there is."

"Well, I ain't standing here arguing with you. Come on into the house. You look like you could use a meal. How about a drink of water? Tin cup there on the wall."

Hannah lunged, filled the cup and drank greedily. So they were leaving, Hannah thought, as she entered the house to find cardboard boxes and satchels piled everywhere.

Ben's wife, Susan, met her with glad eyes, a wide, welcoming smile. "Oh Hannah, we're going back. I'm so happy, I'm counting the days till the train departs for eastern civilization."

"Good for you." Spoken abruptly, devoid of warmth.

Ben glanced at her sharply. "Do you have time to make a cup of tea for Hannah?"

"Of course. Oh, of course. You do look hungry. Susan bustled around her kitchen, talking, putting yellow cheese on a blue platter, some cured meat, saltine crackers, and small, brown cinnamon-speckled cakes.

Cheese. Saltine crackers. How long since she'd eaten either one? For a moment, Hannah thought of comforts, things she'd always taken for granted, the butter on her bread, the eggs from the hen house, flour and sugar and coffee. It would certainly be easy to settle into the old way of life, but that was precisely why she resisted.

It was too easy. Life as dull and tasteless as vanilla pudding without sugar. Going back to Lancaster, marrying someone, having many children, she knew no cheese or butter or saltine crackers would ever spice her life to anything interesting.

"Let's go," she said to Ben.

"You should give me an idea how badly the windmill is damaged," he said.

"It's wrecked some."

"Is the main structure still standing?"

"Yes."

Ben drove the spring wagon loaded with tools. At the homestead, he eyed the battered windmill and said he'd need help, he couldn't begin to do the work by himself. He paced the area around the windmill, repeatedly lifting his gaze to the battered paddles, talked to himself, and finally drove off in the spring wagon pulled by two tired horses, saying he'd be back with more men, a welding machine and, he hoped, lots of luck.

This was all said without the usual rolling good humor, leaving Ben Miller as dry and brittle as the surrounding plains, which struck fear in Hannah as she stood in the wind, watching him drive off.

He returned the following morning with Ike Lapp, Jake Fisher, and Jerry Riehl, the spring wagons piled with tools. They brought a galvanized milk can of water, warm and tasting of metal, but it was blessed water, slaking their thirst as they drank cupful after cupful.

Ben Miller took Sarah aside, stood in the yard, in the heat of the late morning sun, the wind tugging at Sarah's skirts, flapping the edges of Ben's straw hat.

Hannah paced the kitchen, the sight of the two people talking in the yard drawing her to the window repeatedly. What were they saying?

The conversation went on too long. At one point, Sarah reached into the pocket of her skirt, produced a handkerchief to wipe her eyes. Ben was going back. Would he persuade her mother?

The men swarmed the windmill like black insects, crawling up the rungs as loosened paddles occasionally fell to the ground in chilling spirals. What if the wind caught one and flung it haphazardly to slice into the body of an unsuspecting victim?

They repaired, hoisted, welded, all day. By nightfall, the windmill was spinning, the giant arm pumping fresh water from the underground stream. It poured from the pipe, sloshed into the tank, bringing the thirsty cattle in a headlong dash, jostling and shoving into position, drinking for a long time.

Hannah stood, her arms crossed, noticed the beginning of the falling off of the cattle's flesh. They were thin. Thin and thirsty, unable to escape this heat and brittle grass. She asked Ben Miller for a bill, proudly, her eyes boring into his with a fervor he could not understand.

"Hannah," he said quietly. "I know you don't have the funds to pay me. I'll strike a bargain. You agree to give up and return to Lancaster County with us on the train, and your debts are paid. There is no way on earth anyone will be able to make a living, let alone survive in these conditions."

Almost, Hannah let go. Let go of hope and determination, let her dreams evaporate like steam on a cold winter morning, allowing the sight of the ribs with the cowhide stretched over them to determine her choice.

But, what if? What if it rained? What if this arid, dusty prairie turned into the lush paradise her father had envisioned? Each new day there was a chance the rains would come. There was water now.

She shook her head, met Ben's pleading gaze, shook it again. "No."

Ben sighed, looked off toward the house. He felt a deep widespread pity for the widow Sarah, and her son, faced with an awful decision. But so be it. He had his own family's welfare to consider.

Jerry stayed behind, sent Jake with Ike Lapp and Ben Miller. He asked Hannah to walk with him, he wanted to talk to her. Her first impulse was to refuse, but the thought of the broken windmill and the cow's ribs had softened her somewhat, so she told her mother and Manny that she was walking with Jerry.

The night was dry, wisps of heat rising from the dust on the road. The stars above them were blinking on and off like tiny white lanterns in a sea of night, the wind rustling what remained of the waving prairie grass. There was no moon, but the road was discernable by the bright light of the stars.

They did not speak. The silence stretched between them, taut as a bowstring, uncomfortable. Hannah cleared her throat, pushed a strand of dark hair behind an ear. She bit her lip, her hands hung loosely at her sides. What did he want?

Jerry stopped, turned. "Hannah," he began softly.

She made no reply.

She heard his sigh, or was it merely a sound of the wind?

"I'm so afraid I'll mess this up."

Still she did not answer.

"I want you to know that I'm not forcing a decision on you. I just hope that somehow I can find the right words."

Her heart fell. Was he asking her to marry him? Her breathing stopped for a long moment, then resumed, leaving her light-headed, her heart clattering in her chest.

"You know and I know . . ." He stopped. "We both know there are dire conditions here. It will be tough for anyone or anything to survive. I'm not sure it's possible."

She cut him off. "It's possible."

He chose not to challenge her response. She felt him reach for her hand. She withdrew it, fast. His hand came in contact with her skirt, then fell back.

They walked on in silence.

There was no yipping of coyotes, no howling of wolves, no prairie hens skittering through the grass by the side of the road. Only a barren silence that stretched for many miles on either side of them, a wide circumference of a pitiless stretch of forgotten land, blessed neither with rain or snow. It was a land that threatened to creep into a heart or soul, rendering it barren as well, creating human beings who stopped feeling and experiencing life fully, turning them into dull, lifeless versions of the prairie itself.

Jerry felt a rising alarm as they walked. Hannah seemed as firm and as obstinate as ever. Would she clench the bit in her teeth, headstrong and self-willed until she met her own doom? The thought of a future without the presence of Hannah in it was simply not possible.

"Wisdom easy to be entreated." These words were put into his mind. He took a deep breath and tried again.

"I know what your ranch means to you."

"No, you don't."

"Maybe I don't."

"You don't. Not if you're planning on returning to Lancaster. You have no idea."

"Did I say I was going back?"

"Yes."

"I'll stay, if you'll stay."

She stopped walking, startled. "Everyone else is going back. My mother wants to return as well."

"And you?"

"I'm staying."

"Jake is going back."

"So?"

He turned and grasped her shoulders, his grip firm, drawing her toward him until she could smell the steel and oil of the windmill, the perspiration of the day's heat.

"Marry me, Hannah. Marry me while Ben Miller is here to perform the marriage. We can get a license from the courthouse. We can live together, but don't necessarily have to, well, you know, live as man and wife. We'd be married in name only, and you would have a man to help you with the cattle, protect you from the riff-raff that ride around and prey on out-of-luck home-steaders. I know you don't love me, Hannah. You love only the land. You don't have to love me. We'll just live together, try and make a go of it, if that's what you want."

Hannah could always draw on the strength of anger, swat any choice or confrontation aside like an annoying insect. Anger and rebellion were her strength, especially with people. They served her purpose well, to hide the weakness beneath, erase the softening, the opening of her heart, and the trust that went hand in hand with love.

But now, they fell from her grasp. It was, by all means, a solution. Could she do it? What if she fell in love with him and he could never love her, stick thin and mean as the old cow that had killed her father?

He drew her closer. She wriggled out of his grasp, stepped away, breathing hard.

"Don't do that."

"What?"

"Touch me."

"All right. I won't."

"I will do it if you promise not to touch me or try to kiss me the way you did before. Married in name only. The only reason I am allowing this is to save the homestead. Do you have money? Means of surviving the drought?"

"Yes, I have some money put by."

"Then yes, I will marry you."

Jerry's heart sang, lifted the song to the heavens and danced with the stars, leaped from star to star, flinging the notes with abandon. He wanted to hold her, and yes, of course, kiss her, pledge his undying love for all eternity, now and forever, with God's richest blessings bestowed on both of them.

He put his hands in his pockets and said, "It's settled then."

"You understand, of course, that this is a marriage out of necessity. It will save the homestead. So don't go around thinking I'll fall in love and be a real wife, because it is not going to happen."

"I know. I agree to keep my part of the contract." It would be enough to sit across the table from her, three times a day. It would be enough to talk to her, every day. Learn her ways, learn the reason she was as hard to please as a wild horse, and as untamed. He looked forward to the challenge.

Suddenly shy, she fell silent. The wind whispered the words of promise neither one could say.

The following morning, Sarah sat down weakly, Hannah's words like an approaching cyclone. She threw both hands in the air, wagged her head back and forth, disbelief clouding her eyes.

Manny reacted with a stare, and silence.

"Are you sure?" Sarah finally uttered.

"You're going back, aren't you?"

"We are."

"Well, then. I'm staying. We are staying. We're going to try and make it through the drought."

The ceremony was held the following week. Heat shimmered across the prairie, but the summer breeze flapped the curtains in the living room as Ben Miller preached the Amish wedding sermon of creation, Ruth and Boaz, Samson and Delilah, and the story of Tobias from the Apocrypha.

Hannah sat, dressed in a blue Sunday dress and a black cape and apron, which replaced the white Swiss organdy normally worn by the bride, simply because it was not available.

She was breathtaking in a neat, white covering. Her hair was done loosely, combed in waves and darkly shining. Slim, sitting with natural grace, Jerry stole glances of admiration all through the service.

Hannah looked at him once, then kept her eyes averted. She was going to have to watch out. Dark haired, dark eyed, with that long, tanned face and wide mouth, he was startlingly handsome in a white shirt and black vest and trousers.

They were pronounced man and wife, given the blessing of old, the same vows that had been repeated for hundreds of years, a tradition that would stand the test, and be carried on until the end of time, a precious heritage, the birthright of the Amish.

Now, of course, Hannah was blind to this, her eyes covered by her own will and determination to save the homestead at all costs. Her vows were spoken without love or spirituality. This was the only way of obtaining what she most desired.

If the drought continued, they'd get by. He had money. She would tell Betsy she was quitting at the café, which was a joy of enormous size, not having to make that long, hot ride into town.

The wedding meal was simple, mostly supplied by the remains of Susan Miller's pantry, and most of Jerry's. Potatoes mashed with milk and salt, the usual *roasht* made with only bread cubes and onion. Thin gravy made with a whisper of chicken broth.

There was wedding cake, however, made with lard and white sugar, eggs and white flour, a rare and special treat.

Hod Jenkins sat with Ken and Hank, uncomfortable in stiff collars, Clay with a red-faced, sweltering Jennifer. The Klassermans sat side by side, perspiring great splotches on their Sunday finery, madly fanning themselves with white handkerchiefs, wondering if this service would ever end.

There was a general upheaval afterward, packing, hauling things to the rail car in Pine, an endless, wearing task as the summer heat mounted. But the day came when it was time to go, time to part, time to leave Hannah in the care of her new husband.

Sarah swallowed her tears, put on a brave face, knowing any display of emotion would only draw out Hannah's indignation.

Manny shook their hands, taller than Hannah now, wished them both *Gottes saya,* then turned to search the small crowd for the petite Marybelle, already awaiting the promise of a rosy future in Lancaster County.

Mary sniffled a bit as she clung to Hannah, produced many facial contortions as she desperately tried to keep her tears to herself.

Eli said he was going to raise pigs in Lancaster County and have bacon at every meal, then shook hands gravely, like a well-mannered little preacher.

Hannah held Abigail's small form, soft and pliable, molding her into her own body, kissing her soft cheeks over and over, before handing her to Sarah, tears dangerously close to the surface.

The train whistle blew, a short, sharp blast, followed by another. Ben Miller's family boarded the passenger car. Jake Fisher shook hands, clapped a hand on Jerry's shoulder, thought for the hundredth time that Jerry must have become mentally ill out here in this forsaken, dry land. No one could pay him enough to marry Hannah Detweiler.

As the train pulled slowly out of the small, dusty station, the whistle sounded again, high and piercing. Steam poured from the underbelly of the locomotive as black smoke poured into the hot sky.

Hannah did cry, a great gasping sob as she saw her mother's face pressed to the dusty window, a handkerchief to her nose. Crying. Her mother cried to leave her with Jerry. This knowledge brought her own unstoppable sobbing.

Jerry heard and turned away quickly, jamming his hands into his pockets to keep from reaching for her.

Hannah snorted once, lifted her defiant eyes to his and said, "Let's go."

Jerry followed her to the spring wagon, and they rode off across the desolate prairie, sitting side by side on the hard, wooden seat in the bright morning sun, with the dust and tumbleweeds blowing ahead of them.

GLOSSARY

Ach du lieber—Oh my goodness!

Ausbund—The book of old German hymns written by Amish ancestors imprisoned in Passau, Germany, for their Christian faith.

Aylend—A poor work ethic; unconcerned about work.

Dichly—A triangle of cloth worn by women instead of a head covering.

Fa-sarked—To take care of.

Frieda—Peace.

Gottes saya—God's blessing.

Grosfeelich—Arrogance stemming from pride; hubris.

Herrn saya—God's blessing.

Ivva drettung—Overstepping set boundaries.

Knepp—Thick, floury dumplings.

Nein—No.

Ordnung—Literally, "ordinary," or "discipline," it refers to an Amish community's agreed-upon rules for living, based on the Bible, particularly the New Testament. The *Ordnung* can vary in small ways some from community to community, reflecting the leaders' interpretations, local traditions, and historical practices.

Ponhaus—Scrapple.

Roasht—Chicken filling.

Rumschpringa—Literally, "running around." A time of relative freedom for adolescents, beginning at about age sixteen. The period ends when a youth is baptized and joins the church, after which the youth can marry.

Schenked und fagevva—To forgive.

Schmear kase—Spreadable cheese for bread.

Sei—His.

Verboten—Forbidden.

Vissa adda unvissa—To know or not know.

Voddogs—An everyday shirt or dress, patched again and again, then handed down to a younger child.

Voss in die velt?—What in the world?

Wunderbar—Wonderful!

Yusht da vint—Just the wind.

Zeit-lang—Homesick.

OTHER BOOKS BY LINDA BYLER

*Available from your favorite bookstore
or online retailer.*

"Author Linda Byler is Amish, which sets this book apart both in the rich details of Amish life and in the lack of melodrama over disappointments and tragedies. Byler's writing will leave readers eager for the next book in the series."
    –*Publisher's Weekly* review of *Wild Horses*

LIZZIE SEARCHES FOR LOVE SERIES

BOOK ONE   BOOK TWO   BOOK THREE

TRILOGY   COOKBOOK

SADIE'S MONTANA SERIES

BOOK ONE

BOOK TWO

BOOK THREE

TRILOGY

LANCASTER BURNING SERIES

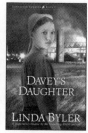

BOOK ONE

BOOK TWO

BOOK THREE

TRILOGY

HESTER'S HUNT FOR HOME SERIES

BOOK ONE

BOOK TWO

BOOK THREE

THE LITTLE AMISH
MATCHMAKER
A Christmas Romance

THE CHRISTMAS
VISITOR
An Amish Romance

MARY'S CHRISTMAS
GOODBYE
An Amish Romance

BECKY MEETS HER
MATCH
*An Amish Christmas
Romance*

ABOUT THE AUTHOR

LINDA BYLER WAS RAISED IN AN AMISH FAMILY AND IS AN ACTIVE member of the Amish church today. Growing up, Linda loved to read and write. In fact, she still does. Linda is well-known within the Amish community as a columnist for a weekly Amish newspaper.

Linda is the author of four series of novels, all set among the Amish communities of North America: Lizzie Searches for Love, Sadie's Montana, Lancaster Burning, and Hester's Hunt for Home. *Hope on the Plains* is the second book in the Dakota Series, preceded by *The Homestead*. Linda has also written four Christmas romances set among the Amish: *Mary's Christmas Goodbye*, *The Christmas Visitor*, *The Little Amish Match-maker*, and *Becky Meets Her Match*. Linda has co-authored *Lizzie's Amish Cookbook: Favorite Recipes from Three Generations of Amish Cooks!*